FALLEN

AN ENOCHIAN WAR NOVEL

LUKE MITCHELL

For anyone who's ever been stuck between a rock and a hard world.

NATURAL BORN

"We've got 'em," crackled a gruff voice in Two's earpiece.

He perked up, downing the rest of his watery caffa and chucking the cheap cup. "I might need a location with that spot of sunshine, Ordo..." What was it, again? Ordo Franklin? Ordo Fenner? Scud if he could remember the officer's name.

"They're holed up in the back docks, sir," came Ordo Whatever's reply. There was the muffled sound of movement in the background. "Sending nav now."

Two straightened the fingers of his left hand, and his palmlight map sprang to life a second before the red blip appeared at the southeastern edge of Divinity, right alongside the Red River. "Got it. Perimeter?"

"Moving into position now, sir."

A bitter smirk pulled across Two's mouth at the tone of the Ordo's voice. The one good part about working with legionnaires: they didn't ask questions. This guy didn't have a clue who the scud Two actually was, and it didn't matter. Two's people pulled the strings, the orders came down from above, and Ordo Whatever hopped to Two's command like a happy hound, tail-a-thumping.

"Great work, Ordo," he said, perhaps a tad mockingly. His amusement drained quickly enough. "Sit tight until I get there, huh? These two aren't your everyday apostates."

Two killed the connection and raised his palmlight to hail an autoskimmer. For a split second, he thought to relay the apostates' location to Watchtower control, just in case the worst should happen, but then he remembered that the nav pin had been sent to his palmlight, which meant they already knew. Watchtower was—appropriately enough—always watching, after all.

Fifteen minutes later, Two was soaring over the lower industrial area, skirting past the head docks straight for the dilapidated mass of rotted wood and blighted permacrete that was the back docks. The place was like a rodent's nest of walkways, winding their twisted paths between the hundreds of tiny scuddy huts where poorer-than-dirt fishermen and scavengers squatted between their measly attempts at producing something of value. It was exactly the kind of place Two hated—not because of the dirt and the squalor, but because there were just too damn many winding paths and hidey holes to complicate his life.

Then again, he decided as he climbed out of the autoskimmer to the waiting reception of three ragged homeless men, he didn't love the dirt and the squalor all that much either. They watched with a kind of stern expectation, brows furrowed and hands outstretched, their fingertips blackened and reeking of fish and sweet tar.

Tarheads. Charming.

It was his fault he was here at all. There was no getting around that. He should've nabbed the apostates back in the slums, but one of them had spooked far too quickly. Which meant she—or maybe *he*, but his gut said *she*—was well-attuned. And when a demon actually knew enough to catch Two's probing and slip capture once...

Maybe he should've called for backup.

But grop that. He didn't need Three—or, Alpha be cursed, One—stepping in here and trying to control his every move. No. He was perfectly capable of handling a couple rogue demons on his own. And if not... well, maybe today would be the day.

With that cheery thought in mind, he stepped forward—only to have his three waiting tarheads shuffle in a little closer, walling him in, frowns darkening. Half-beggars. Half-robbers. Even more charming.

He half-thought about reaching for his power and scaring them properly, but he quelled the idea as soon as it surfaced. That was the road to losing control—to letting the demon take over for good. So instead, he calmly pulled his jacket open and showed them the sidearm holstered under his left arm. Frowns turned to dark scowls, and the tarheads scattered with a few choice curses.

Two opened his palmlight map and set off with his own internal curse, wishing he could dismiss the men as savages. It was easy enough, letting the blind hatred roll in. Justifying it was a bit harder. Condemning beggars and drug addicts for their flaws when he was the one carrying an honest-to-Alpha demon astride his blackened spirit?

"Shut up," he muttered to no one in particular. He shook his head, trying to clear it. He was close. They might've even felt him already.

Time to let the demon out.

He was reaching for his palmlight to reestablish contact with his tail-thumping Ordo when the gruff voice crackled in his earpiece.

"Sir, we're picking up movement. The apostates appear to be—scud!"

Before Two could ask what in demons' depths was happening, the report of a gunshot split the fishy air. Even in the relative quiet of the pre-dawn hours, it was faint. A rifle, he thought, but maybe suppressed. A sniper? That probably wasn't good.

"Ordo, I need you to—"

Another gunshot, followed by the Ordo's barked orders—something about *contain that specialist* and *I said cease fire*.

Two barely registered the Ordo's words. Adrenaline spiking through his veins, he took off at a sprint, mind racing, wobbly walkway creaking underfoot.

This was why he hated working with clueless squads.

He needed a team that understood what they were up against. But Seekers didn't get teams. Didn't get friends. And as he rounded a corner and caught sight of the cramped muddy yard outside the target fishing shanty, he decided he wouldn't want these softsteel sippers as teammates anyway.

They were already moving in.

He registered that fact just in time to watch the legionnaire on point turn around and open fire on his own squad.

Two took off with a curse, vaulting one last rickety railing and crossing the path to the muddy lot at a run, unable to look away from the perverse spectacle. A pair of legionnaires fell to the friendly fire almost immediately. The rest reacted as trained soldiers should and disarmed their maddened teammate, pinning him and dragging him roughly down the steps to where he wouldn't be obstructing the squad's avenue of ingress. Over it all, Two was vaguely aware of Ordo Whatever's steady stream of barked, curse-heavy commands, telling the squad to move in, telling others to properly restrain their apparently mad point man.

Except it wasn't the legionnaire who'd pulled that trigger. Nor would he be the last. Two knew it, just as he knew he was the only one here who could do anything about it. So he braced himself, closing his eyes, pushing down the sick feeling in his gut.

And he let the demon out.

The world exploded out around him. Rotting wood and cold mud, damp air baking a degree more fishy in the first beams of the morning sun, the flicker of a dozen legionnaire minds scrambling for order—all of it cascading through his senses in the bare instant before he directed his focus toward the inexplicably trigger-happy point man. His brotos were slapping the restraints on him now. Two reached for the real problem.

He could feel it there, like a black serpent coiled around the man's very spirit—the influence of a wild demon, freed of its chains by one of the pair inside who was either too desperate, too ignorant, or too stupid to understand what manner of evil they were playing with. And given the strength with which the demon resisted Two's initial attempt to pry it from the point man, he was guessing desperation had something to do with it.

He wasn't going to win the fight for the legionnaire's mind. Not directly. He could feel that much. So, Two turned to attacking the demon at its source instead. He traced the long tail of that black serpent in his extended senses, up the steps and into the crumbling fishing shanty. The cramped space was dark inside. There was an aura there, a sinister cloud of wild rage and black hatred. Two pushed past it, fixing onto the source of the demon in his senses. A woman—he was sure of it now.

And she could feel him too.

Her demon crashed into his with the unerring speed of a striking viper. No warning. No mercy. Anger flared deep in Two's chest—a primal rage that swelled just as surely as if she'd gone and sucker punched him right in the mouth. The bitch.

He flexed his defenses tighter, the world of his physical body and the muddy yard outside shrinking from mind as he sank deeper into the one that belonged to his demon. Sometimes, he almost felt for these tragic abominations. Today, he had a feeling, would not be one of those days—if for no other reason than that he didn't have the capacity left to worry about anything other than surviving.

Her demon was strong. Stronger than he'd ever felt from a wild one. Maybe as strong as One's. Definitely as strong as his own. It was nearly overwhelming at first, the panic at finding himself equally matched. The realization slipped its icy fingers through his mind—numbing his thoughts, tripping up his reactions. Her demon didn't miss the opening.

The fighting was tight and violently rapid. Her demon darting circles around him, striking from seemingly all directions at once. Him twisting to keep pace, balance faltering another sliver with each attack.

Then the onslaught abruptly ended. Two had all of an instant to catch his figurative breath before realizing what that meant.

He leaned back into his physical body just in time to find Ordo Whatever leveling his sidearm right at Two's face. The man most certainly didn't have that thumping-tail look anymore. Or any look, for that matter. He was vacant. Possessed.

Two caught the ordo's wrist and shoved the weapon aside just as the first shot roared, nearly deafening his left ear.

No time for tact. He grabbed the possessed ordo's throat with his free hand and let his demon ride the contact in. It was forbidden. It was despicable. But in that moment, he didn't know what the scud else to do. He threw his demon forward and pushed the ordo down into a deep sleep like flipping a switch. The ordo hit the mud with a wet, squishy thud. Two looked back to the shanty, where the legionnaires were already moving back in. Or had been. Half of them had stopped.

And they were pointing their rifles right at him.

For a second, Two couldn't help but marvel at the power of a demon that could take the minds of half a dozen soldiers at once. Then it dawned on him that they might be acting of their own accord—that they were probably simply turning their weapons on the stranger who'd just dropped their ordo like a bag of softsteel.

Alpha be damned.

"Wait!" he cried. Or tried to, before her demon found him again.

He fell to his knees with the ferocity of the attack, clinging onto control by the barest edges of his fingertips. The worst of it, though, passed surprisingly quickly as something else vied for the apostate's attention. The legionnaires, Two realized. One fireteam was moving toward him now, coming to apprehend him, by the looks of it. But the rest of the squad had finished ascending the rickety stairs and were stacking up on the shanty door above, preparing to breach.

Good. If he could just keep that Alpha-cursed apostate and her demon under control for another few moments...

He sank back into their stalled contest, taking advantage of her distraction to spring a far more concentrated attack. She gave ground. Too much ground. He could feel the tenuous hint of her breaking point—was mere moments from claiming her mind and bringing a halt to this madness.

Then something yanked him away from their battle—away from her dark shanty and back to his physical body, right into a quickly soaking front side and a face full of cold mud. The legionnaires, driving him to the ground. Working restraints onto his wrists. Telling him to take it easy, buddy, and don't try anything funny.

Funny?

Two pulled his defenses tighter and tried to gather enough control to tell the four goat-groppers where they could shove their funny business. Before he could, though, the shanty door exploded outward with a splintering boom, taking two legionnaires down with it.

After that, things degraded quickly.

Soldiers barked orders at one another, regaining their wits and pressing forward only to be tripped up or smacked aside by some invisible hand. When the first legionnaire inexplicably went flying over the walkway railing and plummeted to the mud below, the fireteam of barking hounds sitting on Two's back finally decided maybe he wasn't the real threat here. They stormed off to help their allies, all but the one who kept his bulk pinned on Two via a knee to the shoulder blade, looking around like a frightened pup.

"Let me go, you idiot," Two growled.

Curiously, the legionnaire's decision only pended as long as it took the demon to telekinetically hurl another of his squad mates from the walkway above. Two pushed to his feet, his entire front sopping wet and heavy with mud. But that hardly mattered.

"That's it," he muttered. Then he threw his demon at hers like a feral hound to a bloody steak.

Alpha damn her blackened spirit, she somehow managed to catch his attack, even extended as she was. But she certainly gave ground. Enough that the telekinetic maelstrom above ceased completely—so abruptly that the legionnaires almost seemed too surprised to act.

"Shoot her!" he cried.

Three of the less doltish legionnaires sprang to action at his words, sweeping into the dark shanty, weapons at the ready. The apostate was positively wild now, her demon bucking against his like a force of nature. Two held on with grim determination, strengthened by the knowledge that it was already over at this point.

A rifle cracked twice above, and made it so.

One of the shots must've found her head, judging by how immediately she disappeared. One moment, a raging storm of bitter fury and demonic presence. The next, nothing but... screaming.

The kid.

Alpha's blessed body, he'd forgotten about the kid—had been too wrapped in their mental wrestling match to remember there was a second apostate up there. In his defense, the kid's demon had barely picked up when Two had sniffed them out earlier that night. The fact that the kid hadn't helped his partner seemed to confirm that his demon was still too young to be a serious threat. Except now...

There were several crashes within the shanty. Shouted curses. Gunshots. Above it all, the screaming continued.

"Son of a bitch," Two muttered, right before what few windows there were in the shanty exploded outward in a demonic gale of howling wind.

He took the stairs three at a time, ignoring the wide-eyed looks the legionnaires shot him, and the wind whipping at his mud-caked jacket.

Inside, three legionnaires were down in addition to the apostate woman they'd killed, all four of them sprawled throughout the room in kind with the rest of the overturned furniture.

The kid had found one of the legionnaires' sidearms. He thrust it at Two's chest, his hands visibly shaking with fear or rage. Probably both, Two decided, as the storm began dying around them, strangled out by the spirit of cold murder hanging in the air. Two reached out and calmly ripped the gun away with telekinesis. The look on the kid's face as the weapon left his hands was almost too much to bear—the wide-eyed, slack-jawed epiphany, two parts panic, one part hopeless, morbid fascination.

It was the look of someone truly realizing they were about to die, and now he'd seen it one too many times.

"Restrain him," he said, bending to pick up the gun. He probably should've neutralized the kid's demon before doing anything else, but he was pretty sure the thing had already lashed out with everything it had. He'd heard tell that it happened sometimes, these untrained outbursts, but they were categorically brief and usually out of the young apostate's control.

For now, the kid was probably harmless.

In the splintered doorway behind, the legionnaires were hesitating. Two was about to snap at them when they found their wrinklies and swept in. After that, they had the kid restrained and on his knees in the blink of an eye. Two checked over the sidearm, making sure it was loaded, the safety disengaged.

Alpha, he was tired. Straight to the bones.

Probably, he should've just skipped the next part. But he couldn't. For the will of Alpha, and for his own sanity, he had to check.

The kid's mental defenses were like soggy bread next to those of his fallen partner—or master, rather, Two saw as he broke into the younger apostate's mind and began rifling through his life's memories. She'd found him on the streets a few seasons after he'd escaped the father whose need for the bottle had been increasingly rivaled by the man's enthusiasm for offloading the pain to his son, physically and otherwise. She'd protected him. Taught him. Loved him.

Corrupted him.

It was unmistakable. But Two swept over the kid's mind again, just to be sure, ignoring the legionnaires' looks of growing discomfort with the odd silence. He didn't blame the kid for having fallen prey to a demon while living through the kind of abuse he'd so clearly experienced. If the Sanctum had found him sooner, maybe... but they hadn't. And there it was, nestled at the core of him like a dark ink stain on his very spirit, undeniable.

Too old to be trained as a Seeker. Too dangerous to be left alive.

"Why are you doing this?"

The kid's voice was shaky with fear in Two's mind. It almost made him flinch.

He didn't answer. Just finished his inspection as best he could. He'd tried before to explain himself to his marks. But there was no use. It made no difference in the end.

"I'm going to kill you." This time, the kid spoke out loud, his voice brimming with a heartbreaking attempt to pass off fear as anger. "I'm going to gropping kill you!"

This was going to be one of those days, it turned out. One of the days when Two would lie awake questioning himself and his place in ending these tragic abominations. But Enochia was counting on him, whether they knew it or not. His own brothers and sisters, too.

Alpha was counting on him.

So he stepped forward, raising the gun.

"Alpha grant you peace, fallen."

He pulled the trigger before the legionnaires could finish asking what the scud he was doing. And like that, it was over.

Two tossed the gun and turned to leave, mindful of the incredulous stares piercing him from all sides. They thought he was a monster. And they weren't wrong. But they didn't know the whole story. Didn't know that there'd been nothing else to be done for the kid. That he'd been corrupted by a demon, and that there wasn't a single brig on Enochia that could've held him once he learned to control his curse.

But Two couldn't exactly tell that to the two legionnaires who stepped in to bar his exit from the wrecked shanty. They glanced at each other, neither one sure what to say, only sure that they couldn't simply let this monster walk away. The entitled bastards.

"Check your orders," Two growled, wanting nothing more than to be out of this shanty, and alone. "You'll find I'm to be excused for my actions here. That I was never here at all, in fact."

Another uncertain glance between them, then a look back to one of their squad mates outside, who looked up from his palmlight and gave a hesitant nod.

"As much fun as this has been," Two said, shouldering his way between the legionnaires, who stiffly shifted just enough to let him past, "I hope no one will take offense when I say I genuinely hope I never see you assholes again."

There was a curse and a rustle of movement from behind. Two glanced back in time to see one of the doorway legionnaires catching his partner before he could throw himself at Two.

Two shot the snarling man a smirking salute and turned for the stairs.

Only once he was well out of their sight and alone in a dark alley did he allow his hand to drift to the thin black collar at his neck, as it always did after a kill. Only then did he remind himself that it wasn't just for the good of Enochia and for the will of Alpha—that he'd also lose his own head if he refused.

But that didn't really change the fact that he'd pulled the trigger again. That his hand hadn't even shook this time.

So maybe Alpha willed it. So maybe it was all a little less black and white than those legionnaires would imagine when they talked about this over their ale tonight. But either way, it was getting hard to deny.

He was a natural born killer.

CHANGES

The whip snapped tight, raking the familiar lance of searing pain across Two's back.

One for the woman. He didn't know her name. Never bothered with the names. They made the fallen seem too human—too redeemable—which was a dangerous line of thought in his area of work. Hence the whip. Hence the fact that he'd not resisted when they'd taken his own name and left him with nothing but a roster slot.

Two. That was all the name he needed anymore. Because at the end of the day, fighting the good fight or not, he was fallen too, wasn't he?

He took a breath and swung the whip over his shoulder again. The second blossoming line of fire was for the boy—or, rather, for Two's own transgression of violence against another living person, demon or no. It wasn't easy, being Alpha's first and only line of defense against the demons. Especially when he was harboring a demon of his own inside. Things got confusing. Hence the third and fourth strikes, slashing across his back in dedication and reverence to Alpha—two small pleas for the strength to hold the demons, both within and without, at bay.

He stayed on his knees for a while after that, as he usually did, taking some small comfort from the coolness of the permacrete beneath him, and the quiet of his humble little quarters. He breathed carefully—slow, shallow breaths, designed to not exacerbate the lines of fire howling across his back. There was no escaping the pain, but nor did he really want to. He greeted it like an old friend. A grumpy old scud of a friend, maybe, but a friend no less. One who took him by the inflating ego, yanked him back to the ground, and told him the truth about what he was, and what that meant.

Pain was a good friend.

So for a while, he knelt there, taking in their little chat, relishing the slow tickle of warm blood tracing down his bare back. For a while, he was at peace. Then the door hissed open, and a cold, female voice shattered it.

"Word around the Tower is you bagged two for one today."

One. Splendid.

Two forced on his best smirk before turning to face her. "Jealousy doesn't suit you, you know."

The form-fitting training skin he found her wearing, on the other hand, most certainly did. But all it took was one look at those frosty blue eyes to cure his weaker bits of any notion that this was a woman to be desired. Judging by the sneer that curled her lip, though, his attention hadn't gone unnoticed.

One prowled into his room, decidedly uninvited—never mind the fact that visiting another Seeker's quarters was forbidden, or at least strongly frowned upon, to start with. Two thought to rise but hesitated a second too long. Her hand settled on his bare shoulder before he could. Cold and calloused as it was, it still felt surprisingly good. But that was probably just on account of it being the first non-violent human contact he'd had in cycles. Fire flickered across his back as she shifted more weight to the hand, leaning down to inspect his work.

"Oh dear, those are good ones. You never hold back, do you?"

"I like it hard and fast, what can I say?"

He hated himself for the pathetic quip as soon as it left his mouth. But that was all he and One seemed capable of. Never had a sincere word been spoken betwixt them.

"Maybe you say you're ready to let me take care of you," she murmured, her lips nearly brushing his ear now, her breath deliciously warm against his skin. "Maybe something for the pain."

Case and point on the sincerity thing.

Her proposal was expressly forbidden, on both accounts. And also almost certainly insincere. But somehow, neither that fact nor the pain in his back managed to keep the blood from rushing below. For a second, he couldn't stop the thoughts flashing through his mind. Her hard, lithe figure pressed beneath him, pale blue eyes locked on his, full of some pulse-pounding mixture of lust and hatred. He couldn't help thinking about turning her around, grabbing a handful of her short dark hair, and—

Pain exploded across his back.

He clenched his teeth and barely managed to wrestle his yelp down into a growl. She'd slapped him, he realized dazedly. Taken advantage of his distraction and slapped him in some twisted parody of a caring pat on his bloodied back. He cursed himself for falling for her touch and her suggestive words. Or maybe she'd even pushed those thoughts his way telepathically, just to butter him up. Maybe. It was always hard to tell where swiving was concerned.

"What do you want, you miserable bitch?" he growled, rising carefully to his feet, his back pulsing with the aftershock of her slap.

She touched a hand to her chest as if his words had actually affronted her. The look didn't come close to reaching her cold eyes. "I just wanted to swing by and pay my compliments to a dear friend."

Whatever hatred flickered across his face put a cold smile on hers. It was the most sincere thing that had passed between them yet.

"Don't worry," she cooed, her smile turning absolutely derisive. "I also came to say goodbye. Six's replacement is getting shipped up from the minors today. Looks like you're holding the fort with the children."

Well there was a piece of decent news, at least.

Just in case their years of training and the ever-present explosive collars weren't enough to encourage them to keep their demons under control, their Sanctum handlers also thought it wise to ensure there were never more than three Seekers together at a time. The rule of three. Safeguards on safeguards. Two might've found it more exasperating if he wasn't so intimately familiar with just how much damage a rogue demon was capable of inflicting.

Plus, if they meant One getting shipped out on long assignment, the rules couldn't be so bad, right?

"Best news I've heard all season," he said, not having to force the smirk this time.

She narrowed her eyes at him.

He just shrugged and moved to return his whip to its customary hook on the plain wall. "Speaking of news, have you heard anything about the High Cleric?"

The look that came over her face at that question made his stomach dip. The High Cleric had been out of commission with some undisclosed ailment for over a cycle now. Well long enough to worry—especially when people started making strange faces. But on second thought, One's expression didn't read *bad news* so much as it was just... odd.

Quick as it had come, though, the expression slid from her face, leaving only a cold, blank slate.

"He's back," she said simply. "Better than ever."

And with that, she turned to go.

Something was off about the entire interaction.

"Always hate to see you go," Two said in a last-ditch attempt to kick something loose.

When she glanced back at him over her shoulder, though, her mask of frosty amusement was firmly back in place.

"But you just love to watch me leave, don't you?"

He couldn't prove it, but he could've sworn she tilted her hips just a degree or two as she said it, popping the already lovely curve of her forbidden backside out that much more for his viewing pleasure.

It was a trap. The most dangerous swell on Enochia. He knew that. But she also wasn't wrong. He had to admit that much. And yes, there was the threat of death for consorting with fellow demons to consider. Technically, they weren't even really supposed to be talking outside of the field, but no one went out of their way to reinforce that rule since they did indeed operate together out there sometimes.

But these things were all extraneous.

It was the look in her eyes. That was all he needed to ground himself to the facts that really mattered—all he needed to remember that One was every bit the monster he was. Probably more so. And as lovely her backside was, that look in her eyes reminded him that, no matter what manner of twisted sexual tension might've crept in between them over the years, she hated him to his core. Just like he hated her.

One would just as soon kill him as grop him. Of that, he had no doubt.

She turned to leave, then paused.

"I hear the new girl's pretty," she said, turning back to shoot him the strangest look yet. "Don't go forgetting about your number One while I'm gone."

Back still aflame, brow furrowed in confusion, Two watched her go, trying to fathom what in demons' depths was going on in that cold, dark head of hers.

Kill him just as soon as grop him. No doubts. None at all.

Definitely.

***

SLEEP DIDN'T COME that night. It happened sometimes, afterwards. Or *had* happened sometimes in the first few years of Two's career as an arcane killer. He'd thought he'd gotten over it. The past few marks had gone down easily enough, and with nary a bad dream after the fact. It had actually bothered him a bit, how easy it had started to feel, ending lives—even if those lives were plagued by demons.

But this one had been different.

Lying awake in the darkness of his cramped utilitarian quarters, Two couldn't shake the thoughts of the boy and his... what, his teacher? Guardian? Friend? Two didn't want to think about it. He'd glimpsed enough of the kid's story when he'd broken his mind. Maybe that's what was bothering him so much. The kid had been his youngest yet. But it was more than that, wasn't it?

Maybe it had bothered him, seeing two demons so clearly care for one another. Or maybe it was just that the wild bitch of a master had damn near broken his defenses. She'd been strong—the strongest he'd ever hunted. Alpha knew what might've happened if she'd won their mental wrestling match. And the panic he'd felt in those first moments of her attack...

Was he rattled? Did he *get* rattled?

Maybe. Maybe not. All he really knew for sure was that today had been too close a call, and that the whole ordeal had left a seeping uneasiness in his gut.

Why are you doing this? The kid's frightened voice drifted to him in the darkness. Always with the questions. Who was he? Why was he doing this? Why couldn't he leave them be?

Like they couldn't understand that they were dangerous. That all of them, Two included, were walking time bombs—the most dangerous bombs on Enochia. Never mind that half of them could barely lift a pebble with telekinesis when Two or one of his teammates found them. The Seekers were simply staying ahead of the curve. Because eventually, no matter what, the demon always won.

He blew out a long breath and readjusted his bedding, trying in futility to find a position that would alleviate the fire from his whipped back.

Halfway there. He was halfway there, give or take. Another four years, maybe. Six or seven if he was... well, *lucky* wasn't the right word. Either way, whether it happened in the field or by the High Cleric's orders, Seekers rarely made it more than a year or two past twenty-five, and certainly not beyond thirty. Past that, things got too dangerous. There was only so long one could expect to rein in the demon—especially once they'd gone through the training and fully awoken the thing.

That was the price they paid.

Some days, the thought still filled Two's gut with cold dread. But the point remained. A few more years, and he could finally rest. For good this time.

He held onto that thought, and the peace it brought him. Felt the tension begin to drain from his body, sleep coming to carry him away from his heavy thoughts. He was just on the verge of nodding off when the voice came to him.

"Well hi there, neighbor. Can't sleep either?"

Alpha be damned.

Female. Unfamiliar. The new Six?

"I was about to," he sent back, not bothering to mask his irritation, *"before you interrupted me."*

"Hey, you called me, scudboots, whether you meant to or not."

That gave him pause—mostly because it could've well been true. Their demons had a way of wandering off into the outside world during sleep, exploring, or scheming, or whatever the scud it was they did. It creeped Two out to no end, but at least the bastards didn't seem to be capable of doing any heavy lifting without their fallen's waking cooperation. Linking that fallen's mind to another's, though...

"Whatever," he sent. *"I didn't mean to. And I'm trying to sleep, so grop off."*

"Well, I was trying *to before a certain grumpy scudboots came knocking on my door, so to speak. Was almost there, too. Imagine my shock."*

"I..." Was she messing with him? Who just freely admitted something like that? He swallowed, heat spreading to his cheeks—among other places—and tried not to think too hard about it. *"Well carry on, sweet cheeks,"* he sent, trying to affect an indifferent mental tone. *"I'm going to sleep."*

"Yeah, so says your lips. Alpha's mighty beardsplitter, I can feel you stirring from here. What did that cot ever do to you?"

"Would you just—" He took a deep breath, willing the frustration down. He needed to disengage.

"Hey, no need to be embarrassed," she sent, and he could feel the amusement bubbling at the surface of her mind. *"It's no small wonder, really. This whole celibacy business is way gropped up. But we're all friends here, right?"*

"We'... Look, we're really not. We aren't even supposed to talk like this. If the clerics found out—"

"I know, I know. Off with our heads. I think I saw that one listed right beside the whole 'no fun' rule."

"This isn't a joke, kid. There is no fun for us. Not out there. Not in here."

"Yeah, not with that *attitude, there isn't. You let your demon out for work, right? Maybe you just need to let him out to play a little."*

Let his demon out to *play*? How the scud had this girl passed training?

Probably the same way he had, he realized. Because he hadn't really been all that different when he'd been bumped up to the rank of Seeker four years ago, had he? Maybe not.

Alpha, it was irritating.

"The demon's play is *the work, kid. Give it a few years and you'll understand. Provided you make it that long."*

She was silent long enough that he might've thought she'd given up had he not felt her there, lingering at the edge of his mind.

"You're the one who took down two fallen today?"

"I did my job, same as any other day. So what?"

Another pause. *"You're hurting."*

He was about to ask what she meant, and how she could even tell, when the warmth began to creep in. He barely noticed it at first, like a soft trickle of sunlight on a cool Harvest day. But then it deepened and grew, lapping in on gentle waves.

"What are you... Stop that."

"It doesn't feel good?"

Another wave of warmth rocked in, this one more substantial, enfolding him. Teasing him.

"That's not the..." His breath was getting ragged, light tingles arcing through his body, pulsing in his groin. *"It feels fine. We just can't..."* Another wave hit him, and suddenly he was so hard that it hurt—some wild voice in his head demanding he leap from the cot and start knocking down walls until he found this woman. It was like lightning in his veins, crackling through an ocean of pure bliss. It was—

"Stop it. Now."

He was almost surprised he managed the words at all. Once they were out, he almost wished he hadn't. It felt so Alpha-damned good. For a long moment, he teetered there on the edge, conscious of her hesitation—his brain demanding that she stop while his body screamed for her to push him over. He couldn't move, conflicting desires holding him rapt at her mercy. Couldn't breathe.

Then the sensations began to recede, lapping away as gently as they'd drifted in, lowering him from a crackling cloud of bliss to his dark quarters, where he was panting to catch his breath, a light sweat on his brow and back, residual tingles shivering up and down his aching body.

"I was just trying to help."

He took a few more breaths to compose himself and tighten his mental defenses before answering.

"I'm not sure who that was supposed to help, but I need to make one thing clear. You can't pull that scud here. They'll kill you. Scud, I'll kill you. Our demons aren't Alpha-damned toys, girl. Don't try that again."

He felt the faintest overtones of the reaction rolling through her. Anger, maybe. Or indignation. He'd never been great at the empathetic side of telepathy—or the empathetic side of anything, really. When she finally replied, all he could say about her mental tone was that it was short.

"Fine. Okay. Got it."

He debated saying more, though he wasn't really sure what there was to be said. He almost felt bad for coming down on her. *Did* feel bad. Why the scud did he feel bad? Shutting down this bullscud from the start was the only move here, for both their sakes. But even so, he found himself needing to say something more.

"Get some sleep, Six. They'll probably put you on your first mark as soon as possible."

And hopefully they'd send Seven to oversee the operation instead of him. Let *her* deal with reining in this overeager rookie.

"Sure," she sent back. *"Sounds as good as any of my other choices."*

It was a bitter joke, of course. Choices were not something Seekers got to make, outside of things like what to eat from the fab and which weapon they'd use to expire their marks. But that wasn't about to change anytime soon, and no good would come of commiserating over it, so Two decided to leave it at that and try to take his own advice to find sleep.

It took a while, wired as he still was from whatever the scud she'd tried to do to him. He'd never felt anything like it. By comparison, Six's sensuous aura made One's suggestive imagery from earlier that day seem like a boring sleight-of-hand trick—all flash and no substance.

In a word, it was dangerous.

He didn't need any more assurance of that than the fact that he now found himself wondering what she looked like. What she smelled like.

Stop that, he chided himself.

Those thoughts were more dangerous than Six's uncanny ability. Because at the end of the day, she was one of the fallen. Her demon was every bit as vile as the rest of them—every bit the equal to the ugly beasts that he and One carried inside. It hadn't even truly been *her* pushing that telepathic temptation on him just then, he reminded himself. It had been the demon.

The thought made him feel even more unclean.

He held onto that feeling, prodding at it like an open wound, categorizing its nauseating depths to be used later, in case of hormone-induced stupidity. It didn't matter how sweet she might seem. She was a monster, just like him. And one way or another, this fanciful nature of hers would pass. It was a small miracle that wild spark of hers had even survived through the training at all. But she was a Seeker of the White Tower now.

This place would beat it out of her quickly enough.

How gropped up was his life that *that* was the comforting thought that finally settled his mind enough to start drifting toward sleep?

Whatever. He didn't fight it. Just welcomed the alluring promise of a break—however long—from what had been one flaming scudbucket of a long day. Finally, sleep came for him, carried in on the wings of one last quiet whisper.

"Nice meeting you, Two."

3

SHIVER

Two woke from a dream that made his spirit feel even more tainted than it already was—the kind of dream he would've laid there recounting for a while with a blushing afterglow and a strong inward chiding had he been alone.

But he wasn't.

He didn't have to turn his head to feel Cleric Verner standing there, watching him like a crusty old hawk.

"Sure, come on in," Two muttered, not quite under his breath, moving to push himself up from the cot and then quickly relenting at the fire the movement raked across his aching back. He groaned and tried again more slowly.

"You were dreaming," Verner said, his tone flat. He was staring down his long nose at Two without a detectable hint of any emotion, outside of general disapproval. No worry or sympathy for Two's clear pain. And certainly not a shred of respect for his privacy.

What privacy?

Two couldn't count the number of times Verner and his fellow handlers had marched into his meager room at whatever hours of the night or morning suited them—sometimes to deliver an assignment, sometimes just to remind him that they could.

"You were dreaming," the cleric repeated, as if it should mean something.

Two hoped to Alpha's immortal light it didn't.

"Yeah, that tends to happen from time to time." He thought about asking if he'd said or done something odd, but given what he'd been dreaming about, it seemed unwise. Consorting with demons. That would've been putting the dream's content lightly.

Definitely best they move on.

"Do you need something, Cleric?"

Verner turned his disapproving stare around the room, to the bare permacrete walls and the single chair at the plain desk. "There is little I need, fallen, but for the light of Alpha. Least of all do I need reason to check on my fallen charges."

And Two would do well to remember it. Right.

He bowed his head, a familiar mix of fear, resentment, and deference swirling through his gut. "Of course, your holiness. I only meant to ask if there is some service I might provide this morning."

When he finally deemed it acceptable to look back up, Verner's expression was still mostly stony, but the cleric gave a fractional nod of approval. "There is, child. Six's replacement arrived yesterday evening and is in need of acclimation. You are to show her to the relevant facilities and see to it she understands her boundaries here."

Something about the way Verner said the word, *acclimation*, made Two's stomach wriggle. But maybe that was just the post-dream guilt talking. Or, more likely, it was the sinking suspicion that the fates and Alpha above were set on pushing him straight toward what could only be bad news.

"Your holiness, with respect, I think Seven might be better suited for mentoring a new fallen who's..."

He was about to say *so impetuous* when he caught himself. He couldn't know that she was impetuous and severely boundary-deficient. They weren't supposed to have even met yet.

"... well, the females seem to do better with female guidance, yes?"

It was a bullscud cover-up. The only Seeker who might've hated One more than he did was Seven. And she and Eight weren't exactly friendly, either. Verner didn't say as much, but Two saw the edge of suspicion in his hawk-eyed stare.

"Forgive me, your holiness, it's just that I've never been the one to bring on a new member. I'm sure Seven would—"

"Seven departed this morning on assignment," Verner said, each word biting and slow. "And you will do as you're told, fallen."

Two swallowed. "Yes, your holiness. Of course."

He kept his head bowed, silently hating the rush of fear that still clawed at his gut whenever a cleric—especially Verner—took that tone.

Their handlers weren't bad people. He knew that on a rational level. They'd merely been tasked with the impossible. How could anyone—even a cleric—be expected to hold anything but disdain and contempt for someone like him, a broken spirit who'd fallen straight to demons' depths and back?

It was for this same reason that most of the Seekers despised each other—which was, in a twisted way, exactly why Two understood how Verner and the other handlers felt. What else could you feel for a monster? Pity, maybe. And Two was pretty sure their handlers *did* pity them, just as he pitied his own Seeker brethren. But, holy or not, there was no room for men like Verner to treat them with affection. It was simply too dangerous.

"If you require food or the privy," Verner said, "I will wait."

So maybe there was room for the smallest of kindnesses, at least. Two couldn't quite decide if the gratitude that swelled in his chest at Verner's offer was well-earned, or merely proof of just how perverse their arrangement here was.

Life got complicated, living with a demon on board.

He considered the fab in the corner of his small room and decided food could wait. Much as he appreciated the option, he hated eating with an audience, and despite his offer, Verner was clearly ready to complete his task and wash his hands of demons for the day. So instead, Two rose from his cot, ignoring the protests of his swollen back, and went to hurriedly splash some water on his face and pull on fresh clothes.

In the hallway outside, Verner's four-man detail of Sanctum Guard greeted him with their eerie stares, their opaque golden faceplates perfectly concealing the wary looks with which they no doubt regarded him. Two resisted the urge to point out that he didn't need help finding Six's room

—that, if he were to extend his senses and focus carefully enough, he could've told Verner not only where she was in the White Tower, but also what she was doing. Alpha, he could've told him what she was wearing.

And just like that, the dreams came back to him, sending the first excited thrill through his chest. He set his jaw and did his best to look his normal apathetic self as he marched along at the center of their procession for the nearest mag lifts. Outwardly, he was pretty sure it even worked. Inwardly, though...

No matter how much he wanted to be pissed about it, he couldn't totally drown out the foolish, drooling corner of his man brain that was excited to see the girl who'd nearly made him stain his linens last night. The *fallen* girl, he reminded himself, shuffling into the service lift beside Verner and the guards. It made him sick.

"I'm sure I don't need to remind you the transition can be disorienting for new Seekers," Verner said as one of his men tapped the lift controls. He fixed Two with a grave look. "Just as I need not remind you that you are not to be her friend, but merely a guiding hand."

"Yes, holiness," Two replied, with a deferential nod.

Disorienting was probably an understatement. To say the Seeker candidate training facility was a warm or nurturing place would've been an equally gross overstatement, but in the years between being conscripted to serve and either failing out—terminally, of course—or passing on to become Seekers, the place had at least been a source of some stability. Never mind that that stability had been painful more often than not. They'd been taught the true extent of the evil lurking inside each and every one of them, and given the tools to bring their demons under control. The whips, wielded always by their own hands. The explosive collars, fashioned from an elastic polymer so that they could grow as their young wearers did.

No, it had been far from a warm and fuzzy family estate. But to the kids who'd survived the horrible accidents, the abuse, and whatever else in their pasts that had primed them to join the ranks of the fallen, in a twisted way, that training facility had almost felt like a home.

Two still remembered the day he was told he was to graduate his training and become a true Seeker. He'd thought he'd been ready, thought he'd understood the job. On that day, he'd burned with pride. But then he'd gone to sleep that night and simply woken up in the White Tower. They didn't get to be conscious for the move—Two guessed because the clerics didn't trust their demons not to try to reverse engineer the location of the training facility, which was a carefully-kept secret none of the Seekers were privy to.

Either way, he'd woken scared and alone. Then Cleric Verner had come to him with the rumor of a man who'd been luring women into dark alleys and leaving them with even darker memories and strange reports of having been mentally present but unable to control their own bodies. Almost like a demon had crawled in and forced them into submission.

Find him, Verner had said, *and see to it Alpha's will is done.*

It hadn't been a clean job. Two hadn't been remotely ready. For any of it. Which was why he knew that, wise as the clerics might be in the ways of Alpha's Enochia, Verner had no idea what he was talking about when it came to what Six was going through. Then again, after last night, Two wasn't positive he did either. Six hadn't exactly seemed a frightened pup— indeed she seemed to be taking the change in stride.

But hadn't he put on that same external appearance when he'd first arrived? Calmly sarcastic on the outside, a trembling fountain of loose scud on the inside?

Whatever. It didn't matter, Two decided, as they filed out of the service lift. Because Verner was right. She wasn't his friend, and he wasn't hers. He'd make sure she understood that. He'd show her around, answer her questions, and then it'd be done. Simple as that.

Still, as they proceeded down the hall toward the room he already knew was Six's, he couldn't help but think he should reach out and give her a telepathic heads-up before Verner burst straight in like Two was sure he would. It was nothing more than common courtesy, right? Maybe. But he'd also be doing her no favors to blunt an important lesson that they were never really secure here.

Always alone, but never in private.

It turned out to be a lesson she was on top of. Verner was reaching to palm the access panel when the door hissed open in its tracks. And there she was.

Two had all of a second to process golden waves of hair and the outline of a pleasing figure beneath the roughspun trainee garb before her eyes flicked past Verner and caught him straight by the spirit.

A shiver ran through him. Or was it through his demon? He didn't know. Couldn't tell. His brain was too numb, those soft brown eyes too alluring.

"Two," Verner's voice snapped him back to his senses like a lash to the back, "meet the new Six."

Her lip quirked, presumably at his dumb stare, but she pulled it under control quickly enough and gave him a perfectly neutral wave.

Good. She wasn't stupid enough to tease him in front of a cleric. Two, on the other hand...

He composed himself, returning her dispassionate wave and turning to Verner. The cleric was watching him with that look that gave little away, outside of the general suggestion of judgment. He held Two's gaze for a second before turning back to Six.

"Two will be showing you to the relevant facilities today, as well as answering whatever questions he deems prudent to answer." He turned back to Two. "See to it she makes it to Kada by the tenth bell."

Two nodded wordlessly, not having to dig far to recover his demeanor of general displeasure at being here. Verner watched him for a second too long—or maybe that was just Two's paranoia setting in—then bid farewell to both of them, spoke a few quiet orders to the Sanctum Guard, and departed down the hallway post-haste, his cream and gold robes swirling gently in his wake.

"So, where to first, goodfellow?" asked a warm, sultry voice behind him.

It nearly sent another shiver through him.

Alpha, what was it with this woman that every facet of her seemed to call to his blood? It felt almost preternatural—enough so that he wondered for the second time if it wasn't something to do with her demon calling to his. It didn't seem impossible. He'd heard of some fallen forming exceptionally tight bonds out there in the wild. But he'd never had this kind of reaction to a fallen before. Not even with those whose lives might've been prolonged or even saved by managing to twist his mind with lust or sympathy.

He did his best to drop the thought and emulate Verner's dispassionate mask as he turned back to her, careful not to actually meet her eyes.

"We'll start with breakfast down in the messes, if that suits you."

She gave a slight shrug—Alpha, even the way she shrugged was alluring—but said nothing, her gaze flicking to the four Sanctum Guard at his back before returning to him, waiting to see if he'd add more. He was about to ask if she'd like to change before remembering that he was probably supposed to bring her to Kada because she didn't *have* anything to change into.

"If you'd like to clean up, or..." He waved a helpless hand, unsure where he was going with this train of thought, or why.

She glanced down the front of her roughspun tunic and back to him. "Sarentus' mercy, am I in need of cleaning, Seeker?"

"No. I was merely being... Never mind. Let's go."

She didn't argue, just gave another one of those delicious little shrugs and stepped out into the hallway. Didn't even bother to close the door behind her.

Alpha, it was going to be a long morning.

4

THREE LESSONS

"Your quarters are... adequate?" Two asked as he palmed Six's door closed and turned for the lifts.

It was a pointless question. Her quarters were a carbon copy of his humble lodgings, just like all the Seekers'. No one found them adequate, aside from maybe Four, whose brooding spirit seemed meant for bare permacrete walls, and Eight, who, as far as Two could tell, didn't really take enjoyment in much of anything aside from honor and duty.

"It's a cot and four walls," she said, her tone perfectly demon-may-care.

It was a facade he recognized all too well. Or at least he thought it was. But it wasn't like he was going to tell her she could cut the bullscud and tell him how she was really feeling. Not with four Sanctum Guard wordlessly trailing behind them—here not so much to keep them in line, Two knew, as to observe and report to Cleric Verner on any concerning behaviors.

So he said nothing at all until they sat across from one another at one of the white polymer tables of one of the smaller, more private White Tower mess halls, picking at eggs and grains in what felt like some kind of unspoken competition to out-casual one another while their four watch hounds sat at the next table over with their helmets removed so they could join the game and pick at their own plates of food.

"Typically, you'll take your meals alone from the fab in your room," Two said, when he judged everyone to be sufficiently settled.

Six returned from some distant thought and considered him, taking her time to finish her bite before replying. "Sounds isolating."

"That's kinda the point," Two said, watching the closest Sanctum Guard out of the corner of his eye. "Lesson number one: you are not a part of this community. You know you exist on the fringes to keep the monsters at bay. I know too. But to them"—he waved his fork in a small but all-encompassing circle—"you have to be nothing. You are not an acolyte. Not even an acolyte's boot licker. You don't exist."

Six wasn't chewing now, or even picking at her plate. "Shouldn't be a problem," she finally said. In his mind, she added, *Aren't you supposed to be comforting me or something?*

"No, I'm really not."

"Good," he added out loud, for the benefit of their silent watchers. "Then finish your food, and we can move on to lesson two."

He had to suppress a satisfied smirk as the Sanctum Guard at the edge of his vision relaxed, his wary suspicion temporarily assuaged by the seeming pause in their little exchange.

"But speaking of things we're supposed to be doing," he sent while pointedly shoveling the last of his eggs down, *"what the scud was that back there at your door?"*

Her brow started to wrinkle in confusion, but she managed to cover the slip-up by leaning in and inspecting some imaginary oddity on her plate. *"What the scud was what?"* she sent back. *"Are you always this tense?"*

"Only when naive little recruits think it's funny to play their head games in front of the Alpha-damned head of our handlers. I told you not to try that scud again."

Something flashed in her eyes—something that looked like amusement until she lurched forward, coughing up eggs into her hand linen.

That got the attention of the Sanctum Guard right quick. Not that they moved to help. Just perked up, listening more attentively.

"Sorry," she groaned after a couple smaller coughs. "I'm just... wrong pipe." She touched a delicate hand to her abdomen. "My stomach doesn't seem to be handling all this change well."

"I didn't do scud back there, Two," she added.

Maybe it was the grimace on her face, or the way the placement of her hand conveniently seemed to draw the eye straight to the generous swell of her chest, but their guards seemed more or less appeased by her explanation.

Two wasn't.

"You'll get over it," he said, gathering his plate and rising from the bench. "Come on."

"These people will kill you, Six," he sent as they went to deposit their dishes in the mess' wash receptacle. *"And they'll kill me too if you keep dragging me into these games."*

"Look, I don't know what you think I did up there, but I feel the need to point out that you're the one gropping cots in the midnight hour. Maybe you just think I'm cute, man."

He pulled open the receptacle's cover. *"I think you're trouble."*

"I think you have serious issues with women," she sent, scooting in and sliding her plate and cup down the chute.

"I think I should tell Verner to throw you back and find a new Six."

She paused in turning away from the chute, searching his face. He didn't mean to meet her eyes. Had been deliberately avoiding it. But suddenly there they were, studying one another, and even here, in plain sight of four Sanctum Guard and another couple dozen acolytes and citizens, his head buzzed with the closeness of her.

"Then why don't you?" she sent softly.

He turned without a word, barely caring at this point whether she was quick enough to keep their crumbling act together for the benefit of their observers.

This was not good.

His heart picked up at the sight of one of the Sanctum Guard holding his palmlight to his ear before glancing in Two's direction and giving a slight nod, as if he'd just received some communication and was confirming... confirming what? That they were finishing up in the mess hall? That Two was off the rails and needed to be put down immediately?

The guard slid his helmet back on, his golden faceplate hiding all thought and emotion from sight. A tingling itch crept across Two's neck, right at the line of his collar. His hands clenched, resisting the urge to reach for the damn thing. Was this it? He felt like he was going to explode. Maybe *was* going to explode.

Then something soft and perfectly languid crept through him, like a warm cloud settling at his center.

"You definitely have issues with women," came Six's voice. He turned to find her watching him expectantly, like she was waiting to see where they were supposed to go next. *"And you're really not a very good tour guide, either."*

Across the room, the other Sanctum Guard were all pulling on their helmets while the one Two had been sure was the herald of his doom gathered their dishes and went to drop them in the wash receptacle.

He almost could've laughed. Had he really been imagining the whole thing?

Before he could finish chiding himself for being a panicky fool, some of the warmth crept out of him. Too much.

He looked back at Six. "Did you just...?"

She shrugged. "You kinda looked like you might explode just now. I can't imagine that would've ended well for me."

Two started to open his mouth, clenched his jaw instead. Never mind that it was the truest thing she'd said all morning and that he should've been relieved to find she wasn't utterly clueless about how dangerous this place was. She'd worked her abilities on his mind again. And worse, it seemed his baseline defenses weren't worth a damn against her special brand of telepathic manipulation.

"Come on," he said. "We're leaving."

He caught the eye—or general faceless attention, rather—of one of the Sanctum Guard and tilted his head toward the door. The Guard nodded. They could've talked, of course. Eventually, anyone who spent long enough in the mini-city of the White Tower started to catch on anyway that there was a small group of nondescript no-names who shared an unusual relationship with the Sanctum Guard—occasionally almost seeming to be their commanders, but most of the time looking more like their prisoners. Luckily, the faithful servants of the Sanctum asked as few questions as the loyal hounds of the Legion. Even so, Sanctum Guard and

Seekers tended to only speak when necessary—mostly because neither was particularly fond of the other.

And right now, Two wasn't particularly fond of anyone. Least of all the blonde time bomb hurrying to keep pace on his flank.

"Look, I don't know what you want me to say," she sent, her thoughts steeped in exasperation.

He'd show her the necessary stops, he'd get her to Kada, and that would be it. She'd be someone else's problem—all set to deconstruct what little life she had left here as a Seeker without dragging him into it. That thought even let him conjure up a polymer smile as she shuffled into the lift next to him, their four guards on her tail.

"Fine," she sent. *"You want me to admit I'm all scared and lonely? I am. Does that help you pull your manhood back in one piece?"*

Two punched the command for the Great Hall, all the way up—the pinnacle of the White Tower. The jewel of the Sanctum. The place where the good people went to be closest to Alpha, and the apostates went to meet his justice.

It seemed an appropriate place to start.

"No?" she sent. *"Scared lonely girl not doing it for you?"*

He consciously refrained from clenching his fists and resisted the impulse to look at her. *"You have an interesting choice of nocturnal activities for a scared lonely girl."*

"See, I think it's interesting that you think that's interesting."

"What I think is that you're not ready for this job."

"Come on, you're telling me you don't like to punish the wicked when you're lonely?"

"The fact that you'd even think about calling it that tells me you're definitely not ready for this job."

"Well Alpha be sweet, then. Guess I'd better march on over to Verner and let him know. I'm sure the lecherous old bastard would think of something to do with me, don't you?"

His reaction this time was only masked by the slowing of the mag lift and the chime announcing they'd arrived at their destination.

"That's a cleric you're talking about, fallen."

The bite in his mental tone took him by surprise. Why did this girl's every word make him so angry? Probably because half of the things that left her mouth were pure blasphemy. But it wasn't like the same couldn't have been said about him when he'd first arrived here at the Tower. And maybe therein lay the root of his irritation.

"That's also a human I'm talking about," she sent as they stepped out of the lift, her tone more subdued now. *"A man, too. And lest my feminine intuition deceive me, a man who takes... a certain pleasure in that which he deems heretical."*

"You're full of scud."

"I sure hope so," she said slowly, staring at their surroundings in awe, *"the way this is all going. Sweet Alpha."*

He didn't bother responding. Just let her drink in the illustrious majesty of the antechamber they'd arrived in. Rich ivory tiles, veined with gold. Intricate darkwood etchings working their way up the abundant open wall space, all the way up to the angled duraglass ceiling high above. The room was enormous. Even after being here as many times as he had, it was hard to believe a place of such splendor could even be in the same building as his hundred and fifty square foot permacrete prison.

And this was only the antechamber.

The wonder on Six's face as she took it all in sparked the first glimmer of hope in Two's chest. Maybe he could still bring this whole thing under control. Maybe all she'd needed was the right perspective—a reminder of the Sanctum's power, and where they stood in the eyes of Alpha.

"Come on," he said, starting for the mouth of the dark stone path that led through two towering rows of mighty columns to the Great Hall beyond. "It's time for lesson number two."

"Which is?"

"You must never forget who it is you serve."

Six didn't reply, only followed quietly along, her lips parted in perpetual awe, her eyes tracing every inch of the expansive decor. It was the first time their trailing Sanctum Guard actually seemed somewhat at ease, as if they had no fear any evil could befall them in this place. Two almost began to relax himself, save for the glowing ember of unease that he always felt in any worship hall—the guilty weight of the knowledge he was tainting a holy place. He reached the opening between the two massive column lines, and that perverse swirl of guilt and satisfaction only deepened.

He hadn't been sure if the gallows would still be there. The ceremony had only been last night, but usually they were quick about removing the unsightly relic, especially on those occasions when it was actively used in the ceremony. Last night, though, its function had been only symbolic—a reminder of the justice that had been served on Alpha's behalf. But there it was in the distance, on the second plateau of the massive four-tier head of the Great Hall, in the process of being prepped for storage by half a dozen acolytes.

Two felt the subtle shift in the weight of the room behind him as Six caught sight of the barbaric device in the distance. She didn't say anything at first, and he was content to let her soak it in as they proceeded down the dark stone path to the Great Hall proper, dwarfed between the great stone columns. When they finally cleared the column line and the full extent of the Great Hall exploded out around them with its vast expanse of stonework and its towering duraglass windows, Six stopped walking, a trace of fear mixing with the reverence on her face.

"I... understand why you brought me here," she sent finally.

The meekness in her tone felt odd after the rest of their exchanges. But that was exactly what he'd wanted, right?

"I know life at the training facility was no joke, but you need to understand stepping up to this place... just because you have more freedom doesn't mean you're any more free than you were back there." He looked around, his gaze settling on the gallows at the head of the hall, and the point felt almost too well-made. *"The only difference here is that they willingly give us enough rope to hang ourselves with."*

Her gaze followed his. *"Yeah, that's... graphic. But I get it."* She turned back to him, searching his face with those lovely brown eyes. *"So help a girl out, huh? What are friends for?"*

With a significant force of will, he pulled his eyes away from hers and realized they'd been doing a scud job of maintaining their charade of conversing out loud for their guard detail. The four Sanctum Guard, though, hadn't seemed to notice their silent interaction. Their faithful attention was directed to the activity at the head of the Great Hall. When Two looked, a couple of them were tracing Alpha's sigil over their breasts.

"I've been trying," he sent back. *"You're just bad at listening."*

"Hey, maybe you're bad at teaching," she snapped back, with a trace of her earlier spunk.

Two bristled, but her face was already falling.

"I didn't mean—I'm just... being difficult, I know. I'm sorry." She looked back up at him. *"So what's next? What's lesson number three?"*

Two gazed around the enormous hall, looking for *what* exactly, he couldn't have said. A sense of righteousness, maybe, or even just simple purpose. But as he looked around, he couldn't seem to find anything but the blunt, inescapable reminder that, after having stood four long years ago almost exactly where Six was now, he was every bit as trapped as she was. More so. And the part of him that had once longed for that freedom he spoke of? That was the worst part.

He couldn't seem to find it anywhere.

And there was Six, watching him, waiting like some scolded pup for him to give her a pat on the head and tell her in soothing tones that it was all right and that he hadn't meant to be so rough—that if she was good she could soon play to her little heart's content. Waiting for lesson three. Like he knew what the scud he was talking about. Like four years' worth of fallen blood on his hands made him someone to be listened to. It was sickening. Infuriating. He couldn't stand that look on her face.

Lesson three?

"I'm glad you asked, Six, because lesson three is really quite an important one."

He held her eyes, not bothering to try to hide the depths of misery roiling in his tainted spirit.

"Lesson three: I am not your gropping friend."

5

THE JOB

The rest of the morning passed by incident-free, if not exactly pleasantly. Lesson Three in the Great Hall decisively marked the end of their clandestine telepathic conversation. From there, Two showed Six to the armory, introduced her to the few analysts she might have cause to occasionally work with in operations, and lastly took her to see the skimmer bay where they kept their own small fleet for Seeker use.

Part of him wanted to apologize for lashing out earlier. Most of him wanted to see that mischievous grin return to her lips. But it hadn't been for random maliciousness that he'd said what he'd said. They really couldn't be friends. Not if they wanted to live. And so, when the time came to deliver Six to Kada, she arrived fully intact but lacking any comforting words from him and noticeably depleted of all apparent spunk. By all means, holy and otherwise, that should've been that.

She didn't bother him as he lay in his cot that night. Only in his dreams.

Still, the next day he woke with a kind of burgeoning lightness in his chest. Or at least the closest thing to lightness he was used to feeling. For now, it seemed, he was in the clear, all set to keep his head for another few years. Not that that was purely happy news, but it was at least reassuring. He felt stability returning like an old, disinterested spouse—in it for the long haul, just please don't interrupt my storyvids, thank you very much. After a cold shower and a bowl of thick breakfast grains from the fab, he was actually starting to feel kind of good.

Then his palmlight buzzed and rectified that bullscud right quick.

A message from operations—which, he knew, almost certainly meant a message from Verner, whether directly or not.

<ASSIGNMENT: *First mark support for Six.*>

What followed was a list of what little information they'd gathered on the mark, a preternaturally lucky dice roller who'd apparently set up shop right in the slums of their very own Divinity. Not a good move on his part. The report was little more than rumors and speculation, but there was a decent chance they were on to something. It'd be easy enough for Six to figure out once she was on site. It was what she'd have to do about this dice roller if the rumors panned out that was the real problem. Which was exactly why Verner had opted to send Two for support, of course.

Because how the scud else could this situation with Six get any more confusing for him?

The first mark was never easy. Not even for a sadistic psychopath like One. Which was why there was always a second Seeker present for the first kill. For insurance in case of weak stomachs—and, more often than not, for a few words of comfort after the fact. No amount of logic and faith that you'd done a good thing—that you'd eliminated a demon from the world—could completely override the tiny fact that there'd been a human life lost in the balance. If ever there was a time that one Seeker was meant to be a friend to another...

"Scud," he growled softly at the remnants of breakfast grains in his bowl.

The grains didn't have much to say on the matter, so he tossed the bowl into the sink, pulled on his jacket, and left the room, heading for the service lifts, and one of the smaller, more private worship halls after that. The briefing they'd sent him had indicated they wouldn't depart on this operation until nightfall, when their lucky dice roller was rumored to be active.

Normally, Two would've saved his ritual worship hall visit until closer to mission time, but somehow, he was more nervous about this job than he had been about any of his own in years. Killing people was never going to be easy, but pulling the trigger on demons had certainly grown a lot simpler after he'd gotten over the initial hump. Babysitting someone else through their first kill, though?

His stomach was churning just thinking about it.

He thought about reaching out to Six to see how she was handling the news of her first mark arriving so quickly. But that was a bad idea. For one, they might've told him before they'd told her. For another, he needed her to believe what he'd said yesterday. If Verner was going to push him into being her support, he'd give her the right word or two when it was time. Just enough. Nothing more.

Then he'd get back to despising his own miserable life on his own— just the way he liked it.

Luckily, the cleric on duty in Two's habitual worship hall—more an alcove than an actual hall—was one of the many who didn't know what Two was. Not that the odds had been against him or anything. Very few of the clerics—probably less than one in a hundred across Enochia—were even aware that true demons actually walked among them, much less that they were able to do far more than just tempt and corrupt. If they'd known that fallen like him were real, and that they could literally bend the shape of reality and the minds of men as readily as soft clay...

That knowledge alone probably would've had the clerics rousing the public into a zealous and no doubt poorly-executed demon hunt across Enochia. The knowledge that the Sanctum kept a dozen such demons in their service, on the other hand?

There was a reason very few were privy to that information. Only a few handfuls of living clerics at a time, as far as Two could guess. It didn't matter that the Seekers were serving Alpha as best they could—that they existed only to hunt that which couldn't feasibly be hunted by any other. If knowledge of the Seeker core ever hit public circulation, Two didn't want to imagine what manner of scudstorm would erupt. From a certain point of view, it might've even seemed funny, to think how much power the Sanctum had inadvertently placed in the Seekers' laps. Not that Two or any of the other twelve would ever dare attempt to apply that leverage.

Their spirits were already stained enough as it was.

Two nearly jumped when the cleric of the small hall appeared in front of him. He hadn't heard the slender man coming—had barely even noticed himself taking a seat on one the benches toward the back, lost as he had been in his own thoughts.

"Holiness," Two murmured, bowing his head.

The cleric—Two couldn't remember this particular one's name—laid a gentle hand on his bowed head. "Something troubles your spirit today, child?"

Despite everything, Two couldn't help but share a bitter grin with the rich, cream-colored carpet at that. "Your holiness... You have no idea."

THE REMAINDER of the day passed uneventfully—albeit slowly, thanks to the incessant churning in his gut—and by the time the tenth bell of the evening rang, Two had yet to hear from Six. He got ready to head out, dreading what was coming but also eager to get the whole thing over with —provided it was still on, of course. Verner almost certainly would've had operations tell him, had plans changed, but he'd still started to wonder when he'd sat down for a light supper still having not heard so much as a telepathic peep.

Maybe she was too nervous to ask for consolation. Probably, she was just too bitter or proud to come to him at all after his harsh words yesterday. Scud, maybe she was sitting there cool as a kukra melon, having convinced herself she was actually ready for this. He doubted that last one, but either way, it wasn't going to do anyone any good, him sitting around pontificating about it. So he set off for the lifts, heading for Six's room first.

She wasn't there—or didn't answer his knock at least.

He reached out with his senses to make sure, then moved on to the armory to grab a sidearm—a step that never ceased to feel ludicrously pointless to him. Because if his demon ever actually managed to slip his control and take the reins, it was hardly going to need a sidearm to wreak destruction, and even if it wanted one, it wasn't like the couple Sanctum Guard on armory duty were going to be able to stop it. But for whatever brain-touched reason, the protocol was one in the very long list of precautions that made the handlers feel better. Two suspected this particular protocol was much more about the reminder of what the Seekers were and who they belonged to than it was about the actual act of restricting their weapons access.

Still, it was hardly the worst of his troubles, he decided once he'd procured a weapon and was on his way to their skimmer bay, where this morning's missive had instructed they should meet their detail of Sanctum Guard—yet another bitter wrinkle in tonight's scud fest. Not that having Sanctum Guard along was all bad. He preferred hunting alone, and often times was allowed to these days, but if he had to have backup, he'd take Sanctum Guard over legionnaires or anyone else nine times out of ten.

But tonight was definitely that tenth time.

Keeping a new Seeker safe and stable through her first job would've been bad enough. But doing it under the watchful eye of Verner's hand-picked rat squad?

Alpha help them if anything went sideways.

He arrived at the skimmer bay fifteen minutes before their designated meeting time. Whether out of nerves or some unexpected respect for punctuality, Six was already there. Probably the nerves, Two guessed, judging by the way she was sitting on a skimmer hood, eyes distant and hands clasped in her lap. Her gaze snapped to him as he stepped into the bay, and something flickered across her brow as she took him in. Was it irritation? Disdain? He couldn't quite figure it out before she disengaged and pointedly returned to staring at the far permacrete wall. Then he took in what she was wearing, and for a few seconds, it was all he could do not to deteriorate into a gaping, slack-jawed swell hound.

He stared with a tight jaw instead.

Cleavage. Merciful Alpha with the cleavage. It wasn't even that the forest green blouse Six had chosen for tonight's mission was particularly low cut. It was just that her swells seemed to leap out anyway, throwing the tendrils of their curvaceous presence straight across the room, sure as any demon, and snagging him straight by some spot deep in his core, below the viscera. The bare skin of her legs didn't help matters either, where it lay exposed between the tops of her dark boots and the frilly hem of her...

"You, uh..." He shook his head, trying to clear it—trying to stop tracing the soft curves of her bared flesh and extrapolating the tantalizing image of what lay beneath. He couldn't believe Kada would've fashioned these garbs, or, more importantly, that Verner would have approved of them—out loud, at least.

Six, for her part, had seemed content to continue staring at the plain gray wall as if he didn't exist—a probable sign, some corner of his brain suggested, that she was still angry with him about yesterday—but at his stuttered start, she shot a frown his way. "What?"

He tore his gaze away from her lovely legs. "You're wearing a skirt."

Her eyes widened, jaw slackening in a look of surprise his swell-muddled brain didn't quite register as mocking until she pointedly gaped down at said skirt and back to him.

So they were back to the childish games already?

Two resisted the urge to rise to her baiting and roll his eyes. Instead, he glanced over her once more. It wasn't exactly like the outfit would put her in harlot territory out on the streets of Divinity. With the chic brown leather jacket and the way she'd arranged her golden hair, she'd probably fit right in actually—would probably in fact have half the bachelors in Divinity sniffing after her. But that was the problem, wasn't it? She was going to draw attention, looking like that. Especially in the slums, where many of the so-called bachelors left more than a bit to be desired in the realm of manners and impulse control.

"It seems ill-advised," he finally said, "walking into a potential combat situation in a skirt."

"I wasn't planning on getting into any fights."

"You might not want a fight. I get that. But you *always* plan for one."

She shot him a sweet acid smile that did strange things to his insides. "Is that lesson number four?"

"That's just the job, kid."

It felt kind of perverse and more than a little impotent, calling her *kid* while he was just shy of pulling a muscle trying to keep from staring at her tits. She seemed to notice, too, because that smile of hers only sharpened as she leaned back on the skimmer hood and reached back to support herself on her hands in a way that only put the generous curves of her breasts on display that much more. He did his best not to squirm under her silent stare.

"So what's your plan, then?" he asked, waving a hand at the spectacle. "You're just gonna flit around, catch this dangerous criminal's eye, and..." He waved his hand some more, unsure how to finish the thought.

She just gave a salacious little shrug, her smile sweetening. "Pretty much, yeah."

"Forgive me if I fail to see how the scud that's actually a plan at all."

"Well, we're supposed to play to our strengths, right?"

"Sure, but—"

"Well I'm not that great with telekinesis, Two. Not particularly strong, either. And I'm certainly no master at arms." She gave him a pointed look. "What I'm good at is driving telepaths wild." Her lips twitched, and for the first time, the bitter edge in her expression gave ground to real amusement. "What I'm good at is making big strong Seekers explode on their linens with a thought and a wink."

His cheeks burned at her casual amusement, but he forced himself to hold her stare. "That's a far cry from killing a man."

She dropped his gaze, but the small hint of victory that swelled in his chest quickly staled at the way her smile brittled, so clearly surface-deep at this point. All traces of amusement gone, she pulled a slender flask from an inside coat pocket. "That's what this is for."

He frowned at the flask. Poison? Probably. The thought made him uneasy, as did the deeper implications of what she was saying.

Verner had trained a venom-fanged seductress. Or had signed off on one being trained, at least.

It felt wrong.

Using the Seekers' demons to fight fire with fire was already bad enough. Using them to ensnare the fallen, though? To twist their minds and desires and lure them in like slobbering bulls only to slip them poison... somehow, it seemed worse. Out of the twelve, Eleven was the only one who'd occasionally employed poison in the past, and that had always been markedly different. This...

This was just going to have to happen, he realized, as the sound of boot steps at the doorway announced the arrival of their Guard detail. But not just their Guard, he saw with a flicker of surprise.

Verner himself had come to see them off.

And was it just Two's imagination, or had the good cleric been stealing a peep at Six's forest-green-bound cleavage when Two turned?

"Holiness," Two murmured, dipping his head as Six echoed the greeting behind him.

"You are ready for this, child?" came Verner's voice.

Two looked up to confirm Verner's words had been addressed to Six. She all but wilted under his attention, eyes falling, shoulders rounding, hands returning to clasp one another in the fold of her lap. It was some combination of impressive and heartbreaking, how quickly the presence of a cleric flipped her modesty switch.

Two understood completely.

"Of course, your holiness," she said softly.

"Good," Verner said, looking satisfied. Very satisfied indeed, Two couldn't help but notice, as the cleric studied her a few seconds longer. "Very good." He turned to Two for the first time. "You will confirm the mark's affliction before any action is taken. Outside of that, you will assist only if it becomes absolutely necessary."

Two had already known his duties running support on a first mark, of course. He'd thought he'd made peace with them. But now his insides churned at the thought of watching Six lure some grizzled fallen off into a dark corner, barely able to contain himself, ready to fall to his knees—to do anything—to please her. Watching her reel him in, her hand casually finding its way to his chest, right over the man's bounding heart. Would she smile as she offered him a drink? Would she offer more? A kiss? How far would it go before—

"Do you understand, fallen?"

Verner was watching him with that same suspicious look he'd worn when Two had first officially met Six the day before. Two did his best to keep his face empty as he nodded, trying not to betray his guilty thoughts by wilting as Six had.

"Of course, your holiness."

Verner surveyed them both for another few seconds before giving himself one last satisfied nod. "On with it, then. Alpha be with you both."

Not for the first time, Two sincerely hoped that the cleric's blessing carried more than the weight of its words alone.

6

THE HARDEST PART

The smell of chronic body odor and ill-contained human waste was like a living thing trying to crawl its way from the cloying Divinity air right into Two's tightly-closed mouth. Next to him, he felt Six readily match his increased stride, hastening them past the patchwork doors of the particularly pungent vagrant den and down the filthy alleyway.

"Oh how sweet, to be home again," Six sent.

He ignored the comment. Unpleasant as it was, the smell was hardly the worst he'd ever experienced, having spent his fair share of time on the streets throughout his shattered childhood. Given Six's comment about being home again, not to mention the fact that pretty much every Seeker trainee was gathered from the streets, he imagined Six had experienced plenty worse too. Still, he felt her relief almost as clearly as his own when a strong whiff of smoke swept down the alley, helping to wash some of the human stench from their nostrils. Not that whatever was burning ahead smelled especially wonderful either. But that was the slums for you, right?

He started to open his mouth, then glanced back over his shoulder, to where he could feel the Sanctum Guard following by his prickling neck hairs alone. Would Verner be sitting in Watchtower control, listening in? Was he watching right now? He'd certainly seemed interested enough in this mission. Or in Six, at least. Two pushed that thought down as quickly as it rose, right along with the confusing mess of... whatever it was that the thought stirred up in his chest.

"You sure you're ready for this?" he sent as they drew close to the mouth of the narrow alleyway, the voices and bustle of the gathering ahead washing over them now like a stinking wave of alcohol and greed.

"What does it matter?" she sent back, pausing beside him. *"Not like I have a choice. Or a friendly ear to hear my woes."*

He stopped, turning to face her in the dim, flickering light. She was staring through the gathering ahead with a distant look, her jaw tight.

"Nervous?" he asked.

She stiffened, like his words had startled her. *"Of course I'm nervous, you ass."*

"Well why didn't you say so sooner?"

She fixed him with an incredulous stare.

"What?"

"Lesson number three," she sent, her mental tone pure acid. *"Remember, scudhead?"*

He bristled, anger roiling through his chest, priming his tongue to spit out half a dozen different shots about *maybe if she hadn't acted like an impulsive child from the very start,* and *did she really gropping think he had even the slightest desire to be out here right now? Laying his neck on the line beside the girl who'd worn a gropping skirt to come slay a demon?*

But he was here now. His neck *was* on the line. And she was afraid. He could see it in her eyes.

"Okay," he sent softly. *"Okay, just, never mind that for now. We're going to get you through this thing tonight, and then we can worry about the rest later. Deal?"*

She chewed her lip for several seconds and didn't quite nod, but didn't outright tell him to grop himself, either.

"Let's confirm we actually have a fallen on our hands before we get too carried away, yeah?"

This time she did nod, meeting his eyes with renewed focus, and he felt a sliver of the tension in his chest give way to something else. She started toward the mouth of their dim alleyway and the raucous slum square gathering beyond, but he reached out and caught her by the elbow to stop her. She didn't pull away, just looked from his hand on her elbow up to his face, a question in her eyes.

He let go quickly, hoping none of their Sanctum watchers had seen the contact. *"Better to sweep for him from here. Not that this is exactly a dinner party at the High Praetors, but even these people might notice if you go vacant in the middle of the party."*

Another nod. *"Good point. You'll keep watch here?"*

He nodded, and her eyes slid closed. Somewhere at the edge of his senses, he vaguely felt her start to reach out, but with her attention so completely focused elsewhere, he was too ensnared in the soft curves of her cheeks and the fullness of her lips to notice much else. He watched as those lips drew tight in concentration, her brow lightly creasing. It was the first time he'd been able to really look at her without feeling like he'd have to do battle with her stubborn wit over it. It almost felt wrong, staring so openly. But also exhilarating. The seconds ticked by, her breath rising and falling, and he couldn't look away. He wanted to reach out and touch her —was all but paralyzed by the irrational desire, his heart thundering at the perverse impurity of his feelings for this demon-ridden girl.

Then her eyes slid back open.

He swallowed, trying to pull himself together, hoping he wasn't actually salivating. She searched his face for a silent moment, her brow crinkled ever-so-slightly.

"Anything?" he sent, desperate to deflect any impending questions.

"Something. I'm pretty sure he's out there. To the left from the alleyway, two fires down, right in the middle of the big game."

She was still watching him with an odd look. But maybe that was just his own confused conscience talking. It didn't matter. They had work to do.

Briefly, Two closed his eyes and confirmed her findings. She hadn't been exaggerating when she'd said the mark was right in the middle of a big game. Two's stomach sank. The bastard must've been surrounded by fifty people out there. One of them clapped the guy on the back while Two was feeling the scene out. Two drew his senses back to the alleyway, not wanting to set off the mark's inner alarm. Or his demon's alarm, at least. The mark himself seemed more than a little preoccupied—slightly drunk, by the feel of it, and shouting and taunting with the best of them as he prepared for another roll.

When Two came back to his physical senses in the alleyway, Six was still watching him, but his misgivings at what he'd felt out there killed any of those ludicrous flutters from taking off in his stomach. Crowds were never good news, and especially not crowds of which your mark was the life of the Alpha-damned party. Give him a reclusive nomad any day—the ones who drifted from hideout to hideout, always alone, always in quiet places. Made things a scudload easier. Looking at Six, though, he decided that maybe this was exactly the kind of job she was suited for. A crowd might not be such a problem when you could probably get most men to follow you straight off a sheer cliff.

"What are you thinking?" came her voice in the middle of his thoughts.

"I'm thinking it's way too busy out there. Can you get him alone?"

The faintest grin tugged at those sensuous lips of hers. He felt her confidence building now—felt it somewhere right below his stomach and above his thighs.

"Wouldn't you follow me into a dark alley?" she sent.

He suppressed the urge to swallow. *"Technically, I already did."*

She tilted her head. *"Fair point. So are we doing this?"*

"You're doing this. Verner wants to see that you have what it takes to do it alone. I'll be close, though. Watching the whole time."

The news didn't seem to throw her newfound confidence. If anything, it just added a few degrees to the sultry heat of her grin.

"Well, I hope you enjoy what you see, Two."

His head buzzed with the intensity of her eyes on his. Was that just him, or was she already turning on the demonic charm in preparation for her debut? Impossible to tell. But one thing was certain. As she turned from him and strode out of the alleyway, skirted hips swaying with each mesmerizing step, he couldn't deny it.

He enjoyed the scud out of what he saw.

AN HOUR LATER, Two was enjoying what he saw a whole scudload less. Not because things were going poorly. Quite the opposite.

Six was clearly a natural in these kinds of situations, as evidenced by her current place at the roaring heart of the dice crowd, with that sleazy bastard's dirty arm draped around her waist. Two watched from the dirt-caked window of a depressingly small and abandoned apartment as the fallen raised his dice to Six's lips with a wide, scud-eating grin beneath his mangy beard. Six obliged all too willingly with yet another blow on the dice. Grin widening, the fallen threw yet another roll. Yet another win.

He celebrated with a nice firm handful of Six's skirted ass.

Two's hands, already in fists, clenched tighter. Six just shot her fallen vagrant a mischievous grin, and ground her hip into his. Was that actual enjoyment on her face? Or was she just that good at her role? He couldn't tell.

By and large, killing fallen was something Two did out of methodical necessity. It was a job. An important job, but one that he never took any particular pleasure in.

With this guy, though, he might actually enjoy it.

Except it wasn't his kill to make this time, was it? It was Six's.

He found himself almost wishing she'd trip up, just so he could have the satisfaction of ending that ever-grinning, dice-tossing, ass-grabbing scudbucket. But that wouldn't do. If Six failed here tonight, it wouldn't necessarily mean the end of her run as a Seeker, but it most certainly wouldn't land her on firm ground, either. Still, he had a feeling it was a moot point. Thus far, Six had worked her way into the dice-roller's circle like an Alpha-damned natural. Every man down there wanted her, and probably half the women too—the ones who weren't too busy shooting her dirty glares, at least.

Scud, the way some of the men were eyeing her, Two thought they might be contemplating killing the dice-roller themselves just to get their own shot with her. Those ones made him nervous. Because as easily as she'd worked her way into the crowd, he still wasn't sure she'd be ready if the scud hit the turbines.

She *was* wearing a skirt, for Alpha's sake.

So he watched with a steady tension, ready to leap in if need be, and ever wary that the Sanctum Guard were doing the same—two from the rooftop of his building, and two more from the building across the fire-lit square this flock of vagrants, lowlifes, and common criminals had gathered in for their night of drinking and gambling and Alpha knew what else. Several times, he thought about reaching out to Six and making sure she was okay, that everything was going according to plan, and that the mark's dice-stroking fingers weren't getting too adventurous for her liking. The desire grew even stronger when he noticed that she was glancing up to his window every few minutes, but he refrained by sheer force of will.

This was her job. She'd call if she needed help. And he *wasn't* her gropping friend, right?

The seconds crawled by, scraping their scuddy way into minutes and, eventually, another half hour—Six grinding against her mark all the while, laughing at his scuddy jokes, whispering Alpha knew what into his ear. The guy had to realize by now that she was like him. Fallen. Or gifted, as the less educated amongst their unlucky kind tended to call themselves.

Two could only imagine what manner of indulgent bullscud Six had shoveled the man to put him at ease. Probably, she'd told him that she'd felt his power from afar. That she'd needed to come and be with someone like her, someone who could take care of her in a way no normal man could.

Two had heard more than a few rumors about the magnitude of bliss two fallen might share if they were depraved enough to let their demons bond during a swive—pleasure beyond what any mere human could ever dream of attaining. He couldn't have said, himself. He'd never had that particular human experience, with a fallen or otherwise. But watching the two of them now, Six's face lighting up with yet another laugh—a fake one, if Alpha was merciful—the thought made him sick on multiple levels.

Finally, for the love of Alpha, the dice roller gave into the growing insistence of Six's affections and disengaged himself from the game. That the scuddy bastard had taken as long as he had made Two want to punch him all the more. The fallen wasn't exactly ugly underneath that mangy beard, but Two was a toe-dancing haga beast if the bastard was even within five leagues of Six's beauty, and...

And why the scud was he even thinking about this?

They were on a job, dammit. And the mark was moving.

Two cursed himself for the distraction and watched them disentangle from the dice crowd. Once he was reasonably sure he knew which way they were headed, he turned for the door and took off at an easy run. He was pretty sure Six had it in the bag at this point, but this was also the moment it'd be easiest for her to let a bad case of empathy and nerves blow a sure thing. Better he be within striking distance to see the deed safely through. He just hoped he didn't have to see more than that.

Back on street level, he reduced his speed down to a brisk walk as he cut through the fire-lit gamblers' square. No reason to draw undue attention. He seemed to draw enough as it was anyway—maybe because even his battered street clothes were a touch upscale for the locale, or maybe just because half the men there were the kind of macho degenerates who were chronically compelled to mark their territory with challenging glares and confrontational body language. It was a small miracle Six and the dice roller had made it out of this place without one of these charming goodfellows attempting to assert himself between them, like a haga beast challenging another alpha for mating rights with his females.

Two couldn't help but smirk at the cheeky morons as he strode past, feeling that familiar itch, almost like he wanted them to make trouble, to try to hurt him. *You could break them,* his demon whispered to him. *You could tear them apart.*

And Alpha, would it feel good.

He pushed on, suppressing a shudder, and cleared the far end of the gathering without incident. He couldn't see Six or the dice roller as he reached the dark alleyway, but a quick sweep revealed they were quite close to one another ahead, tucked into a quiet little alcove around the corner a little ways down.

He felt the dice roller's hands on her body, tracing toward the hem of her skirt. Felt a ripple of amusement from Six. And was that her breathy laugh he heard as well? Sometimes it was hard to separate his senses and the demon's when he was scanning over distance like this. Either way, she seemed to be at least giving off the appearance of having fun—enough to shoot another pulse of nausea through him and convince him he'd rather not make direct line of sight quite yet.

Why she'd even dragged it out this long, he wasn't sure. He couldn't imagine she'd have much trouble getting a man to drink from her flask, so to speak. She probably could've made her move as soon as they'd made it to the alley. Allowing it to go on like this felt cruel. Did she actually enjoy this game? Or was she just too nervous to end it?

Maybe he should just stroll right over there and force her hand.

He was halfway ready to do just that when he felt a jolt of alarm from Six... and from the dice roller too? Scanning further down their quiet little side alley, Two understood why.

Five men were approaching them from the far side of the alley.

And something told him they weren't there to wish Six and her scud-eating mark good fortune and a happy swive...

7

CONTACT

Two started down the dark alleyway with a muttered curse, checking his sidearm and leaving the holster strap unclipped so he'd be ready to go if it became necessary. Judging by the tone of the voices as he drew up to the cool permacrete corner and paused to listen, though, it was sounding more like a *when* than an *if*.

"—fair and square, goodfellows," someone was saying.

"Not today, Joda," growled a gruff voice. "You've shipped your scud downstream for the last time. Now you're gonna pay up."

A shakedown. Wonderful. Of course whatever scudstorm of retribution this dice-rolling idiot had coming would strike right when Six was in the middle of quietly taking him out.

"What do I do?" Six's whispered in Two's mind, her voice tight with fear. *"He already drank the stuff."*

More than *in the middle* of taking him out, then.

"It's gambling, man," the first voice—Joda the dice roller—was saying. "Sometimes the dice don't fall your way. That's the game. I don't know what you want me to do abou—Hey!"

Two heard Joda's cry of alarm just as he felt one of the burly newcomers yank the man away from Six and drive a strong fist into his gut.

"Get out of there," Two sent. *"Tell them it's none of your business, that you don't want anything to do with the cheating bastard. Let the poison run its course, just get out."*

There were a few moments of Joda's wheezing and more threatening demands for him to pay up. Two was about to step in when he felt Six slowly start moving. For some reason, no one seemed to notice. Not until...

"Hey, what the scud?"

"What?"

"The pretty bitch. She disappeared!"

"She didn't disappear."

"I watched her disappear!"

"She run?"

"Find her," the gruff voice growled.

He felt the men scattering through the alleyway; felt Six trying to maneuver between them, apparently unseen. Then one stepped too close. There was a grunt of pain from the first one, a few curses from the others, and then one caught her from behind.

"Agh! What the scud?" the first one was crying. "She came outta nowhere!"

"She got one of those shrouds or somethin?"

"You try'na hide from us, honey?" asked the one who had her pinned to his chest. "What else you hidin' in there?"

"Sorry, boys," came Six's admirably level voice. "Looks like I wandered into the wrong party. Don't let me stop you, though. I just met this guy tonight, so whatever you gotta do, I'll leave you to i—"

He felt her alarm and her sharp intake of breath as the towering brute who seemed to be the leader of this merry band of assholes seized her by the throat and leaned in close.

"You're right where you oughta be, sweet thing. I can't think of anything sweeter Joda here coulda brought us."

"Part of the payment plan," another voice added. "Right, Joda?"

A thunk and a cry of pain.

"He asked you a question, scud bucket."

Two tried to think, but couldn't focus on anything but the feeling of Six struggling against the two men.

"Just relax, sweet thing," said the guy holding her from behind. "Just let it—Gah!"

Two felt the impact as Six stomped a booted heel down on the guy's toes hard enough to break bones. She whirled to catch him in the ribs with an elbow, but their tree of a leader proved unsurprisingly accustomed to dirty fighting. He was already yanking her off balance by one wrist, swinging with his other hand. He caught her with a heavy smack that put her on the ground, groaning in a disoriented wash of pain and grimy alley water. Around her, the assembled goon squad guffawed.

That was it.

Two had stepped around the corner before he knew it, striding straight toward the moronic pack, his demon whispering dark encouragement in his ears, begging him to let it take over completely. He wanted to let it. Before, he'd been trying to think of a way to extract Six and himself from the situation—to let events run their course. But now...

"Hey!" one of the dead men snapped, catching sight of Two and pointing out his arrival for the others. The rest turned to face Two, their oak tree of a leader stepping in to head him off. Big tough guy.

Big tough dead guy, sneering at the demon.

"Who the grop are you supposed to—"

Two caved in the big man's knees from behind with a slap of telekinetic force, then grabbed his big scudspouting head and drove his right knee into the man's face before he could sputter so much as a surprised curse.

The big guy hit the ground beside Six like a falling tree, unconscious or close to it. Two stalked forward, relishing the looks of shocked fear flashing across their faces—his demon latching onto that fear like it was the only nourishment on the planet. The one man who drew a gun quickly found his weapon ripped from his grip by the invisible hand of telekinesis. The other two hesitated at the sinister winds suddenly gusting through the alleyway. Two hadn't even meant to conjure them. He did, however, mean to grab the next of the dead men with telekinesis and slam his head into the hard permacrete of the alley wall. And slam he did.

He reached for the next one. Something smashed into the back of his head before he could, and his world exploded into a dancing light show. Bizarrely, it barely even hurt as Two whirled around, preparing to unleash the demon on the bastard he'd somehow passed by without noticing. But the blow had left his head spinning, and no amount of righteous anger could seem to pull his focus back in place. Not before the scudbucket tackled him into the wall, at least.

They hit hard enough to drive the air from Two's lungs and snap his head back for a smack on the permacrete that left his vision dancing. He was surprised to find he'd kept his feet at all, but he didn't linger on the discovery. Not when the guy threw a hard punch into his gut. Not when he saw his attacker's friends approaching, two of them holding knives, and the third going for the gun Two had ripped away a moment earlier.

Two let loose, then, handing the reins to the anger; not pausing to think. He absorbed the next punch and drove a knee into the man's groin. Followed up with a kick that shoved him back into the wall and sent his attacker sprawling across the alley. He ripped his sidearm free from the holster just in time to put a softsteel slug into the right thigh of the first man who came to stab him. The second hesitated at the thunderous gunshot. Two grabbed the man's knife with telekinesis, ripped it from his hand, and launched it at their third as the thug bent to scoop up his own gun. The knife buried itself up to the handle in the back of the man's shoulder, and he stumbled to the ground, screaming.

Two raised his own gun, ready to kill every last one of the bastards, but they'd had enough. The two who were still in any condition to walk were snatching up their wounded friends, dragging them away from him. Two nearly jumped when he caught motion to his right, but it was just Six, laying a hand on his shoulder, her lips moving with something that only seemed to come to him as buzzing tones.

He must've hit his head harder than he'd thought.

The left side of Six's face was red and puffy where she'd been struck. And she was holding a gun, he realized—the same gun he'd torn from that thug's hand. The thought yanked his disjointed attention back toward the far end of the alley, where the four men were hastily retreating. They didn't seem to notice they'd left their tree of a boss in an unconscious heap on the grimy alley floor.

"Gropping freaks!" one of them cried, just before they disappeared around the corner.

In the silence that followed, the pain in Two's ribs and the spinning ache in his head only intensified. Six was saying something. He tried to straighten, tried to stand off the wall, but his legs went weak and he found himself leaning against it more heavily than ever, sliding down the perma-crete until he was sitting on the alley floor. It was only then that he noticed the other body.

Joda lay dead on the ground not far from the unconscious thug, blank eyes staring up at the sliver of night sky above the alleyway.

"How about this?" a warm, wonderful voice interrupted his humming thoughts. *"Are you with me, Two? Sweet Alpha, say you're with me."*

"—mmm withya," he heard himself mumble, more by the vibrations in his skull than anything else, as if he were talking with his ears plugged.

"Sweet Alpha," Six breathed. She was kneeling beside him now. "That was... That was..."

Two stirred, his senses pulling back into something like coherent focus, the pain in his ribs and skull sharpening by the second. "Another job well done," he groaned, gesturing toward Joda's lifeless form. "Congratulations, Seeker."

She blew out a disbelieving huff. "But I didn't... That wasn't..." She touched a hand to her chest. "Alpha, my heart won't stop."

"I sure as scud hope not," Two groaned, pushing himself up straighter. "Not after all that."

He leaned closer to inspect her bruising face, lightly brushed a thumb across her cheek before he could think better of it. The contact rippled through him in a way that had little to do with what his fingers were feeling. Reflexively, he started to withdraw, but she wordlessly caught his hand in hers and pressed it to her soft cheek, her eyes searching his.

"Are you okay?" he managed through his parched mouth, his head still spinning from everything. Or maybe just from her, as she dropped his gaze and lightly shook her head, squeezing his hand tighter to her cheek.

"You were right," she said quietly. "I was stupid. I didn't think they'd —that we'd..."

"Hey..." Somehow, his other hand found its way to her cheek, his hands framing her face, forcing her eyes to his. "Hey, I was stupid, too. When he hit you, I... I mean, when it looked like you were in trouble, I..."

He could kiss her right now. With her soft eyes mere inches from his, the thought came as naturally as her sweet breath filling his senses, and with all the stomach-tugging gravity of a high-altitude skimmer dive.

He sucked in his breath and withdrew his hands from her cheeks, cursing himself for the momentary weakness.

"I was reckless," he said, turning his gaze away from her and down the dim alleyway. "I shouldn't have let that goat-gropper get behind me."

"You saved my life, Two," she said quietly. Then, before he could stop her, she leaned in and planted a kiss on his cheek, her lips warm and wonderfully tender.

He needed to pull away. Couldn't seem to move. Couldn't seem to drown out the part of him that burned to turn and kiss her back. It sent tingles down the back of his neck. Tingles like... like...

Like someone was watching.

Cold dread in his stomach, he pulled away from Six, already looking up, already knowing it was too late. And there they were. Two dark silhouettes looking down from the opposite rooftop, their compatriots no doubt lurking nearby on ground level.

"I just wanted to say thank y—"

"Shut up," he snapped at her mind.

She recoiled, anger flashing across her features. He didn't care. She'd figure it out as soon as she looked up. He'd gropped up. He'd let his defenses down, allowed himself to forget what she was, what *he* was.

And the Sanctum Guard had seen everything.

8

HIGH PLACES

They knew. They had to know.

Two stood at the base of the four mighty plateaus at the head of the Great Hall, just outside the living quarters of the High Cleric. He was flanked by four fireteams of Sanctum Guard, and three of the High Cleric's own Onyx Guard stood at the entrance to his quarters, their deadly attention no doubt fixed on him behind those faceless black masks.

He hadn't slept last night. He'd refused to respond to Six's never-ending telepathic onslaught of questions and apologies—had spent the entire night reminding himself that she was one of the fallen; that, sweet or not, she was a monster inside. Just like him.

Somehow, though, he was still having trouble letting go of the feeling of her soft lips on his cheek. But oh well. It didn't matter anymore. Verner was in there now, talking with the High Cleric, which could only mean one thing.

Two was going to die.

He didn't know exactly what the Sanctum Guard had told Verner—wasn't even completely sure what all they'd seen. But it would've been enough. Had to have been. And Alpha only knew how much Watchtower control had seen or heard on top of that. What else would they have brought him here for? Why else bring so many men? Demon or no, he wasn't taking down sixteen Sanctum Guard. He wasn't even sure he could've taken the three Onyx Guard. And even if he somehow did all that, all it would take was a few palmlight commands from the High Cleric, and *boom*—off with his collared head.

Escape was not an option. Forgiveness was not an option.

And so he was going to die.

Despite everything—despite the countless nights he'd spent staring at the dark ceiling after a kill, counting the years until he could lay down to rest for good—the thought filled him with a hopeless, nearly frantic dread. He couldn't lay down and accept the end. Not even for Alpha's sake. If it came to it—if Verner walked out of that great stone doorway and told his soldiers to seize him, or to open fire...

He'd let the demon loose. Alpha help him, he'd do it. And even with that dark self-admission weighing on his spirit, when he closed his eyes, it was somehow still Six's face he saw, her lips he felt on his cheek.

Alpha damn that woman.

He was just sinking into a long list of the reasons she made him want to tear his own eyes out when the sound of Verner's voice snapped him back to the Great Hall. The cleric was getting closer, headed his way— most likely to give the order. Two tensed, gathering his focus, his breaths coming faster than a galloping hosa, heart hammering like the hooves to match. Around him, he felt the Sanctum Guard responding to his tension, adjusting stances, shifting weapons.

Ahead, the central of the three Onyx Guard glided to the side of the open doorway, moving more like a ghost than a man, and snapped to attention as Cleric Verner appeared in the opening.

Was this it?

The silence hung. Verner's expression was unreadable. Two couldn't breathe, but that didn't stop his heart from hammering on, each beat all but rocking him on his toes. Verner kept staring. Two found himself reaching for the demon, cold nerves on the verge of snapping. Why didn't the bastard say something? For the love of Alpha, why wouldn't he—

"His holiness, the High Cleric, wishes to speak with you, fallen."

It might've been a good ten seconds before Two registered Verner's words—a few seconds more before he finally allowed himself to let out a tight breath.

The High Cleric, speak to *him*? It wasn't completely unheard of. They'd met once, years ago, shortly after Two had put down his first mark and officially joined the ranks of the Seekers. But to be granted an audience with his holiness now, after what Verner had undoubtedly just finished telling him...

Was the High Cleric toying with him, or was there still hope?

Either way, he didn't really have any choice but to find out. So he forced himself to start forward, doing his best to keep his shaky legs from buckling. If Verner or any of the guards had anything to say about his unusually slow response, they kept it to themselves.

Two felt the hidden stares of the Onyx Guard piercing in from either side as he drew close. Alpha, they gave him the creeps. Something about the way they moved, and the odd weight of their attention. He knew for a fact the Onyx Guard were positively lethal killers. Rumor had it they were also among the extremely short list of non-fallen humans who'd been trained to repel telepathy, like Verner and the High Cleric himself. He had no idea if the rumor were true—or how strong they could possibly be even if it were. He had even less interest in ever finding out, he decided, as the Onyx Guard permitted him to pass through the round stone entryway.

Calling the High Cleric's quarters opulent would've been like calling the oceans wet. Plenty true, but it kind of missed the full scope of the thing. For one, the rooms themselves were richly constructed, similar in tone to the antechamber of the Great Hall, with its gold-streaked marble floors and its intricately carved darkwood walls. The living space was also impressively large—far larger than it seemed to have any business being, nestled as it was beneath the four plateaus at the head of the Great Hall.

But the grandeur of the place wasn't in the size or the quality of its walls and floors. It was in the decorations that lined those walls and populated the numerous tables—or shrines, really. There was the crown of the first High Clerics, from back when they'd actually worn crowns. The mighty stone of what was said to be the first sigil of Alpha ever hewn. The original holy text of Sarentus, the divine prophet. Dozens more he could only guess at. Two only knew enough to understand it was a place most scholars of history and the arts would've given anything short of life and limb to visit.

Just like he would've given pretty much anything to not be there right then.

But he didn't have a choice. The ghostly presence of the three Onyx Guard falling in behind him was a painfully clear reminder of that. So he forewent the step of gaping at the splendor and headed to the back of the grand entry hall, where a slender acolyte was waiting, pale and gaunt beneath his flowing robes. The acolyte said nothing as Two approached, just stepped aside and waved him through the rich darkwood archway into the hallway beyond.

Two hesitated inside the threshold, on the verge of asking the acolyte where he was supposed to go, then headed for the door on the far right that was manned by a single Onyx Guard instead. It was starting to drive him crazy, this dead-silent death march, but at the same time, he decided, he'd be damned if he was going to be the one to break it.

If they were going to kill him, it would make him feel better to know he'd gone forth in stoic silence rather than simpering insecurity. The door at the end of the hallway, though, seemed to be the last in the line—for now, at least. It hissed open at a touch from the Onyx Guard.

And there was the High Cleric.

He sat inside, waiting behind a stone table that was so substantial as to make the cleric—arguably the most powerful man on Enochia—seem small and frail. The two Onyx Guard on his flanks, however, killed any illusion of the cleric's vulnerability.

He raised a single hand and gestured for Two to join him at the table, the gold and cream of his robes flowing like a second shimmering skin. Two stepped forward uncertainly, distantly aware of the four Onyx Guard sweeping into the room behind him but too caught up with the High Cleric to care about much else.

The cleric was getting on in his eighties, his papery skin wrinkled and spotted with age, his once blond hair wispy and thinning. His eyes, though, while a bit rheumy, seemed to cling to their sharpness much more tightly than did the rest of his aging body. Those pale blue eyes watched, their expression inscrutable, as Two approached the table.

Two pulled out a heavy wooden chair, sat across from the High Cleric, and tried not to squirm as the four Onyx Guard formed up on his flanks, within easy killing distance.

Why was he here?

The thought played through his mind, over and over.

Why, why, why?

The silence stretched.

Then the High Cleric roused, as if he'd been asleep or utterly lost in thought rather than staring at Two for the past minute. It was an odd little episode, but Two forgot about it as soon as the cleric fixed him with a new, more curious stare, and spoke.

"Are you happy here, Seeker?"

A jolt ran through Two. He couldn't help it. The question was that unexpected. "I... I don't understand, your holiness."

"Happy," the High Cleric repeated. "Does your life here not fulfill you? Does it not satisfy your every need?"

Dread seeped in. He understood now where this was going.

"Of course it does, your holiness. I... I'm striving to satisfy the will of Alpha. I need nothing more than that."

"No? What do you have to say, then, of the need for food, for water? What of the need for sleep? What of the needs of the flesh?"

Two said nothing, icy fingers tracing up the back of his neck, reaching around to the spot where Six had planted her Alpha-damned kiss on his cheek.

"Come now," the High Cleric said. "We can't be expected to be purely creatures of service, can we? Therein lies the establishment of slavery, does it not?"

Two clung to silence, hoping the High Cleric would simply continue speaking. When it became clear that he wouldn't, Two forced the words from his mouth.

"I do not claim to know, holiness. I know only that I strive to uphold the will of Alpha, and in my eyes, that's all that matters. For me, it's enough. I know nothing else, nor do I want to."

For several long, tense seconds, the High Cleric studied him. Then his thin lips quirked in a faint, kindly smile, and he actually raised his slender hands to give a pair of claps.

"Very good. Very good. It's a just answer, to be sure. Very honorable." He cocked his head, his brow furrowing. "It's bullscud, is it not?"

Something about his tone chilled Two to the core. This wasn't merely some tentative prodding. The High Cleric knew. He knew that Two had fallen prey to another demon's charm—and that that was one too many demons for any one man to be allowed to entertain, Seeker or no.

"Your holiness..." Two started, uncertain what he could say—how he could possibly defend himself when he'd so clearly failed the Sanctum. Because he had, hadn't he? He'd spent all of last night thinking himself in circles about how events had been misconstrued, and how those Alpha-damned Sanctum Guard had just happened to see the wrong thing at exactly the wrong time. A momentary misunderstanding.

But they hadn't misunderstood a thing, had they? Sitting here, under the piercing stare of the High Cleric and Alpha himself, Two finally had to admit that. He'd broken stride, truly fallen off. He'd *wanted* to kiss Six —still did, despite the fact that the thought twisted his insides on multiple levels, so far that they felt wrung dry.

And now the High Cleric was watching him, nodding slowly to himself, a faint smile pulling at his wrinkled face.

"Bullscud, to be sure," he said slowly, "this life of slavery."

What?

Two stared at the cleric, trying to retrace the conversation. Had he just... Was the High Cleric screwing with him? Trying to trick him into thinking they were in fact of similar minds just to get him to confess what he'd done—what he'd wanted to do? What would be the point?

"Or so I've always thought, at least," the High Cleric continued before Two could arrive at any satisfactory answer. "Haven't you? Have you never found yourself thinking that one so wise and powerful as Alpha would be a cruel deity indeed to demand his subjects denounce such worldly plea-sures just to leave this life with his favor?"

"Your holiness, I—"

"Does it not strike you as cruel, child, that our deity would choose to damn one such as yourself when it was undoubtedly within his power to spare you from becoming fallen in the first place?"

Two hesitated, surer and surer that the High Cleric was driving at some point, but far too confused and terrified to figure out what.

"If I ever had such thoughts, your holiness, I've long since buried them. It is not my place to question the will of Alpha."

"No, child. Nor is it mine." He leaned forward on the stone table, his sky blue eyes taking on a note of reverent wonder. "And yet I have seen it. Felt it. A shocking truth, whispered to me straight from the mouth of Alpha whilst I prayed on my retreat these past cycles."

A retreat? That's where he'd been all this time? Then why all the rumors that he'd taken ill? Two couldn't help but wonder if he was lying, if maybe the High Cleric *had* suffered some sickness—the kind that might've touched his mind.

"What truth is that, holiness?" Two asked, too engrossed in where this was going to worry about the preposterousness of his asking the High Cleric of the Sanctum to explain himself to a lowly fallen. Besides, the cleric was clearly willing to do so. He even looked a little eager as he leaned forward another couple inches, like he was preparing to present a fine new artifact for the collection outside.

"Touch my mind, Seeker."

"What?" Two glanced at the Onyx Guard, half-expecting to see them trading confused looks, but they remained as silent and steadfast as their jet-black namesake. "Holiness. High Cleric, I cannot—"

"Go on." The High Cleric waved a hand at himself in invitation. "It's quite safe. You will not be punished, I swear it."

Something had happened to him. Two was sure of it now. Perhaps it had been a fever that burned too hot. Maybe he'd simply had a psychotic break. Either way, divine chosen or not, the man must be brain-touched. He was human, after all, wasn't he? His mind just as fragile as anyone else's?

Clearly so if he was asking Two to touch it.

Two wouldn't—*couldn't*—obey the command. He couldn't say whether the fear was of holy origin or simply of the death that would doubtlessly come if and when something went wrong with the High Cleric's game. All he knew was that the thought scared the scud out of him. He would *not* touch this man's mind.

But the High Cleric didn't have to know that, did he?

With little other in the way of choices, Two allowed the distant, unfocused look to settle over his face, pretending even to himself that he was letting the demon free, casting its feelers out toward the waiting mind across the table. It wasn't like anyone would be able to tell the difference. No one but a fallen could do that. So Two took a few moments, letting the act sink in, then said, "It is done, your holiness, but I dare not look inside far enough to—"

"I said you will not be punished for the act, Seeker. I did not say you may lie to me."

The words fell like physical blows, each one a violent kick to Two's gut, each one paling in comparison to the shock that spread through him when his brain caught up and registered the most important detail of all—the detail that changed everything.

The High Cleric's lips hadn't moved.

He hadn't spoken at all. And yet Two had heard him—had heard him as clearly as if he'd been speaking right inside Two's head.

Telepathy.

That had been telepathy. Which could mean only one thing.

The High Cleric of the Sanctum was harboring a demon inside him.

9

REVELATIONS

*"*You *look as if you have some questions, my child."*

The High Cleric's voice was unmistakable in Two's mind. Around them, the Onyx Guard remained at rigid attention, their perfect discipline only amplifying the silence pounding in Two's ears.

How was this possible?

"Speak, child. Ask what you will."

For several seconds, Two could only stare, his mind effectively blank for the sheer volume of thoughts trying to race through it. "I..." he started out loud, then realized the Onyx Guard were no doubt listening, even if they were too disciplined to blink at the odd silence stretching between himself and the High Cleric. He started again, casting his thoughts in the cleric's direction, too petrified to reach out and connect more substantially. *"How did you... How long have you been... Have you fallen?"*

The cleric raised one pale, wispy eyebrow. *"On the contrary, my child. I have risen. And as to your other question, suffice it to say, my absence these cycles past was not the result of some common illness. Alpha came to me as he never had before. He showed me the truth of things."*

"But you're... we're..."

Alpha be damned, the High Cleric had lost his mind. No. Not lost.

His mind hadn't been lost. It had been *taken*. And if the High Cleric had fallen...

For one wild second, Two saw the darkness unfolding, clear in his mind's eye as the sunlight had been through the duraglass ceiling of the Great Hall. They were all damned. An insidious evil had spilled into the heart of their Sanctum, unbeknownst to anyone. And how *could* they have known?

No one could have seen it coming.

He eyed the distance between himself and the High Cleric. Scanned for something to use—anything that could be weaponized.

Only him. Only another fallen.

He wondered how many fractions of a second he might have to pull it off before the Onyx Guard took him down.

Which was why he had to do it.

Six world-class killers, an enemy demon, and an exploding collar all arrayed against him. He'd lose. No question.

But maybe not before he stopped the monster who'd invaded their High Cleric.

He focused in on one of the untouched water glasses in the center of the stone table. If he shattered the glass... if he was quick enough with the shrapnel, then maybe, maybe...

"It would be unwise to test me, Seeker."

Two flinched. He couldn't help it. His focus slipped, his will to act sluicing away right along with the reservoir of energy he'd been drawing in.

"You worry that I have been corrupted," the cleric continued. *"That it is no longer your High Cleric speaking, but some wild demon."*

"A fallen is a fallen, High Cleric, regardless of their station."

"And so I thought too, before Alpha shone his wisdom upon me. We have strayed, my child. The Sanctum has done this world an inexorable amount of good, but we are not without flaws. We have erred. I have erred. There is no changing that. But now is the time to right our course. And with faithful servants like you and One by my side, we can save Enochia from the true threat of darkness. I have seen it."

The way he mentioned One, it was almost as if she were already on board. And thinking back on their last conversation, and the look that had come over her when he'd asked about the cleric... Alpha, did she already know what had become of her beloved High Cleric? Had she actually listened to him? Two glanced at the Onyx Guard, unable to quell the uneasy thoughts.

Had she simply realized that the High Cleric's *long assignment* might well have been rearranged to *permanent retirement* had she not accepted?

"Do your Onyx Guard know what you are? Does anyone?"

"My Onyx Guard do as they're told." His wispy eyebrows wrinkled. *"Unlike others among my flock of faithful servants."*

"Whatever Cleric Verner told you, I—"

He waved a dismissive hand. *"My goodfellow Verner has yet to learn what I have learned. If he had, his feathers wouldn't be so ruffled with you presently. Frankly, though, I don't believe he is ready to hear the truth, or ever will be. The fear is too strong in his heart."*

"Shouldn't it be?" Two sent before he could stop himself. *"What we are..."*

"Is Alpha's one defense against the true demons of Enochia."

"We are the true demons of Enochia, cleric."

"And where have you heard that, but from the mouth of your handlers? Where have you seen it written in the holy texts that all who are different are to be condemned?"

"It is not my place—"

"Not your place to question the will of Alpha. And yet you question your own High Cleric?"

"But you're—"

"Tell me, my child, do you truly believe Alpha would allow this establishment to be so thoroughly corrupted? That our omnipotent savior would allow the High Cleric of his own Sanctum to be infiltrated by the very darkness we were founded to resist?"

Two couldn't say. Couldn't seem to do anything but grind his teeth in a futile attempt to ground his spinning head to a single sensible thought.

"We have been given a gift, Seeker. A gift that's been mistaken for a curse for far too long now. And I need your help in fixing that."

"My help in... in what exactly? In pretending that demons don't exist?"

"Don't be absurd. You know that they do. You have no doubt slain several of them these past years. They are drawn to men and women of excep-

tional power—individuals such as you or me. The mistake lies in assuming that every one of us must be tainted by evil, that to be gifted alone is to be fallen to their dark power."

Two stared at him for a long time, lost in a torrent of thought, wanting to refute his claims—or, better yet, to wash his hands of all of this, forget he'd ever met Six or heard the High Cleric's arguably demonic telepathy. He wanted to go back to his tiny quarters and his stiff cot, where the world made sense, and his lash was waiting at his bedside, ready to cleanse him of the sort of dirty thoughts the Alpha-blessed High Cleric of the Sanctum was telling him not to shut out anymore.

"Why are you doing this?" he finally asked. *"Is this a test? Is this because I failed last night?"*

The High Cleric hardly seemed to notice his questions. *"Ask yourself this, child. Has this so-called demon you imagine riding your spirit ever once rebelled against your use? Has it ever once resisted your desire to use it in service to the will of Alpha?"*

"No, but—"

"Has it ever once sought to twist your mind, to turn you from the path of goodness?"

"I've killed people. Many of them."

"In service to Alpha."

"There's a darkness inside me, High Cleric. A black anger that burns with no end. I've felt doubt. Self-hatred." Two forced himself to meet the High Cleric's eyes. *"I've felt lust, your holiness. The darkness whispers when I close my eyes at night. I live in constant fear of the day my strength might fail."*

Alpha be damned, what was he doing? Twenty minutes ago, he'd been standing on legs of gelatin in the Great Hall, ready to fight like a wild animal against the holy execution he'd been sure was coming. Now he was trying to convince the High Cleric that he was indeed a dark threat, liable to explode at any moment?

Maybe he *would* explode at any moment, said the light tug of the collar at his throat. Maybe Alpha *had* forsaken them, and a demon had taken the throne, and this was all some sick game the creature would play right up until it decided to end his stubborn life. The High Cleric certainly looked amused enough, that soft smile pulling at his papery cheeks.

"Darkness, you say? Constant fear?" His smile widened. *"Then you are indeed a child of Alpha, Seeker. To struggle with the darkness inside is to be human. So too have I struggled against my baser desires and emotions. So too has any who's set aside many worldly delights for the sake of Alpha. It's the fact that you still fight at all that proves you harbor no demon."*

"And you expect me to simply take your word on that? To throw a thousand years of our own teachings out the window on the word of one High Cleric who claims to have had some revelation but shows every sign of having fallen?"

Two realized his words were sliding from informal straight to outright disrespectful, but it hardly seemed to matter. High Cleric. Demon. Whatever the frail-looking man in front of him truly was, Two had no doubt they were beyond polite formalities right just then.

"I expect that you'll trust Alpha's guidance when you lie in the dark weighing my words tonight. I trust that you'll find in the depths of your spirit that I speak truth. I am not the first of this new wave, child. Alpha has shown me. A change is coming to Enochia. Others like us have risen within the ranks of the Legion, within the halls of the praetors. All across Enochia, our kin rise by Alpha's design, set in places of power to defend our world against the true threat."

Some part of Two wanted to roll his eyes at the vague, theatrical prophecy of doom—yet he couldn't ignore the sickly weight the High Cleric's words left sitting on his chest. *"And what threat is that?"*

An image began to form in his mind's eye, cloudy and nebulous at first. When Two realized what the High Cleric was doing, he allowed the telepathic connection to reach a little deeper—still keeping his defenses plenty tight, just in case. The hazy mental image began to resolve into the shape of an unassuming man with slender features and calm, pale eyes that almost looked gray. He was dressed to match, all in simple grays, and his hair was far too white for his age, which couldn't have been more than a year or two past thirty. Along with the image, came a single word, wrapped

Carlisle.

"Who is he?" Two asked.

"The acting general of all demons' depths, if his actions of late are any indication."

"What did he do?"

"The question is not what he did, but what he is doing. Waging war against the very foundations of Enochia."

"By himself? What real danger can one fallen possibly be to an entire world order?"

"I don't believe you need any lessons on the dangers of a loose demon."

The High Cleric was right. Two had regretted his words as soon as he'd thought them. He knew all too well what manner of havoc a single demon could wreak, given the right opportunities. It reached far beyond the obvious physical dangers. Left unchecked, even one demon could bend the minds of hundreds—thousands, even, if they had enough time. With a thought, they could compel their helpless human prey to grant them power, hand over wealth. Hand over anything. Which was exactly why the Seeker core did what it did.

And exactly why Two couldn't trust this thing sitting across from him in the High Cleric's skin.

"And he won't be alone long," the High Cleric added, not seeming to notice Two's renewed wariness. *"There are others out there, and their numbers are growing. Trust me. They will flock to his cause like tavern hounds to the drink."*

"Even if that's true, why tell me any of this? Why not just hand out the assignments and let me go on with my life?"

"Because I need you to understand what is at stake here, Seeker. And because it is time to cast aside the baseless condemnation and let the truth be known. This is not my will, child, but Alpha's."

"And if I still don't trust you?"

The High Cleric considered that. *"Then touch my mind, Seeker, and tell me what you see."*

Two studied him, searching for any sign of deceit or an impending trap. He found none. Why he was so nervous, he couldn't have said. A High Cleric the man may be, but Two had never come across another telepath he couldn't at least stand his ground against. And besides, if the High Cleric had wanted to attack his mind, he hardly would've needed to wait for Two to come sniffing.

Maybe he was just afraid of what he might find. But how much worse could it really get?

Pushing that thought aside, Two reinforced his defenses and began to reach out, slowly, cautiously drifting the tendrils of his demon across the stone table to the man who insisted it was no demon at all inside him, but a gift of Alpha. The ripple of denial had barely finished passing through him when his extended senses reached the High Cleric.

It was like staring at the light of Alpha.

Where other telepathic minds shined to his senses like candles in the dark, the High Cleric's mind blazed like a blinding beacon. It felt... vaster. Fuller. More extensive than any mind he'd ever sensed.

It felt divine.

"You're... what are you?"

"I am Alpha's General in the coming war, my child. There are evils out there, evils the likes of which have not been seen since the days of Sarentus. Evils we will not withstand a second time. And make no mistake, if we do not stop them, men like Carlisle will see these evils brought to bear on Enochia once again."

Two braced his hands on the cool stone table, the clenching of his jaw no longer sufficient to steady his spinning head. He'd never been one to faint or swoon at any level of violence, but now his vision was dipping oddly, his stomach churning like a skimmer in heavy turbulence. *"I... I thought you were going to have me killed,"* he finally managed to send through the tumult.

It was only once he admitted it out loud that Two finally allowed himself to entertain the new idea that he might actually walk out of here alive today. The High Cleric seemed to read the blossoming hope in Two's eyes, and a look of paternal sympathy crinkled his papery brow.

"I know this is an unfathomable amount to take in all at once. You should take a day to gather your thoughts, my child. Eventually, we will talk about what happened with Seeker Six, but for now, you have bigger questions to ponder. I will be here when you are ready to discuss what comes next."

Some part of Two tried to stand, insisting he flee the room immediately, before the High Cleric could change his mind. His legs and arms, however, were deaf to his mind's frantic pleas. *"I'm... free to go?"*

The High Cleric extended a hand toward the door in an open invitation to leave. "Thank you for your time, Seeker. You are free to leave. Unharmed."

It took Two a second to realize the cleric had spoken out loud—a gesture to ensure the Onyx Guard understood he was free to go, no doubt. It hardly calmed his nerves. In fact, the reminder of their guards' unwavering discipline in light of what had no doubt looked to them like a long, silent staring contest only deepened Two's unease with the situation. But he forced himself to stand anyway.

"Thank you, your holiness," he said with a bow. Surely there was more to add—entire volumes of questions and clarifications and grateful platitudes to be spewed—but now that he'd gained his feet, that insistent voice telling him to get the scud out of there was stronger than ever. He turned and hurried for the door.

"Two."

He froze and turned back, half-expecting to find a firing line of Onyx Guard standing with weapons raised, ready to pull the trigger at the end of what had been the longest, cruelest joke of Two's life. But the High Cleric was only watching him, appraising him.

"You need not atone tonight, nor ever again so long as you walk the path of Alpha beside me. Keep your whip as you keep up appearances in the coming cycles, my child, but do not take it up against your own flesh. Do you understand?"

Words failed him. It was too much to process. Too much even to manage a silent nod, but he did his best and found himself stumbling down the illustrious hallway some moments later, unable to recall whether he'd succeeded, or even to recall having turned back to the door, for that matter. It was all a swirling mess in his head. All he really knew for sure was that the walls were crumbling around his little world.

And he had no gropping idea what lay beyond.

10

GOOD FAITH

Two found himself staring at the door of his quarters almost before he knew it. He couldn't remember having pressed the button on the service lift to bring him to this floor of the White Tower. Couldn't even remember his exit from the Great Hall, or whether the sixteen Sanctum Guard had still been waiting there to end him at a moment's notice.

No one had shot him. He was pretty sure of that, at least. Though he couldn't quite say yet whether that was a kindness or a curse.

The High Cleric of the Sanctum, a... what? Not a fallen, according to the man's own holy word, but certainly a telepath. Certainly powerful.

Certainly mind-groppingly unexpected.

He almost wished the Onyx Guard would've just put him down, he decided. That would've made things simpler. Scud, maybe he should've just gone to Six's room the first night she'd beckoned and forced their hand before any of this scudstorm had exploded into his life. At least he could've died happy. Because demons and hardened street thugs, he could handle. Violence and telepathic warfare, fine. But this anxious uncertainty? This raw bundle of abraded nerves that felt to be hanging out of his open chest right just now?

Grop that. He'd take a bullet any day.

His heart was still racing like he'd sprinted the forty-seven stories down to his floor rather than ridden the mag lift in stupefied silence. He'd just finally found the slack-brained will to raise his hand and palm his door open when something else brushed at his attention—the faintest wisp of a presence.

Six?

He palmed the access panel, and the door hissed open to reveal his living quarters—tragically tiny and barren by comparison after his stint in the opulence upstairs. The room was empty. No Six. But he was sure he'd felt something. He was reaching out to sweep the room with his senses when her voice came to him.

"I didn't... I, uh... Can you just come in and close the door, please?"

Several features of her words stood out at once. For one thing, *come in* seemed to imply that she was also in the room, which didn't appear to be the case. For another, he got the immediate impression that she was about to complicate his life yet again. At the very least, she was definitely telling him what to do. That alone made him want to snap after the day he'd just had.

But something about her mental tone swept it all aside.

"What happened?" he sent, reaching out with his extended senses. *"What's wrong?"*

He nearly recoiled when he found her sitting on his cot—clear as day to his extended senses, yet clearly *not* there according to his apparently faulty eyeballs. Except... No. There was something. A slight distortion in the air, like an unmoving heat wave. And the cot itself, deforming under some invisible weight. How in the—

"Just... The door. Please."

With a sinking feeling, Two stepped into his room and closed the door behind him, trying to appear casual. *"How the scud are you doing tha—"*

But the words died mid-thought as he turned back and found her plainly visible on the cot now, sitting with her arms wrapped tightly around her knees and her head bowed. So he hadn't lost it. She could turn herself invisible—and pretty damn convincingly, as well.

"That's... I've never seen anything like that," he admitted aloud.

The confusion he'd heard when she'd tried to slip away back in that alleyway scuffle suddenly made a lot more sense. For a second, his brain filled itself with questions about how she was doing it—bending light? Absorbing it? Creating some kind of subtle telepathic illusion?—but then his better judgment caught up, and he realized he had a gropping fallen in his bed. A fallen whom he was already reported to have had forbidden contact with. And even if the High Cleric—or whatever the scud he was now—wasn't overly concerned about that, Verner would still be watching them.

"You shouldn't be here," he said.

For a long moment, he thought she hadn't heard him. Then she stirred, raising her head from her knees only far enough to take a quick glance at him. He barely had time to glimpse her puffy, tear-streaked eyes before she buried her face once more.

"I know," she sent. *"But I didn't know where else to go."*

He studied her balled-up form. She wasn't quite trembling, but something was clearly not right.

"Did, uh..." He took half a step toward the cot, thinking to sit beside her, then rethought that move and pulled his quarters' single chair over to sit facing her instead. "Did something happen? Did Verner—"

She tensed at the cleric's name. Two paused, not really sure how to proceed. Had Verner threatened her after what'd happened between them? Degraded her as she'd been made to atone by the whip? Should he ask, or would that only make it worse? He didn't know, so he sat there in silence, frozen, wanting nothing but to disappear.

When Six finally looked up, her eyes were wet with fresh tears.

"He said they were going to kill you."

"Oh." He thought about the look Verner had given him as he'd passed him on his way into the High Cleric's quarters—the controlled hatred, the disgust he could never seem to quite hide from his otherwise inscrutable eyes. "Oh... Well"—he gestured weakly at himself—"I'm still here, mostly in one piece, so no need to go crying on my account."

She shook her head like he was missing something obvious, her expression bittering. *"He said they were going to do it* because *of me. Said it was going to be my reminder not to let my harlot heart wander."* She closed her eyes, bitterness giving way to despair as her lips trembled. *"He said that's why he was... teaching me my... my lesson."*

A twinge of nausea twisted Two's gut. Something about the way she said it...

"What did he do?"

Her eyes snapped open, full of hatred, her face pulling into a snarl. "What do you think he did? What else am I good for?"

The sick feeling deepened, his head threatening to start spinning again. "I... But he's a cleric. He's..."

"Yeah," Six growled, nodding too emphatically. "Yeah, you're right. He's a cleric, right? How could he possibly give in to his human impulses? I'm sure that's exactly the kind of bullscud reasoning they've all been hiding behind for the past thousand years whenever someone felt like taking a sample of the goods."

"But... But Verner... He hates us."

She showed him a bitter smile. "Turns out that really does it for some guys. Especially the kind of sick scudbuckets who spend their lives publicly depriving themselves of..." She shook her head and scooted to the edge of the cot, moving to stand. "You know what? Never mind. You're right, I shouldn't be here. I sure as scud don't need you questioning what did or didn't happen to my own—"

Two caught her wrist as she rose and tried to storm past his chair. She stared down at him, surprise overtaking the anger on her face. He considered his own hand on her wrist, a little surprised himself, still trying to wrap his head around what she was saying. It was impossible. Unthinkable. Every cubic inch of his Sanctum-trained brain insisted it had to be. But another part of him, the part that Six had remotely stirred to a cot-gropping frenzy that first night, knew the truth.

"He really...?"

Her face tightened, her eyes full of pain and guilt and he couldn't say what else. For a second, he thought she might cry more. Then she shook her arm free and sank back to the cot with a heavy sigh. *It's hardly the first time a cleric's thought to use my body.*

Again, he wanted to dismiss the claim as impossible, but he felt that truth again, deep below his conscious knee-jerk beliefs. Of course it was possible. Scud, it was barely even surprising after what he'd learned about how much the High Cleric was hiding.

"Did he force himself on you?" he sent, at once not wanting to know the answer and yet feeling some dark need to.

She dropped his gaze and scooted back on the cot until her back was against the wall. She pulled her knees to her chest, the anger bleeding from her eyes as she stared off and gave a faint nod. *"It's not like I can fight back. We both know what would happen if I did."* Her lips quivered, hatred seeping back into her eyes. *"Scud, they probably convince themselves I like it. Probably think I'm asking for it just for existing."*

More questions hovered in Two's mind. How many times had this happened? She was barely nineteen, right? How long had this been going on?

A storm of confused feelings raged inside him. Stomach-turning nausea at the thought of Verner lying prostrate on Six, thrusting his miserable old body on hers, whispering that this was her fault, that she deserved it. Betrayal that their handlers—trusted superiors, if not exactly friends— could even conceive of treating their subjects with such disgusting apathy. Fear that it would happen again.

But over it all, rage. Sick, desperate rage.

Verner's disgust for the fallen was one thing. His perpetually cold attitude toward them, his dispassionate, hard-edge leadership of the Seeker core. That was all forgivable. That was his damn job, keeping them and their demons under control.

But this?

His knuckles cracked, begging him to action.

This was utterly, irrevocably unforgivable.

"I'm going to kill him."

He didn't remember standing, so he was surprised when Six surged forward and grabbed his hand as he turned for the door.

"Then they'll kill you."

"I don't care anymore. I can't keep doing this. Not..." His mind went to the High Cleric, and his arguably demonic new talents. Demons or no, they all felt pretty damn fallen right now. All of them. *"They have to pay."*

He started to pull for the door again, not wanting to stop and think it through. Wanting nothing more than to find that crusty old hawk Verner and make him beg for the mercy Two no longer had it in his heart to give. Wanting to storm through this tower of lies, ripping it to pieces until the

Sanctum Guard managed to bring him down and send him to whatever eternal torture might await his spirit beyond.

But Six held tight to his hand, refusing to let go.

"Please don't go. I just..." She shook her head, her eyes pleading with his. *"Don't leave me here."*

His resolve wavered, and she seemed to feel it, pulling on his hand in a silent plea for him to sit.

"Can we just... Can we please just talk about this, at least?"

Two didn't want to talk. Didn't want to have to stay here a moment longer with the day's gropped up revelations mixing and churning and burning a hole straight through his gut. He wanted to hurt someone. And he wanted it to be Verner. The cleric had to pay. Two was as sure of that as he was that, if he didn't make it happen sooner than later, Verner might well still be the death of both of them.

The thought brought the familiar itch to his neck, right at the collar line.

"If you kill him," came Six's quiet voice in his head, *"they'll kill us both. Alpha, they might just flip the switch on all twelve Seekers and start with a fresh batch of trainees. They almost had enough back at the facility. Just... Will you just sit for a minute?"*

He teetered there, already knowing deep down that he couldn't go off and do something that might doom them all, but hoping he might just find the danglers to do it anyway. Finally, he gave in to her gentle tugging and allowed her to pull him down to the cot beside her. Wordlessly, she wrapped his arm in both of hers and buried her tear-streaked face in his shoulder. He hardly noticed at first. He felt sick with rage. Utterly impotent, despite all his power.

He had to do something. But what was there to be done? He couldn't kill Verner. Couldn't whisk Six up and make some grand escape. If he attempted either, they'd probably find themselves freed from both their collars and their heads before the sun rose tomorrow.

He wanted to scream.

He'd been trapped ever since the Sanctum had found him on the streets and taken him in to begin grooming him into what he was today. His life was a prison. There was no arguing that. But never before had he so clearly felt the cold steel bars pressing in on him.

His heart was still racing—hadn't stopped, he realized, since he'd left the High Cleric's.

The bars were pressing in, all right—the very walls falling down on top of him. But not just him, he remembered, as Six shuddered against his arm. She was shaking with silent sobs, plagued by waking nightmares of her own. Nightmares he could barely begin to imagine. Even just trying to, his heart broke for her.

He'd reached over with his free hand before he knew what he was doing. Human contact wasn't something he'd had much practice at—any at all, really, outside of the violent kind—but somehow, it felt easy to lay his hand on the back of her golden head and pull her closer to him. It felt natural. He couldn't imagine touching One like this. The thought alone nearly made him withdraw his hand. But then Six responded to the touch, nestling just a bit closer, and he forgot about anyone but her.

Her and Verner.

"He's never going to hurt you again," he sent. *"I won't let him. Any of them. I promise."*

She looked up, her face wet with tears and scrunched in an expression of doubt—not at him or his intent, necessarily, but more at the impossibility of the statement. As she searched his face though, some of that doubt began to fade, as if she could see that he meant what he said. And he did mean it. Meant it with an intensity that surprised even him.

Storming up to Verner's quarters like a rampaging demon was one thing. Stupid. Suicidal. But if that grimy bastard came for her again... the rest didn't matter. Two would break his mind, boil his eyes, and tear the bones straight from his feeble old body. Consequences be damned.

Whether it was the look in his eyes, or simply the crushing weight of everything else, Six cried with renewed desperation then. Two held her as she did. He didn't know what else to do. A few times, he stroked her back in an attempt to sooth, but it felt inconsequential. How could such a trivial gesture mean anything after everything she'd been through? He was sure it couldn't. And yet each time he did it, she clung to him a little tighter, so on he went.

At some point—he couldn't have said how long, and didn't care to check his palmlight—he realized by the end of her shaking and a change in her breathing that she'd fallen asleep against him. That was fine, he decided. Never mind that it could be grounds for their execution if they were found. He wasn't making her go back to her quarters—back to the place where Verner had violated her, and where he might feasibly seek to get back at her whenever his cold, twisted heart desired.

For a while, he simply sat there, taking some small comfort from Six's warmth, and the gentle rhythm of her sleeping breaths. Then slowly, carefully, he lowered her to his cot, using telekinesis to keep the movement smooth enough that she didn't wake. She did stir slightly when he moved to pull away from the cot—not quite waking, but letting out a distressed murmur and flopping one hand in his direction.

He settled on the edge of the cot and took her hand in his, too exhausted now to feel much more than empty dread as he stared at the door, absentmindedly stroking her hand with his thumb, wondering if this would be the end.

How the scud had this happened?

One new Seeker. One routine job. Two gropping days, and now this. The High Cleric, turned some kind of deranged prophet, touched either by the power of Alpha or that of a demon the likes of which Two had never before encountered. Cleric Verner, turned demon in his own right, powers or no. And Six...

He sat there for what felt like hours, watching the door all the while, waiting for a small army of Sanctum Guard to come calling for their heads.

How the scud had this happened?

And more importantly, what in demons' depths was he going to do about it?

11

THE PATH

He was already dead.

That was the first thought Two had as he snapped awake to stale yellow lights and the undisputed champion of all stiff necks. But he *had* woken, he realized the next instant. In his room. Still fully clothed.

And with Six's warm body pressed against his like the world's loveliest spoon.

As soon as he registered that, he jerked around to the door, expecting to find Verner watching them, finger poised on the collar detonator.

He wasn't.

The door was closed. No one there.

Movement and sleepy murmurs drew his attention back to Six as she let out a long yawn... and stretched. Merciful Alpha, did she stretch. Her hips shifted against his, driving her lush backside straight into his groin. Even aroused as he'd already been on waking, he somehow grew twice as hard in the space of a breath. Six made an appreciative noise that sounded only half conscious and turned, blinking the sleep from her eyes.

She smiled dreamily when she saw him, and despite everything—despite the catastrophe of the previous day and the puffy redness in her eyes from last night's crying—he was still gripped by an irresistible desire to kiss her.

"Hey, there," she purred. Or started too, before the blissful ignorance of sleep drained from her eyes, carrying her smile with it—no doubt on the back of the memory of where she was, and why she was there. Her eyes flicked around the room, then to her clothes. Then his. Then the door.

She didn't launch into a storm of *what should we do* and the couple thousand related questions like he'd expected—like he himself was on the verge of doing. She just turned back to the wall and collapsed to the cot with a muttered, "Gropping dreams."

Two pointedly removed his hardness from her vicinity and had to pull himself into a seated position on the edge of the cot before he felt comfortable speaking.

"Are you, uh..."

Okay, so maybe he still didn't feel comfortable speaking.

"What? Okay?" She rolled over to face him, and waved at the door as if to say *What, with the rapist's firing squad lining up out there?*

He swept the hall with his senses to make sure it was actually clear, then bowed his head, trying to gather his thoughts. They needed a plan. Which was exactly what he'd been thinking when he'd apparently fallen asleep. How had he been so careless? Never mind the army of Sanctum Guard. It was a small wonder Verner himself hadn't walked in and slit their throats with his own lecherous hands last night.

As if he'd need to. As if there were anything Two could do if Verner got permission to trigger the detonators. More than once last night, Two's thoughts had drifted to the impossible daydream of waking Six, disabling their collars together, and getting the scud out of there. But it was just that: an impossible daydream. Because even if they'd both somehow managed to telekinetically remove their collars without setting them off— a questionable venture at best—they would've had to do so with the heavy knowledge that their selfishness would cost ten loyal Seekers their lives. They'd been told many times how thoroughly the intricate sensors of their twelve collars were interconnected. And while Two might not have shed a tear for a monster like One, he wasn't ready to pull the trigger on ten of his fellow prisoners.

Which brought them back, as all paths seemed to at the moment, to their uncomfortably gaping lack of a damn plan. His head was whirling with half-formed scraps of ideas when Six's hand settled on his.

"Two."

He turned, the scudstorm in his head suddenly silent, and met her soft brown eyes. Alpha, it was embarrassing—not to mention dangerous—the way her touch affected him, the way those eyes took him by the throat and held him.

"Thank you," she said quietly. "For last night. For everything. But you don't have to worry about me moving forward. I see your engines spinning over there, but I can take care of myself."

A part of him wished he could've simply agreed—said *good knowing you* and moved on. But with each passing second he failed to look away from her eyes, that idea felt more and more unthinkable. It was too late to bother trying to distance himself anyway. Verner already wanted his head, and the only thing staying his hand was probably... the High Cleric.

The thought hit him like a flash.

After everything—after what Six had said last night about Verner's words, *He said they were going to kill you...*

Verner had actually thought it was all over, hadn't he? Thought he was seeing Two for the last time as he'd left him in the Great Hall to go pay his visit to Six. Yet Two's head was still attached, which meant... was the High Cleric actively protecting him and Six?

It seemed like the only explanation, short of Verner having some change of heart.

But then what was the High Cleric waiting for? What did he want Two to do next?

"You still with me in there?" came Six's voice.

He shook himself out of his reverie and forced himself to pull away from her. "Look, I meant what I said last night. No one's ever going to lay a hand on you again."

"No one?" she said, arching an eyebrow at the hand he'd just withdrawn.

He saw the teasing joke she was reaching for, and the lascivious allure her face so readily exuded. But where before he probably would've missed it, he also saw the subtle misting of her eyes, the slight quiver of her lips. She was shaken. Touched, even. He couldn't decide if that was a good thing or a bad thing. Didn't have time to think about anything but the one thing that might be able to pull them out of this mess.

"I have to talk to the High Cleric."

That caught her by surprise. "Why? Didn't you see him yesterday for..." She frowned. "What was that for, actually?"

"It's a long story." He didn't add the part where it was a long story that might also get them killed. He was still too unsure of his footing to know who or what to trust. But she seemed to read some of that sentiment on his face anyway.

"I'm getting the feeling this is a little more complicated than an accidental kiss on the cheek."

"A little bit."

Her delicate fingers traced to the dark collar at her throat. "Dangerously complicated?"

He stood, avoiding her eyes. "I'm going to speak with the High Cleric. You should..."

Should what? There was nowhere for her to hide. Not really. But he didn't want to irk the High Cleric by bringing another unsuspecting telepath into his vicinity—not when they needed his good graces.

"... go hang low in the mess, or one of the worship halls. Somewhere public."

There was real concern in her eyes now. "You're that worried?"

"Come on," he said, turning for the door, "I'll see you to the lifts and—"

He froze at some whispered warning on the edge of his senses. He took a breath, focusing in on what had caught his attention, and...

There.

Someone was coming—nearly at the door already.

Without thinking, he grabbed Six by the hand and yanked her to her feet, then he snatched up the chair beside the cot and darted over to his desk, waving his node display to life. He'd just dropped into the chair when the door hissed open and a stout cleric he didn't recognize walked in.

Two didn't have to try hard to act surprised. "Cleric. Can we help you?"

He couldn't tell if the man was a handler or just running an errand for one. The handlers didn't exactly wear badges announcing their clandestine positions. Scud, the man could've just wandered into the wrong room. But something about the way his slightly narrowed eyes flicked between the two of them made Two doubt that.

"You're together," he said, as if his meaning should be perfectly clear by those two words alone.

Two studied the man. "You're a handler?"

The cleric nodded, unflinching. "I am. Cleric Kellen, of Serenity."

Two bowed his head in the appropriate gesture of deference—and also in an attempt to cover up any confusion on his face. What in demons' depths was a Serenity handler doing here?

"Six had her first mark last night, your holiness," he explained. "I was offering my counsel on her conflicted feelings." He turned his attention back to Six to finish the lesson he'd never actually begun. "Reminding her that it's natural to feel what she's feeling after the first mark. That, at the end of the day, we survive by remembering what a fallen will inevitably do if left to their demon's devices."

She nodded reflectively, falling into her role with admirable grace, despite her sleep-tousled hair.

"Very well," said Cleric Kellen, appearing remarkably disinterested now that his initial curiosity had been sated. "I'm here to speak to Six about her new assignment."

Six looked as startled as he felt.

"Why not Cleric Verner?" he asked quickly, hoping to distract Kellen from her reaction. "Your holiness," he added at the reproving stare Kellen turned on him.

"That is between Six and myself, Seeker, if you'd be so good as to leave us to it."

It was only then that Two registered Kellen had come here looking for Six. Here, to his room.

What the scud was going on?

"Of course, Cleric Kellen," Two said, rising to his feet.

"You're leaving?" came Six's tense thought.

"He thinks this is your room."

Not that there was anything to cue him otherwise, Two decided, glancing around. Their rooms were all equally barren.

"But what does he want?" Six sent.

That was a damned good question.

"Stay mindful of your guilt, Seeker," Two said to her out loud, "and remember who it is we serve."

"Find out what he wants," he added mentally. *"I'll be close."*

Six nodded her wordless acknowledgment, stepping back to let him pass. Cleric Kellen frowned at him, but scooted aside to grant him access to the open doorway. Outside, Two hurried down the hallway to the first empty room he found, five doors down—a storage closet, by the feel of it. He'd just coaxed the locking mechanism open, thinking to slip inside and monitor Six's situation remotely, when the brush of a new telepathic presence against his senses made him jump.

"Calm yourself, Seeker, and come see me. There is something we must discuss."

The High Cleric's voice was unmistakable. Two hesitated, his mind racing with far too many moving pieces to even begin making sense of. Verner's inaction. Kellen's arrival from Serenity. Now the High Cleric calling him to discuss... what, exactly?

He glanced back toward his room, apprehension churning through his stomach.

"You need not worry about Six's safety," the High Cleric sent. *"You have my word."*

It didn't lessen Two's unease, feeling like the High Cleric could apparently see right through him, even at a considerable distance, but he wasn't sure he had any choice but to obey. So, reluctantly, he sent an affirmative in the High Cleric's direction and reached for the shining flame of Six's mind, five rooms over.

"The High Cleric is summoning me."

For several seconds, there was nothing, though he could feel them there in the room, both still standing at a conversational distance from one another, discussing something.

"Go," came her reply finally, sounding slightly distracted. *"I'll be fine."*

He hesitated, wanting to say something, but not sure what. He couldn't help but think that *fine* was looking less and less like a word that belonged in their lexicon. But the High Cleric was waiting, and he was out of options. So he turned for the lifts, unable to do more than wonder when this scudstorm would end.

———

To Two's surprise, the High Cleric met him in the entrance of his Great Hall quarters, looking up from an artifact and waving Two in like an old friend when he paused at the threshold of the massive stone door. There were at least four Onyx Guard posted at the edges of the room, but none of them broke their statue-like discipline as Two started cautiously forward, the High Cleric still waving him on.

It all felt rather informal, and not a little bit bizarre.

"How did you sleep, my child?" the High Cleric asked as Two approached. "You look ill at ease."

"Where is Cleric Verner?" Two asked—or maybe demanded—before he could stop himself. He drew up short, immediately regretting his tone and his utter lack of grace with the man who might be the only thing keeping Two's head attached to his neck right now.

But the High Cleric didn't look particularly upset by his poor manners. In fact, Two couldn't read his expression at all.

"Cleric Verner has gone missing," he said slowly.

Something about the way he said it sent a chill through Two. Missing? After one night? "And you're sure he didn't take a skimmer to watch the sunrise, or—"

"Cleric Verner has gone missing," the High Cleric repeated, and his tone this time left little room for interpretation.

Two glanced around at the Onyx Guard—motionless as ever. *"What did you do to him?"*

"Nothing less than he deserved."

Two waited for the grim satisfaction to pour in with the knowledge that the lecherous bastard had paid for what he'd done to Six, but it didn't come. Instead, he felt only a vague sense of nausea, and the uneasy prickling of the question hanging at the edge of his mind. He didn't want to ask. But he needed to know for certain.

"You had him... removed?"

As many times as he'd pulled the trigger himself, Two couldn't bring himself to ask the High Cleric of the Sanctum if he'd had a man killed.

But the grim look on the High Cleric's face was all the answer he really needed. *"Cleric Verner was never going to accept the truth about our kind, nor did he have any intention of leaving Six unmolested once he'd known the pleasure of her flesh. I saw it in his mind."* He finally turned from the display he'd been admiring and faced Two with his full attention. *"It was not a decision I'd wish on anyone. Had he stayed, he would've driven Six to the grave, and had I told him what Alpha has shown me, he would've gone to the public, used what he knew to fight us, to spill fear across the planet. And so he had to be removed. Permanently."*

Two was silent for some time, trying to digest that and decide how he felt about it. The High Cleric waited patiently, having presented his case and once again seeming confident that Two's own intuition would guide him to the truth more readily than would more persuasive words.

"You chose a Seeker over a cleric," Two finally sent, feeling flat, unbelieving.

"I chose the wronged over the wrong-doer, my child, just as I would expect any loyal servant of Alpha to do."

"I don't know what to say."

"You needn't say anything at all."

"Thank you." It felt like a dirty thing to say, considering what he was thanking the man for. Dirtier still because he knew that, deep down, he meant it. *"I have to ask, though, was this because of me?"*

The High Cleric looked up at the ancient wooden sigil of Alpha hanging at the head of the entry hall before answering. *"Our actions are all intertwined in one way or another. Whether you ask of blame or credit, it's impossible to say where one man's ends and another's begins. I trust in Alpha to show me my path. Beyond that..."* He shook his head. *"Beyond that lies little but narcissistic madness."*

"And what of us who do not see the path so clearly as you, High Cleric?"

The cleric turned back to Two and favored him with a gentle smile. *"We all see the path, my child. It comes in the quiet moments, and in the joyous ones. It comes in the deep sadness of those who acquire much but value little. The path is clear, always. Some simply grow more skilled at ignoring its call."*

Two considered that for a length of silence, his mind drifting to the feeling of pulling the trigger, the pain of the lash at his back afterward. The guilt and atonement. The sleepless nights. Verner coming the next day—or cycle, or season—to tell him to do it again.

"Why did a handler from Serenity come to my quarters looking for Six?"

If the question caught him off guard, the High Cleric didn't show it. *"Because I sent him there."*

After their discussion yesterday, Two wasn't overly mystified about how the High Cleric might've sensed he and Six had spent the night together in his quarters, but he couldn't decide if it made him relieved or uneasy, the High Cleric's seeming willingness—eagerness, even—to be forthcoming about his each and every thought and move.

"Six is being temporarily relocated to Serenity," the High Cleric added before Two could ask. *"For her safety, and your own."*

Panic gripped him, sudden and startlingly intense. For a second, it was all he could do not to turn and sprint from the room, straight back to his quarters.

The High Cleric raised his hands in a soothing gesture. *"I understand that this comes as a shock, that you two have grown attached to one another. For the life of me, I don't see how we ever convinced ourselves we'd be able to prevent such bonds forming between young Seekers forced into life and death situations. I see now that we have been terribly wrong, about a great many things. But the handlers do not. Not yet. And Cleric Verner was not the only one who knew what transpired in that alleyway. Appearances must be maintained but a little longer."*

Two forced himself to nod. What else had he expected? That he and Six would be free to fly off into the sunset? That was a daydream fantasy. Scud, him keeping his head was a daydream fantasy. To hope that he and Six would be allowed contact after what had happened between them was just plain ludicrous. And even so, he couldn't quite silence the voice in the back of his head that kept asking, over and over, *How long is 'a little longer?'* He thought about asking, but he held back, not trusting himself to mask the edge of panic that might creep into his tone.

That girl...

For the first time, he allowed himself to truly entertain the things the High Cleric was saying. That a change was coming in the Halls of the Sanctum. That maybe someday—maybe someday soon—things could be different. Between him and Six. Between all of them.

It felt wrong—especially knowing that Verner's bones were already buried in the foundations of this new world. But so what? How many bodies already littered the Sanctum's foundations? Two couldn't even begin to fathom. And Verner had been far from an innocent, cleric or no.

Freedom...

He couldn't deny he wanted it. And why shouldn't he? This was the High Cleric blazing the way—Alpha's chosen voice on Enochia, not some fallen street urchin. This was the path—the silent calling his spirit had whispered to him on all those dark nights, trying to sleep after a kill. This was the answer. The next step.

"What would you have me do, your holiness?"

The High Cleric's gentle smile was short-lived. *"I would have you stand by my side against the coming darkness, my child, as I have already said. I would see you help to usher in a new era. One where those who are capable of wielding the light against such darkness are celebrated rather than damned."* He pointed to the collar at Two's throat. *"Treasured rather than threatened. Already, I fear our numbers dwindle precariously. But I would have you put your trust in Alpha to guide us through."*

"And the rest of our Seekers?" Two asked, thinking of Six.

"Not all are ready to hear this truth, as I'm sure you would agree. Our steps must be deliberate, well-planned. Eventually, though, they will all see the light."

"Then tell me where to start."

"Soon, child. One is already attempting to track one of our true enemies, the demon known as Carlisle. I may have you join her, depending on how the search goes, but for now, you should gather your strength. Say your farewells to Six, if you would, but do not tell her of this. Not yet."

"She's not ready?"

"It is Cleric Kellen and the rest of his Serenity sect who are not ready. Soon, they too will come to see. But for now, we must be careful."

Two bowed his head in silent acknowledgment. The High Cleric dismissed him with the assurance that he would call upon Two when it was time. And for the second time in as many days, Two turned for the Great Hall and the lifts beyond, as sure that his life had just markedly changed as he was unsure exactly what that might mean in the days to come.

1 2

IDENTITY

Six was still in his quarters, Two sensed as he stepped off the lift forty-seven floors later. He was pleased by the knowledge, though he couldn't say exactly why. What excitement he did feel, though, died quickly enough when he reminded himself what he was preparing to do.

It was time to say goodbye. For now, at least.

The thought shouldn't have filled him with so much dread. They'd only met four days ago, for the love of Alpha. But those four days had somehow expanded—blown out into something truly significant to his life. Something substantial. He'd experienced similar dilations before, he supposed. Especially on long jobs that'd left him staked out with a fellow Seeker or a chatty Legion fireteam for days and days. But never quite like this.

Four days, and he somehow felt like he'd known Six for years. Like she was his closest connection on the planet. And really, when he thought about it, maybe she was. Never mind that they barely knew each other. When it came down to it, Two barely knew anyone. Seekers didn't get friends. But that hadn't stopped Six from worming her way past his defenses. Maybe that was just her charm, her intrinsic abilities at work. Or maybe the things the High Cleric had told him had gotten to his head, coloring his recollection of the past several days.

Either way, he didn't want to think about how long it might be before he saw her again. Isolated and global as their assignments tended to be, the Seekers often went several seasons—sometimes years—without seeing one another. And that wasn't even to mention the Sanctum's careful practice of never keeping more than three of them in one place at a time, lest they begin to grow too close and get ideas about changing things.

The thought of their handlers' fears pulled an eager smirk across his lips. Because things were going to change now, weren't they? Slowly at first, maybe, but he had the High Cleric on his side. It wouldn't be years before he saw Six again. Seasons, maybe, but that was probably for the best. Or so he told himself until he palmed the door open and found her sitting on the edge of his cot, staring off into space.

She looked so lost, so dejected, that it was all he could do not to march in and wrap her in his arms—an impulse he couldn't have imagined even thinking about had it been someone like One or Eight sitting there. Instead, he stepped into the room, closed the door, and pulled his chair over to join her face-to-face.

"They're... relocating me," she said slowly, still staring past him with unseeing eyes.

He took her hands in his, surprising himself. Had it really only taken four days and a few mind-gropping chats with the High Cleric to push him to so casually break all of the rules? The fickleness disturbed him. But not enough to stop. Not when her hands felt so right in his.

His touch brought her back to him, her soft brown eyes glancing down to their connected hands then searching his face, perhaps for some hint as to his newfound boldness. She didn't shy away from the contact. Only squeezed his hands and held his eyes as she spoke again.

"They're moving me to Serenity."

"I know," he said quietly. He didn't see the point in lying about that, even if he couldn't yet tell her everything that he'd learned about the High Cleric and their new path moving forward.

Her brow wrinkled a little at his comment, and she was clearly curious as to how and why he could already know that, but she didn't ask him to explain as he'd expected.

"I've only been here four days," she said.

"I know." Despite everything, he couldn't help but smile a little at her echoing of his own thoughts. The flicker of amusement, though, only seemed to dishearten her more.

"Did Verner tell them to move me? Did... did you? Is that why the High Cleric..." She trailed off, hanging her head, her hands going limp in his. "I'm sorry, I don't know what I was thinking back in that alley. I never should've..."

He squeezed her hands, trying to pull her back from whatever edge had caught her tongue. When that got no response, he surprised himself again and cupped her cheeks in his hands, directing her eyes back to his. As soon as her eyes met his, though, and he saw her surprise at the touch, he lost his nerve and returned his hands back to the safety of his own legs, dropping her gaze as well.

"It's not your fault," he said, trying to push past the awkward feelings in his chest and focus on the important points. "If anyone should've taken control, it was me. But it's okay now. Verner's not going to be a problem anymore. And this move isn't forever. I think the handlers just need to be sure we're under control. I didn't want you to... I mean I don't..."

He forced himself to meet her eyes. She stared back with a silent question that dropped his insides into free fall.

"I don't want you to go, Six. I never would've asked for it."

She held his eyes a few seconds longer, searching for something. Maybe weighing his words. He couldn't tell past the warm haze swirling faster and faster through his brain as the gaze lingered. Finally, she nodded to herself, breaking the spell.

"When are you leaving?" he asked quietly.

"Soon, I think. Cleric Kellen went to visit a colleague to give me a little time to pack. Said he'd message me when he was done." She glanced at the gear bag Two hadn't noticed at the foot of the cot, which was probably large enough to hold whatever clothes Kada had supplied her with. "Not that I needed much time."

"Right." He looked around at the bare permacrete walls, searching for something to fill the sudden pressing silence of their dwindling time together. "So he still thinks this is your room, huh?"

A smirk pulled at her lips. "You men aren't really all that hard to fool. The eyes start to stray a little too far and..." She shifted on the cot, trying to get comfortable. "Annnd there you go. Right back to home base."

Two realized his gaze had drifted to the lovely swell of her breasts as she'd moved. He tore his eyes back to hers, the heat rushing both above and below as she met him with a victorious grin. Then something passed between them, like the cold ghost of Verner himself, and the warmth of the moment died in an instant at the memory of what had happened to her just yesterday.

"Six... You need to be careful in Serenity. Keep your head down. Please. And if anything happens..." He woke his palmlight, swiped up for an ID exchange, and offered his hand to her, palm up. "I meant what I said."

"You're sweet," she said, her tone and eyes mocking. But she woke her palmlight and held her hand over his. The exchange finished, and she looked at her updated palmlight and said softly, almost to herself, "I don't know how you're so sweet."

He wasn't sure what to say to that, aside from to agree with the implications. Because he *was* a killer, after all, wasn't he? Whether he was a demon or Alpha's chosen or whatever the scud else, nothing changed that. But when she looked back up to meet his eyes, it wasn't with the expression one reserved for a killer.

She just looked sweet. Almost abashed. Like she was preparing to say something she wasn't used to saying.

"Can you do one thing for me, then, if I promise to be a good girl over there?"

He eyed her warily, not quite able to stop himself from matching her suddenly shy smile. "What's that?"

"Can you tell me your name, so I don't have to keep calling you gropping Two? Your real name, I mean. The one they took away from you."

He felt himself rock back in his chair. The question was so unexpected that, for a second, all he could say was, "Oh."

It took another moment staring at the floor to realize that the name she spoke of didn't come to him immediately. He actually had to think about it. Which maybe wasn't so surprising given how thoroughly—and literally—it had been whipped out of him over the years. Still, it was an odd thing to realize. His old name, nearly lost to him. He'd grown so used to being called Two. Or Seeker. Or fallen. For years before that, it had mostly been *trainee,* or sometimes *initiate* by the older, sterner handlers.

"You don't have to tell me," Six said, looking embarrassed for having asked. "I know it's painful enough for me to think about, and I'm barely out of training. I just thought…"

She trailed off at the look on his face as he met her eyes again. He wasn't sure what it was she saw—was barely even sure what was going through his own head in that moment. All he really knew was that, whether it was truly his or not anymore, the name held some piece of who he'd once been. And he wanted her to have that much, at least.

"Garrett," he sent, feeling that the name was somehow safer thought than spoken. But grop that. What was the point of giving her that piece of himself if he didn't damn well mean it?

"My name was Garrett," he repeated out loud.

"Garrett," she whispered, and he only noticed then how close they'd drawn to one another—so close he could taste the sweetness of her whispered breath. It made his head spin. Or maybe that was just the feeling of her saying his name.

He didn't try to resist the urge to reach out and stroke her cheek, nor did he need to ask why her eyes were clouding with moisture. He wiped the first tear from the corner of her eye, understanding completely.

"Garrett," she repeated, still at a whisper, her smile beautiful and tragic. "I was Alexia."

"Alexia," he whispered, not sure if he was leaning closer or she was—only that they were inches apart now. A tiny shiver passed through her at the sound of her name. He leaned closer still. She didn't shy away, just held his eyes, questioning, as he froze a scant inch from her lips.

We shouldn't, he thought to say, but his lips wouldn't comply. He hung there, drawn by her scent and the wonderfully smooth warmth of her cheek in his hand. Drawn by gravity itself. Her breath tickled his mouth, maddening. He fought with every bit of his will to rise above the spell and back away before he made things irrevocably more complicated.

Then she tilted her head and brushed her lips faintly against his, their eyes still locked, and he lost control.

He slipped his hand around the back of her head and pulled her soft mouth to his, closing his eyes and losing himself in the flood of wonderful sensation. Her lips parted to his, welcoming him with a soft, pleased sigh that rippled through every inch of his being, begging him to attack, to sink into her with his everything.

He wasn't quite sure if he pulled her or she came of her own accord, but she'd left the cot and settled on his lap almost before he knew it, straddling him on the chair. The kiss only deepened once she was on him. She pressed her body to his, her hands running through his hair, her tongue finding his, coaxing his blood to sing until he was so hard against her that it hurt. He didn't care. Didn't care about anything but getting closer. He rose to his feet, her legs straddled firmly around his hips, and was about to take her to the cot when her palmlight buzzed against the right side of his head.

Even knowing what the buzz meant and having heard the High Cleric's revelation that he and the Seekers were not true demons, the vibration still felt like a ping from Alpha himself, telling them to stop before he had to resort to divine intervention. They paused, breathless, foreheads pressed together, as she checked her palmlight.

The message, unsurprisingly, wasn't from Alpha, but from Cleric Kellen, who was ready and waiting to depart.

"I can't seem to control myself around you," he sent weakly, trying to gain control of his ragged breaths as she slid down from his hips and went to collect her bag.

She looked a bit flushed herself, but her smile was lascivious. *"I think my demon likes yours."*

Much as her smile made him want to throw her down on the cot and resume their activities—consequences be damned—the thought of demons sobered him. For a harebrained second, he thought about telling her what the High Cleric had said, what His Holiness had become. But even if Kellen hadn't been waiting for her, he knew now wasn't the time.

"I think I like you," he sent instead.

She searched his face for a long moment, her smile somehow widening while also taking on a bittersweet edge.

"So you're saying you are *my gropping friend?"*

He blew out a laugh, remembering his harsh words to her on their first day together and marveling once again at the whirlwind of ups and downs these past days had brought them. *"I really don't think I have a choice in the matter."*

Her smile turned satisfied. Then she slung her bag over her shoulder, marched up to him, and pulled him into a kiss so intense that he nearly collapsed onto the cot when she pulled away.

"I think I like you too, Garrett."

Alexia.

His head spun with her closeness as he tried in futility to document her every perfection—every line and dimple of her face, every twinkle and depth in her smiling brown eyes.

Sweet Alpha, Alexia.

He watched her turn for the door, wanting to stop her, wanting to tell her that he wasn't ready to watch her walk away and that they'd find some way to change the handlers' minds. But he couldn't seem to find the words. Couldn't seem to do anything but watch as she palmed the door open. Stepped forward. She paused on the threshold, looking frozen herself, like she was waiting for him to say something, or convincing herself not to.

Unable to conjure words, he reached for her with his senses only to find that she was already doing the same to him. Their senses—their demons, their whatevers—brushed against one another midway, rolling and swirling like two gentle waves coming together on still water. He sank into the contact, imbuing it with everything rushing through his heart and mind in that moment—his desire to be with her, to keep her here with him. His promise they'd be together again someday. The gratitude he felt for the girl who'd swept in and somehow shaken him out of the trance his life had become.

Similarly, he felt her own fear at what lay ahead. At the thought that her life and body were not hers to control. He felt her fleeting hope that she might yet escape this curse of hers and someday have a life of her own, free from guilt and darkness.

He opened his eyes, needing to tell her that she wasn't a monster. That she was too good to be caught in this mess. That he was going to win this war for her, see to it she had her freedom one day soon. But something about the look in her eyes stopped him. He watched wordlessly as she turned on the threshold.

And then she was gone.

13

THE GREAT HUNT

Two years later, Garrett was still thinking about that kiss. He stared at the bland gray ceiling of his quarters, ignoring the buzz of his palmlight bracelet just a little longer, lingering as he so often did on the haunting finality of those last moments with Alexia. Finally, he rose from his cot with a heavy sigh, staring at the message he'd just received—one eye on the present, and one on the past, with Alexia, as it so often was.

It was preposterous. All of it. Preposterous that he should let such an ephemeral spark—brilliant as it had been—shine on in his life, even after so long. Preposterous the he hadn't seen that final moment for what it had been back then. Or maybe he had. Maybe that was exactly what had barred his tongue from speaking the full truth to her back when he'd had the chance.

Either way, he hadn't told her. About the High Cleric. About the dream they might one day be free together. About any of it. And as the seasons had crept by, their sparse messages—already emotionally barren as they were by the necessity of their handlers' ever-vigilant eyes—growing less and less frequent, Garrett had found his once optimistic thoughts sliding more and more to the deadening realization.

He'd lost Alexia, and he wasn't getting her back.

No, whispered that stubborn voice in the back of his mind. *Things are just taking longer than expected—that's all.*

He rolled his eyes at his own naivety, and its failure to die even when he saw it for what it was. Because even if they did get things under control enough for the High Cleric to make good on his promises to let them free, it had surely been too long. Expecting that Alexia would still be thinking of him as he thought of her... that was like hoping a passing cyclone might be kind enough to leave you dry and spotless. He didn't even want to think about how many so-called fallen her new handlers in Serenity might've had her take down by now, or the things she might've done to get them within range of her poisons, or whatever she was using these days.

He felt sick just thinking about it.

But then maybe he should do something about it. Because he wasn't a helpless victim here, was he? If he and the few other Seekers in the know could've actually done their jobs by now and killed this brewing scud-storm before it broke, maybe he wouldn't be here. Maybe he and Alexia and all the other Seekers could be working their way toward better lives.

But their enemies were crafty as... well, crafty as demons. And the storm was getting ready to break—if it hadn't already.

They still didn't know exactly what the demons were up to, aside from sowing general chaos across Enochia. Aside from a few whispered rumors and a single run-in that had left One and Five thoroughly humiliated, no one had even come close to apprehending the demon known as Carlisle. Of course, it might've helped if the High Cleric would've brought all the Seekers in on their Great Hunt, but he continued to hold to the line that most of them—and especially their handlers—weren't ready for the truth.

Garrett didn't have much time to think about it. He'd been too busy getting his own ass handed to him while trying to track down another mysterious player: one Andre Kovaks. He stared at the name on the palm-light message that'd just roused him from his troubled half-sleep. It might've helped, having had the man's name before now. But it didn't matter anymore, if the news was true.

Because Kovaks had apparently been apprehended last night. Without Garrett's help.

Wonderful.

He read the rest of the way through the mission update and his stomach only sank further. Here he'd been, rightly claiming that Kovaks was damn near impossible to trace—that he hadn't felt so much as a hint of the man's telepathic presence even the one time it'd turned out he'd been close enough that it should've been easy. Kovaks was like a ghost, he'd told the High Cleric.

And now the crazy bastard had gone and gotten caught doing something as stupid as trying to break into Vantage's biotech research facility? The place was a veritable fortress, located northeast of Divinity and, from what he'd heard, armed well enough that it could've given a Legion outpost a run for its coin.

What kind of madman attacked a place like that? And more importantly, what kind of Seeker failed to catch such a crazy bastard before he did?

As if the High Cleric had needed any more reason to believe he was an impotent oaf.

Point of pride aside, it was good to know that Kovaks was at least off the streets. The man had been causing more than a few problems, lately—or so he'd been told. In truth, while the man was clearly dangerous and seemed to have a particular fixation with trespassing on Vantage property, Garrett wouldn't have seen him as much more than a public menace if the High Cleric hadn't made it clear that Kovaks was an important servant of the enemy. The danger wasn't in the grade of his crimes, the High Cleric said, but in whom they were meant to expose: their gifted allies in high places.

Garrett still didn't know who these mysterious allies of theirs were, aside from High General Adrian Kublich. That one had come as enough of a shock on its own. The High General *and* the High Cleric both Awakened to Alpha's Gift and conscripted for this demon hunt of theirs? He wasn't sure how they could need any more resources to win this fight, and yet the High Cleric had told him that he and Kublich were hardly the extent of their network of Awakened elites. There were also praetors, powerful business leaders, and more. Garrett just didn't know names—nor did he need too, apparently, when he couldn't even be counted on to bring in his own target.

With another sigh, he slid off the cot and went to pull some clothes on.

He'd need to get over to Vantage quickly. Whatever they'd done to incapacitate Kovaks probably wouldn't keep him tied up for long. Had the High Cleric not been burning to question the man, the smart move would've been to simply kill him on the spot. Demon-touched or no, those with gifts weren't easily held by traditional shackles. That was why Seekers almost never took prisoners, unless the fallen was deemed young and stable enough to be considered for Seeker training.

Fallen.

The word put a bad taste in the back of his mouth. In the two years since the High Cleric had first revealed himself, Garrett had started to come around to the idea that many with Alpha's Gift were not in fact demon-touched as he'd been taught to believe. But with that acceptance came the burning question: just how many innocent gifted—or Shapers, as they liked to call themselves out there—had been killed in the name of Alpha just in these past two years? How many might've been saved if the High Cleric had taken a more aggressive role in ushering in this new age of his?

It was disturbing to think about. And yet the High Cleric held his course of secrecy.

The others were not ready for the truth, he'd said, time and time again. He'd done what he could to minimize the number of groundless casualties, but taking larger steps, coming out with the truth and upsetting the balance, was unthinkable. Tempting as it might be, he said, such a perturbation in their ranks was exactly the opening Carlisle and his allies were waiting for. If they rocked the ship now, before the demons had been quelled back to the nether, Carlisle would make damn sure that ship capitulated.

It didn't make it any easier to stomach the thought of innocent blood being spilled. But the casualties of this holy war were not Garrett's to stomach, the High Cleric had told him. The weight of those lives, he'd said, was his burden to bear, and his alone. Alpha had shown the High Cleric the vision, and now it was up to him—and him alone—to find the strength to have faith in it, no matter the cost.

No one could've questioned the High Cleric's nobility—that was for damn sure. Still, no matter what his holiness said, Garrett couldn't imagine any of this scud was going to stop eating away at him until they'd bagged Carlisle and all his demonic friends and brought some inkling of peace to Enochia. Whether that made him noble as well, or simply just stupid, he couldn't have said. All he really knew, as he finished pulling on his boots and started for the skimmer bay, was that he had a job to do.

And this time, he was going to see it through.

14

KOVAKS

Something was wrong.

That was the first thought that rang through Garrett's head as he settled the skimmer to an easy landing in the courtyard. But what was it? He looked around at the preposterously tall permacrete wall that surrounded the considerable perimeter of Vantage's premier research facility.

How the scud had Kovaks even made it in here?

He shook the thought off as unimportant. The fallen had their ways. But that wasn't what was bothering him. Nor was it the heavily armed greeting party marching out to meet him with a skimlift in tow, bearing a limp, chained form that could only be Andre Kovaks. Clearly, they intended to hand their prisoner off and turn Garrett away before he even saw the door. Were they really so suspicious of a Sanctum agent?

That was... interesting. And definitely unwarranted. But this *was* where probably at least half of Enochia's past few decades of major medical breakthroughs had occurred, so maybe it was understandable.

What was actually bothering him though, he realized, was the fact that he couldn't feel a single flicker of telepathic presence radiating from the ragged figure being born to him via skimlift. Was Andre Kovaks already dead?

As if in response to his silent question, the figure stirred, raising his head from the skimlift's flat platform in a weak attempt to look around.

Not dead, then. So why couldn't he feel him?

Garrett climbed out of the skimmer, trying to decide what manner of trickery was at play here. The procession of guards picked up their pace, as if they were embarrassed to leave him waiting for a proper reception. Or, he decided as one peeled off to hustle straight up to him, like they didn't want him poking around more than a few yards outside the range of his own skimmer.

That might've raised his eyebrow, had he not been fixed on Andre Kovaks' approaching form, sweeping his senses over him again and again. It didn't make sense. He felt the skimlift, felt Kovaks on it, alive and shallowly breathing. But no telepathic presence. No demonic darkness.

Unless Garrett was missing some trick, Kovaks was just a man.

Before he could start properly pondering how that was possible, the lead guard finished beating her hustled way over to him, drew up to her full height, and locked him with a dark visor stare. "Where would you like him, sir?" she asked in a hard voice.

"Back seat's fine," he said, eyeing Kovaks' restraints and still trying to decide if—and if so, *how*—this was possible. "Might ask to borrow your chains."

Couldn't hurt, even if he was just a plain old boring man.

"I wager that's a smart move, sir," she said, gesturing to her men to get started on the transfer. She turned back and thrust a small dark something his way. A dark leather purse, he realized. The kind wary travelers used to keep their coin close to their bodies and out of the hands of pick-pockets.

"He had these on him," she explained.

He took the purse, unzipped the main compartment, and peered inside at a few metallic objects he couldn't make much sense of in the poor lighting.

"What are they?"

"Not sure, sir."

Well wasn't she helpful?

He closed the purse and tucked it into his jacket for later inspection. "Just out of curiosity, how'd you bring him down?"

"Stunner, sir."

"Any idea how he made it past your wall?"

"It's under investigation, sir."

"Any idea what he was looking for?"

"Under investigation as well."

Yep. Real helpful.

He looked around at the dark corners of the yard, untouched by the faint hint of the coming dawn, then to the well-lit front entrance of the massive research building, wondering what in demons' depths Kovaks had come here for. *To expose our powerful allies,* he was pretty sure the High Cleric would've told him. But expose what, exactly? Was there something happening at this facility? Something to do with the war between the demons and Alpha's Gifted?

He wanted to continue with the questions, but the flat emptiness of the guard leader's dark visor said quite plainly that he wasn't going to be getting any meaningful answers from her. For a half-second, he thought about reaching into her mind and taking them anyway, but then his better judgment caught up, and he recoiled at the thought. Alpha's light may have been shining through him for now, but he'd fall to the darkness like anyone else if he was ever foolish enough to start abusing it like that.

He looked back to where the guards were loading a once-again limp Andre Kovaks into the back seat of his skimmer. The brief brush with temptation had left an uneasy feeling in the pit of his stomach—a prickling tickle that shivered straight up to the back of his neck. He took a calming breath, but the sensation only grew like a soft pressure settling over him. It wasn't just internal uneasiness, he realized.

He was being watched.

He allowed his extended senses to trickle out, opening himself to their influence, letting them guide him. His eyes traced upward by their own accord, settling on the line of the rooftop in the darkness above. His heart leapt when he spotted the lone silhouette standing there, looking down on the scene. Staring at him. He was sure of it, though he couldn't see a single feature of the distant shadow's face.

Pulse racing, he focused his senses, reaching out and—

"I said that'll be all."

The harsh voice snapped him back down to the yard, where the guard leader was watching him, her stare somehow seeming to intensify even through the opaque visor.

"Unless you have more to add, sir," she said, only slightly less stiffly.

It was almost impressive, the verbal gymnastics of how convincingly she used the honorific, sir, while keeping the underlying sentiment to a clear, *Kindly get the grop off our compound, scudbucket.*

Garrett glanced back up to the rooftop. The shadowy figure was gone. He focused back on the verbal gymnast. "I think that'll be all."

She pulled a little more of that passive-aggressive magic—a subtle shift in the pitch of her feet and the puff of her chest—to let him know that right just now would be a prime time for him to be on his scudding way. He suppressed the urge to throw a mocking salute just to ruffle her feathers.

What the scud was up with these people? Were they really that uptight about him catching an accidental glance of some lab experiment he wouldn't even understand, or had Vantage just found a niche in hiring up all those tight-asses who hadn't quite cut it for Onyx Guard?

And who the scud had been watching him from the rooftop like an Alpha-damned shadow monster?

Garrett pulled the skimmer door closed behind him with the frustrated thought that, whatever evil deeds Andre Kovaks was guilty of, he could at least understand why the man had been curious to poke his head in here. Something was up with Vantage.

He glanced at Kovaks in the mirror. The guy looked rough, his face dirty, his dark clothing ragged. Of course, that might've all been on account of his mishap here at Vantage, but something told him the rough look wasn't out of the ordinary for Andre Kovaks. His face was too lined with somber misery, his beard too grizzled, his hair too unkempt and greasy.

Garrett swept his senses over the man one more time, just to be sure.

Nothing.

Not fallen. Not gifted.

Just a man.

"What the scud were you doing here?" he muttered to himself.

To his surprise, Kovaks stirred at his voice.

"Still alive?" he croaked. "...'ll be damned."

So now he had company for the flight home. Wonderful.

He turned to the front, half-thinking of asking the verbal gymnast and her tight-assed guard brigade for another hit of that stunner, but they were all standing at rigid attention, weapons not quite pointed his way, but held at the ready, their leader standing with arms crossed at the end of the firing line.

Whatever.

He powered up the engines and took off, taking less care than he normally would have to avoid ruffling them in the wake.

He needed to find out what Kovaks knew anyway. If the man truly wasn't fallen, though, that sort of complicated the original plan of telepathically duking it out for control. Plain old man, plain old talk. It felt like kind of a stupid line to draw at that moment, but then again, that was probably exactly the kind of thing most fallen had said before they'd made whatever poor decisions had opened them to demonic invasion in the first place.

For the moment, Garrett just focused on guiding them out of Vantage's perimeter and getting the autopilot set so he could focus on the potentially violent madman chained up in his back seat. The skimmer cabin settled to a cold, dim blue as they left Vantage's light show behind for the first waxing light of dawn. He was wondering where he might start, or if Kovaks was even still conscious, when that rough voice croaked through the quiet cabin again.

"Are you one of them?"

Garrett remained facing forward but watched the man's dim outline in the mirror. "One of what?"

"Them," Kovaks said, as if the meaning should be obvious. "The invaders. Infiltrators." Chains rattled, and Garrett could just make out Kovaks lifting his bound arms and tapping at the side of his own head. "You know, the string pullers. The mind benders."

It was the last two words that made Garrett's pulse pick up. The rest of his words could've easily been generic madman rambling. Scud, even *mind benders* sounded plenty like more of the same. But it was the first sign he'd seen that Kovaks might actually be anything other than a wild street dweller who'd just somehow managed to bust into Vantage seeking drugs or Alpha knew what else. The first sign other than the High Cleric's warnings and the purse of Kovaks' mysterious metallic *whatevers* that was still tucked away in Garrett's pocket, at least.

Garrett studied Kovaks' outline, wondering how to answer his question. Probably, he should play along with the man's vague accusations, right?

Kovaks let out an explosive sigh before he could, rolling his eyes so hard his entire head tilted back to match. "Of course you're one of them. Why else would you have come?"

"Maybe I want to know what you were looking for back there."

He chuckled. "Want to know what I *think* I was looking for back there, you mean." He flopped his arms as if he'd meant to throw his hands wide but forgot they were chained. "Why ask at all? Why not just rip the answers straight outta my sad little head? What, you get off playing with your food? Pretending to be one of us?"

One of us?

"What else would I be?"

"Oh, yes..." He tapped his head again, chains rattling. "Very good, very good. So clever, aren't you? So convincing."

What in demons' depths was this guy getting at? He seemed to be at least vaguely aware of the existence of telepathy, but the rest of it? *Playing with your food? Pretending to be one of us?* It was like he thought he was talking to a demon.

Maybe Garrett could work with that.

"Fine," he said, hardening his tone. "I'm saving you for my master. Does that make you happy, mortal?"

That at least got a response out of Kovaks. He went still in the backseat, watching Garrett with rigid attention.

"Now tell me," Garrett continued in the same cold tone, "what were you after at Vantage? Did Carlisle send you there?"

"Who?"

"Do not play games with me," Garrett snapped. "What did Carlisle want from Vantage?"

"What are you?" Kovaks whispered.

"Answer the Alpha-damned question!" Garrett roared.

For a second, he thought that had done it. Then Kovaks' startled expression shifted, slowly giving way to a dismissive frown. "You know what? I know who Carlisle is about as well as you know what the scud you think you're pretending to be right now. Nice try, though."

What was it with this guy? Garrett couldn't decide if he was dangerously clever or just gropping insane. Maybe it was both. Either way, Garrett was losing his footing, and he only had one more idea to try.

He slipped into his best street tone. "Fine. You wanna know the truth? I'm a gropping enforcer, man. What the scud did you think I was?"

"Full of bullscud, mostly."

"Yeah, funny, I've been thinking the same thing since you first opened your mouth. Look, broto, I don't know how the scud you managed to get inside that perimeter back there, but you have about fifteen minutes before I drop your ass at the White Tower, and you've said just enough to freak me out. If you're caught up in something dangerous... if you know something... well, I've got another fifteen minutes to decide what's what. After that, you're off my plate whether I like it or not. So do with that as you will."

Crazy or not, Garrett was pretty sure the glint of hope in Kovaks' eyes was genuine. Wild and a little frightening too, maybe. But genuine. Garrett watched him in the faint light of the coming dawn. The man's lips worked furiously beneath his grizzled beard, clearly chewing through his options. Garrett considered saying more, trying to tip Kovaks into spilling, but something told him he'd already done everything he could. Any additional attempts would probably only startle Kovaks back into his crazy paranoid shell.

Though judging by the look on Kovaks' face, Garrett had a feeling the guy had just slipped back into crazy town without prompting. The ambient light of the coming dawn was just bright enough now to make out Kovaks' lips quirking into a bitter grin.

"You're a Seeker, aren't you?"

They might as well have been broadsided by another skimmer. Garrett did his best to cover up his surprise, to close his gaping mouth before it was blatantly obvious. Too late.

In the back, Kovaks' grin only widened. "Ah, I see. Interesting. I don't believe I've ever spoken with one of you in person. What an honor. Tell me, which ones are pulling your strings? Is it your cleric masters? I know they have some in the Sanctum, just like they have some in Vantage, and in the Legion, and gropping everywhere else."

His tone had grown agitated by the end, chains clinking tight as he lost his composure and struggled to break free.

"How can you be so blind?" he shouted when his futile attempts at freedom failed.

Garrett tensed, preparing to push the crazy bastard into deep sleep telepathically if he had to.

"You can feel them," Kovaks croaked, chains rattling slack as the fight drained from him. "You can feel them in a way I can only imagine. You have to know something's wrong. You have to feel that, don't you?"

"What the scud are you talking about?"

"The invaders," he said, again in that tone that said this should all be obvious. "They're like you. Telepaths. Powerful ones. Don't tell me you didn't notice the people telling you to murder your own brethren had gone and come back with the very same gifts?"

The High Cleric's face sprung to mind, unbidden. How in demons' depths did this madman know these things? For a second, panic nearly gripped him.

Then it occurred to him.

Carlisle.

Kovaks might not have been a telepath himself. He might not have even genuinely known who Carlisle was—either because he never had, or because Carlisle had been careful enough to telepathically blank the man's memories in case he fell into enemy hands. But given the things he knew, Garrett was certain Andre Kovaks must be working within the network of that demonic bastard's influence. It was the only explanation.

Which brought them back to what the scud he'd been after tonight.

"Why did you break into Vantage, Kovaks? What were you looking for?"

Kovaks blew out a humorless chuckle. "Would you believe me if I said I don't actually know?"

Garrett frowned at him, wondering if Kovaks was screwing with him until it occurred to him that Carlisle and whatever other demons Kovaks served might actually prefer to run operations that way. Telepathically compelling someone to complete an objective without explaining the true purpose sounded like a pretty good way to make a field agent who could do the job but couldn't spill the secrets, even if they were captured by another telepath.

It was insidious. And damned ingenious.

"Perhaps you should go back and have a look yourself," Kovaks said, his tone serious. "I'm not quite sure what it is yet, but something dark is happening behind those walls. You should see what it is your masters are up to."

"Something dark..." Garrett repeated slowly, taking some comfort from the fact that Kovaks' words were sliding from disturbingly poignant straight back to madman drivel. "Something these invaders of yours are up to?"

"These invaders of *ours*, Seeker."

"Yeah. Right."

Chains jingled. Kovaks leaned forward as far as he could, until Garrett could smell the stink on his breath when he spoke.

"You won't be scoffing when you're watching the darkness consume everything you've ever known or loved."

It was unsettling, how intense and completely assured Kovaks was in that moment, but then he settled back into his seat and seemed to deflate, defeated.

"Yeah," Garrett said softly. "Well, I haven't really known or loved all that much, so I think I'll be okay."

Kovaks gave an exasperated huff. "And a small wonder that is. Forgive me if I don't join in weeping for you, murderer, when you have allowed yourself to become the very vessel by which your kind have been oppressed for a thousand years."

"That's... not what I am," Garrett snapped before he could think better of it. "Not anymore."

"No? Perhaps not. Perhaps your new masters have turned you to an even more sinister purpose. Perhaps they promised—"

"Alpha, will you shut up?"

To his surprise Kovaks complied, looking a touch self-satisfied, maybe, but mostly just tired.

"If you're so confident back there, why don't you tell me about your masters? Did Carlisle tell you to say all this? Did you never think he could be the one who's lying to you?"

He sighed. "I told you, I don't know who you're talking about. I'm pretty sure *you* don't even know who you're talking about."

"Bullscud. I know who you serve."

"Then search my mind, Seeker. Tell me I'm lying."

It was only by a significant force of will that Garrett refrained from plunging into Kovaks' mind then. Once he'd mastered the initial rush of the urge, though, he couldn't help but wonder if he was being foolish to abstain. He wouldn't have held back if it were life and death, would he? No, he wouldn't have. But sitting here in a quiet skimmer cabin with a chained madman, it was hard to convince himself the stakes were high enough for such a dangerous abuse of power. Especially when there'd be no way to even tell which parts of Kovaks' memories were real and which had been twisted or injected whole by a nefarious demon set on bending the man to its will.

Nothing in Kovaks' mind could be truly trusted.

The realization left his insides tingling with an itch he didn't know how to scratch. Why couldn't the bastard have just been a demon?

He pushed the dark thought aside as the distant blip of Divinity grew near enough that he could just pick out the sliver of the White Tower, ascending to the top of the city skyline.

The High Cleric would know what to do.

"We'll get the answers out of you, one way or another," he said, as much to himself as to Kovaks.

Kovaks said nothing, letting the silence stretch as the lights and sprawling permacrete towers of Divinity drew into plain view, the sky growing light with the coming sun. Garrett stared ahead, his eyes only distantly taking in the approaching skyline, and the glimmering lanes of early-morning air traffic.

He couldn't say why, but he found his thoughts drifting to Alexia—to the night when he'd found out about the High Cleric, when Verner had committed his perverse barbarism with Alexia and sought to end Garrett's life. To the way it had felt holding Alexia in the wake of that scudstorm, her arms clinging to him just as surely as his own sinking certainty that they'd been forsaken and that it would be just the two of them against the world from that point on.

Alpha, he wished she were here now.

"They're going to kill me," Kovaks said softly, drawing his attention back to the skimmer cabin. "Aren't they?"

It was Garrett's turn to let the silence stretch.

"Can you promise me something?" Kovaks asked, when it became clear Garrett wasn't going to answer.

Garrett forced himself to meet Kovaks' eyes in the mirror, not quite able to say the "no" hanging on his lips.

The look in Kovaks' eyes struck straight through to Garrett's spirit.

"I won't ask you to help me. I won't ask you to stand up and rebel. All I ask is that you find the courage to question what's happening around you. Question it silently, in the sanctum of your own head. But question it. Ask yourself who it is you're fighting, and why. Ask what it is that might be driving them. Forget what you've been told, if only for a moment, and ask these questions as if you do not already know the answers. Find the courage to lay your demons and your fears to the side, look at the cold, hard facts, and draw your own conclusions. That is all I ask."

Garrett considered his words quietly. "And if I do as you ask, and still arrive at the same conclusion?"

Kovaks showed him a humorless smile, and for a moment, Garrett had the odd thought that, had they met in another life, under completely different circumstances, he might have actually liked this man.

"What do I care?" Kovaks said, shrugging and tilting his head back to rest on the seat as they entered an air traffic lane bound for the White Tower. "I'll be long dead either way."

15

APOSTATE'S FOLLY

When he'd first set out to find Andre Kovaks, not even yet knowing the man's name or anything other than that he was a servant of the enemy, Garrett had expected the moment he returned with his inevitable prisoner would be one of triumph—an important victory, well won. But as he watched the team of Sanctum Guard preparing to escort Kovaks off to the holding cells, he didn't seem to feel much of anything at all. Aside from unsettled.

For one thing, he wasn't used to taking prisoners. Fallen and other gifted sorts didn't make for compliant captives—not when they could pick a lock or bribe a guard with little more than a few focused thoughts. But Kovaks wasn't a fallen. Not in the conventional sense of the word, at least. Whether or not he was a servant of the demons, though...

It didn't matter. Garrett had done his part. Not that he'd really been the one to catch Kovaks or anything. But he'd brought the man in and saw to it he was safe to be held captive. He'd make his report, and the High Cleric would see to it the rest was handled. Simple as that.

But that wasn't really what had him unsettled, was it? Or not the entirety of it, at least. No. It was all the bullscud Kovaks had been spouting on the way over that lingered in Garrett's mind, staining the walls with doubts he couldn't quite ignore and questions he couldn't answer.

"Was there anything else, sir?" a tentative voice cut through his troubled thoughts. The head Sanctum Guard of the escort team was watching him from behind his inscrutable gold faceplate.

Garrett shook his head distractedly. Two years ago, it would've filled him with a rush of power to hear a Sanctum Guard call him sir, awaiting his instructions. And indeed, it had been nice the first few seasons, having his small sect of Guard who'd been informed—albeit vaguely—that they were to defer to his orders as if he were a cleric. But the novelty had faded quickly enough.

And at the moment, he was too busy watching Kovaks, wondering where in demons' depths the man had learned the things he had. Whoever Kovaks had been working for, he definitely knew far more than anyone outside the White Tower should. For a brief second, he couldn't help but wonder if Kovaks had once been a cleric—a handler, even—but that was ridiculous. Carlisle was the most likely answer. That gray-haired demon and his ilk no doubt knew of the Seekers existence to some extent. Garrett and his allies had been hunting the man for at least two years now, after all.

But how had Kovaks actually known the word, Seeker?

Garrett scowled at his own paranoia. There was an explanation. Clearly, there was. But it didn't matter anyway. He'd done his part, remember? All that was left for him to do was bid farewell to this strange man with his raving mad bullscud and his odd little...

The purse!

He'd nearly forgotten about Kovaks' bag of trinkets, lost as he'd been in the man himself.

"Guard," he called, drawing the small leather bag from his pocket.

Out of the corner of his eye, he saw the procession halt at his call. That would've been another rush two years ago. Now, though, he was too busy staring at the dark leather purse, curiosity guiding his fingers toward the zipper.

Back at Vantage, he'd barely had time for more than a dim glance at the purse's contents, but even the clean lighting of the skimmer bay couldn't help him make sense of the first item he slid out of the bag. The metallic cylinder was maybe nine or ten inches long and about an inch in diameter, but by far, the most notable thing about it was the network of silver symbols inlaid here and there across its surface. They were surprisingly delicate and something about them reminded him of... he wasn't quite sure what. But something. He eyed the odd little stud near the middle of the cylinder, instinctively feeling it must be some manner of trigger. He glanced around, half-tempted to see what would happen if he pushed it.

It was only then he noticed that the head Sanctum Guard had marched back over and was patiently watching him behind his golden faceplate.

"Sir?" he asked when he noticed Garrett's attention on him. "Was there something else?"

Garrett held up a finger for the man to wait while he rifled through the other contents of the purse. There wasn't much. A few equally odd trinkets, also inlaid with the strange silver markings, a moderate handful of coins, a spare energy cell, and...

And a holodisk.

He stared at the plain lightsteel disk with an odd mix of curiosity and fear, considering what manner of madness its internal circuits might contain. Info about Kovaks' mission at Vantage? Footage from within the facility itself? Scud, it might just be empty.

"Have a listen," a rough voice called from across the bay.

Garrett looked over in time to see Kovaks opening his mouth to say more, but one of the guards gave him a firm cuff to shut him up and turned him back toward the door, brandishing a stun rod in his face. The rest of the golden faceplates turned to Garrett, waiting to see what he had to say to Kovaks' proposition.

Which was a damn good question.

He pinched the holodisk between his fingers, weighing his options. What could be on it that Kovaks would want him to hear? More of the man's bullscud rambling, most likely. He didn't need to hear that. No one needed to hear that.

And yet his fingers lingered, Kovaks' last request echoing uncomfortably at the surface of his thoughts. *Question what's happening around you. Draw your own conclusions.* But that was exactly what he was doing, wasn't it? Drawing his own conclusion—that he didn't personally need to hear whatever was on that disk. Because that was the real question here. Whose word did he trust between the High Cleric's and that of the dirty, stinking madman who'd been caught breaking into a medical research lab?

It wasn't much of a question.

He slipped the disk back into the purse with the rest of the items, zipped it closed, and handed the entire kit to the guard. "See to it that the High Cleric receives this. See to it personally. Understood?"

The man somehow seemed to stand a little straighter, despite already being at military attention. "Understood, sir."

"That's all," Garrett said, waving the Guard on and trying to ignore the trickle of guilt he felt as they formed up and dragged Kovaks out of the bay. Out of his hands. But not out of his mind.

IF NOTHING ELSE, the next few days proved two things. First, that Garrett had been right to trust his gut. And secondly, that Andre Kovaks was inarguably, profoundly insane. Garrett still wasn't sure how the man had known some of the things he did. The High Cleric had agreed with him that his master Carlisle likely had something to do with it. But when Garrett heard the manner of wild delusions contained on that holodisk...

Perhaps he shouldn't have been surprised. Kovaks' accusation that the ruling class of Enochia had been corrupted by forces beyond the people's comprehension was exactly the kind of move they'd been expecting Carlisle and his ilk to make all this time. It might have even given Garrett a second's pause if it had ended there. But then Kovaks had gone on, muttering to himself from what sounded like some dank back alley about how they weren't alone in the universe, and about how the very planet itself was at risk.

Aliens. The crazy bastard actually believed that a ship full of aliens had landed on Enochia and somehow taken over the planet without anyone noticing, that they were planning something using companies like Vantage to do Alpha knew what and, ultimately, to wipe out life as they knew it here.

That alone would've been enough blasphemy to condemn him—the teachings of Alpha were quite clear on the existence, or lack thereof, of life outside of Enochia. But then there'd been the actual break-ins, and the slander against the Legion and the Sanctum. Of course, maybe it wasn't complete slander if there was a small grain of truth nestled within his madness. There *were* unique individuals in high places, after all, guiding Enochia toward a better future—but those were Alpha's gifted chosen, not some three-headed extraterrestrials hiding in the shadows. Garrett had confirmed as much with his own senses, both in the High Cleric and in High General Kublich the few times they'd had cause to cross paths over the past year.

He was fairly certain he would've noticed if the leaders of their quiet telepathic revolution were anything more or less than gifted humans.

Still, it was this small grain of truth in Kovaks' ramblings that made Garrett wonder why the High Cleric had released the logs to the WAN at all—and especially why he'd permitted them to be broadcast on the reels. Sure, maybe the exercise would send a message to Carlisle and set an example for any other would-be blasphemers out there that the Sanctum would not be so openly challenged without consequences. Still, Garrett wasn't sure it was worth the questions the whole ordeal would raise. And beyond that, he couldn't help but think it seemed oddly cruel.

Either way, Kovaks had been right about one thing: whatever else happened, he wasn't going to be around to see it.

By the time his execution date was set, the reels were alive with talk of the mad blasphemer and his wild alien conspiracy theories. Garrett watched the situation unfold with a frustration that grew like the festering of a splinter he hadn't even known was there to begin with. He couldn't say what it was that so upset him—whether it was the exasperation at watching the reels evolve into more outlandish lies with each iteration, or simply the mindless barbarism so many thousands of clueless citizens saw fit to personally hurl at Kovaks over the reels.

The man was already sentenced to death. Wasn't that enough?

Maybe that was what was bothering him so much. Maybe Garrett just understood a little too well what it felt like to be a pariah. Or maybe he was just upset because here he was, joining in with the same crowd who would turn and eat him alive if they had the slightest inkling about what he actually was.

He tried not to think about it when the time came for Kovaks' execution, but he couldn't ignore the unaccustomed flutter of apprehension as he took the service lift and slipped discreetly into the gathering crowd in the Great Hall. Of the many executions he'd attended over the years, this one felt undeniably different—probably not in small part because he rarely saw his own targets killed in such an official setting. Unless you were planning on training a fallen, you didn't capture them—and you sure as scud didn't bring them into crowded rooms.

Seeing Kovaks on the worn old gallows at the head of the immaculate Great Hall, though, and knowing that he'd put him there, Garrett somehow felt more conflicted than he ever had about pulling the trigger in the field. It hardly made sense, and yet there the turmoil was, twisting in his gut and driving him to pass up the spots he'd normally take at the fringes of the crowd and to instead press into the thick of things, where he'd be lost in the sea of faces—just another mob-goer, here to watch the madman die. And Alpha, were they ready...

"—aliens. Merciful Alpha, how much sweet tar is he on?"

"That's an insult to sweet tar. This scudbucket's beyond cracked."

"—eir necks really break when they fall, daddy?"

"Did he really live in a dumpster?"

"I heard he lived under a bridge with a goat for a wife."

"Poor goat."

"—hope he suffers. My children will be talking about this nonsense for seasons."

These gropping people.

On and on it went with each group he passed. Garrett pushed on until he found a spot between two off-duty legionnaires who were silent and looked about as grim as he felt. He couldn't help but wonder why they'd care more than the rest of these automatons—wondered to the extent that it made him half-suspicious. But maybe there were a few decent spirits left on this cursed planet.

Soon enough, the High Cleric arrived and ended the babbling anyway. He appeared, as he usually did, at the precipice of the fourth and highest of the huge plateau steps at the head of the Great Hall, ferried up there by the mag lift from his quarters below. It was surprisingly reassuring, seeing him take the high plateau—that of Alpha, preceded first by the three levels of mind, body, and spirit. The man looked the part, gazing over his flock in his ceremonial robes of cream and gold.

If there'd been any lingering doubt that the High Cleric was indeed the worldly mouth of Alpha, it was washed away by the feeling that settled over the room as he spread his arms in welcome—as if Alpha's very presence were flowing into the silence left by the crowd that now stared attentively, hungrily, up at their High Cleric, awaiting their ministration.

And by the love of Alpha, did he give it to them.

The High Cleric had always had a special talent for speaking, but ever since his own awakening two years ago, when Alpha had shown him His vision for the future of their kind, his skill at touching a crowd had become otherworldly. Listening to him speak of duty and faith and stability for Enochia, Garrett couldn't help but wonder if Alpha wasn't reaching down and channeling His own grace through the cleric right before their eyes. He forgot about the ignorant cruelty of the crowd around him. Forgot about the crowd completely. Forgot, even, about Kovaks up until the High Cleric steered the ministration back around to the many ways the foundations of their existence could be challenged by the demons and apostates of the world.

It was the mention of demons that jarred Garrett out of it, as it usually did—the unwelcome reminder that, no matter how much deeply he hid himself in this crowd, Garrett would never be one of them. To these people, demons were conceptual—fae tale constructs they used to help make sense of troubling temptations or to scare their children into behaving. And true, most still believed that demons might sometimes reach up and momentarily seize those who'd strayed, force them to commit terrible atrocities in the moment. But they had no idea how literally that darkness could manifest in their world. They wouldn't dream of the existence of men like Carlisle, whose spirits were blackened and bound to the nether.

Not yet, at least.

When the High Cleric reached the customary point of asking, it turned out that Kovaks did have last words to share. A lot of them. They spilled out of him in frantic bursts, first in pleading tones then in growing agitation. He called for them to open their eyes and see what was happening to their planet right under their noses. The reverent silence the crowd had held for the High Cleric did not extend to Kovaks, though, and soon his words were drowned out by a respondent wave of cries for him to go grop his goat, return to the nether, die already.

The High Cleric ended the tumult, killing Kovaks' line to the amps and silencing the rising tide of the crowd with a wave of his hand. Garrett could still faintly hear Kovaks' unamplified voice spouting on. He gave up soon enough, though, when the High Cleric resumed with his own final words. Garrett knew the wild look in Kovaks' eyes in that moment. It was the look of one realizing the arrival of their own death, yet unwilling to go, their business unfinished. Those wild eyes tore through the crowd, possessed, desperate.

And settled straight on Garrett.

The look in Kovaks' eyes in that moment struck him so deeply that he forgot to breathe. Beneath his grizzled beard, Kovaks' lips moved, mouthing something over and over—some whispered prayer Garrett couldn't make out by his lips alone.

"Alpha grant you peace, Andre Kovaks," came the High Cleric's solemn farewell.

Then the portly hangman threw the lever, and Kovaks' eyes went wide with terror.

He didn't die neatly. Sometimes they didn't. But somehow, Kovaks found it in him to keep his eyes fixed on Garrett until his red face turned to blue, and his focus drifted off somewhere beyond—distant, and then gone.

Garrett came back to his own thundering heart and spinning head and realized he hadn't breathed the entire time. He gulped in a few lungfuls of air, drawing odd tingles through his oxygen-deprived body, and even odder stares from those around him. He didn't care. He watched Kovaks' body, still swinging from the gallows, the creak of the wood and the taut rope slowly giving way to the building volume of murmured voices.

Garrett barely heard them. Barely saw anything but Kovaks' lips in his mind's eye, mouthing that silent prayer, over and over again, holding Garrett's eyes until the end, holding to hope until his final moments that a complete stranger—the enemy who'd brought him to his death—would heed his last words.

Wake up.

SEVERAL HOURS LATER, Kovaks was still swinging from the gallows in Garrett's mind—his limp form swaying back and forth in the darkness as Garrett lay awake in his quarters. *Wake up,* it whispered to him, as it had been all night. *Wake up.*

He was pretty sure he knew what that night's nightmares would consist of if he actually managed to fall asleep at any point.

With a sigh, he rolled over and woke his palmlight. As he often did on troubled nights, he swept into his ID log and pulled up Alexia's entry—though it wasn't labeled *Alexia,* but *Six.* He'd thought about changing it a few—or maybe a few hundred—times, but even that simple little affection had always seemed too much of a risk for both of them. It didn't matter anyway. He knew who the ID belonged to, and ridiculous as it was, that alone brought him comfort. He wasn't even sure why he thought of her on nights like these, but he'd often stare at that string of numbers, fantasizing about a time when he'd be able to simply contact her without fear.

He didn't have the first clue what he'd say when that day came, but it was a nice thought anyway. Almost as nice as the thought that he might be with her again someday. Someday soon, even.

Alpha, what he would've given to feel her hands on him again, to taste her lips.

His fingers traced absentmindedly to his collar, the familiar loop of daydreams springing to mind as surely as if that collar were a controller for a holodisk buried in his brain. He'd vanquish this growing shadowy threat. Earn the eternal gratitude of the High Cleric and the forgiveness of Alpha. Maybe the High Cleric would go on to usher in this new world where people like them no longer had to hide their gifts. Garrett hardly cared about that anymore. He'd be gone. He'd pull Alexia out of whatever twisted jobs they had her running in Serenity under the guise of Alpha's will. They'd run away together. It didn't matter where. Only that they'd be together and that, for the first time, they'd know true peace. Someday. Someday soon...

Wake up.

He jerked back to full alertness at the ghostly whisper in his head, having nearly nodded off staring at his palmlight. Alpha be damned if he was going to get a minute's peaceful sleep tonight.

For one impulsive second, he nearly threw demons to the wind and hit the call icon beside Alexia's ID. Just to hear her voice for a second. Just to think about anything other than the look in Kovaks' eyes—the helpless, frantic madness of those final moments, the dull, glassy sheen of death, creeping in even as he held Garrett's eyes from across the Great Hall.

Consequences be damned, he needed something to pull him away from that memory.

But it couldn't be her. Not yet. It didn't matter if the Divinity handlers were slowly being trained by the High Cleric's careful instruction to be incrementally more lenient with him and a few others. Off with her Serenity handlers, Alexia might as well have been on a different planet. He couldn't put her at risk. And besides, he wasn't even sure she'd want to talk to him.

And for the love of Alpha, how in demons' depths was he thinking about her right now after what he'd watched today?

Because she was the only thing he *could* think of. The only thing that didn't make him want to rip his own hair out, or pull his old lash out of its two year retirement.

Why had Kovaks had to pick him as the object of his insane pleas? And why did he even care at all? He'd killed over twenty people with his own bloody hands. Why was he lying here haunted by the dying breaths of a troubled mind?

There was no reason. It was pointless—worse than pointless.

"Gropping crazy bastard," he muttered at the darkness.

Wake up, it whispered right back.

16

MAD HOUNDS

The following day came and went in a haze. Garrett was as surprised he'd slept at all as he was unsure he'd even truly woken up. Everything felt just... off. Off in the way things often felt in those hyper-realistic dreams that sometimes left him confused the next day about what had been real and what had been an uncanny figment of his troubled night-time imagination.

He needed to center himself. Find something to pour his mind into before it went wondering someplace it might not come back from—or, worse, someplace it might come back from bearing a demonic passenger.

He needed to get his head right—which meant, he decided, that he needed to speak with the High Cleric. From what little he'd told Garrett the morning of the execution, Kovaks had largely been a dead end. Interrogation had at least gotten the man to admit to his connections with Carlisle, but what little he'd seemed to know about the man had been, as Garrett expected, deemed unreliable given that it was all vulnerable to telepathic manipulation.

Hunting Kovaks, in other words, had been an unproductive waste of an entire season's worth of Garrett's time. Which was why it was time to move on to the real target.

He knew One was already on a full-time hunt for Carlisle. She hadn't made any effort to hide her *legitimate* contribution to the mission—as she'd pointedly put it to him every chance she got—since her joyous return to the White Tower and to Garrett's eternal misery. And while Three and Five had been much less obnoxious about it, he was pretty sure they were running support for her at times—at least when they weren't busy tracking their own targets.

Why Garrett had seemingly been left to the minor jobs, he couldn't have said. He was every bit as capable as One—and more so than Three and Five—and he didn't think he'd ever given the High Cleric cause to doubt him. It was *because* he was a faithful servant, in fact, that he'd never deigned to make a point of it in their discussions. But it was time now.

The darkness was building out there. He could feel it like the electric tingle of a coming storm. The handlers could even sense that something was up. No one had said a thing when the High Cleric had brought a fourth Seeker home to the White Tower, breaking the steadfast Rule of Three.

Kovaks had been the opening shot. For two years this storm had been brewing, and now it was about to break. Faithful servant or not, it was time Garrett made his voice heard. It was time for the High Cleric to send him after Carlisle. Except the High Cleric wasn't there when he arrived in the Great Hall, brimming with self-actualized conviction, ready to fight for his case. Not as far as his extended senses could tell, at least. The hall itself was half full with Alphasday attendants, entranced in their own silent worship between the morning and midday sessions, but inside the High Cleric's quarters, he felt nothing but Onyx Guard and a few attendant acolytes.

That seemed odd. Had he stepped out between worship sessions?

"Excuse me, goodlady," he said quietly to a passing worshiper on her way out, "might you know if the High Cleric is expected to return for the midday?"

She shook her head. "Apologies, my goodfellow, but I cannot say. His Holiness was absent this morning, though they did not say why. Cleric Amadeus led the session." She looked disappointed by the fact.

He bowed his head and thanked her, chewing that over as she moved on.

Definitely odd.

Briefly, he considered messaging the High Cleric, making it known that he required a meeting. But, while the High Cleric had never explicitly said as much, it was implicitly understood that that wasn't how it worked. The Seekers provided mission reports and any other relevant updates. The High Cleric decreed when a meeting was required. Whatever was going on, it looked like Garrett might have to wait.

Deflated, he returned to his quarters for a bland meal he hardly tasted. He spent the afternoon combing through the reels and the Legion's own secure intel network, too distracted to even notice he was looking through records he'd already seen earlier that cycle, much less to draw any insightful conclusions. In the evening, he was staring at his open palmlight, weighing his choices between messaging the High Cleric and attempting to just butt his way in with One when his palmlight buzzed.

An incoming call.

And it was the High Cleric.

He stared at the ID in surprise for two full buzzes. The High Cleric didn't call. Had never called. Still staring, Garrett forced himself to swipe the connection on.

"There's been an awakening," came the High Cleric's terse voice—no preamble, no greeting. "I need you in the streets. Now."

"Yes, High Cleric," he said reflexively. Then, processing the oddness of the order, he added, "An awakening, your holiness? Is there something..."

Something what? Unusual? Special? By their estimates, there were at least five or six awakenings across Enochia every cycle—one every few days, on average. Which didn't exactly make it a common occurrence by most standards, but it was hardly something one normally received a call from the High Cleric over.

"He was Legion-trained," the High Cleric said. "A promising servant of Enochia. And he's been captured by Carlisle. From within Sanctuary."

Shock ripped through him. "Carlisle was in Sanctuary?"

"He just tried to kill the High General."

Garrett gaped at his palmlight.

That *was* special. And unusual. And gropped twelve ways to demons' depths.

"Tried?"

"Kublich is alive," the High Cleric said. "But never mind that. I need you on the streets. Right now. I need you to find Haldin Raish and pull him from that demon's clutches."

"Yes, High Cleric." Garrett was already on his feet, going for his jacket, filing away the name, Haldin Raish. "Where were they last seen?"

"It's Carlisle," the High Cleric snapped with more ferocity than Garrett had ever heard. "They *haven't* been seen since he attacked the High General in Raish's home. Get out there and start sweeping. Bring a fireteam, but for the love of Alpha, keep it inconspicuous. Find the boy. He may yet still be of use to us if you can pry him away from the demon."

Garrett hesitated. "And if I can't?"

"Then Carlisle must not be allowed to sink his hooks into the Raish boy. Do whatever you must to see it doesn't happen."

"Yes, High Cleric," Garrett said, striding for the door with more purpose than he'd felt in seasons. "I'll see it done."

DESPERATELY AS GARRETT wanted to prove his worth to the High Cleric in light of the Kovaks dead-end, sweeping an entire city for one telepathic mind was not a quick and easy feat. Especially not when one was lacking a more refined starting point than that his quarry had been in Sanctuary earlier that evening. Which is why Garrett nearly missed it when the faintest telepathic light flickered in his senses to the east.

"There," Garrett hissed, his eyes snapping open in surprise.

"Where, sir?" asked the Sanctum Guard beside him, glancing away from the skimmer controls.

Garrett closed his eyes, focused to confirm, then opened them back up and pointed through the permacrete buildings to the east. "That way."

Behind his golden faceplate, the Sanctum Guard nodded and guided them to begin merging with the next eastbound air traffic lane, trusting Garrett's word more than Garrett did. The presence had been faint, and nearly beyond the reach of his senses. When he sank down and reached out again, though, he felt it with growing certainty. Definitely a telepath. Definitely moving through the streets of Divinity.

But was it Raish?

He wasn't sure. For one thing, the chances of his having found the boy after twenty minutes of random cruising seemed laughably low. Though it wasn't like there was an abundance of telepaths running around in the city.

The main question was, if it was Raish they were flying toward now, then where the scud had his kidnapper gone?

Was it possible Raish had escaped him? Or was Carlisle setting some kind of trap, lurking nearby to strike down anyone who came looking for his victim? Given how regularly the man had slipped between their fingers, Garrett had started to wonder if Carlisle might not have some dark secret to hiding his mind from their detection.

But that didn't matter now.

Garrett would find Raish, and then he'd do what he had to, just like the High Cleric had said.

"Slow down," he said to the driver, casting his senses back out.

The telepath was close—and definitely a *he*, Garrett decided now. A *he* who was full of powerful, dark emotion—chaotic and barely controlled. It didn't feel at all like a mind that was ready to talk reason, but that only made Garrett more sure they'd found the boy who'd just been abducted by a demon.

"Drop us there," he said, pointing to the mouth of the busy pedestrian pass their target had just entered.

The Guard diligently obeyed, flicking on the landing indicators and guiding the skimmer gently down to one of the designated drop-offs. While he did, Garrett pulled up his palmlight and swiped a quick message to the High Cleric.

<Might have him.>

He added a nav pin on his location, then reluctantly added One, Three, and Five to the list of recipient IDs as well. Pride be damned, if this was some devious trap of Carlisle's, he wasn't going to be so stupid as to try to wrestle the demon down on his own.

"Circle the block until I say otherwise," Garrett instructed, slipping in an earpiece and swiping on his palmlight to open a channel with the driver.

"Understood, sir."

Garrett nodded and turned to the four Sanctum Guard in the back seats. "Let's move, boys."

He didn't need to say more than that. They knew who they were looking for, just like they knew not to ask questions.

The five of them moved into the thick crowd single file, doing their best not to stir any fuss over the presence of armed Sanctum Guard in the streets. Dressed in their Alphasday finest and brimming with righteous self-importance, most passersby hardly seemed to notice at all. That was fine by him. He kept his senses extended and his defenses tight. The kid had stopped halfway down the side alley ahead, which at once calmed Garrett's need to hurry and doubled his apprehension that this could all be a Carlisle-induced trap.

Only one way to find out.

"Down here," he said to the two Guard closest to him as he steered out of the foot traffic for the empty alleyway.

"How can you tell, sir?" one of them asked.

Garrett and the man's squad mate both stared him down.

So maybe they didn't *all* know not to ask questions.

"Just trust me when I say he's nearby," he said, starting down the alley-way. "And gropping be ready."

Detached from the stream of foot traffic, the racket of the crowd quickly grew to a dull roar behind them. Ahead, the alleyway was quiet. Clean, too. Well-lit and well-paved. The alleyways in this part of Divinity were probably nicer than the main streets in the slums.

And there, behind the first of the boxy blue dumpsters, Garrett could feel the boy hiding more clearly than if he'd seen him with his own two eyes.

"Come on out, kid," he called. "No need to hide with the garbage anymore."

There was nothing—no jump or surprised gasp—but Garrett swore he felt the kid tensing like an electric charge in the air. He swept his senses out uneasily, checking the surrounding area again for any sign of a lurking Carlisle.

Nothing.

"Come on, kid. I swear we won't bite."

He felt the Sanctum Guard shifting behind him in the tense silence that followed, either uncomfortable about what they might be facing or—more likely—wondering why the scud he was bothering with talking at all when they could surely take one measly little kid, dark tyro or not. All they really knew was that this was a capture or kill mission, and right now, Garrett seemed to be soft-footing it.

He ignored their shuffling, feeling what they couldn't. Raish was deliberating.

Slowly, the kid leaned out from behind the dumpster.

He looked like a stereotypical Legion tyro—buzz cut, firmly set jaw, plain clothes. But the look in his eyes said something different. There was a glimpse of fear there in the first second, like he half-expected to find an enraged haga beast bearing down on him, but once he caught sight of them, he mastered that fear, and there was nothing left but suspicion and cold calculation.

This kid wasn't going to be an easy sell, Garrett decided, as Raish's gaze scanned over the Sanctum Guard behind him and finally settled on Garrett himself.

"Well there he is," Garrett said, holding his hands out to show they were empty while he reached out to try for a better read on Raish's mind. "Alpha be praised, right boys?"

Raish looked less than relieved at the arrival of would-be friendly forces. "What do you want?" he called, taking only a half-step out from the cover of the dumpster.

"Sanctuary reported a tyro abducted on base." Garrett took a few steps forward, hands still held peacefully at his sides. "One Haldin Raish. Some kind of home invasion."

He watched Raish's face, searching for any reaction to help him gauge what had happened, and where Carlisle might've gone.

"You know the drill from there," he continued. "Teams were dispatched to find you and bring you home."

"I do know the drill," Raish said, nodding slowly. "Which is why I'm wondering who the scud you are to be leading a fireteam of Sanctum Guard."

Damn Legion brats.

Garrett tapped a few commands on his palmlight and held up his falsified credentials for Raish to see. "Undercover patrol," he explained, as

Raish wasn't close enough to make out the details. "Called for assistance when I spotted you and it looked like you were still running from someone. Wasn't sure if we'd be needing the backup. What happened to your abductor?"

He took another step forward but paused at the look in Raish's eyes. The kid was about to bolt.

"Look," he said, softly as he could manage, "I get why you'd be shaken up after getting nabbed, kid, but you're safe now."

He eased closer, reaching out with his senses, preparing to shut Raish down if he tried to run. The kid clearly didn't trust a single word coming out of his mouth.

"You know what?" Raish said, backing away from them, past the dumpsters. "You're right. I'm safe. I got away from them myself, and I appreciate your, uh, concern, but I can get home myself too."

"You know we can't let you do that, kid. I have superiors too. I can't just report that we found you, said all is right, and left you to fend for yourself in the streets."

"How about this?" he said, still inching backward. "How about you call my father, Captain Martin Raish, and tell him you've found me. He'll send a skimmer for me."

Garrett studied the kid, sure he was being tested, but not really sure how or why. Had Carlisle put him up to this, or had he legitimately escaped somehow? It didn't matter. The others would be here soon. It was time to stop gropping around.

"Okay, kid. Let's do it the hard way, then."

Raish turned and ran, but that didn't matter either. Garrett was already inside his head.

He thought hard about going rigid as a board, and Raish's body complied. The kid toppled face-first to the pavement, his young mind blazing with wild panic as he fell and then with pain as he hit. Even as a secondhand observer in Raish's head, it was unpleasant. But they needed to get him off the streets and back to the White Tower.

"Grab him," Garrett said, wanting to check their surroundings but needing to focus. "Hurry it up."

If ever there was a time for a trap to fall, this was probably it.

Whether the kid knew what he was doing or not, Raish was fighting against Garrett's control. And maybe it was just the fear and the panic, but the kid's mind was surprisingly strong for having just awoken. Garrett found himself actually having to concentrate to keep him contained while the Sanctum Guard marched over to get him.

He felt Raish's fear as the boot steps approached from behind. Felt him trying to thrash, trying to cry out. Trying not to lose it completely.

"I know, I know," Garret sent as the guards hauled him up. *"Pretty disconcerting, right?"*

Perhaps Garrett was being cruel. The addition of his telepathic voice only made Raish struggle that much harder. Garrett felt the kid raging to attack the Sanctum Guard manhandling him, wondering if he'd cracked completely or if they'd just tagged him with some kind of ultra-powered muscle relaxant when he'd turned to flee.

"Nothing so pedestrian," Garrett sent.

He felt the renewed surge of panic, coupled with the flicker of shock as Raish realized the strange voice in his head seemed to be aware of what he was thinking. Garrett turned his own thoughts to a more productive use, sweeping quietly for thoughts of Carlisle while Haldin panicked at the two Sanctum Guard handling him, and the other two flanking Garrett —or Smirks, as he could hear the kid calling him in his thoughts. Raish noticed the vacant look on his face.

"Well I AM a bit occupied," he growled, frustrated now, preparing to take off the kid gloves and push deeper into Raish's mind. He could feel the ice creeping through Raish's thoughts as clearly as if they'd been his own. The kid was starting to understand. He was quick.

"There it is," he confirmed, carefully splitting some of his focus back to his own body to add to the guards, "Call the skimmer, boys. And bring him here."

The sooner they got out of here, the better.

Garrett sank back into Raish's head as the Sanctum Guard started forward. He took control and marched Raish along with them, ignoring the mental cries of protest as the kid felt his body moving by Garrett's will. He felt for the kid—for the powerless fear and rage at the demonic sorcery being worked against him. But Garrett was too busy pushing into Raish's memories to let it stop him. Raish drew into himself, trying to protect his thoughts and once again doing a surprisingly good job of it.

But Garrett had the upper hand. He was already sliding through Raish's scant walls.

There was a flash of something red and terrible in Raish's mind. Beastly eyes, alight with demonic fire. Then a movement in the darkness above caught their combined attention. Something falling.

Someone falling.

Garrett tore back into his own body, feeling the telepathic inferno plummeting down, knowing it was already too late.

"Above!" he barked—just as the dark figure touched down beside him and exploded.

That was the best sense Garrett's concussed mind could make of it. One second, a demon was falling from the shadows. The next, Garrett was flying through the air, smacked clear by what had either been a bomb or the hand of Alpha himself.

He hit the wall with a jarring thud that knocked his entire brain loose. The alleyway spun around him, dipping in odd swirls. *Telekinesis,* some corner of his mind reasoned. He'd just been hit by a telekinetic blast.

A telekinetic blast from Carlisle.

Fear pierced him. He spat a curse, scrambling drunkenly for his feet, trying to get his bearings. Strong hands found his shoulders before he could—followed almost instantly by a devastating knee strike to his diaphragm. He gasped, reaching for the hands—Carlisle's hands—on his shoulders. He caught a glimpse of gray hair and pale eyes.

Then those eyes narrowed, and Garrett found himself sailing through the air again. This time, he crashed into something with a little more give. One of his guards, he realized.

He hit the alleyway floor in a stupor, pain racking through his body. Carlisle was already dismantling the guard he'd just hit, raining blows with nearly preternatural speed. The other guard who'd been with them was already down, slumped against the permacrete wall.

Down the alleyway, Raish was beating a third limp guard into the same wall with a ferocity that would've frightened a wild animal. He didn't stop when the last guard rushed in and tackled him down. Just shifted his focus and kept fighting. Garrett tried to get up. Tried to gather his defenses. But watching those two pummel the last of his Sanctum

Guard into the cold pavement like a pair of mad hounds, he was gripped by a fear like he'd never known.

Demons.

This was what true demons looked like.

And now that he'd seen it, Garrett was going to die.

His mind flashed to Alexia. Stupidly. Uselessly.

Then Carlisle thrust a palm to the side of his head, and Garrett knew no more.

17

———

CLEANUP

A warm hand cupped Garrett's cheek, gentle and caring. *Alexia.*

He knew it was her. Finally, after all this time.

"Wake up," she whispered against his ear.

He leaned back from her tickling breath with a wide smile. A smile that died on his lips when he saw who it was he faced—not Alexia, but Andre Kovaks, still dangling from the noose, his eyes glazed over and his lips motionless even as he whispered again, "Wake up."

Something jerked Garrett's leg. Someone kicking him.

"Wake up, scudboots."

He snapped to, blinking his eyes open against bleary lights, and looked up... straight into One's cold blue eyes.

"You," he groaned. "What happened?"

By way of reply, she glanced around pointedly. "I take it you had some difficulties here."

He lifted his throbbing head enough to take in their surroundings and it all started flooding back in.

Carlisle. That freakish demon and his gropping... what? Apprentice? Had Raish been working with him, or just fighting for survival, or telepathically compelled, or—

He silenced the whirlwind of questions, focusing in and taking stock of his own body first. He seemed to be more or less in one piece—achy and throbbing as that piece was. He sat up with another low groan. The alleyway was filled with enforcers and even a few medics, legionnaires standing guard at either end. He'd woken up in the middle of a teeming little crime scene.

"We haven't found him," One said in response to his questioning look. "Either of them. I was close enough to feel Raish when they..." She frowned. "Disappeared."

"Disappeared?"

She turned the frown on him. "That's what I said."

"Disappeared how? Where?"

To his surprise, One actually offered him a hand up. "That's the question, isn't it?"

Maybe Carlisle had scrambled Garrett's brains with whatever he'd done, or maybe Garrett had just hit his head too hard whilst being blasted around by the demon, but somehow, he didn't see it coming when One started to take his weight and then dropped him straight back to the cold pavement, where she leaned over his aching body to make her point all nice and dramatic-like.

"You really think I'd be sitting around here waiting for your sorry ass to wake up if I knew the answer?"

He sighed, too tired and confused to be properly angry. "You're a real bitch, you know that?"

The fact that *that* was what got her to smile for the first time that night spoke volumes about One's character.

"So when you say disappeared..." he said, crawling to his feet on his own wobbly strength this time.

She bobbed her head like she knew exactly what he was thinking. "Not *ran away out of my range*. Not *knocked unconscious*. Just..." She snapped her fingers. "There one second, gone the next. Like—"

"Like Carlisle's packing some kind of telepathic shroud."

"Exactly like that," she said, looking annoyed that he'd interrupted her big reveal.

"How is that possible?"

She just gave him a look that made it plain she wasn't going to dignify that with a response. *Because if she already knew that...* and so on. As if he'd needed a reminder about why he couldn't stand this woman.

"Guess that might explain why you've been having so much trouble finding the bastard," he said, half under his breath, but still loud enough that he knew she'd hear. Alpha knew why that didn't brighten her mood.

"Has there been word from the High Cleric?" he added before she could get any sinister ideas.

"He's been updated," she said, watching the alleyway activity as if she couldn't be bothered to find their conversation interesting enough to actually look at him. One of the medics, having noticed Garrett was up, was rushing over.

"And?" he said quickly. "What's the next move?"

One deliberately waited until the medic was too close for her to disclose anything overtly secret, then she swept a hand around in an all-encompassing gesture at the city around them.

"Welcome to the hunt, scudboots."

THE FOLLOWING days were neither happy nor encouraging. Whatever manner of demonic sorcery Carlisle had or hadn't cooked up, one thing quickly became quite clear: Raish and Carlisle had indeed disappeared. And as far as any of them could tell, they'd done it without a single trace.

Garrett was assigned to the hunt full time, just as One had implied. The High Cleric was too busy in the first few days to confirm as much by anything but a quick message, but Garrett hardly minded. Finally, he was going after one of the targets that really mattered—maybe *the* target, as far as they knew. He felt something returning that he thought he'd lost—a thrill for the chase, maybe, but that wasn't the entirety of it. There was something more.

A deep conviction in what he was doing, maybe. That was it.

Because as much as he'd previously wanted to believe in the High Cleric's grand vision for Alpha's Gifted and their new lives on Enochia, he realized now that a part of him—and maybe not a small part—had been holding on to the teachings of his past life, clinging to the belief that he and the others were all still monsters, and that they'd all one day burn for having had the gall to deny that. But he'd seen a true demon in action now. It had scared the scud out of him.

And now he knew what he had to do.

So he took to the streets with an energy he hadn't been able to muster since his first year as a Seeker—sometimes flying by skimmer with his fireteam of Sanctum Guard, sometimes walking the streets with them. He worked day and night—sweeping, always sweeping—stopping only to return to the White Tower for food and a few hours of sleep here and there. And he wasn't the only one.

One, Three, and Five all prowled the streets with similar tenacity. After what had happened to Garrett in that alleyway, none of them argued that pairing up would've been the wise choice, but Divinity was a big city, and their individual ranges could only stretch so far. Spreading out meant covering more ground and thus meant a better shot at finding Carlisle. Simple as that. For the most part, this meant they stuck to the air, sweeping as much city as possible from the safety of their skimmers. When they did take to the ground, though, they quickly fell into the habit of doing so all at once, staggered every few blocks in a telepathic hunting line whereby any mysterious disappearances could be quickly felt and converged upon.

Day after day, it went on like this. They even stumbled across a few unexpected telepaths—one vagrant in the slums, one passing traveler on the major mag line that connected Divinity with its sister cities, and most shockingly, one high-ranking praetor, a woman named Anetta Oberton. Garrett had a strong suspicion that Oberton might've been one of the High Cleric's previously unnamed allies, but there was no way of telling in the moment. In a past life, none of them would've dreamed of walking away from any fallen like that—praetor or vagrant or otherwise—but the High Cleric's instructions had been clear. No targets without his say-so.

And right now, Carlisle and Raish were the only targets in Divinity.

So they soldiered on, despite the fact that they had been at it nearly a cycle now and had still gotten nowhere. Loners by nature, they didn't talk more than necessary. But there were two things in particular that they *especially* didn't talk about—pointedly refused to talk about, even, though Garrett was sure they were all ruminating on the problems in their own heads.

For one, there was the question of what had happened to Haldin Raish. Even buried in the hunt as he was, Garrett didn't miss the barrage of stories on the WAN reels covering up Carlisle's attack on the Raish household in Sanctuary. According to the stories, some undisclosed failure of the house's backup energy cells had led to a tragic accidental house fire. According to the stories, the entire Raish family had perished in the fire.

They hadn't gotten much more than that out of the High Cleric. All they knew was that the Raish family appeared to have been dragged into this mess simply because High General Kublich had been dining with his old friend, the legendary Captain Martin Raish, when Carlisle had decided to make an attempt on Kublich's life. That the boy, Haldin, had turned out to be gifted... they weren't sure if that was some freakish unfolding of random chance, or if Carlisle had somehow known all along.

One had broken their silence on the topic to make it known that she liked the theory that Haldin Raish had in fact been the one to help Carlisle onto the base—that he'd been corrupted by Carlisle's demon even before the attack, and that sacrificing his parents had been some kind of sick initiation rite.

Vicious as the kid had been as he'd fought for his life back in that alleyway, Garrett was pretty sure One's own gropped-up sensibilities were coloring her speculation a little too heavily there. He still wasn't entirely sure whose side Haldin Raish had been on that night in the alley. Probably, the kid had simply been fighting to survive regardless of sides after what'd happened to him. But Garrett was pretty sure about one thing.

The kid had been a wreck.

Garrett had felt Raish's pain himself—was still haunted by the brief flash he'd seen in the boy's memories, demonic red eyes piercing the darkness. Even now, he shuddered just thinking about it, and remembering how utterly powerless he'd felt when Carlisle had descended on him in that alley.

What horrors was Carlisle wreaking on that poor boy's spirit while they were out here flying around like a bunch of blind dung fowl? If he hadn't killed Raish outright—which seemed unlikely, given that he'd bothered kidnapping him in the first place—would Carlisle be seeking to turn him? Garrett couldn't imagine a fiery tyro like Raish would even consider serving the creature who'd killed his parents. But who knew what kind of darkness Carlisle might be feeding him. Who knew how that demon might twist and distort Raish's memories, and buy his loyalty with lies and promises of power and vengeance.

It made Garrett sick to think about. Another gifted spirit, fallen to darkness. Another inevitable name on the High Cleric's list of marks.

And this one was Garrett's fault. Because if he'd only been more careful—waited a little longer for backup, been a little more empathetic to the kid who'd just lost his parents... Well, who knew. But it didn't matter now. Because he hadn't been more careful, and now it was done. In all likelihood, alive or dead, it was already too late for Haldin Raish.

Either way, they needed to find Carlisle and stop him before he managed to bend a powerful new ally to his side. But that only brought them to the second of the two unspoken quandaries: Carlisle's mysterious vanishing act.

If One's report of Haldin disappearing from her senses was accurate—not to mention her report of Carlisle's failure to ever appear in her senses at all, even when Garrett knew the man had been there in the alleyway—it seemed safe to assume that Carlisle had some method by which he could completely shroud his mind from them, and that this new sorcery could also be applied to another. Intriguing as the development was to them, the far more important takeaway was that they might well be gropped no matter what they did.

Even the High Cleric had admitted that Alpha hadn't seen fit to show him past the demon's shroud. His Holiness took this to simply mean that the will of Alpha was that his Gifted should ply themselves to the hunt and trust in the fact that this was the function he'd intended of them. Garrett didn't argue, refusing to give up when they didn't yet know if any of this was actually true, but he couldn't help wonder: could they ever hope to find a telepath whose mind was invisible? Had they already passed him by in the streets, utterly unaware of the fact?

There was no way to know. But given that the Legion and the Sanctum had both already allocated significant resources toward finding Carlisle by more conventional methods, Garrett stayed the course, ignoring the whispered voices in his head insisting that the demon probably wasn't even in the city anymore, and that Garrett wouldn't be able to tell the difference if Carlisle were halfway across Enochia or standing right behind him anyway. For an entire cycle, they kept hunting like a pack of hungry wolves.

Then, in the bleary-eyed, pre-dawn hours of the Honorsday thirteen days after Raish had gone missing, Garrett got the call—or, rather, the knock.

He snapped out of his feverish half-sleep and rolled off the cot with a grumbled curse. A glance at his palmlight confirmed he'd only been asleep for two hours—which brought him to a grand total of about one full night's sleep in the past five days. But he couldn't complain to the person he felt waiting at the door. Three had slept just as little as he had.

He swiped the room lights up and palmed the access panel. Three was already dressed for battle, sidearm holstered at his hip beneath the black long coat that only made his slender form seem that much longer. Garrett could smell the wet leather of his dark boots, which hadn't had a chance to dry since they'd last been out.

"They hit Vantage," Three said without preamble, his dark eyes weary, and his hair mussed from what precious little sleep he'd had. "The High Cleric wants us in the air. Now."

18

CHAIN OF COMMAND

Tired as he was, Garrett couldn't seem to silence the wild racing of his thoughts on the way to the Vantage research labs. He couldn't help but think about his unsettling flight with Kovaks, and the fact that whatever might be happening at Vantage was apparently important enough for Carlisle himself to get involved—and to drag his new apprentice into it, even. Because that's what was really bothering him about all of this, wasn't it?

Garrett hadn't needed to ask what Three meant when he'd said *they* had hit Vantage. He'd wanted to ask—had wanted his gut feeling to be proved wrong. But it would've been a waste of breath. He'd already known deep down that this was the inevitable outcome of his failure back in the alleyway. Three had confirmed as much.

For whatever reason—after Alpha only knew what dark terrors had rent his spirit into submission—Haldin Raish finally appeared to be working with the demon.

Garrett flexed his fists, imagining what it would feel like to pull the trigger when it was time. Because, tragic victim or not, he was almost certainly going to have to pull that trigger on Raish now. It didn't matter if it was the kid's fault or not. Or even Garrett's. If Carlisle had turned him, if Haldin had fallen, then he had to be put down right beside his mad hound of a master. Simple as that.

Garrett glanced over at Three in the driver's seat of the skimmer and wondered if his fellow Seeker shared any of his remorse for what needed to be done. Probably a sliver, at least, he decided. Three wasn't a psychopath like One. But he also wasn't nearly friendly enough for Garrett to even think about broaching the subject with him. So Garrett kept his whirling thoughts to himself until the lights of Vantage came into clear view.

And Sweet Alpha, were there a lot of them.

The place was lit up like a small city—which, taking in the extent of the domestic facilities and ancillary buildings sprawling out behind the main research building, Garrett decided it basically was. But it wasn't just the scope of the compound that had him gaping.

"Scud," he muttered, trying to count the Legion transports hovering around the area and marshaled in the open yard inside the perimeter wall. "They weren't gropping around with the reinforcements, were they?"

"Should they have been?" Three asked, not looking away from the controls.

Definitely not the man he wanted to go talking about feelings of remorse with.

For some reason, Garrett turned to the back seats to gauge the reactions of the four Sanctum Guard they'd brought along, but they were unsurprisingly unreadable behind their golden faceplates. Three was slowing the skimmer, clearly debating where he should try to land, when a voice came to Garrett.

"Come to the rooftop."

It was a voice he'd only heard a few times before, but it was distinctive enough in its calm authority. What was less clear was what in demons' depth the High General of the Legion was doing out here.

Garrett traded a look with Three and saw that he'd heard Kublich's voice as well. He looked as surprised as Garrett felt, but neither of them said a word as he steered the skimmer around and started for the rooftop of the main research facility. Garrett hadn't noticed the transport that'd already landed up there. A dozen or so legionnaires were gathered loosely around the vehicle, looking bored. Perhaps fifty yards farther across the long rooftop, a small force of Vantage's private security goons watched them, their territorial hackles clearly raised.

And roughly midway between the two groups, in the splash of the transport's floodlights and the few rooftop lights, Garrett spotted two figures who appeared to be deep in conversation—the High General, he could feel, and another man in a dark suit. Another telepath, he realized. They were just close enough to make out the two men turning to look their way when the suited one jabbed a finger at the High General and started stalking away for his security team.

Some kind of argument?

Three guided the skimmer down close to the Legion forces, which was probably a good call from what little experience Garrett had with the hyper-vigilant Vantage crew. Garrett climbed out into the muggy night. High General Adrian Kublich was already striding their way, his face grim. But not as grim as the guy he'd just been talking to. Garrett only caught a quick glimpse as the dark-suited man paused to look back over his shoulder, but that glimpse was all he needed.

It was Alton Parker, the CEO of Vantage. And he was staring straight at Garrett like this was all his fault.

That look made Garrett's insides squirm for reasons he couldn't begin to explain, but at least it didn't last. Parker was already turning back to his people, storming off for the nearest rooftop access point. He and his troops swept into the stairwell and disappeared, leaving Garrett staring at empty rooftop, one thought turning over and over in his numb brain.

Alton Parker was one of Alpha's Gifted.

"I appreciate your coming," came the High General's voice, snapping Garrett out of his staring contest with the empty rooftop. "But it's too late," Kublich continued, drawing up to face him and Three. "The intruders are long gone, and I'm afraid Vantage is less than open to the prospect of outsiders conducting any investigation within their facility— Legion, Sanctum, or otherwise."

Garrett glanced back at where Parker had disappeared to, wondering for the hundredth time what in demons' depths they were up to in this facility.

"Of course, High General," Three was saying. "We understand. Don't we, Two?"

Garrett pried his eyes away from the closed door and back to Three and Kublich. "Yes, of course." He looked at Kublich, hesitating, then pushed on. "Did Citizen Parker at least confirm it was indeed Carlisle and Raish, or disclose anything about what they might have been after?"

Three, in the middle of gesturing at the Sanctum Guard to stay put in the skimmer, shot him a severe look, like he shouldn't be asking such direct questions of the High General. Maybe he was right. But Kublich didn't seem to mind.

"It was them," he said, staring off into the dark sky. "We arrived just in time to see them flee. As for what they were after..." He shook his head and focused back on Garrett. "As I said, Vantage is choosing to exercise their rightful privacy in the matter."

"Even though Alton Parker is one of us?"

Garrett sent the thought to Kublich against his own better judgment, needing to know what was going on but figuring he could at least dull the boldness of the move by keeping it silent and between him and the general. Kublich masked his reaction so completely that Garrett wondered if he'd heard him at all. Three's dirty look, on the other hand, seemed to indicate the Seeker had at least noticed Garrett was up to something, even if he wasn't sure exactly what.

Kublich studied them both for a handful of seconds before speaking.

"Are you two willing to do what it takes to catch these demons, no questions asked?"

Garrett traded a glance with Three and saw his own drive reflected in his fellow Seeker's eyes, the momentary disapproval forgotten.

"Yes, sir," Three said.

"Of course," Garrett added.

Kublich watched them for another intent few seconds before nodding to himself. "Good." In their heads, he added, *"Then take the day and the night to rest, and meet me in the Sanctuary tunnels tomorrow night."*

"With respect, High General," Three sent, clearly as uncomfortable as Garrett with the thought of their simply checking out from the hunt without leave, *"the High Cleric—"*

"Let me speak with the High Cleric," Kublich sent, leaving no room for argument. *"For now, go back to the Tower and get your rest. You're going to need it."*

"Thank you for coming," he added out loud, though none of the troops were close enough to hear anyway. "That will be all, for now."

With that, Kublich spun on his well-polished boot heel and strode off for his transport.

"That was... unexpected," Garrett muttered.

He looked over and found Three watching him with a stern expression. Three turned without a word and went back to their skimmer. Garrett spared one last glance at the door by which Alton Parker, telepathic CEO, had made his exit, shook his head in wonder, and turned to follow Three back to their ride.

"If they're going to force us to work together," Three said the instant Garrett's butt touched the seat, "I'm going to need to know that you can keep your impulses under control."

Even two years after the fact, Garrett's mind still flashed to Alexia and their forbidden contact before his rational mind took over and reminded him that, for one, Three—and the other Seekers, for that matter—almost certainly had no idea what had happened between him and Alexia and that, for another, Three was obviously referring to Garrett's impromptu questions outside.

Which kind of irritated the scud out of him.

"You want me to ask before I wipe next time, too?"

Three was unamused. And, apparently, too careful to say anymore in front of their Sanctum Guard escort, who sat in obedient silence, waiting for them to have it out. *That depends on if you're going to insult the High General while you're at it. The High Cleric has been clear about his position in our chain of command.*

Garrett resisted the urge to roll his eyes. Briefly, he considered asking if Three had noticed what he had about Alton Parker, and where he supposed the CEO of Vantage fell on his beloved chain of command. But he doubted that would improve the boot licker's mood.

Alpha, what he wouldn't have given to swap Three for Alexia right then.

"Fine," he sent back. *"How do you suggest we proceed, then, partner?"*

Three wrinkled his nose at the word, glancing out through the windshield. *"I guess we follow the High General's instructions until we can check with the His Holiness."*

Ahead, High General Kublich turned to look their way almost as if he'd noticed their attention, and despite the darkness where they'd landed and the thick tint of their duraglass windshield, Garrett had the distinct feeling that he could see straight through to them. It made his insides squirm a little.

"*Yeah,*" he sent back to Three. "*I guess we do.*"

WHAT WAS SAID between the High General and the High Cleric, Garrett could only guess at, but somehow he wasn't all that surprised when he received word from Three that they were on to meet with Kublich beneath Sanctuary that night. Which left the rest of the day for an amount of sleep that felt positively decadent after the cycle of ghost shifts they'd been pulling.

Somehow, though, he still felt tired when he woke that night to go meet Three. But maybe that was just the chronic unease that seemed to have seeped into his bones ever since Kovaks, or the new ripple of worry at the fact that it was Three he kept hearing these updates from, and not the High Cleric himself. Had Garrett crossed some line, fallen out of the cleric's favor? Had it been his failure to stop Carlisle and secure Raish back in that damned alleyway that had left a stain on his previously good standing?

He didn't know. And he was pretty sure asking about it would only make things worse. So he went to meet Three as if all was right with the world, unable to quell the feeling that it most certainly wasn't. Why else would they be meeting Kublich in such a seedy underbelly that hardly anyone else alive even knew it existed?

He didn't know the answer to that one, either. But it was time to find out.

The flight to Sanctuary was a short one, even by the circuitous route Three took them on. The Legion fortress stretched the northwestern corner of Divinity, by all means a small city in its own right behind its dark, towering walls and its legions of sharpshooters ready to drop anyone foolish enough to sneeze the wrong direction anywhere near the perimeter.

He doubted any of those sharpshooters saw them coming as they skimmed over the dark waters of the Red Sea, right along the sheer cliff face that led up to the level of Divinity proper.

By all common knowledge, if one didn't have the requisite preexisting ID to land, there was only one way into the fortress of Sanctuary: the massive darksteel gates which, while always open in times of peace, could never rightly be called vulnerable. By *uncommon* knowledge, on the other hand, there was another way—an ancient way that was known by almost no one and that looked and smelled about as nice as it should've, considering.

Not for the first time, Garrett wondered what it was Kublich needed to show them. Given that their skimmer was outfitted with a valid ID pass for Sanctuary, it must be something of the utmost secrecy. Garrett had personally met with Kublich three times over the past couple years, but the only time they'd been relegated down to the tunnel had been the first encounter, when Kublich had revealed his true gifted self to Garrett and One. Even that easily could've happened above, in the plain sight of Sanctuary. Telepathy was, after all, telepathy. But the High General had wished to speak freely and without caution on that occasion. And now...

Garrett's fingers itched to be at the skimmer controls as they drew even with Sanctuary above and Three guided them up the cliff face in search of the hidden entrance.

"If you need help finding the hole..." he said quietly.

Three didn't dignify that with a response, but his frown of concentration did take on an irritated edge in the dim light of the skimmer displays. Soon enough, though, he found what he was looking for. Garrett did his best to avoid tensing as Three guided them over one jagged outcropping of the dark cliff face, under another, and into the short tunnel burrowed beyond. Only then did Three activate the headlights, bolstering the windshield display's limited efforts to render visibility from the nearly complete darkness.

Garrett couldn't ignore the feeling that he was being swallowed whole by the mountain rock—the same mountain rock that was the underlying foundation of much of Divinity. Maybe there was something to be said about the interpretive validity of that sentiment. He didn't have time to decide.

The High General was waiting for them ahead.

Garrett couldn't see him yet, but there was a faint trickle of light coming from ahead, and it was hard to miss such a powerful telepathic presence once he opened his senses. There was something else there, too. Two *somethings*, he decided. Kublich had brought along two people. That was unexpected. And something about them felt... odd.

Three eased the skimmer through the remainder of the tunnel and into the small skimmer bay that looked to have been carved straight out of the rock. The headlights washed over the High General and his two escorts, all of them standing impressively still, waiting. Three set them down, angling the skimmer so the headlights would reflect off the walls and add to the light of the lamp one of Kublich's lackeys was holding instead of blinding them all.

"Greetings, Seekers," came Kublich's voice.

"High General," Three sent.

"Sir," Garrett added, opening the skimmer door to the cold, damp cavern air. It smelled of dust and mildew in a way that might've been pleasant if not for the faint odor of the ancient sewer system that connected the bay to the Sanctuary subbasements. *"I see you've brought company."*

He half-expected that might earn him one of those *ask before you wipe* looks from Three, but his fellow Seeker looked equally curious as they went to join the High General and his two extras, who both remained eerily still as Kublich looked from them to the Seekers.

"These are your new allies," he finally sent.

Garrett wasn't sure why they'd bothered coming to the one place they were supposed to be able to talk freely if they were going to do the silent communication dance—until he realized he wasn't sure if the High General had been speaking to him and Three, or to his stationary flank guards.

Garrett took a closer look at the pair. Both wore full armor and had their faces hidden behind dark faceplates. Between the dark armor and their creepy discipline, they reminded him of the High Cleric's Onyx Guard, except... He swept his senses over them and once again came away with the distinct feeling that something was seriously off with these two. He just couldn't say exactly what.

It was only then he noticed that the High General was patiently waiting, as if he'd expected them to be conducting this examination. *"They understand direct telepathic commands better than spoken ones,"* he sent, as if there should be nothing surprising about the outlandish claim. *"The more visual or sensory the command, the better."*

"Sir?" Three said out loud, open confusion and mild alarm on his face.

Garrett didn't blame him.

"Tell them to lift your skimmer," the High General sent, unperturbed by their confusion. *"With your mind. Do it."*

This time, they couldn't resist trading a confused look. What the scud was this? Three gave the faintest shrug, arching an eyebrow. They didn't need telepathy to know what they were both thinking.

Whatever in demons' depths was going on here, they didn't really have much choice but to play along. Because as Three himself had pointed out, the only man they answered to above the High General was the High Cleric himself. If they refused, if they asked too many questions... well, Garrett wasn't actually sure how that would turn out. But he didn't have to find out.

"Lift... lift the skimmer, if you can," Three sent uncertainly, presumably to everyone in the room.

The two dark-clad soldiers cocked their heads as if struggling to comprehend. Garrett swore he could hear one of them breathing a bit harder, like a hound excited at being engaged.

"Show them in your mind," Kublich sent.

Alpha, this was getting weird. But Three complied, and Garrett saw his message like a fleeting thought passing by—the faint impression of the two soldiers taking to each end of the skimmer and hefting its thousand-plus pounds of hardware up with comical ease.

As one, the two soldiers sprang into action, running over to the skimmer—one to the front, one to the back. They both bent, scooping under the hood and rear hatch for handholds. Garrett tensed. There was no way. They were going to hurt themselves. They were going to—

As one, they heaved. And a thousand-plus pounds of skimmer lifted smoothly from the stone floor.

"What the scud?" Garrett hissed, taking an involuntary step back.

It wasn't physically impossible that two highly-trained men might budge a small skimmer. But the ease with which they'd just done it, the hungry eagerness with which they turned to Three, awaiting further instruction... it was unnatural.

"That will do, I think," the High General said behind him. Whether he added some telepathic command, Garrett didn't know, but the two *things* carefully set the skimmer back down with that same impossible ease.

"What are they?" Three sent, still staring at the two obedient soldiers.

"They are our best hope—our only hope, maybe—of finding the demon Carlisle and his bright new disciple."

"I don't understand..." Three murmured.

"Are they... human?" Garrett added, careful to send the thought only to Three and Kublich.

"Of course they're human." Kublich frowned at him. "What else in Alpha's Good Grace would they be?"

Garrett dropped his gaze, feeling foolish yet unable to shut out the memory of Andre Kovaks raving like a madman about sinister aliens.

"They've simply been enhanced," Kublich added, looking proudly at his silent soldiers. "And we need not speak privately around them. They are perfectly loyal."

Garrett was too confused to worry about speaking at all—privately or otherwise.

Enhanced? What the scud did he mean, enhanced? Was this some new, secret phase of Project Sentinel? It had barely been a decade since the Legion's last attempt at a quasi-supersoldier stimulant had ended with multiple test subjects falling prey to a host of severe mental issues—many of which had led to quite messy, and quite public, incidents. Would the Legion really dip back into those murky waters so soon?

Then another thought occurred to him.

What if it wasn't the Legion at all? Could this have something to do with what they were working on at Vantage? That would explain why the High General himself had decided to respond to the breach the other night, wouldn't it? He stared at those dark faceplates, wondering what might lie beneath.

Silence had held the skimmer bay for too long now, but the High

General seemed content enough to let them puzzle through their thoughts at their own speed.

"How are these soldiers supposed to help us find the demon?" Three finally asked, apparently deciding that the rest of the major *what the scud* questions could wait.

The High General favored him with a smile. "I'm glad you asked. As you see, they are quite strong, and capable of receiving our communications. But that's hardly the extent of their talents. Their physical senses are also worlds beyond ours. They can track a scent better than the finest hounds." He looked meaningfully between Garrett and Three. "They could track a man for miles on a torn scrap of clothing alone."

Garrett couldn't stop gaping. "That isn't..."

"Isn't possible?" Kublich asked, quirking one dark brow. "Take one. See for yourself."

That, at least, put some hesitance back on the eagerness that'd been creeping into Three's expression.

Garrett traded a concerned look with his so-called partner. "As in..."

"As in take control of one's mind," Kublich said, "and see what they can see for yourself."

"I'd rather not," Garrett said, more quickly than what might've been deemed polite or respectful. He hardly gave a damn.

"It is forbidden, sir," Three added in a much more measured tone.

The High General looked between them as if their reluctance came as a sincere surprise. "You say you're ready to do what it takes? This is what it will take. The demons hide their minds? Then we will track their bodies. We will do whatever it takes to stop them, because they must be stopped."

"But this—"

"This is a necessary step in ushering in our new world," Kublich said.

"But this..." Garrett waved a hand at the enhanced soldiers, who still stood by the skimmer, preposterously motionless. "Are two men really such a threat for us to go this far?"

The High General smiled at that—not quite mocking Garrett's question, but clearly confident that he was missing something important.

"The Dorrin Uprising began with two men. Did you know that? Most of the stories begin well after that, once two had grown to two dozen, and two hundred, and so forth. But it was two who sparked the fire. Two discontented spirits. And they were merely men—neither gifted nor fallen. Carlisle's network is already far greater than that, and as you know all too well, he is far more than a mere man."

Kublich shook his head, pulling himself back from some distant thought. "But that's all beside the point. This work"—he gestured to the enhanced soldiers—"is about far more than hunting down two dangerous demons. This work is the first step to bridging the gap between the people of Enochia. When the time comes, even coming from the High Cleric himself, the revelation of our existence will not be welcomed with open arms by all. We will need intermediaries." He looked at the soldiers, then back to Garrett and Three. "Many of our kind may need protectors in the early days. This is what it will take to build a world where Alpha's Gifted may be accepted and even celebrated rather than hunted in the shadows."

Garrett stared at the enhanced men, turning the words over. There was some sense there. It was hard to argue that. But where had these new guardian hunting hounds of theirs come from? He couldn't help but wonder. Had they been volunteers? Defectors?

Could this all truly be part of Alpha's plan?

All is as Alpha plans, my child, he could practically hear the High Cleric whisper in his head.

"Do they talk?" Three asked, eyeing the soldiers with open curiosity now.

Was he actually accepting this?

"Not yet," Kublich said. "The change is... disorienting. They're still adapting, still transitioning, but soon, they will regain their speech. Until then, you can simply integrate with their minds to see what they see. They agreed to as much when they volunteered for this project," he added at the shift in their expressions.

"Are these two..." Garrett started. "Are there more?"

Kublich nodded. "There are others in training."

"Who else knows about this?" Three asked.

"No one. No one but myself, the High Cleric, and those directly involved in the project. I will tell One and Five when the time is right. For now, no one else can know. Provided you are willing, you will pick these two up here each night, and return them here each morning. You may incorporate them into larger teams with your Sanctum Guard, but they must remain out of sight, or at least at a distance." He toed the crate one of the enhanced had been holding earlier. "I've brought optical shrouds to help you with that."

One look was all Garrett needed to know that Three was nearly sold, if he wasn't there already. Staring dumbly at the enhanced creations before him, Garrett wasn't sure what to think. His brain was still caught up teasing at the meaning of Kublich's words—four of them, in particular.

Provided you are willing.

"And what if we're not willing?" he asked, ignoring Three's indignant glare. "How much longer must we hide in shadow, holding our tongues rather than question why we, as Alpha's Gifted, are still treated like prisoners more often than not?"

The words left his mouth like gouts of flame, and he regretted them as soon as they had—not because he didn't mean them, but because the underlying sentiment was true. Chosen or not, accepted by Alpha or not, the Seekers were still in a precarious position in this slowly shifting world order. And Garrett sure seemed to be giving them all a lot of reasons to doubt his worth lately.

But the High General favored him with another knowing smile. "Only as long as you wish, Seeker. That was the other piece of news I wished to deliver tonight. I spoke to the High Cleric, and we both agree that the time has come to put our faith in you into actions rather than words." He looked between them, his smile widening. "Which is why both of your collars have been permanently disarmed."

Garrett and Three traded their most surprised look yet—enhanced super soldiers be damned—both of their hands going straight to the thin dark bands that'd been the most present, oppressive reminders of their imprisonment ever since they'd been brought in as trainees.

Disarmed? Was it possible? He didn't know—was already lost in thoughts of how he might check to be sure, what he might do if it turned out to be true... and the long list of reasons Kublich might be lying through his teeth to them right now.

Only he *wasn't* lying.

Garrett wasn't sure how he knew—and maybe it was just delusion born of the sheer magnitude of his wishful thinking—but something about the High General's demeanor, or maybe even the subconscious feel of his mind, was undeniably open and genuine about this.

"The rest of the Seekers will have to follow incrementally in the coming seasons," Kublich continued. "And we ask that you please leave the collars on for now to maintain appearances until the situation can be properly explained to your handlers. But you are free men. You will do as you choose."

Garrett could only gape at the High General—at the implications of what he was saying, and at the sound of the word, *please*, coming in Garrett's direction from someone other than a clueless civilian on the streets.

It was actually breathtaking. A lifetime of faithful service, cowering in the shadow of the Sanctum, fearing any moment, any misstep, could be his last. Two years since the High Cleric had first revealed himself to Garrett and promised a new life—a better life. Two years wondering if it had all been a wild fantasy, if it had always been too good to be true.

And now he was actually free?

He couldn't believe it. He barely even registered what he was doing as Kublich congratulated them and turned to guiding them through a few exercises to get acclimated with their new human blood hounds. It was only hours later, when they were flying back to the Tower to rest and get their heads on straight for their first night out with their new allies that it occurred to Garrett how much was still riding on his shoulders—how directly his actions moving forward would likely affect his fellow Seekers, and even the world at large. But even that hardly mattered right then.

Because blessed or cursed, bound with the lives of his fellows or not, for the first time in his life, Garrett was free to choose. Free to do the right thing or to grop it all up as spectacularly as possible, like any other sad scudbucket on this planet could—without the fear of instantaneously losing his head.

There was a lot to think about. A lot to confirm.

But for now, in his heart, he was free.

And Alpha, did it feel good.

19

FIRE AND ICE

So began the strangest phase of Garrett's life as a Seeker.

It wasn't that he was unused to creeping around in the shadows of Divinity at nighttime, hunting his prey. It wasn't even that he was all that unused to doing it with a full team. But having Kublich's enhanced soldiers prowling along with them... that took some getting used to. As did the logistics of keeping them out of the way of their Sanctum Guard, and whatever other dregs of Divinity were actually still on the streets in the dark hours. After the first night out, though, they began to find their routine.

Garrett and Three would each direct one of the enhanced to check this corner or that, scenting for any trace of Raish or Carlisle. The soldiers were tremendously fast and strong. Garrett and Three quickly realized it was barely an obstacle to have them jump ten foot gates or scale some of the shorter buildings, where they could catch drifting scents and give the Seekers a better look at their surroundings.

For the first several nights, Garrett left the latter part to Three. Call him superstitious, but something about so casually stepping into another mind, even one that'd volunteered for the link, felt... not necessarily wrong. Just not quite right, either. Luckily, Three didn't share his hesitation. It didn't seem to matter as much to Garrett's partner that the two of them had effectively been granted their freedom to make such decisions. If the High Cleric or the High General said all was right with a thing, then by the light of Alpha, all was right in Three's mind.

More than a few times, Garrett considered asking Three about what he might want to do with his freedom when this was all over. He wasn't entirely sure why he didn't ask, aside from a vague feeling that Three was actively disinterested in talking about such wishy-washy bullscud. Then again, Garrett wasn't all that sure he wanted to talk about it himself, if for no other reason than that it might bring up the fact that he couldn't quite stop wondering if Kublich's declaration of freedom had truly been genuine, and without strings attached.

It wasn't that Kublich or the High Cleric had ever given Garrett any real reason to doubt them. It was more just the uneasy realization that, when it came down to it, there was really no way to ever tell for certain whether the explosive collar at his throat was actually deactivated or not. At least not unless he really wanted to test the boundaries and go check in with his old faceless friends at Watchtower control, where several of the Seekers had long suspected the backbone of their collar trigger system might be housed.

There were only two problems with that plan, the first being that none of the Seekers actually knew where Watchtower control was. Garrett had stumbled upon the likely location by pure accident a year ago, when Cleric Verner's replacement, Cleric Faden, had sent Garrett one of his acolytes and the devout young man had made a careless misstep. Garrett had just as promptly set the information aside, more than a little paranoid that Faden had been baiting him for a trap all along. At best, it would've been suicide if the handlers ever found out anyway. But now...

Now, he wasn't so sure. But as much as that bothered him, he knew he was better off just following Three's example and keeping himself focused on the task at hand. At least until they found Raish and Carlisle. Luckily, there was plenty to focus on.

The enhanced continued to baffle Garrett on a daily basis, and in every facet of their existence. There was the impressive strength, the uncannily sharp senses, and the intensely creepy vibe of their silent presence. But nearly as odd as all of that—and maybe even odder—was their telepathic sensitivity. Garrett didn't have the faintest clue how Vantage (or whoever) had actually gone about amplifying these men's existing physical abilities, but he could at least imagine how such things might be possible. Bestowing the gift of telepathy on someone by way of syringes and test tubes and Alpha knew what else, on the other hand... that was something different. Something else entirely.

Not that the enhanced were even really telepaths in any complete sense. When it came to communicating, they were as mute telepathically as they were verbally. Which was why it was necessary for Three to dip into their minds in the first place—to read their thoughts for whatever intel they'd gathered on the prowl. But the fact that they could receive and understand Garrett's and Three's thoughts at all was perplexing enough. Normal people simply couldn't register telepathic thoughts like that. And if that ability was something that could be manufactured in a laboratory...

The thought made Garrett's skin crawl, though he couldn't quite explain why.

But maybe that wasn't it at all. Maybe it wasn't that the abilities had been *added* so much as that some part of Alpha's gift lay dormant in all of his children, and that Kublich's people—or Alton Parker's, or whoever's —had merely found some way to uncover that bit in the enhanced.

That thought actually brought him a measure of cathartic peace.

Either way, there was little point in speculating. Eventually, he decided, he would find out for himself. But for the time being, they had two demons to catch. So they patrolled, and they patrolled some more. After half a cycle of watching Three integrating with the enhanced and raving—or marveling in a dry, professional way, at least—about the experience of seeing things through their senses, Garrett finally gave in and tried it himself.

Three and Kublich, it turned out, hadn't been exaggerating. Especially not about the keenness of their noses.

It was almost hard to make sense of, at first, the tremendous overflow of olfactory information Garrett was confronted with when he first checked in with one of their silent scouts for a report. To a normal human, it might well have been overwhelming. To Garrett, though, it merely felt like a new dimension of his own extended senses. Not that that made it any less fascinating.

Though it occurred to him that whatever particles were responsible for conveying such scents should feasibly be detectable in his extended senses—at least with enough focus—he'd never even thought to try to "smell" the metal handrails, or the dry permacrete, or the thousand other benign things he suddenly noticed when he stepped behind the nose of an enhanced. And that wasn't even to mention the entire worlds of scents that'd taken up residence on those previously uninteresting surfaces. Every person who'd touched this handrail. Every drunk tavern-goer who'd relieved themselves on that alley wall. Through the enhanced, Garrett smelled them all.

And he did *smell* them. Because he had a feeling that, even if he'd tried such a thing with his extended senses, the experience of *detecting* those odorants wouldn't have lived up to that of actually *smelling* them. It was more than just molecular detection. With each scent came the undercurrent of the scout's emotional reaction—excitement at this scent, curiosity at that one. The entire world became intriguing in a way Garrett hadn't thought to expect. Even the smells of overripe dumpsters became something to explore and deconstruct rather than something to pinch one's nose at.

Garrett couldn't help but imagine he was experiencing something akin to how the average hound saw the world, only Kublich had assured him that the senses of the enhanced exceeded even that. Garrett wasn't sure how one would rightly tell about that. All he knew was that, if they managed to close within a few blocks of Carlisle or Raish, he had faith the enhanced would sniff the demons out from the scents that'd been gathered from the break-in back at Vantage.

And yet, for all that olfactory sensitivity, the nights continued to pass by with empty hours of hunting and nothing to show for it. To say Garrett began to lose hope would've been overly dramatic. Especially when he'd never really had a strong hope to begin with. Hope, he'd found in his years of hunting, had never seemed to lead him to anything but an unhelpful comfort with wasting time on avenues that wouldn't pan out. But that was exactly how he was beginning to view their hunting sessions.

Right up until the night they nearly tripped straight into the demons.

It was a real bone soaker of a rainy night when it happened.

"We should pack it in for the night," Three was saying, trudging down the dark alleyway beside Garrett, both of their boots splashing every few steps in the puddles of the slums, where drainage systems were inadequate and potholes were frequent. *"This is pointless."*

Garrett couldn't really disagree.

Aside from the fact that patrolling during this heavy a rain was abominably miserable, he couldn't imagine how they'd be finding anything tonight, unless Carlisle and his apprentice happened to switch off whatever sorcery had been hiding their minds. That, or stumble straight into their hunting party in this rainy alley.

Unlikely. But probably not much less likely than their chances at catching a useful trail tonight. Even their enhanced sweepers' senses were all but useless in the thick rain.

"Call it once our boys get back?" Garrett sent.

Three nodded.

That was what Garrett typically defaulted to calling the enhanced these days, seeing as words like *men* felt just a little bit off and ones like *hounds* seemed too slippery a slope to forgetting that their silent, eager servants were in fact human, even if they seemed a bit off at times. Or always. Regardless, since the rain drastically shortened their effective scenting range, and since they were fast as all scud, Garrett and Three had sent their *boys* out to run wider sweeps around them, checking in every half hour or so.

Garrett was just reaching out to see if the enhanced were close enough to call back when Three grabbed his arm, his spindly fingers clamping down with surprising strength, hard enough to spark a flare of anger in Garrett's chest—until he followed Three's wide-eyed gaze to the mouth of the alleyway, and his heart nearly stopped.

It couldn't be.

But it was.

Nearly two full cycles of sweeping Divinity, scanning every building they passed, checking every hidey hole. And there the bastards were. Out for a gropping nighttime stroll in the rainy streets.

As far back from the mouth of the alley as Garrett and Three were, Carlisle and Raish passed out of their line of sight quickly, continuing on down the main street. Garrett stared dumbly at the empty space for a precious few seconds before his brain kicked back in.

"Shrouds?"

Three nodded, looking every bit as shocked as Garrett felt. Nearly thirty days of pounding the streets, and it was only then that Garrett realized he'd completely lost hope of actually ever finding anything. They'd been hunting a mythological creature out here.

And they'd just found it.

He turned back to the Sanctum Guard, who were watching them intently, weapons at the ready. He tapped at his chest with an open hand then jabbed two fingers in the demons' direction, indicating it was time to shroud up and hunt. Without hesitation, they all pulled up the thin, translucent hoods of their shrouds, opened their palmlights, and activated the devices. One by one, they vanished from sight, leaving nothing but dark, grimy alleyway behind.

Turning back to Three, Garrett reached back, pulled the thin film hood up and over his head, then activated his own shroud just as Three winked out of sight ahead of him. Aside from his palmlight reading that the shroud was active, nothing really seemed to happen. Nothing aside from the faintest sense of claustrophobia at the way the film dimmed the world around him and trapped the sounds of his own breathing inside with him. But his adrenaline-buzzed brain barely had time to worry about that.

He hurried for the end of the alleyway, glancing back to check on the Sanctum Guard—whom he of course couldn't see—and bumping into Three twice before he had the good mind to use his extended senses instead of his eyes. For the first time, he actually envied the Sanctum Guard their golden faceplates and the array of infrared and other sensors within. Now that he thought about it, he wasn't even sure if those sensors would allow them to see him and Three through the shrouds.

So how were they supposed to communicate?

This was happening too fast.

This was probably why they only gave these things to specters after the proper training. But it didn't matter. He felt the Guard there, and he knew they could at least ping his and Three's locations via their palmlights.

"They're getting too far ahead," Three sent from the corner. *"Let's go."*

Three didn't wait for an answer, just slipped into the main street.

Optical shrouds activated, Garrett and the Sanctum Guard crept out of the alleyway behind him and set off, stalking quietly after their marks in the pouring rain. The street was less dark than the alley had been—not so much because of the sputtering yellow streetlights as because of the countless ad displays beaming their stale blue glow into the falling rain. One heavy rain of water permeated by another of scuddy promises and worthless bullscud.

Gropping slums.

Luckily, it was late enough and miserably wet enough that most of the foot traffic had already thinned out. Aside from a couple they skirted past by the first alley and a few vagrants Garrett spotted further down another narrow side street, it was just them and the two demons.

"We're going to have to take the shots," Three sent. *"Are you ready?"*

Garrett slipped his sidearm from the holster, thinking quiet thoughts. Three was right. They couldn't risk the split second warning they'd be giving Raish and Carlisle with a verbal command to open fire.

"Just say when," he sent back, quickening his pace to catch up.

"Closer," Three sent. *"Until it's a sure thing or we can feel them."*

Garrett sent a silent affirmative, somewhat relieved that Three had so calmly referenced the glaring little detail that had him feeling like a hound walking in boots. It was the strangest thing, seeing Raish hurrying to catch up to Carlisle fifty or so yards ahead—and not being able to feel a damn trace of either of them in his extended senses. But it wasn't just them, either. It was the air and the street and the buildings immediately around them. It was like they were surrounded by a void that nullified Garrett's senses wherever they stood. Even the falling rain vanished from his senses as it fell on the pair.

It was more than a little mind-gropping. But it also didn't matter right then. Whatever demonic power they called upon to hide their minds, Alpha had still seen fit to dish the two straight onto his and Three's platter tonight. Their confidence was going to be their undoing. Raish was Legion-trained, and Carlisle was the most slippery demon they'd ever had the displeasure of hunting. They had to know that wandering the streets of Divinity when they'd both been publicly named as wanted terrorists was plain stupid, no matter how craftily they could hide.

Of course, maybe something had forced them out here, but that didn't really matter either.

All that mattered was that, after too many long cycles of endless patrols, they'd found their marks. Hoods up and heads down, those marks trudged on. And Garrett and Three followed, their Sanctum Guard hugging close at their left flank now.

The range was closing. Garrett felt the moment approaching—felt it with a kind of violent exuberance. All this time, all this fearful talk of the demon named Carlisle, and now he was only a trigger's pull away...

Garrett continued on, reaching ahead to tell Three he was ready.

Then Carlisle slowed and pulled to a stop ahead as if something had caught his attention.

Garrett froze, feeling Three do the same as the Sanctum Guard fanned out on either side of them. He raised his weapon, waiting for the Guard to get in position, sure that Carlisle had felt them. But then Raish drew up beside Carlisle, and the demon stopped him to point up at an ad display that had caught his attention ahead.

They had to be kidding.

For the first time, Garrett found himself wondering if maybe they'd overestimated this Carlisle—if the extent of his threat was that he'd stumbled onto a neat trick for hiding his mind and then merely gotten lucky a few times after that. But then he looked up to see what had so interested the fearsome demons.

An ad display for some kind of feminine product.

"Something's wrong," Three sent, echoing Garrett's own sudden certainty. *"Open fire on three. One... Two..."*

Ahead, Carlisle lifted a foot and stomped the ground with violent speed, like he was trying to break it.

The rainy night exploded with violently blinding light.

Garrett jerked back, trying too late to cover his eyes, a gust of rain and air slapping his face and washing over his body in a wave of magnetic crackles. For a few seconds, he couldn't see anything beyond the dull, pulsing afterburn of what had felt like an entire crate of detonating snap flares. The hint of vision crept back, revealing the five staggering forms next to him—plainly visible, he realized, a few of their shrouds still sputtering out.

Not good.

Without another thought, Garrett raised his weapon in the demons' general direction and fired. Or tried to. The gun ripped from his hand before he could pull the trigger. Then a flicker of motion caught his eye, and he looked up to the blurry sight of Carlisle hurling a thick hunk of *something* straight at them.

He shoved Three aside and dove the other way to avoid the projectile. *Ice,* he numbly realized as the hunk shattered against the building behind them with bone-breaking force. The demon had pulled a head-sized hunk of ice from the rain water as quickly as if he were plucking a pebble from the ground. Garrett scrambled to his feet, vaguely aware of Raish charging the Sanctum Guard to the right, launching toward one of them in an inhuman leap, but much more concerned with the gray haired, pale eyed demon flying straight at him and Three with unnerving speed and grace.

And his demon preceded him.

It was frightening, the cold, calm power that radiated from the man. To the eye, Carlisle shouldn't have struck anyone as particularly imposing. But as Garrett felt that raw telepathic power press against his senses, even with Three at his side, he found himself afraid for the second time. When a gout of flames burst to life in Three's hand, though, Garrett gathered his wits and reached out to pin Carlisle with telekinesis while his partner put the fire to good use.

The only problem was that trying to stop Carlisle with telekinesis felt a lot like trying to stop a charging haga beast. And when Three let loose with his first good blaze, Carlisle somehow swatted the fire aside with a bare hand, closing in on Three.

Behind Garrett, from where Raish had charged the guards, bone cracked with a sickening sound, and someone gave a horrible scream. Garrett didn't have time to look. Instead, he stepped in on Carlisle's side and tried to stomp the bastard's knee in while he was focused on Three. Carlisle barely seemed to move, but Garrett's boot found nothing but thin air, and when he twisted to follow up with an elbow strike to Carlisle's head, he found himself slamming to the rain-soaked street faster than he could make sense of, his neck and torso feeling like they'd just been worked over by a demolition crew.

The bastard was fast. And strong. And as Garrett watched Carlisle turn another column of Three's flames aside as casually as if he were shading himself from an unpleasant glare, Garrett felt something that he'd never felt before—something beyond simple fear.

They were out of their depth, here. Completely outmatched.

He rose to his feet anyway, his pummeled body groaning in protest. With a snarl, he threw a focused blast of telekinesis to sweep Carlisle's legs out from under him. The bastard just went with it, tucking into a neat aerial that landed him straight back on his feet, where he drove a solid kick into Three's chest. Garrett readied another blast.

Something slammed into him like a human cannonball before he could use it.

For the second time, he hit the pavement, this time cursing at whatever had brought him down. An *actual* human cannonball, he realized—one of the Sanctum Guard, thrown or blasted by Raish. They disentangled from one another, and Garrett looked up just in time to see Carlisle closing on him, an ominous glow in the palm of his hand. Garrett rolled around to drive a kick into the demon's stomach from the ground, but Carlisle waved a hand, and a wave of telekinetic force swept Garrett across the rain-slicked pavement a good ten feet.

He drove his upper back into the ground and kicked up off the back end of his slide, but not before Carlisle had closed on the Sanctum Guard and clamped that glowing palm to his helmeted head. The Guard hit the pavement like his strings had been cut. Carlisle was already whirling to meet Three.

A torrent of gunfire from behind snapped Garrett's attention to where the last two Sanctum Guard were opening up on Raish, who stood in the middle of the rain-soaked street without a single scrap of cover—and with a wall of spent softsteel slugs hovering motionless a few feet in front of his outstretched hands, where he'd apparently stopped them all with telekinesis.

It didn't seem possible, that someone who'd had their awakening just cycles ago could even *use* telekinesis, much less stop gunfire. Before Garrett had time to dwell on it, though, Raish belted a wordless cry and hit the two guards with a telekinetic blast that sent one of them corkscrewing to the pavement and the other stumbling for balance—until Raish brought him down hard enough to shatter his golden faceplate on the pavement.

Enough of this.

As the last Guard rose to take his shot, Garrett focused his mind like a battering ram and hit Raish's defenses as hard as he could muster. Focused as the kid was on the Guard ahead of him, Garrett punched in easy, a feral satisfaction spreading through him as the Guard took aim and Raish registered that he suddenly couldn't move or reach out with his abilities.

"Got ya, you little scudder," he growled, fear and desperation spilling over into righteous rage. He reveled in Raish's dread, felt the young demon try too late to fortify his mental defenses. But Garrett had him, and Raish could only watch helplessly as the Guard regained his feet.

The wet thud of Three slamming to the pavement nearly shocked Garrett loose from his hold on Raish. His chest tightened. Carlisle would be on him any second. But ahead, the Guard was leveling his rifle, just one second away from reducing two demons to one.

He felt Carlisle closing on him.

Take the shot, dammit.

He swore he could feel the Guard's finger stroking at the trigger.

Close enough.

He let go of Raish's mind, spinning wildly to meet Carlisle's rush. Too late.

The last Garrett knew was the bark of gunfire, and the terror of Carlisle's glowing palm slamming into his face.

20

BREACHED

Garrett woke to thick thoughts and even thicker bindings. Alpha, his mouth was dry. And after one tug on the ropes binding him, it was painfully clear he wasn't going anywhere by manual strength alone. That didn't stop him from jerking against the restraints a second time, harder, hot anger flashing through his veins, taking control as the budding panic tickled at his insides, slowly constricting.

Then he noticed the man on the table ahead of him, and everything else left his mind for a moment.

Carlisle sat on the table with his legs crossed, completely motionless, his pale eyes fixed on Garrett in an expressionless stare.

"What?" Garrett rasped from his parched throat. "What do you want from me?"

Inwardly, he cringed at the words. He sounded like a frightened idiot, asking the same pointless questions one of his marks normally would've asked. But he couldn't help it. This man rattled him. And the more Garrett's rebooting brain took stock of the current situation, the more he realized just how well-founded that fear was. They had him. They had him... where?

Carlisle just kept on staring, so still and silent that the creepy bastard might've been sleeping sitting up and with his eyes wide open.

Garrett forced himself to look around and get his bearings before opening his mouth and playing further into whatever head game Carlisle was enacting. The room they were in wasn't large, but not especially small either. Plastwall and plain carpet. Nothing in the room but Garrett's chair, Carlisle's table, and a few storage modules in the corner. A home office, maybe?

That didn't exactly narrow things down.

It was hard to tell for sure with his arms tied separately behind the chair, but Garrett was pretty sure his palmlight had been taken. No surprise there.

And Carlisle was still staring.

"Anyone ever tell you you're kind of creepy?"

Nothing. No reaction. It was like Garrett hadn't spoken at all.

Maybe the creepy bastard *was* sleeping with his eyes open.

Garrett reached out to see what his extended senses might be able to tell him... only to realize that he couldn't reach out at all. Not past his own body, at least. He felt the fabric of his clothes in his extended senses, felt the tightly woven fibers of his bindings where they touched his body, and the dense, well-sanded grains of the chair beneath him—wooden, not polymer as he'd expected. Perhaps that tiny little detail could tell him something about his captors. He couldn't say. It was a little hard to think straight when it felt like he'd suddenly lost an appendage.

He was blind. There Carlisle was, sitting right in front of him, and yet Garrett felt nothing. No Carlisle. No table. No anything. Like someone had draped a telepathic shroud across him, and everything outside of that translucent little film had ceased to exist beyond the limited scope of his mundane senses.

His heart raced as he tried again to reach out. Then again, harder, straining to break through that eerie sheet of nothingness in his extended senses, and into the room he could so clearly see all around him.

Nothing happened. Nothing at all.

He was powerless.

The thought sent him into another kicking fit of futile jerks and twists, fighting against the unyielding rope that bound him so tightly to the chair. So tight. Growing tighter. Constricting around his chest and lungs. Terrified, he looked to Carlisle, suddenly certain that the demon was telekinetically strangling him right then and there. But Carlisle hadn't twitched. And as Garrett tired from his struggles and eased back to catch his ragged breath, the tightness began to recede as well.

He was losing it. Letting the fear twist his head around. He needed to get his scud together. Needed to think about how he'd ended up here, and what had happened to Three, and to the enhanced, and...

That was it. The enhanced.

Their talented human bloodhounds hadn't been there when Garrett, Three, and their Sanctum Guard had ambushed Carlisle and Raish, had they? No. The enhanced had been out on an extended run, sweeping the dark streets more closely in the miserable downpour that had dulled the range of their sharp senses. But they would've returned, right? Had they returned in time to find Carlisle and Raish dismantling Garrett and Three's little hunting party? Had Carlisle already killed them?

Garrett had no idea. About any of it. But once the seed was planted, he couldn't help but think that maybe—just maybe—his enhanced allies could be out there, scenting the scene, tracking them to wherever in demons' depths Carlisle had dragged him after the smoke had cleared. He clung to that singular hope, looking around at the confined space with a new purpose of mind.

They would come for him.

His clothes were still wet. Or damp, at least. He couldn't have been out for that long. Maybe it was only a matter of time. Maybe.

They would come for him.

Without any immediately useful action to take, though, the waiting soon became its own kind of agony. There were only so many circles he could think himself around before he lost it to another futile fit of claustrophobic anxiety. A few times, he tried to goad something out of Carlisle, but the man remained positively catatonic aside from the steady, impossibly slow tide of his breathing. So Garrett waited. Painfully. Until at one point, on what must've been his seven-hundredth inspection of the room, he finally noticed the shoddy little pendant hanging around his neck.

It was little more than a disc of polymer scrap and a short collar of steel string, but it was the markings on the polymer that caught Garrett's attention. They were runic, and while he was sure he'd never seen anything like them, the marks had clearly been made with some specific intent. At first, the discovery sparked excitement, and even a glint of hope.

Had he found the cause of his sudden telepathic blindness?

Maybe. Probably, even. But it hardly mattered, he came to realize over the next few hours. Because like everything else in the room, the pendant was securely fastened outside of his physical reach. And somehow, even though it's cursed cloaking field still allowed his extended senses to reach at least the surface of those things physically in contact with his body, the necklace and pendant themselves were both invisible to his senses.

Either way, he was still trapped.

They would come for him.

In the meantime, he waited some more. Eventually, he even made enough peace with the situation to nod off and join Carlisle for a short time in the realm of creepy bastards who slept sitting up. Or dozed, at least. It was hardly refreshing. At some point—he couldn't have said how long into his dozing—a movement from Carlisle roused Garrett back to full alert. It was barely more than a slight straightening and a nearly imperceptible tilt of the head, but after the demon's sitting dead routine, the tiny movements struck like a thunderclap.

Garrett drew his telepathic defenses tight, sensing instinctively that something was about to happen. Mind secure, he blinked the grogginess from his eyes, attempting to settle the swirling storm of apprehension closing in on his chest.

At the sound of the door opening, he resisted the urge to whip around, looking for answers. He took a breath, thinking controlled thoughts, and then there was Raish, stepping into the room, looking from Garrett to the cursed pendant at his throat, and finally to his demonic master, Carlisle. The kid's arm was in a sling, and he looked like scud—like maybe those last shots Garrett had heard before Carlisle reached him had found their mark after all. Judging by the tenderness of Raish's movements, it seemed like a decent guess.

Thinking about the fight in the street only reminded Garrett of how Raish, barely a few cycles past his awakening, had somehow telekinetically stopped a small river of gunfire. It was disconcerting, to say the least. But that hadn't stopped Garrett from telepathically overpowering the kid twice now. That thought, at least, brought him a small measure of comfort. Proof that Raish was probably still human.

Garrett wasn't sure the same could be said of his master.

They would come for him.

Something passed between the two of them as Raish strode into the room and went to lean against the table next to Carlisle. Probably, they were just rehearsing their plan telepathically, but something about the way Carlisle was looking at the kid—with concern and... was that affection? Love, even? Definitely pain, and self-blame, as he looked at the blue sling holding Raish's arm.

Then the unthinkable happened. Garrett had no idea what thought Raish might've shared with Carlisle, but the demon actually grinned—or quirked his lips, at least. For a second, the guy almost looked human. They went on like that for a minute, trading nods and questioning looks, and even a few more affectionate expressions that began to convince Garrett he wasn't just imagining things.

These two cared for one another.

It was... well, he didn't know what it was.

Then they both turned to face him, and their expressions shifted from friendliness to such wary distaste that, for a second, he almost felt like *he* was the demon there. He pushed the thought aside, doing his best to ready what defenses he could. Would they torture him now? Attack him telepathically? Did he even stand a chance if it came to that?

Carlisle shook his head at something.

Alpha, it was maddening not knowing what they were saying. Even though the Seekers were rarely together to begin with, much less more than two at a time, they all eventually learned how irritating it was to be the odd man out while other telepaths spoke privately. When the subject of their discussion was most likely you, though, and when the topic might well be your life and death, well... that was something else entirely.

Whether he could call it lucky or not, Garrett at least didn't have to wait much longer before Carlisle hopped off the table and approached him.

"Time to play?" Garrett asked in his best nonchalant tone.

They would come for him.

Carlisle ignored him, calmly reaching down to adjust the pendant he wore at his breast—a pendant, Garrett realized as he drew closer, that was covered in runes quite like the ones on the polymer disc on his own chest. His mind was still racing to catch up when Carlisle bent down and plucked the polymer chip from Garrett's chest as if he intended to remove the cursed necklace. Garrett half-thought about trying to bite the bastard's hand before he could. Instead, he gathered his will, doing his best to appear outwardly calm as he braced for telepathic attack.

It was only as Carlisle moved to slip the necklace off of Garrett that it occurred to him he stood a far better chance of breaking Raish's defenses a third time than he did of resisting an allied attack from two demons at once. It hardly mattered that making the attempt would mean leaving his own defenses weakened for a moment. He didn't have time to question it. As soon as Carlisle withdrew the polymer chip necklace from Garrett's head, the room exploded back into his extended senses, and he threw his mind at Raish with the full weight of his desperation.

Immediately, though, Garrett saw that this wasn't going to be like it had been back in that rainy street, when Raish had been distracted. Comparing then to now was like weighing the sturdiness of thin plastwall against the darksteel gates of Sanctuary. But now he had no choice. He was trapped here with two demons, ready to do Alpha only knew what to him. No choice. No escape.

So he slammed against the walls of Raish's mind again, and again.

The little bastard held strong. He didn't even seem to be particularly hard-pressed to do so. It didn't make any sense, some baffled corner of Garrett's mind insisted. A kid who was barely two cycles from his awakening, catching gropping walls of gunfire and standing up to Garrett's full on telepathic assault? No sense at all. But maybe this was just what a true demon looked like.

With mounting hopelessness, Garrett withdrew from his failed attack to buy time. He'd kept his defenses raised as best he could while he attacked, ready to retreat back at the first sign of Carlisle's inevitable push. But it was only as he returned his full attention to bolstering those defenses that he realized Carlisle had already made his move—had been at it, in fact, since he'd first removed Garrett's chip. The demon's mind was already snaked around his walls, thoroughly choking out his defenses. Too tightly, he realized, trying to fight back. It was already too late. Just a matter of time.

Then Raish punched into his defenses with frightening ferocity, and Garrett knew even before he properly felt them there that he'd just lost.

Panic froze him. Or maybe that was Carlisle, sinking his icy hooks into Garrett and forcing him to sit still and obedient in the corner of his own mind while they got to work. Whatever the case, when he finally recovered enough of his faculties to even think to struggle, only to then be reminded that he was not only telepathically frozen but also physically tied down, he almost lost it completely. Carlisle didn't seem to mind. Raish, on the other hand... Even limited as Garrett was in his ability to sense the thoughts and intentions of his captors, he could tell that Raish was a little overwhelmed by all of this.

Scud, this might've been the kid's first mind dive.

How in demons' depths was he so strong already?

He winced inwardly, forgetting such questions completely, as Raish found Garrett's true name and whispered it in his head. By comparison to how sickeningly methodical Carlisle's scan felt—how many deep, dirty Sanctum secrets the gray-haired man was actively drinking from Garrett's mind—the concession of his name should've been nothing. But it *wasn't* nothing, dammit. It was *his* name. The one thing that'd truly been his all his life—and the only thing that'd been his to give to Alexia, and to no one else.

He was going to make these bastards pay for that.

Something passed between Carlisle and Raish, and then Raish's awkward prodding took on a more focused edge, turning toward... Sanctuary? Sanctuary and its secrets. They were looking for a way in.

"How about you try the gate?" Garrett growled in their shared mental warzone, hoping to rattle Raish or at least distract himself from making things worse. *"Both of you be my guests and—"*

But, with a thought, Raish pushed him deep into a mental corner until it felt like he was shouting at the kid from the depths of a dark, endless chasm. Raish was learning. Fast. Garrett could feel the kid's search sharpening despite the faint trace of lingering uncertainty at being in another's mind. And then like that, they flashed to memories of his and Three's late night approaches to the cliffs on the northwestern edge of

Sanctuary, and to the hidden passage and the stone-carved skimmer bay, where they'd been returning every night to collect their enhanced scouts.

Garrett felt the indignant surprise ripple through Raish's focus, deepening as he encountered Garrett's knowledge about High General Kublich and his secret gifts. This discovery was personal for Raish, and far more potent than anything that had preceded it. Of course it was. Raish was Sanctuary born. He'd been raised to have the utmost faith in the Legion and his superior officers. But it was more than that.

As unidirectional as their connection was, Garrett couldn't tell exactly what it was, but it was hard to miss the dark cloud of death and overwhelming hatred that hung over Raish's thoughts of Adrian Kublich—so dark and complete that, for a second, Garrett could hardly breathe for the intensity of it, and for the flashes of sick pain and bloody darkness, lit by a beastly crimson glow. Raish pulled himself back under control before Garrett could glimpse anymore.

Garrett's curiosity almost got the better of him then. But even if he asked what the scud Kublich had done to Raish, he doubted he would've been heard. He felt Raish's focus turning back toward him now, burning with the blind question of how Garrett could possibly lower himself to serving such a man.

In that instant, Raish exposed his ignorance. Not that it came as a surprise. How could a silver spoon Legion brat ever hope to understand what Garrett had been through, after all? Raish had been awakened a measly two cycles ago. Garrett had spent a lifetime of toiling slavery under the Sanctum lash, years of faithful service that had never once earned him anything other than his handlers' resentment and and a loaded gun aimed at his back. All until the High Cleric and Kublich and the others had risen up to save them.

Raish would never understand. And he didn't even try to. Garrett couldn't understand himself how someone who'd awoken to such abilities could so readily condemn others of his kind for wanting to live freely, but the kid's thoughts were already bouncing along to who Kublich served, spreading like demon fire seeking answers, or a target he could latch onto and burn. *Burn.* Raish wanted to *hurt* them. Garrett could feel it in the kid's core.

"You won't stop us," Garrett sent, with as much confidence as he could

muster. *"You or that damned wild hound you call a master. This planet has trampled us underfoot long enough."*

MORE OF THAT RIPPLING INDIGNATION. Raish wanted to hit him now. Garrett could feel it. And he had to say, the feeling was mutual. The vicious little bastard had bought into whatever his demon master had sold him so completely that he couldn't even see the damage they were causing. And all the while, Garrett felt the background chill of Carlisle's ghostly presence, scanning through his every fiber with mechanical efficiency.

It was a damn good thing he'd never learned more about the identities and plans of the High Cleric's most powerful allies. No secret of Garrett's was making it out of this encounter intact. Alpha only knew what these two would try to do with what they'd already learned. Garrett could only cling to the hope that the enhanced had found his trail, and that reinforcements would come blasting through the door before these two decided they were finished with him.

He wanted to curse himself the moment he let the thought slip through his mind. But cursing himself would've only alerted their attention to it. Which, considering the sudden silence that had descended through the overturned playground of his mind, he already had. He felt Raish reaching for the stream of his present thoughts, tracing back through everything that had just passed through.

That's when Garrett cursed himself. Doubly so when he realized Carlisle was already sifting through those same thoughts, sneaky as a ghost.

There went the element of surprise. No point in hiding it now. He let the belief hit them like a bursting dam.

They would come for him.

The enhanced would find him. They'd been out there, scenting from the shadows while the rest of the team made their rounds that night. They would have returned to the scene of the fight with their preternaturally sharp noses. Noses that still had Raish's and Carlisle's scents from Vantage. Just like they could've picked up Garrett's scent a mile away.

They would come for him!

Raw excitement flooded through Garrett as he felt Raish's indignant fury falter, blanch, and shrivel, washed away on a swell of growing horror. He could have laughed if he'd still had full faculty of his body. Then he felt Raish tear out of his mind like a burning hare in search of a lake, and that control did return, Carlisle having already disappeared without a trace.

"They're coming!" Raish cried.

No reason to do anything but feed the panic now, even if Carlisle didn't appear quite so easily spooked.

"That's right, you gropping steel sippers," Garrett snarled. "Let's see how you bastards do against—"

But something slammed into the side of his head before he could even think to lie about it, and the world cut to darkness.

Then, somewhere in the depths—where exactly, or how much later, he couldn't have said—Garrett's darkness rippled with the beginnings of a hazy fever dream. One that seemed intuitively bad, and yet filled him with a disjointed sense of peace for reasons he couldn't place.

It was the siren song of a triggered alarm filling the void.

21

WRONG STOP

It was a strange dream to say the least. Walls singing a lilting tune. The floor vibrating with upside-down thunder, even as the darkness above cracked with its own tiny bolts, and with violent shouts of outrage. The happiest, most welcome violence he'd ever dreamed. Maybe not even a dream at all. Garrett couldn't decide. Couldn't seem to hold on to any one piece long enough to string it together with the next.

"—ear me, fellow?"

That was closer. Right at the center of things.

Click. Click.

Snapping fingers?

Yes, that was it. Fingers snapping right in his face. Then the distant thunder of something patting his cheek, right under the blinding fire of the spot that Carlisle had—

Carlisle.

Garrett surfaced from the dream—which is to say he became aware of the room around him, and realized that he hadn't been dreaming at all. The lilting alarm chimes, the explosions and gunfire. Wherever he was, it was a war zone. The room was somewhat out of focus, but he could still count. Four men. Unless he was seeing double. But no, they were definitely wearing legionnaire armor. And one was untying him, thank Alpha.

"I'm a Sanctum agent," he growled. Or tried to. Judging by the lack of any helpful response, he wasn't sure he'd succeeded.

"I am a Sanctum agent," he repeated more carefully, his head spinning with concussion and the rhythmic fiery ache of Carlisle's goodbye blow to the temple. "Where are the targets? Raish and Carlisle."

This time, they clearly understood him. But as his ringing head cleared out enough to take in their wary expressions, he could practically hear what they were going to say before the first one opened his mouth.

"Sir, without your palmlight or any proper identification, I'm afraid we're going to have to—"

Had the entire room not been lurching, Garrett might've had the good sense to say something like, "I'm going to reach for my pocket, now."

As it was, he just jammed his one free hand into his jacket like a street urchin diving for spare coin. Whether the fact that they didn't shoot him on the spot was lucky or not, Garrett honestly couldn't say in the moment. All he knew was that he needed to move his ass. And that it was more than a little satisfying to watch the closest two legionnaires' expressions as they shared a glance at the ID chip Garrett handed them from the inner breast pocket of his jacket.

It was a simple chip. No name. No precise title. No specific identifiers beyond a number, an embedded verification protocol, and a picture. What it *really* was, for anyone even remotely in the know, was a no-questions-asked order not to grop with his business unless they were prepared to bring a messy end to their career over it.

These men weren't.

They gushed apologies, waving furiously for their teammate to finish untying Garrett.

"Do you require any assistance, sir?" one of the legionnaires asked, offering the ID chip back to him.

"Stims," was all Garrett said, shaking his arms loose and waiting impatiently for the legionnaires to finish with his legs.

The look on the legionnaire's face said what Garrett already knew: it was less than advisable, hitting the stims when he could barely see straight from head trauma. But the legionnaire didn't argue as he handed over the slim injector, and neither did Garrett. He needed to operate right now.

Simple as that. Needed to catch those bastards before they lost them again.

"Hold this," he added, plucking the cursed demon pendant from his neck and shoving it into the legionnaire's waiting hand. "I'll be wanting it back after."

Then Garrett pressed the injector tip to his neck and triggered the device. Almost instantly, he felt clashing armies of fire and ice spilling through his veins, spreading further with each rapidly quickening beat of his heart. Electric tingles crackled behind his eyeballs, a copper taste flaring on his tongue. He bounced to his untied feet without hardly thinking to, and nearly straight into the waiting legionnaires.

"Sir..." one started.

"Either watch my back or get out of my way," Garrett said. He turned for the door, not waiting for their answer, more concerned with wrangling the raging bull's worth of energy down into something usable.

At least he could see straight now.

Outside, it wasn't hard to figure out which way to go. There were only two options in the sparse hallway, and the gunfire was clearly pouring in from the right. Garrett turned for the cacophony, lamenting that he didn't have his palmlight to call in the other Seekers. Not that he'd need to. They would've been looking for him. And judging by the sounds ahead, they couldn't have missed this. Right? Right.

Alpha, he was jittery.

He broke into a shaky run past a few more rooms and a rather decadent flight of stairs, and came to a sight he hadn't been expecting. A grand entryway. And "grand" was undoubtedly the right word, with its golden walls and simulated sunshine, and the burbling fountain that, while currently riddled with slug holes and hemorrhaging water, looked to have been perfectly lovely pre-scudstorm. Not that any of that mattered right now.

Garrett followed the sounds of fighting up the plush red carpet of the darkwood staircase, trying to remember if he'd somehow missed the part where Carlisle lived in a freaking golden palace. At the top of the stairs, the red carpet path split to travel along a balcony to the two halves of the upper floor. Gunshots and yelling to the right. And to the left... He wasn't sure at first what it was his buzzing extended senses brushed into, only that his gut told him he needed to investigate.

Of course, that probably had more to do with the line of injured legionnaires laid out along the banister, groaning as a frazzled-looking medic hurried to apply his craft between them.

"—the scud was he thinking?" one asked in a faint voice.

"It's demons, man," came another shaky voice. "I'm telling you, man, we're hunting gropping demons."

Someone else told the shaky soldier to shut the grop up and get a grip, but Garrett was already turning back to the legionnaires who'd followed him up. He silently reached out a hand for a sidearm, nodding in the other direction toward the sounds of the ongoing firefight. "Go. Help your people. I'll check this way."

They weren't in any mood to argue. If anything, they seemed relieved as one volunteer handed Garrett his sidearm and they turned to leave. It wouldn't be their fault, after all, if he went and got himself killed after ordering them to grop off. Garrett didn't mind the sentiment. He just needed to move before the stims burst out of his eyeballs.

He didn't bother asking the five wounded and their medic what the hell had happened. He just followed the trail of destruction. They were too busy trying not to bleed out to question the guy the brothers-in-arms had just escorted upstairs and handed a weapon to.

Down the posh hallway, past the bullet-riddled paintings. It was quiet in this half of the house. Garrett turned the corner, weapon raised, and immediately spotted his destination by the single legionnaire leg draped out into the hallway from the open doorway. The door itself was gone, having been clearly ripped from its hinges. But that feat of brutality was nothing compared to what lay beyond.

The room was a wreck.

A bloody, splintered wreck.

Bodies and overturned furniture everywhere. Shattered, crackling displays on the far wall. Garrett's eyes fixed on the body below those displays, and his breath caught. The man's... the *thing's* face... Alpha be sweet, was that one of the enhanced? Was that what they looked like under those helmets?

He gave his head a jerky shake, sure the stims and the concussion were gropping with his eyes. But no. There was another one of the things further in, on the back wall. Face specked with sickly green scales. Slitted nostrils and sharp fangs beneath its pale, dead eyes. He was so transfixed that he barely noticed the overturned desk just inside the doorway, and the three or four legionnaires who'd been smashed beneath it. At least until he stepped into the room, and one of those soldiers stirred and grabbed his leg.

"Down... the hatch..." the soldier groaned, jutting his chin to the right. "Never seen... anything like it."

Given the freakish dead things just ahead and the fact that he and his brotos appeared to have been struck by a flying desk, Garrett didn't have to make much of a stretch to imagine what the soldier meant by the second part. Nor did he have to clarify the first part, after a quick sweep with his extended senses.

There was a hidden hatch beneath the carpet.

Down the hatch. The rest could wait.

Garrett swept over to the point of open floor space between the wreckage, reaching farther down with his senses this time. There was a ladder. A long ladder, stretching down a square permacrete shaft. Down, down...

There, maybe thirty yards below: the unmistakable flame of a tele-pathic mind. Raish's? Garrett didn't think so. But he also didn't linger long enough to poke around and find out for sure. He withdrew, hoping the quick brush had gone unnoticed. Briefly, he considered flinging open the hatch and unloading his weapon down the way. Maybe even tossing a few grenades down there. But no. The instant he opened the hatch, whoever was on the ladder would probably see. He'd wait a moment. Drop down right behind them. Catch them at close range by surprise.

Because that's been working so great for you up till now.

"Shut up," he muttered to himself under his breath, glancing back toward the distant commotion across the house and wondering who it was they were fighting, and whether he should go find some backup.

Probably. But another quick sweep told him the way was clear below. Alpha knew how long until they were in the wind, escaped by whatever hidey hole they had down there. And he could move faster without backup, anyway. None of that stopped the fear at chasing the demons into the breach after everything they'd done to him. But the stims and the burning pit of anger in his gut helped with that. It was enough.

Garrett opened and lifted the hatch with telekinesis, taking confidence from the presence of his power. He slid quickly and quietly down onto the ladder, and closed the hatch behind him. He focused on the dim, flickering light below, then closed his eyes to listen at the faint trickle of voices.

"What is it?" someone asked. Someone young, and female. Who?

"Come on."

That was Raish's voice. No mistaking it.

Garrett started creeping down the ladder, rung by rung, until another sound gave him pause. The hiss and metallic slide of a door opening, he thought. They were going somewhere. On foot? He wasn't sure. But then the dim light below winked brighter, and a low hum filled the air, punctuated by another slide-hiss.

A vehicle?

No more voices below. No more time to play it safe.

Garrett let go of the ladder, and plunged down the well, using telekinesis to keep himself centered and, ultimately, to soften his landing. He landed in a crouch, looking around the dusty old room, rummaging for his sidearm... and froze.

No sooner had it entered his head that the room looked like an offshoot of the old Divinity underway lines than he spotted the archaic lev tram under the flickering lights. And there, standing at the head of the compartment in the pale interior lights, was Raish, along with a pretty raven-haired girl Garrett had never seen in his life. The telepath he'd felt earlier, he realized.

For a second, he was too frozen even to wonder who she was beyond that. Then his brain caught up, and he realized Raish and his mystery woman would probably barely be able to see him from their brightly-lit tram even if he stood up and waved in the dim dusty room. More importantly, the two were alone down here. No Carlisle.

The realization brought Garrett as much trepidation as it did relief. Whether it was good news or bad news, he wasn't sure. All he knew was that this was his chance to nab Raish once and for all.

Which sounded good and sunny right up until the tram hummed to life, lifted a few inches from the ground, and began to accelerate forward.

Garrett took three running steps, not allowing himself to think about it, and leapt high, grabbing onto his own body with telekinesis and heaving for everything he was worth.

Too high, his frenetic brain registered. *Too far.*

Then some combination of Alpha's divine will and Garrett's ingrained telekinetic reflexes took hold, and he thudded down to the light-steel tram roof just before it whisked into the underway tunnel to be swallowed by startlingly abrupt darkness. He'd lost his gun, he numbly registered. But there wasn't time to worry about that. Or to listen in and see if they'd noticed his landing. There was no way in demons' depths they'd missed it.

So Garrett focused his mind and threw it at their mystery telepath like a pulse cannon slug.

"What was that?" he heard Raish hiss below, before he'd even registered that he'd already broken through the girl's defenses, and that he was in fact hearing it through her ears. She was new to this, he realized as her shock and horror rushed over him—the blind panic at suddenly finding her body an unwilling puppet to his will. He felt the weapon in her hand —a collapsed composite staff, quite sturdy—just as clearly as he saw Raish prowling toward the rear of the tram, taking his gun in his non-injured hand as he reached for that cursed demonic pendant with his sling hand.

"What?" Garrett forced the girl to ask out loud. "I didn't hear anything..."

The girl bucked against him with a raw ferocity. She wanted to hurt him. Wanted him out. Elise, he saw in her mind. Her name was Elise Fields. And she was in love with Haldin Raish.

Which probably explained why his hand had just froze halfway to his pendant. He knew something was wrong. The kid was too damn sharp. They both were. So Garrett took the collapsed staff in Elise's hand and swung it savagely for the back of Raish's head before either of them had time to get clever.

The weapon whooshed through empty air. Raish was already diving clear. He smashed down to the tram seats with a cry of pain, having landed on his injured arm—and having dropped his gun.

"Elise!" he groaned, awkwardly rolling around to face her as Garrett marched his puppet forward, raising the staff for another strike.

"Stop it!" Elise screamed at Garrett's mind. *"Stop it! I swear to Alpha I'll kill you!"*

The desperation in her voice, and the look in Raish's eyes... it was all almost too much. But Garrett had seen what Raish and his master could do. So he steeled himself and swung the staff at Raish's open knees.

Raish rolled back with surprising speed. The empty polymer seating shattered where his legs had been. Then, before Garrett could make Elise swing again, Raish was there, hooking his legs around her torso and arms, firmly immobilizing her. Garrett struggled to break his unwilling assassin free, pushing her screaming voice down into the depths of their shared mental space. But it was no good. Raish had her pinned too completely. And he was reaching for that damned pendant of his—Garrett could only guess what for.

He changed tact, shifting himself toward the back of the tram, careful to keep his hold on Elise and keep her struggling all the while. It was tricky, splitting his attention between two moving bodies, but by the time Raish's plan became clear, Garrett was ready. Or so he thought.

Below, Raish yanked his pendant free and jammed it down around Elise's neck, effectively cutting off Garrett's control, just as he'd expected. What he hadn't expected was the mental shock of the arcane barrier snapping into place with his mind still on board. It cost him precious moments. Moments that were no doubt allowing his prey to recover from their disorientation.

Garrett shook his aching head in a futile attempt to clear it, and grabbed onto the lip at the rear edge of the speeding tram.

"Gun!" Raish shouted below.

Garrett gripped the lip, all too aware of the low ceiling rushing by overhead. He shimmied his feet down, braced to either side of the rear tram door window. Then he gathered his will, kicked off, and swung straight through that window, leading the charge with a spear tip blast of telekinesis.

Glass shattered. Garrett squinted his eyes and flung himself through, releasing his grip above and hoping for the best. He landed roughly, but on his feet, glass crunching underfoot. But he wasn't worried about that. Or about the two demons ahead.

Garrett was focused on Raish's dropped gun.

The moment she saw him, Elise lunged for the weapon, but Garrett was already yanking it to his outstretched hand with telekinesis. Except the gun didn't make it to his hand.

Elise lashed out, faster than Alpha-damned lightning, and smacked the weapon down with her staff. Without pause, she whirled straight for him in attack, clearly intending to make good on her earlier threats. Garrett threw his hands out, unleashing a raw, sloppy wave of telekinetic force. Sloppy, but effective. Elise Fields went sailing toward the head of the tram with wide eyes.

Raish, on the other hand, rolled to his feet, practically aflame with demonic fury. Garrett threw his mind at Raish's on the off chance of catching him off guard, or emotionally compromised. That didn't happen. But it did buy a moment to spot the gun where it had fallen under the seats. Garrett called it to hand with telekinesis. This time, it jerked to a halt in midair, caught between his raised hand, and Raish's.

Garrett rapidly flicked between full power on the mental attack and the telekinetic struggle for the gun, thinking to take advantage of Raish's relative inexperience with a more complex assault. But Raish held on. The little scudder even managed a few steps forward while they struggled on the two mental planes.

Garrett strained harder, losing himself in the mental struggle, pushing aside the indignant voice in his head that cried over and over again that this simply wasn't possible.

Finally, Raish gave out, and the gun sprang toward Garrett's outstretched hand. He caught it just in time to register that Raish was already charging in. The demon caught his wrist as he pulled the trigger, moving faster than Garrett would've thought possible. Where the slug went, Garrett couldn't have said. He was too busy taking Raish's vicious heel kick straight to the stomach.

He staggered back, trying to bring the gun to safety, but Raish followed, prying the weapon from his fingers. Something struck Garrett's head. Hard. Hard enough that he lost track of the beat down until he slammed into the rear wall of the tram and felt the rushing wind of the broken window and the dark tunnel at his back. His hands raised themselves of their own accord, shaking pitifully.

A kid. He was only a gropping kid.

Garrett wanted to scream, but there was no air left in his paralyzed lungs. No strength left in his limbs.

Raish thrust a hand out, and it was over. Garrett thought to counter —tried to counter—but his body wouldn't seem to respond. He was beaten. Beaten by a gropping kid.

So instead he sat back and watched with a kind of weary disembodiment as the telekinetic battering ram punched his body through the rear tram door, sending him tumbling out into darkness. He might've screamed then. He couldn't really tell. The darkness swallowed him, then it reached up and smacked him, over and over again.

When he finally stopped rolling, he was faintly surprised to realize amid the blossoming fire of a thousand impacts that he was still alive. His eyes focused automatically on the only available light in the tunnel—the distant, receding rectangle of the tram lights. He watched it until it disappeared from sight, the busted rear door flapping in the rushing wind as if in pleasant farewell.

22

FAILURE

"Have you lost sight of your dream, my child?"

Garrett looked up in mild surprise, wary at the sudden gentleness in the High Cleric's tone. It was unmistakably at odds with how the conversation had been going up until that point.

They sat in the High Cleric's personal meeting room, just the two of them—and the cleric's ever-present Onyx Guard, of course—discussing the long list of ways the scud had hit the turbines in the past day.

Three was dead. That had been the conversation starter: Garrett's partner was dead, killed by Carlisle. As for the demon and his disturbingly talented underlings, they were all back in the wind. The raid had largely been a failure. Against impossible odds, Carlisle had blown his way out past multiple companies of legionnaires even as Garrett had failed to capture Raish and Elise Fields in the tunnels below. The Legion had, however, captured two of their allies—an information broker named Francesco Fields, Elise's father, and the man whom that rich house had apparently belonged to, and an ex-enforcer named Phineas Hammer, who'd allegedly accepted a long term contract as Fields' private muscle.

What their exact relationship was with Carlisle and Raish, no one knew yet. Apparently they were both fairly resilient to the early rounds of information extraction. If the Legion's initial digging was any indication, though, those two men knew more than a little bit. Especially Fields. Enough so that Garrett had wanted to ask if he might not go extract their secrets himself. But that was foolish thinking. They were in Kublich's domain, held in the brig of the Sanctuary base. There was no reason Kublich couldn't do it himself, and even if Garrett's skill *had* been required, he wasn't positive the High Cleric would've trusted him to even lace his own boots right then.

He'd gropped up. Badly. More than once. And the more he sought to explain himself, the worse it sounded in his own head.

Trust me, your Holiness. There was nothing I could do, your Holiness. He's really quite a strong little boy.

And don't even get him started on Carlisle...

How could he hope to adequately explain any of it to the High Cleric? The ferocity and strength of those two demons. The way they never seemed to stop—never even seemed to consider the possibility that they might not win their fight. He *couldn't* explain it. Other than that they were possessed, and that he, the holy weapon who'd supposedly been sharpened for eight years now to deal with such foes, was woefully ill-equipped to deal with it.

It was pathetic. *He* was pathetic.

But the High Cleric was still waiting for an answer.

Had he lost sight of his dream?

"No, your Holiness. Of course not."

The High Cleric studied him dubiously. "And what of Six, child? Have you forgotten of your affection for her, and of the freedom you both might share in the peace of our new world?"

"I haven't forgotten."

He didn't add that the thought of Alexia had been the only thing that had picked him back up once the tram had left him down in that tunnel. For a time, he'd simply lain there in the darkness, at first trying to take stock of the damage he'd incurred, but eventually turning deeper, reflecting on the general worth of his life, and how completely he'd managed to grop things up at every step of this hunt. Wondering, finally, if he should even bother getting up at all.

How long he'd lain there, he wasn't really sure. All he knew was that it hadn't been preservation or any love of self that had picked him up from tracks and kept him limping through the darkness, multiple miles back to the site of the raid. It hadn't been the High Cleric, or the ever-loving Will of Alpha. It had been Alexia—always Alexia.

And Garrett was growing tired of His Holiness attempting to leverage that fact against him.

"Well then," the High Cleric said, "perhaps your faith is simply unequal to the task at hand."

Garrett clenched his jaw, refusing to degrade himself by spurting more excuses.

"Perhaps the time has come to invite your precious Six to join the hunt." His papery old lips quirked. "Perhaps she could subdue the demons in her own way, as you have so thoroughly failed to do."

The anger faded from his gut, replaced by sickened horror.

"They'd kill her."

"Perhaps." The High Cleric held his gaze steadily. "And yet the problem remains. These demons must be stopped, and you are telling me that you are not the Seeker to see it done."

Garrett forced a breath, trying to keep his voice level. "Who among the twelve do you think stronger than me, your Holiness? I tell you, these demons are beyond any one of us."

"They are human," the High Cleric snapped with startling malice. He set his jaw, composing himself before continuing. "I do not care what demonic power flows through their veins, they are still human. Which means they can be defeated by one of sufficient faith."

"Smite them yourself, then, Holiness, if you think it a question of faith."

The words had left Garrett's mouth before he could remind himself to breathe, to relax. To remember that this was the Alpha-blessed High Cleric he was talking to and that, deactivated collar or no, the man could have his head removed with little more than the snap of his fingers.

As if anticipating that order, the two Onyx Guard on the High Cleric's flanks actually cocked their heads a little. It was the first time Garrett could remember having seen them react to anything at all.

Then the High Cleric stood from his seat across the table, and Garrett forgot about everything else. He watched with deepening dread as His Holiness stalked around the table, suddenly looking decades less old and fragile than he had a moment ago, only stopping when he stood within arms reach at Garrett's side. Garrett stared abjectly ahead like a subservient hound, afraid to meet his master's gaze, simply feeling his dominant telepathic presence roiling there beside him.

"They can be defeated," the High Cleric finally said, quietly. He leaned down close to the side of Garrett's face. "They *will* be defeated. At any expense. Do you understand? The time draws nigh, my child."

Garrett *didn't* understand. Not one gropping bit. But he knew better than to say so.

He kept his eyes forward, tension coiling through every fiber of his body. "What would you have me do, your Holiness?"

The silence stretched with agonizing slowness, raking Garrett with the kind of morbid apprehension he hadn't felt since he'd first been brought to the High Cleric following his alleyway transgression with Alexia. Had he truly fallen so low in his master's esteem? He didn't know. Couldn't know, until the silence stretched too long to bear, and he stole a glance at the High Cleric, only to realize that His Holiness wasn't even looking at him. The High Cleric was staring toward the closed door, paying Garrett no attention.

"Leave us," the cleric said, not looking away from the door.

"Holiness?" Garrett asked, not sure if the order had been directed at him, or who the intended *us* even was, unless he was talking about the Onyx Guard.

"I said leave us," the High Cleric snapped.

Garrett's arms and legs paid heed to the order before his brain could fully process it, pulling him to his feet and turning him toward the door. He glanced at the Onyx Guard and the High Cleric once more, looking for any reaction, any explanation, but there was none to be found. They behaved as if he'd already gone. So, being careful not to make any sudden movements, Garrett left, entirely unsure where he stood, and what the scud had just happened.

At least until he stepped out into the hallway, and his senses brushed against the man who was waiting just outside the door.

Garrett didn't recognize the slender man with gray hair. Indeed, the man looked so unimposing and bland in his simple, tattered gray cloak that he could've passed for a Sanctum acolyte or a beggar in the slums, and probably could've gone unrecognized by his own flesh and blood doing either. But this man was neither a beggar nor an acolyte.

He was a telepath. There was no missing that. Quite possibly the most potent telepath Garrett had ever encountered. Stronger even than the High Cleric, or Adrian Kublich, Garrett estimated by the faint, blinding glimpse he caught before withdrawing into his own defenses. It was like nothing he'd ever felt before. So bright, so overwhelmingly vast, that he almost wanted to reach out and investigate further. Almost. But he didn't dare, for several reasons—not the least of which was that the man was staring straight at him.

If Garrett lived to be a hundred—an outcome that seemed less and less likely every day—he was sure he'd never forget that stare.

It was cold, the intensity of its piercing omniscience matched only by the depths of its frosty apathy, like the man had read the entirety of his spirit at a glance, and didn't give half a damn about any of it. That stare was utterly alien. And it wasn't leaving Garrett's face.

Because he was in the way, his shocked brain finally realized. Still blocking the door. Stupid.

Whatever it was about the man, Garrett found himself stepping aside and bowing his head deferentially without so much as a conscious thought. Maybe he was still just in pitiful hound mode after his talk with the High Cleric. Either way, the supreme stranger said nothing. Just ghosted past Garrett in his shoddy robes, and into the High Cleric's council room, where the door promptly slid shut behind him.

For several long moments, Garrett could only stare at the ornate door, wondering who the scud the man was.

One of Alpha's Chosen, no doubt. One of the High Cleric's inner circle, apparently.

But then why did Garrett get the impression in hindsight that it had been the High Cleric who'd seemed apprehensive about the man's arrival, and not the other way around?

Who made the High Cleric of the Sanctum shake in his golden robe?

Garrett had no idea. But he turned and forced his feet to carry him down the hallway anyway, back toward the Great Hall proper. Whoever that man was, and whatever he was doing here, Garrett doubted he'd earn any loyalty bonus points from either of them by standing outside the door like a clumsy eavesdropper. Wrapped up as he was in his ruminations, he didn't notice the men waiting ahead until he stumbled into the entry hall. Once he saw them, he didn't quite believe it. Not until he'd swept his senses over them, and watched each and every one stir at his mental touch.

A dozen enhanced, all standing at rapt attention among the High Cleric's extensive collection of priceless artifacts.

For a second, Garret was consumed with a sudden, nearly blinding fear that they'd come for him—that Kublich or the High Cleric had sent this small company of enhanced, six times more of them than he'd even realized existed, to settle the balance on his outstanding string of failures. But then his rational mind caught up and noted that the enhanced would make rather crummy assassins for a telepath, seeing as Garrett was pretty sure he'd be able to order them off, or at least turn them against one another. Maybe.

He thought back to the scene of the raid on Fields' home, and the sight of the two dead monstrosities. The sickly green scales and the deformed facial structures, almost like they were sprouting snouts and turning half serpentine. Had those truly been the enhanced, or something else entirely?

Was that what he would see if he ordered one of the ones in front of him to remove its dark helmet?

He glanced toward the front of the room, where two Onyx Guard manned the main door to the Great Hall. They didn't seem perturbed by the presence of the enhanced. But then again, he was pretty sure those automatons would never seem perturbed by anything, unless they were explicitly ordered to.

That thought triggered another disturbing question.

What if the Onyx Guard were actually enhanced behind those onyx faceplates of theirs?

He shook his head free of the notion.

He was losing it. He'd *seen* an Onyx Guard's face before. Once.

"Alpha be sweet," he muttered at himself under his breath, turning for the great stone door to get the scud out of there.

At least no one moved to stop him. But he couldn't stop the whirlwind of questions racing through his head.

What were these enhanced doing here? Had the High Cleric's mysterious visitor brought them? To what end? And how many more of the creatures were already running around out there?

The way the High General had talked, Garrett had assumed he and Three were out there hunting with the first and only enhanced prototypes, that this was all some sort of advance trial. And as hesitant as he'd been about the whole arrangement, Garrett had even been starting to come on board toward the end. Until he'd seen what was under the mask.

He glanced back at the line of dead-still enhanced, wondering one last time if he should take a peek, and settle this right then. But he couldn't bring himself to turn back.

Because if he wasn't crazy... Those things... They weren't human.

And who the scud in their right minds would willingly and knowingly volunteer for that?

They will be defeated, the High Cleric's words echoed in his head above the nightmarish swirl of sharp fangs and pale, dead eyes. *At any expense. Do you understand? The time draws nigh, my child.*

No. He most certainly did *not* understand what was happening here.

And he wasn't sure he ever wanted to find out.

2 3

DREAM TEAM

The spirit of Andre Kovaks haunted Garrett that night. In his dream, the dead man's ghost sat in the back of his skimmer, every bit as wild and frayed in death as he'd been in life.

Wake up, he mouthed, over and over again, jostling his chains to catch Garrett's attention whenever it strayed. *Wake up. Wake up.* Mouthing the words so frantically, so desperately, that Garrett was sure he would've been screaming them if he'd had the voice to do so.

Wake up.

"Shut up," Garrett said.

Wake up.

"I'm trying."

But Kovaks wasn't having Garrett's excuses. On and on he went, demanding Garrett watch. Over and over and over again until Garrett finally snapped and jerked the skimmer controls forward, sending them careening down to the Divinity streets in a fiery explosion, just to have done with it.

Only it didn't end there. No end to the madness. No sweet, blessed reprieve. He just lay in the wreckage, belted firmly to what remained of his seat as the flames licked up his body—alarming for the pain they represented more than for any actual searing sensation they brought in the moment. And there, fixed in place ahead of him, was Kovaks' burning form, still mouthing the words even as his scraggly beard disintegrated from his face.

Wake up. Wake up.

"AND DO WHAT?!" Garrett roared.

Kovaks paused midway to forming his next word, and instead cracked Garrett a wide smile, like he'd finally solved the puzzle. He smiled so wide his burning lips split and peeled away. "What do I care?" he asked, apparently not bothered in the least by the ghastly damage. "I'll be long dead either way."

That was when Garrett finally woke—straight into a nice cold sweat, and to a day that promised more of the same.

He had no orders. He had no partner. He had nothing, really, but the questions eating at his insides, and the equally uneasy impression that his current lack of assignment was no accident. Habit and discipline dictated he get out of his cot, break his fast on a bland meal from the fab, and get on with his day anyway. In the wake of the raid at Fields' home, there were more than enough leads to start sussing out, explicit orders or no.

But for a while, all he could do was lay there staring into nothingness, thinking about Carlisle, and Raish, and Elise Fields. Thinking about what those two demons had learned from Garrett's own head, and what they were doing now. Thinking about the sharp-eyed man who'd visited the High Cleric with plain tatters for clothes and a telepathic presence like an Alpha-damned celestial body. And then there were the enhanced...

The gropping enhanced.

All I ask is that you find the courage to question what's happening around you, came Kovaks' words, burned seemingly forever in his mind by the countless nightmares he'd had since watching the man hang. *Question it silently, in the sanctum of your own head. But question it. Ask yourself who it is you're fighting, and why. Ask what it is that might be driving them. Forget what you've been told, if only for a moment, and ask these questions as if you do not already know the answers. Find the courage to lay your demons and your fears to the side, look at the cold, hard facts, and draw your own conclusions. That is all I ask.*

"Grop off," Garrett muttered to his empty quarters. "Gropping madman."

Only he couldn't shut the thoughts out as he finally pulled himself from his cot and forced himself to break fast on a bowl of tasteless gruel. He couldn't stop thinking about the wild bullscud Kovaks had spouted during his so-called trial about alien invaders from another planet—about how these malicious extraterrestrials had come to Enochia and somehow taken over the planet without anyone noticing. About how they had agents at all the highest levels of Enochia's infrastructure, and how they were using companies like Vantage to do Alpha knew what...

Like engineer scaly mutant super soldiers?

"Shut up," he grumbled into his bowl of gruel.

If he kept this up, he was going to have himself convinced *he* was an alien by the time midday rolled around. Still, ridiculous delusions aside, he had to wonder where the scud those things he'd seen at Fields' home had come from.

Once he'd finished breaking fast, though, he managed to put the conspiracy theories on hold for the morning and focus on doing his job—which he assumed still included finding and stopping the demons, whatever else may or may not have been going on. After the ruckus the Legion had raised in the Fields raid, there was a lot to go on. Everything from legionnaire reports to Divinity security footage to civilian statements.

At first, Garrett had assumed the Legion and the WAN would collaborate to pass the entire catastrophe off as some manner of training exercise. He doubted anyone would be thrilled to hear that the fight had in fact been a full-scale military operation to apprehend two terrorists and that, despite dropping enough heat to level a city block, their main targets had skirted off to terrorize another day. But the powers that be didn't try to hide the event. Instead, they used it like a weapon, aimed at inciting the public and disheartening their enemies. They told the truth. The only part they didn't tell straight was in reporting that Francesco Fields and Phineas Hammer, known associates of the terrorist known as Carlisle, had been killed in the action during the raid.

Garrett couldn't say whether making that small lie was the smart play or not. Perhaps they thought it would reassure the public that the situation was under control. Perhaps they solely intended to goad Carlisle and Raish into acting rashly out of grief. Either way, it didn't bode well for what the Legion intended to do with Fields and Hammer once Kublich or the interrogators had finished extracting whatever information they could out of the pair.

As for inciting the public with the true nature of the Legion's operation, that part worked wonders. An inordinate amount of civilian reports had been flowing in ever since the first broadcast. More than Garrett had ever seen for any one incident, which didn't particularly surprise him in this case. Apostate terrorists were frightening enough to the good people of Divinity. Apostates who could fight their way clear of an entire Legion raid, though?

Civilians were lining up to tell anyone and everyone they could about what they'd seen.

Some even had *actual* information to share. It was sorting those ones out of the rather enormous crowd of wild-eyed panicky types, psychotics, and deliberate attention-seekers that was the trick.

Luckily, it wasn't Garrett's trick to figure out. He had direct access to the filtered version that had at least passed the muster of a tired Divinity enforcer somewhere along the line. But even that list left more than a little bit to be desired. There were scattered reports that Carlisle had been spotted fleeing the scene with one James Bell, another of Francesco Fields' men. Raish and his raven-haired demon girlfriend hadn't been seen at all. There had been one report from New Amestown of a young couple matching their description, but it apparently hadn't panned out. Garrett moved on.

It was mid-morning by the time he came across anything that truly caught his eye. The incident in question wasn't even from the night of the raid, but from only a few hours earlier, in the dead of the pre-dawn hours, right around when he'd been tossing and turning with visions of Kovaks. Scant as the firm details were, there'd been sightings of two men matching the descriptions of Carlisle and the man he'd likely escaped with, James Bell, another one of Francesco Fields' men. Even more interesting than these lone sightings, though, was the fact that multiple reports mentioned an altercation between the two men and another pair of unidentified assailants—a dark-haired man in dark, nondescript clothing, and a woman in much the same, dark hair cut short.

From the sound of it, things hadn't gone well for the second pair.

Garrett was barely halfway through the aggregated reports of the incident but already pretty sure he knew what he'd found when the door hissed open, and One stepped in looking as frosty—and frighteningly attractive—as ever.

"You're with me, now," was all she said, apparently in no mood to mince words. That only added water to his current theory.

Not feeling particularly impressed or glad for her storm-in routine, Garrett took his time in finishing his line in the report, slipping on his finest smirk, and finally turning to face her. "Any chance this report is about you?"

"I'm gonna kill that gray-haired gropstick," she growled, not bothering to make cute or deny his allegations.

"You caught up with Carlisle, then?"

She crossed her arms, skewering him with her frosty glare. "Are you ready to hit the pavement or not?"

"Five?" Garrett asked, ignoring the question.

"In the medica, sleeping it off. Carlisle dropped him off a rooftop."

She didn't bat an eye over the news, just rattled it right off like she was recounting the highlights of a smashball match.

Garrett glanced back at the display more for an excuse to drop her heartless stare than anything else. "Guess I didn't get to that part yet."

He almost asked if Five was okay, but he imagined One would've mentioned it if the medics weren't expecting the Seeker to pull through. Or maybe it really was that Garrett just didn't care as much as a decent person might.

He looked back at One. "He didn't manage to catch himself from the fall?"

"I don't think he was exactly conscious, strictly speaking."

"Right..."

Garrett didn't need to ask what she meant by that, and she hardly looked to be in any mood to explain, shifting her weight restlessly back and forth, one wrong look away from punching anything that moved.

"Will you just get your scud together?" she said, looking impatiently at the door. "Our friends are waiting, and I've got a feeling today's the day."

Somehow, Garrett didn't share her creepily violent enthusiasm. For a second, he even considered poking the psycho haga beast—maybe because she deserved it, or maybe just for old time's sake. Scud, maybe she just knew how to bring out the sadism lurking in his bones. But apparently not *that* well, because some naive part of him actually seemed to take pity on the icy-eyed demoness in front of him—almost as if it thought she *had* feelings to hurt.

Either way, now was hardly the time to be starting a fight with the High Cleric's favorite pet.

"Just a second," Garrett said, waving the display off and standing to go gather his gear. "Sounds like these reports are missing the good stuff anyway."

By way of reply, she only leaned against the wall and tapped her foot impatiently, arms still crossed.

Oddly enough, Garrett felt mildly relieved as he grabbed his sidearm and his faded green jacket. Much as he wanted to sympathize with Five over the all-too-memorable experience of getting worked over by Carlisle's lightning-quick fists, he was mostly just relieved to have some evidence that it wasn't just his personal failure—that Carlisle was indeed a wild demon beyond any of their skills. Not that *that* was a comforting thought, exactly. Especially not as Garrett stepped up to take Five's place on Team Psychopath. But it was still something.

He'd take it.

Unfortunately, that misguided scrap of warm and fuzzy comfort didn't hang around long. Indeed, it began to decay the moment he laid eyes back on One. It was only when they reached the private skimmer bay and he realized what One had meant by *our friends are waiting* that the comforting thoughts burned away completely.

Two of the enhanced were waiting in the skimmer.

Garrett barely needed his extended senses to tell that's what they were. No one else but Onyx Guard would have sat at such silent, rigid attention awaiting their master's return in an otherwise empty vehicle.

"You..." He trailed off, not knowing how to finish the thought without betraying his hand.

In hindsight, he'd probably been a fool to think the High Cleric would have allowed Kublich to bring him and Three in on a secret he hadn't even told his precious One. Of course she knew about the enhanced. Did that mean her collar was deactivated too? He couldn't help but wonder. Was his, for that matter? Was it really? It was all well and good for Kublich and the High Cleric to say as much, but how could he know for sure?

One was watching him like she could see every racing question in his head.

"How long have you been working with them?" he finally asked.

She just showed him that frosty dead smile of hers. "Worried you're falling out of the loop?"

Sensing there was nowhere for the conversation to go but down from there, Garrett climbed into the skimmer without a word, and did his best not to think about the eerily silent creatures sitting behind him. Whether out of mercy or—infinitely more likely—complete apathy, or her burning desire to go find someone to strangle, One didn't press the matter. They just flew, sweeping Divinity with sight and extended senses, stopping occasionally to let the enhanced have a sniff here and there, mostly out of easy sight given it was broad daylight.

The day passed uneventfully, their visits back to Fields' home and the site of One and Five's scuffle with Carlisle yielding next to nothing. The next day passed with a similar lack of excitement. The day after that, it almost started to feel like they'd fallen back to business as usual. In fact, Garrett was pretty sure they had.

There'd been no word from Kublich about their prisoners, which Garrett took to mean the two hadn't known anything useful about how to find Carlisle and Raish. Aside from one check in call, which had decidedly been directed at One, with Garrett being a happenstance bystander, they'd barely heard from the High Cleric either. The public outcry to find the dangerous terrorists didn't exactly die down, but it at least seemed to stabilize somewhat. And meanwhile, they swept on, finding nothing day after day. Business as usual.

Until the the night of the broadcast.

It happened in the dead of night, nearly half a cycle after the Fields raid. They were just getting to that sunken-eyed hour where Garrett's desire to sleep usually began to win out over his weariness at picking a fight with One. The skimmer amps sparked to life of their own accord. At first, Garrett thought he'd imagined it. Then there came the subtle rustling of someone preparing to speak into a voicer, shortly followed by a voice Garrett couldn't have mistaken.

"Hello, Enochia. My name is Haldin Raish, and I'm..."

It kept coming through the amps—something about coming to them tonight at great risk and how he had something they needed to hear. Garrett could only marginally process the words. He was too busy trading a look of pure, unadulterated shock with One.

It was probably the most genuine thing that had ever passed between the two of them.

Then the moment passed. One flicked the skimmer onto autopilot and started swiping through the skimmer's receiver controls, her movement growing more agitated each time Raish's voice cut off only to reappear on the next setting.

"He's on every gropping frequency," she growled, just before Raish's voice tripled, and Garrett realized their palmlights were now receiving the feed as well.

They shared another look, this one of sudden realization.

"An emergency broadcast," Garrett said.

"Only one line in Divinity," she agreed.

Sanctuary.

It was impossible to think Raish could've made it into the heart of the Legion fortress without being caught—even if he had grown up there. What was even more impossible, though, was what Garrett saw when he glanced from One down to the vid feed on his palmlight.

He was looking at where the enhanced had come from. Somehow, Garrett was sure of that even before his brain began to sort out the details of what he was seeing on the small holographic display—the rows and rows of great big cylinders, filled with murky fluid that couldn't quite hide the silhouettes of the humanoid shapes inside. Hundreds of them. Then the feed shifted, and he saw several more rows of sedated human patients, laid out in neat order on a series of dull gray racks and affixed with an array of straps and IV lines and—

"Turn that scud off," One snapped, taking the controls and gunning them through a hard course change, bound for the northwestern quadrant of Divinity.

"It's an emergency broadcast," Garrett mumbled numbly. He didn't have to look up to know this feed was currently playing on every display in the city—scud, on pretty much every connected display on Enochia.

There *was* no turning it off. That was the point.

Distantly, he felt the heat of One's glare on the side of his face, but he couldn't really bring himself to care about that right then either. Not as Raish prattled on about how something called a raknoth had infected the High General of the Legion and forced the man to murder his parents.

"Kill the volume," One said, in a dangerously low voice.

He finally tore his eyes from the abominations to stare at her, sparing only a quick glance to their backseat passengers, who were as doggedly silent and still as ever. "You're not just the slightest bit curious about all this?"

"Oh, please. You're going to take the crooked words of a fugitive demon over those of our own High Cleric? You knew soldiers were volunteering to be enhanced."

Garrett silenced his palmlight with a pinch of thumb and ring finger. "Those people don't look like volunteers. They look sick."

"You know the demons will say anything to disrupt our mission. Those could be blight patients receiving an experimental treatment for all we know."

Garrett said nothing, watching the display as those murky green cylinders began to drain—the vid work choppy now, like whoever'd had the camera hadn't exactly been steady of hand at the sight.

One grabbed his hand and firmly folded his fingers into a loose half-fist, hiding the palmlight display. "I suppose next you're going to tell me you believed Andre Kovaks' delusions too?

He considered completing that fist and testing the durability of One's icy sneer. Considered it hard. But then what?

Did that even matter?

Before he could decide, she released his hand, glanced at her own palmlight, and touched her earpiece to answer an incoming call. "Your Holiness?"

Garrett sobered, but only momentarily. She was quiet for a few seconds, listening. Garrett stared, on the verge of butting in and demanding to know what they were talking about, chain of holy command be damned. But the conversation was over almost as soon as it began.

"I understand, Holiness," One said. "We'll be right there."

She killed the call with a curl of her fingers and immediately began adjusting their heading yet again, guiding them into an air lane that would take them back toward the White Tower.

"What are we doing?" Garrett asked, hating how impotent the question sounded.

"Following orders."

He clenched his jaw, about ready to burst with the boiling frustration of being swept into the corner like a child. "Do you mind sharing those orders?"

"The High Cleric wants us in his quarters."

"Why?"

She frowned over at him like he'd just asked something truly startling. "We do not question why."

"We do when we have our targets caught in the middle of a Legion fortress, ripe for capture."

"We don't even know they're there. Anyone could have put that vid on."

"Right. Because there are so many apostates out there capable of breaching the mother of all Legion fortresses."

One didn't say anything, but the faint, almost subvocal, growls of the enhanced in the back seat suggested she must've thought something. Garrett glanced back at the creatures, wondering how far his frosty partner was willing to go right now, and what would happen if he countermanded whatever order she'd just given them.

"This is bullscud," he said. "We're blowing the best shot we've had in two years."

"Trust in our High Cleric, Two."

The moment stretched like a frayed suspension cable. Garrett teetered on the edge, looking down at the prospect of catching Raish with nowhere to run on the one side, and the continued shame and dread of being slowly strangled out of his position of favor on the other. He teetered, and finally let the tension bleed out, leaning back into his seat but keeping his senses alert, just in case.

Trust was not something he was sure he could afford to give to anyone right now. Even himself.

Too many lines had been crossed. Too many questions, and too much hand-waving bullscud for answers.

Too many bad feelings churning in his gut.

If One took his silence for loyal submission, she would've been mistaken. But now wasn't the time to do anything rash. Soon, maybe. But not now.

Something stank at the heart of all of this. Something he realized now had been festering there all along. But until he knew what it was—and, more importantly, until he could figure out how to get Alexia out and make sure they wouldn't lose their heads in the process... Until then, he'd play their game.

And not a moment longer.

24

CIVILITY

Garrett woke late with the kind of disoriented start he'd only ever experienced after having been knocked unconscious. He blinked, looking around his quarters for some explanation, feeling a buzzing sense of urgency—about what, he couldn't remember. Only that something important had happened.

Raish.

That was it.

He slid off his cot, padded over to his desk, waving the display to life, and breathed a sigh of relief. That was definitely it. The same topic dominated the reels up and down.

Raish had been captured last night, heading an assault on Sanctuary.

An assault?

That was right. Alpha, why was he so groggy? It was hard to forget the shock upon returning to the White Tower last night only to learn that Carlisle and his apprentice weren't alone in Sanctuary. They'd brought friends. Where those friends had come from, Garrett still wasn't sure, but they'd somehow whipped up enough firepower to create a proper diversion while Raish and Carlisle had waded into the middle of the Legion fortress not only to commandeer Sanctuary's uniquely connected emergency broadcast bunker and distribute their propaganda worldwide, but also to rescue Francesco Fields and Phineas Hammer while they were at it. It had even worked, right up until the part where Raish hadn't made it out of there with his friends.

The Legion had made short work of the larger assault force too, of course, and had subsequently locked Sanctuary down to finish the clean up. But the damage had been done. And Carlisle had escaped.

Which was why the High Cleric had called him and One back last night, he remembered with sudden clarity. With the situation coming back under control, his Holiness had been worried Carlisle might just be mad enough to strike at the White Tower itself while they were all focused on Sanctuary. Which, considering what the crazy bastards had just finished pulling off, might've been a fair concern.

Garrett blinked, trying to remember what One had said last night when their wild propaganda broadcast had started. Something important, he thought. But apparently not important enough to remember.

The broadcast itself was officially being classified as an act of high treason after the slanderous, verifiably false claims about the leadership of the Sanctum and the Legion, and the fact that the vid footage itself had since been identified by analysts as a skillfully manufactured fake. Not that Carlisle and Raish had been lacking on grounds of treason to begin with —or pretty much any other high crime under the stars. But that much, the reel headlines all agreed upon. From there, the details in each story began to diverge, picking up all manner of extra features and speculation.

Garrett sank into his chair, completely absorbed in the reels, flipping from one article to the next. There were several interesting tidbits, some enlightening, others just plain wild. One freelancer had written a rather frantic piece about the beastly howls he'd heard carrying over the walls of Sanctuary, claiming that it was "as if the gates of demons' depths themselves had opened wide and spewed their evil onto the Legion's doorstep."

If only he knew.

Still, for all of the madness, Garrett felt a tenuous sense of calmness settling over him as he reviewed the situation. Raish had finally been captured. Had been brought, in fact, to the White Tower, Garrett seemed to recall, before he'd fallen into the sleep of the dead so deeply he'd nearly forgotten his own name. Sweet Alpha, he'd been tired. Why had he been so tired?

And more importantly, he thought, sitting up straighter, did Raish's current captors understand how dangerous it was to hold a demon of his strength in captivity at all? Quickly as the worry rose, though, so too came the memory of his own imprisonment at Carlisle's and Raish's hands, and of that cursed little pendant cutting his gifts and extended senses down to the confines of his own body, shrouding the outside world completely. Garrett still didn't quite understand how such a thing was possible, but he trusted the High Cleric was shrewd enough to see to it the demon's own device was used against him. Right?

It wouldn't hurt to go check. But even the low-grade pang of worry in his gut couldn't tarnish the rare spirit of hope rising up in his chest like the morning sun.

Raish was captured. And with that leverage on hand, for the first time in a long while, Garrett actually felt confident that Carlisle would soon be following his pupil.

He stood and went to get dressed with a sense of purpose he hadn't felt in cycles, certain that they were closer to the freedom of their new world than they'd ever been.

FINDING RAISH'S cell wasn't hard. Unsurprisingly, there weren't that many of them in the White Tower, and given how rarely ceremonial executions actually happened these days, the staff and Sanctum Guard tended to use the same one each time, down in the sub basements where casual observers never ventured. Garrett hadn't bothered asking before he came down to check on Raish. In hindsight, it might've been wise, but he also didn't love the idea of asking permission to do his job.

Still, that didn't keep him from tensing in the empty service lift when his palmlight buzzed with a message from One.

<Where are you? We have guests to escort upstairs. Loading Bay C.>

That was what had been nagging at the back of his mind since he woke. He was supposed to meet One to help with... he frowned. With what again?

With moving the new unit of enhanced soldiers up into the High Cleric's quarters. That was it. For the grand unveiling—the announcement, following Raish's death, that the enhanced had been the ones who'd made the demon's capture possible. Seeding the public with the notion of safety from the gifted before the full scope of their existence was revealed. It was a good first step toward their new world. He was sure of that, even if he'd been too tired to remember much else from the conversation.

But first, Raish.

Consciously pressing aside the feeling that he was doing something wrong, Garrett stepped off the lift, wondering if he should message One back or just hurry it up here and then go meet her. The faint buzz of voices ahead caught his attention before he could decide. They were coming through the open slit on the cell door.

He drew up to the closer of the two Sanctum Guard posted outside the door. "Who's in there with Raish?" he asked quietly.

"Barbara Sanders, sir," the Guard replied. "Private interview."

Barbara Sanders the WAN reporter? Probably so, if the faint edge of excitement in the Guard's voice was any indication. She was a minor celebrity.

What the scud was she doing here?

Beside him, the Guard stiffened, as if only then remembering himself.

"She had the proper authentication, sir. It all checked out."

"It's fine," Garrett said, waving the Guard down and wondering once again whether it was wise, allowing this thing to blow up into such a public spectacle rather than just ending Raish in a quiet corner.

But the High Cleric knew what he was doing. Garrett trusted that much. The people needed to see the wicked punished before they could feel safe again. And especially before they could be expected to even begin to come around to the idea of Alpha's gifted living among them. Still, Garrett had a feeling he wouldn't be shedding the tension from his shoulders until this was all over.

He stepped closer to the door, listening in.

"I've heard a lot of interesting rumors, actually," came a familiar, soothing voice. That was definitely Barbara Sanders. "I want to know what you believe happened."

Garrett felt two more Sanctum Guard inside the cell, watching over the so-called private interview.

"It doesn't matter what I believe," came Raish's voice. "All that matters is the truth."

"You would have made a fine reporter."

Silence stretched in the cell. Garrett felt the two guards inside shifting uncomfortably. He raised a palm toward the access panel, but stopped himself, curious to see where this was going.

"Let me ask you this," Raish finally said. "When's the last time you saw a teenager sentenced to hang by the High Cleric himself just for trying to spin tall tales?"

"You did break into a Legion base, Mister Raish. A base that's apparently so badly damaged from... well, badly damaged enough that they closed the gates for repairs."

"That wasn't our doing," Raish said. "I can tell you that much."

Yeah, well then whose doing was it, you little scudder? Garrett nearly called through the slit. He held silent, though, waiting, curious for some reason to see what the kid would say.

"An ill-timed uprising then," Sanders finally said. "Fine. But that doesn't explain the multiple other counts of terroristic activities on your file. Are you suggesting those claims are inaccurate?"

"Do I seem like a terrorist to you?" Raish asked, the agitation rising in his voice. He sounded... righteous. Too righteous. Delusional or not, it made Garrett uncomfortable.

He'd heard enough.

"Yeah, yeah," Garrett said, letting the derision bleed through his voice. He palmed the access panel and stepped into the cell. "Work the sob story, kid. See what good it does you."

He almost wavered when he took in the pair inside the cell. Though there wasn't much left to see beneath the chains and the long, dark execution robe they'd already dressed him in, Raish still plainly looked like he'd been trampled by a pack of haga beasts. And the look in his eyes when he caught sight of Garrett...

If ever Garrett could've been intimidated by the stare of a seventeen year old Legion brat, it would've been then.

As it was, he was too busy suppressing his panic and drawing his mental defenses tight.

Raish's mind was decidedly *not* contained.

No arcane shroud. Not even any sedatives. Yet he lay there, chained and helpless. Why?

Garrett brushed against the flat, disc-shaped pendant resting on Raish's chest beneath his dark robe. Was it possible the thing was incapacitating Raish without cutting him off completely? He had no idea, but when he drew his senses back, Raish didn't follow. Garrett forced himself to take a breath. And a calm few steps toward Raish, just in case, putting himself in easy striking distance as he turned to Barbara Sanders.

On the surface, Sanders looked composed as ever, with her neat suit, and her dark curls and cute little upturned nose. But her eyes were pensive as she glanced between him and Raish. Troubled.

"Listen," he said, adopting a tone of reason, "this kid's not some harmless little pup who accidentally scudded the carpet. He's put half a dozen guys I know into the medica." Not that he knew their *names* or anything. But still... "Scud, he threw me out of a damn lev tram and left me to die in an abandoned underway tunnel. He's dangerous, and you should just be glad he's not out there to hurt anyone else."

"Barbara," Raish said, his eyes never once leaving Garrett, "allow me to introduce you to Garrett, the human scudspout who's willing to sell his own kind to—"

Garrett wasn't sure what secrets or bullscud tales was preparing to spill out. He wasn't even sure why the righteous condescension in the kid's tone and eyes shot so violently under his skin in that moment. All he knew was that he'd smacked the little bastard's mouth shut before he could even stop to register how bad it might look to the civilian reporter.

"Hey!" Sanders cried.

Oh well. It wasn't like she'd ever be seeing him again. And however she'd managed to score access to Raish, it was far too late for her sympathies to make any difference here anyway. If anything, Garrett was more concerned with the way Raish glared up at him, taking the strike in dead silence, like it nourished some dark part of him. There was violence in those eyes. Violence, and the kind of indomitable will that nearly made Garrett take a step back despite Raish's generous shackles and chains.

"Merciful Alpha," Sanders added, "let's be civil here!"

For a moment, Garrett swore Raish was thinking about spitting in his face. He kind of hoped the kid would, just to show Sanders that he was in fact the animal Garrett claimed him to be. Instead, the little bastard decided to take the high road. Garrett hung there hesitating, off balance by the entire situation, and not really sure how best to determine whether Raish was in fact fully bound by the pendant at his breast.

The cell door hissed open before he could.

"That's quite enough, Garrett," came an all-too-familiar voice from the hall.

Garrett froze at the sound of that voice—at the sound of his *name* on that tongue. His feet backed him up against the far wall, next to the two Sanctum Guard, and he bowed his head in some combination of guilt and fear, knowing he'd been caught. Never mind that he'd come to assuage valid concerns. He'd been caught.

He felt, rather than saw, the High Cleric step slowly into the room. Just like he felt the blinding astral body of telepathic presence that stepped in beside His Holiness. What were they even doing here? Garrett glanced up, careful to keep his head deferentially tilted, but desperately needing to see. And there they were.

Gone was the strength the High Cleric had sometimes shown during their private councils. He shuffled into the cell like a frail old man, hanging on the supportive arm of the gray-haired, shoddy-robed man Garrett had seen in His Holiness' quarters following his shameful return from the failed Fields raid.

And last night, too? Had this dark stranger been there during last night's council with One and the High Cleric?

Garrett stared at those sharp pale eyes, and couldn't remember. Something rustled at the edge of his mind. Something he couldn't put his finger on. The feeling only deepened when he noticed Raish's reaction. The kid had gone as pale as the bruises on his face would allow. Fear. That was fear in his eyes. Fear like Garrett had never witnessed from the demon, even back in that alleyway, when he'd had the kid cornered barely an hour after his awakening.

This seemed to please the High Cleric, though he kept his expression fairly neutral. The cleric's mysterious companion, on the other hand... He might as well have been walking dead for all the emotion he showed. He simply ghosted along beside the High Cleric, offering support with such silent disinterest that it was as if he was barely there at all.

The High Cleric paused to allow Sanders to wish him good blessings and kiss the ring of his office, then he turned to face Raish, the golden flow of his ornate robes antithetic to the boy's dark execution robes and the red serpent emblazoned on his chest.

"We will speak to the fallen alone," the High Cleric said, clearly to the entire room, though his gaze lingered solely on Garrett.

Something about that look...

The two Sanctum Guard started for the door without question. Garrett thought about reaching out to telepathically ask His Holiness if he might stay. If they were here to speak with Raish about his master, after all, shouldn't he be here to help, and to hear the kid's answers? He didn't see why not. Yet something about the look in the High Cleric's eyes started his feet moving toward the door anyway, his good senses telling him now was not the time to incur His Holiness' displeasure with any hint of disobedience.

Sanders lingered behind only a moment longer, looking at Raish uncertainly, but then she followed too. The cell door hissed down behind her—but not before Garrett caught the look the High Cleric's escort shot him with those frighteningly sharp eyes of his.

That look, just like the High Cleric's...

The door finished closing, and the open slit slid shut faster than the cleric or his man could've possibly reached it. Telekinesis, Garrett assumed. It hardly mattered. Clearly, whatever they had to say to Raish, they wanted it to be private. Then again, Garrett wasn't really sure there'd be words involved at all. Maybe they'd simply come to break into Raish's mind. And the look they'd both given Garrett... like he'd crossed a line. Like he'd made one misstep too many.

His gut squirmed uneasily in the silence of the hallway, and the unwanted company of Barbara Sanders and the four Sanctum Guard.

"Is this standard procedure?" Sanders asked quietly.

The Sanctum Guard all exchanged faceless golden looks, none of them wanting to ignore Barbara Sanders, probably, but none of them sure what they could faithfully say. It didn't matter. Her tone said she already knew the answer to her question, and her attention was fixed directly on Garrett anyway.

"What are they going to do to him in there?"

Garrett looked at the cell door, more to shirk her persistent gaze than anything else. Thinking about Raish alone in there with the High Cleric and his mysterious ally, though, he couldn't help but ask himself the same question. What were they going to do to Raish?

And what were they going to do to *him* once they'd finished with the apostate?

Garrett turned for the service lift, suddenly sure that he did not want to be found loitering out here when the High Cleric had finished with Raish.

"Hey!" Barbara hissed, falling in on his flank. "Hey, where are you going? What's going on here?"

He kept walking, ignoring her, head spinning with the sudden and inexorable certainty that something was wrong here—something he couldn't see or point out, maybe. But something.

Something he couldn't remember.

The thought sent a flash of sickening, crimson pain washing through the center of his brain, flooding out everything else—even sight and sound —so abruptly that he thought he might've sprouted a brain bleed. Quickly as it came, though, it washed away, leaving him on wobbly feet, panting and staring out of the lift car at a disgruntled Sanders, who'd paused just outside the lift, staring right back like she thought he might drop on the spot. So she'd noticed, apparently. Noticed *what*, exactly?

Sanders gathered her wits and moved to follow him into the lift before he could sort it out.

"Do yourself a favor, lady," he growled, stepping up to bar the way. "Just stop asking questions and tell these people what they want to hear. Do you understand?"

He wasn't really sure why he said it, or what he cared at all, what she said. But the words came out all the same. She searched his face with dark, inquisitive eyes, her fair skin pulsing oddly to his eyes in the discolored aftermath of whatever the scud had just wracked his brain. Finally, she relented and gave a curt nod.

Garrett held her gaze a few moments longer, until he was sure she truly did understand, then he stepped back into the lift and punched the controls for a floor halfway up the Tower. He didn't even notice which floor. Just needed to move. Get somewhere and think.

That flash. That... emptiness. Something he couldn't remember. Something brought on by the look in that strange man's eyes down below. The eyes. Judgment. Failure.

A flash of crimson pain.

Garrett jammed the urgent halt button and scrambled out of the lift in a half-blind panic, not knowing where he was going, unable to care. He hurried down the hallway, his feet carrying him by motor memory and old habits rather than any conscious thought, until he fell unseeingly onto the stone bench they led him to. He buried his face in his hands, trying to catch his ragged breath, to center his screaming thoughts.

What was this? What was happening to his head?

The sound of approaching footsteps nearly made him bolt on sheer animal instinct. But when he whipped around, it was only a passing acolyte, eyeing him with timid concern.

"Alpha's blessing to you," she said, with an inflection that made it sound like more of a question than an empty platitude.

Do you need help? that tone asked. *Might you lay your burdens down on my shoulders?*

Somehow, Garrett wasn't sure this kind acolyte was ready to receive his burden—and definitely not ready to learn that her High Cleric was a... telepath, and that last night he'd...

"And to you," he distantly heard himself say, far more concerned with the way his mind filled in the details of last night's conversations, too hyperfocused on certain words and particulars, too disjointed at the edges. Like a cheap polymer knock off. "Good day," he mumbled, noticing the acolyte was still watching him.

She took the hint and continued on her way with a polite nod, leaving Garrett alone with his spinning thoughts in the small alcove his scrambling feet had brought him to of their own accord—one of the many worship shrines that dotted most every floor of the White Tower, little more than a stone bench and an Alpha sigil to receive wandering prayers and more than a few guilt-ridden sinners' penitent breakdowns.

Not a bad place to have a quiet.... what? A quiet panic attack? No. Maybe. He didn't know. He'd never had a panic attack before.

But then again, up until last night, he was also pretty sure he'd never had his memory wiped, either.

2 5

———

LOOPHOLES

A memory wipe?

He was imagining things. Being paranoid. Had lost it completely, even.

But as Garrett stepped into the service lift—having first cut across the Tower just to avoid the chance of intersecting the High Cleric and his sharp-eyed friend on their way back up from visiting Raish—he couldn't deny that it also felt like he was making the right decision, from the core of his instincts right down to his little toe.

Which was probably exactly how a paranoid madman always felt when they were swimming in the depths of their insanity.

But it didn't matter. The idea had caught, and he couldn't turn away from it now. Not without at least checking a few pertinent details. At worst he'd realize his paranoid delusions were accurate, and then... Well, scud, he didn't even know what then.

And this was all assuming that One didn't find him first, anyway, and murder him for leaving her to handle their duties in preparing for tonight's grand unveiling.

She'd just have to get over it. Or not, if this ludicrous hunch of his turned out to hold any water. Scud, she could have even been the one who'd done this to him.

You're being crazy.

Last he could remember, she'd—

Crimson pain flashed through his head, born on a crackling wave of angry static noise, the memories in his head fighting back like entrenched soldiers realizing that the act was indeed past, and that their very existence was now under attack. That reaction alone probably told him all he needed to know. Probably, he should've headed for the nearest skimmer bay, flown straight to Serenity, and extracted Alexia before anyone noticed he was gone.

But he couldn't. Not until he knew they could actually make it out with their heads attached.

And besides, none of this actually proved anything. Odd headaches and fuzzy memories? Maybe he'd just cracked under the stress, downed a bottle of firewater, and gotten too rip-roaring drunk to remember anything. Maybe he'd been drugged for another reason. As beaten and sleep-deprived as his body was, he wasn't sure he even would've noticed the aftereffects of any such drugs. And there was that sleep deprivation itself to consider. Not to mention the serial string of physical and psychological traumas he'd been through.

None of that exactly added up to a stable mind.

Yet, as the service lift slowed to his target floor, some part of him was sure of it, deep down, on a plane well below cold logic and conscious memory: something was wrong here. And he was going to get to the bottom of it.

He stepped off the lift and turned for a section of the White Tower where no Seeker had ever been intended to set foot—the out-of-the-way cluster of offices where, if that clumsy acolyte's intel had been genuine on that fateful day, Garrett would find the tech-heads of Watchtower control.

He still wasn't really sure how he was going to spot what he was looking for when he got there. He'd never seen these people, after all. And much as the handlers' dominion in the White Tower had languished since Cleric Faden had taken over where that lecherous bastard Verner had left off, he doubted the clerics would take kindly to it when they inevitably heard about this.

But Garrett didn't have a choice any more. Times had either changed, or they hadn't. He supposed that was really the heart of what he was here to find out. Just like he should've done the day after High General Kublich had guaranteed that he and Three were free men, and that the collars at their throats would never again be anything but a convincing fashion accessory to keep their "handlers" at peace until the High Cleric's revolution was revealed.

And maybe that was all true. Maybe Garrett really had lost it.

But by the light of Alpha, he was going to have his answers today. Just as soon as he found his target, with nothing to go on but an office wing and the single voice that'd spoken to him over the Lights on the few rare occasions when direct Watchtower support had been necessary in the field. He didn't even know the name that had belonged to that voice. He'd just called him Watchtower. But he was at least pretty sure it had been the same voice each time. He just had to trust he'd know Goodfellow Watchtower when he saw him.

At the front of the wing, the office cluster had the same faded white polymer monotony that Garrett had come to expect from the world of the tablet pushers and the data-fondling administrators—the world that somehow continued to cling to its dreary existence despite the fact that the majority of its output might well have been node-automated over a century ago.

This office front looked every bit as bland and lifeless as the rest. It was the look in one plump, dark-haired servitor's eyes that told him he was indeed in the right place.

She recognized him. And she just as clearly tried to hide that fact after her initial flash of wide-eyed surprise, dropping her gaze and reaching with forced casualness for her tablet.

Garrett reached out with his extended senses and severed the device's connection with its energy cell before she could thumb whatever alarm she might've been reaching for. The servitor froze, unable to keep the shock out of her eyes this time as she turned silently back to Garrett. A few other bored administrators glanced up from their nodes at the new entry. Most stayed riveted to their displays. None of them seemed to recognize him.

Scud, most of them didn't even appear to be fully conscious.

Was this really Watchtower control? Did these people even know what they were doing here—who it was they were keeping afloat whenever they reached out to sweep away a suspicious report here, or to provide a blind Sanctum security pass there?

The servitor's eyes said yes. But if the rest of their reactions were any indication, most of Watchtower control didn't have a clue what he was, or whose trails they were keeping clear on a daily basis. Only that Alpha—or the High Cleric, at least—willed it.

Garrett stifled his incredulity and calmly strode to the servitor's desk. Whatever *she* might've known about him was at least enough that she looked like she might scream. Her wide brown eyes darted back and forth from Garrett to the closed door on her left. Across the way, all but a few of her colleagues puttered on with their nodes, blissfully ignorant of the existence of anything outside of their data sheets.

"He's expecting me," Garrett said to the servitor on a hunch, waving down her feeble objections and pausing only long enough to shoot her his best demon-eyes stare. "See to it we aren't interrupted."

Or else, he added with the demon eyes.

Then he continued on for the door she'd so clearly denoted with her frantic glances, not waiting to see whether or not she'd coax a response from her trembling lips. He couldn't help but feel a bit of smug satisfaction at the effect. Much as he didn't fancy himself a sadist, it was kind of nice to know he wasn't the only person in this Tower who had to deal with the fear of his existence.

Would his good friend, code name Watchtower, feel the same way?

At the door, Garret made a show of raising his hand close to the access panel even as he reached out with his senses to manually trigger the opening mechanism, just as he'd done with the door to the office cluster outside. Out of all the doors in the White Tower, he would've been shocked if this one wasn't off limits to a Seeker access profile, and a chiming red "Access Denied" wouldn't really lend credence to his act.

On some level, he also wanted to think the precaution would double to cover his tracks should anyone be monitoring the access logs throughout the Tower, but he was pretty sure that particular skimmer had set sail the moment he'd stepped foot in this office. There was no way his presence here wouldn't be reported the moment he left—if not sooner.

But he'd deal with that later.

The door hissed open, his palm still hovering an inch from the panel, and he stepped inside, ready for answers. What he found instead was a bolt-upright tech-head watching him with a deep furrow in his ebony brow and an expression of shock even more pronounced than the servitor's outside. He was slender, and trembling. And kind of pathetic.

Could this be the voice of Watchtower? Was this really the man whose every word had once sent cold tingles radiating down Garrett's collared neck?

Garrett took another step forward, allowing the door to slide shut before the shaking tech-head could shout or give voice to his clear shock. But the man didn't make a peep. He just sat there, his shock slowly bleeding off, replaced by some silent mixture of helpless apprehension and sinking dread, like he knew exactly what came next, and had in fact been awaiting this day for years.

"I'm not here to hurt you," Garrett finally said, when he was sure the man wouldn't jump or scream at the sound of his voice.

The man just shuddered instead, nervous twitches jolting through his head and neck, eyes furiously blinking. "Not supposed to—Sorry— Not supposed to be here at all," he gushed out, blinking jerkily all the while.

And that was it. Even through the shaky panic, the voice was unmistakably that of the man Garret knew only as Watchtower.

This trembling tree of lanky limbs. This was the man who'd stood by at the trigger nodes all this time?

"Sorry," the rattled tech-head continued spitting out, flinching under Garrett's scrutiny. "You're just..." *Blink. Blink. Twitch.* "... Just not supposed to ever be here. Not supposed to..." *Blink. Blink.* A look of sudden horror as he remembered himself and focused back on Garrett. "Uh, sorry. Please don't... I mean..."

He couldn't even manage the words that were so clearly written across his every feature. *Please don't kill me.*

Alpha, it was pathetic. So pathetic that Garrett almost couldn't believe he was correct about the man's identity, voice match or no. Granted, it wasn't like Watchtower had ever been a burly-voiced pillar of gruff, but he'd at least seemed calm and collected most of the time—and disconnected more often than not. Not at all like the sputtering mess in front of Garrett now.

Garrett wasn't sure whether to be pissed or pitying. He settled for a long sigh. "Look, I just need to know the status on two of the collars. Answer my questions, and we both go on with our days like nothing happened."

Or not. But the promise would suffice to start. Only the man known as Watchtower was already shaking his head—quickly, frantically, like he didn't even know he was doing it.

"I'm not asking," Garrett said, taking another step forward.

"I know! I know!" Watchtower blurted, holding up his hands in surrender. "It's just that, uh..." He scanned Garrett's face apprehensively, clearly not excited about what he was about to say. "It's just that there haven't been any changes to the system since, well aside from..."

He cowered back at the flash of anger in Garrett's eyes, unable to finish his sentence.

"Check the system," Garrett said, pushing aside the cold dread seeping into his gut. He didn't know for sure yet. This sad excuse for a Watchtower was clearly not thinking straight. And someone else could have carried out the High Cleric's order anyways, right?

"Check," he repeated, hot anger flickering higher and higher with each pathetic shake of Watchtower's head. "It only happened a couple cycles ago. Two deactivations. Check it, damn you!" he half-shouted as the head-shaking intensified. He clenched his jaw, silently cursing the outburst that might well have been heard in the office outside. But at least it got him somewhere.

"I, uh... Okay. Yeah. Yeah," Watchtower said, sinking down to his high-backed chair and swiveling slowly to face the wall of displays, his hands held high in plain view the whole time. "I... I'm doing it."

"Hurry it up," Garrett said as the man begin to swipe his way through his node controls, his movements gaining speed and stability as he sank into the familiar task. The command was wasted breath, anyway. If Watchtower was right—if the sinking feeling in Garrett's gut was right—it made no difference whether the man hurried it up or not. Because Garrett would still be trapped in his explosive noose. Trapped. Just like he'd always been.

"Please, I don't know what to say," Watchtower said while he worked. "I don't know what they told you, but I don't have the access authority to deactivate anything. No one does, as far as I know. It's just you guys and the High Cleric, man. I swear."

"Then what are *you* here for?" Garrett growled.

"Just—Just monitoring, mostly. Just keeping an eye on things. Running manual checks. Flagging erratic activity. That kind of thing." He glanced guiltily back at Garrett. "And standing by to assist in the event that the, uh, recovery protocol should become necessary."

The *recovery* protocol? Was that what this twitchy bastard and his tablet-pushing friends called blowing twelve human heads clean from their necks?

"Look," the tech-head pressed on, glancing uncomfortably toward the door, unaware of Garrett's building rage. "I might know more than most about the Seeker initiative, but that doesn't mean I know much." He turned back to his work on the displays. "I don't know where you came from or what you did before. Most of the time, I don't even know the specifics of what you're doing out there. No one in this operation gets a single scrap more than what we need to do our parts, so I just want you to know..."

In some distant corner of his mind, Garrett was aware that the trembling man known as Watchtower was still talking, prattling on about how and why this whole big mess wasn't really any of his fault, and how he had a family, and how it was nothing personal. But Garrett barely registered a word of it. He was too busy staring at the green text lines of the list that had appeared on the central display.

SEEKER INITIATIVE - Status Report

One ... Active, In-Range (0.23 m; 33.49573, 37.89552)

Two ... Active, In-Range (0.01 m; 33.49533, 37.89491)

It went on down the line, every single collar reading green, active, and in-range across Enochia. All except one, whose line of red text stood in stark contrast to the others.

Three ... Deactivated (manual), Deceased (killed in action)

Garrett stared at the display in numb shock, his eyes tracing over the two most important lines again and again until they ceased to have any meaning at all in the thickening mess of his fragmented thoughts.

Two ... Active, In-Range (0.01 m; 33.49533, 37.89491)
Six ... Active, In-Range (1,082 m; 8.79453, 31.23241)

"This isn't right," Garrett finally murmured. The sound of his thin voice reminded him where he was, and what that apparently still meant for his mortal safety.

"This isn't right," he repeated, less shakily this time. "Reload the report. Update it."

"This is real-time," Watchtower said, avoiding Garrett's eyes. "I'm sorry, man."

Sorry? He was *sorry*? This tech-head civie who played Alpha with twelve human lives, insuring they were ready to pop at the press of a button, even now eyeing Garrett's collar like he expected it might blow at any second?

"I'm really sorry," the cowering heap of scud known as Watchtower confirmed. "But if you don't want the High Cleric to find out about all this, I'm going to have to insist you—"

Watchtower got his explosion then, albeit not the one he'd feared.

Garrett barely even thought about reaching out or drawing the requisite energy. He just raised a clenched fist in Watchtower's direction, and suddenly the man was floating several feet above his chair, suspended by nothing but the crushing embrace of Garrett's wrath.

"What the—" the tech-head hissed, hands scrabbling frantically for something to grab onto. "How the—"

Garrett squeezed harder, and the struggling stopped—out of sheer terror or physical necessity at the increasing pressure, he wasn't really sure. Nor did he particularly care.

"Please..." Watchtower gasped with clear effort, eyes bulging now. "Please, I don't... What... What... are... you?"

Garrett let up on the pressure more out of surprise than sympathy. Maybe the man really didn't know a thing about the Seekers. Garrett wasn't sure whether that made his compliance in managing the collar system more deplorable, or less so. It wasn't like he could really judge anyway, after all the lives he'd ended on the Sanctum's say-so.

All that mattered now was getting the freedom he'd been promised by those lying bastards.

"Daveen?" a female voice crackled from the Watchtower's node. "Is everything okay in there?"

The servitor, checking in, obviously worried she'd done the wrong thing in letting him pass. Garrett was mildly surprised she hadn't just hopped straight to calling the Sanctum Guard the moment he'd left her alone. But then maybe he'd been more convincing—or intimidating— than he'd hoped.

He lowered Daveen the trembling Watchtower back to his chair with telekinesis, and held him on the end of a dangerous stare instead. "Tell her, or I'll make you tell her."

Head spasmodically bobbing more than actually nodding, Daveen reached for the node's holo controls and fingered a comm icon. "We're in the middle of something," he snapped, terrified nerves spilling over nicely into the tone of an irked superior. "No interruptions, Deborah. Please."

With a few flicks of his fingers, Daveen threw the feed from an outside camera up onto one of the corner displays, just in time for them to watch the mollified servitor arch a brow at her own display and dismiss her boss with an annoyed shrug.

"Smart choice," Garrett said, meaning it.

With an explosive sigh, Daveen's rigid posture collapsed down into a sad heap, every ounce of willpower leaving his body. "Please, I don't know what you're caught up in, or what you were hoping to find here. I don't even know..." He shook his head weakly, eyes still on the floor. "I thought it was all just... ghost stories, the things they say about you and your team. They told me you're all criminals and murderers, all demon-touched. I didn't think..."

He shook his head more violently, then looked up at Garrett, eyes full of desperation. "I don't want to know what's going on. I don't even want to stop you. So please don't mistake what I'm about to say as my attempt at playing tough, but, well... you can't threaten me into deactivating your collar, if that's what you're after. I'm sorry."

His hands shot up in pitiful surrender like they were rigged on a pressure sensor to Garrett's tightening jaw.

"I'm sorry, I can't!" he hissed. "The system was built to be immune to exactly this kind of thing. Even if I wanted to help you..." He shook his head helplessly. "There's just no way to do it. No way to shut it down without triggering the recovery protocol. Not without the High Cleric's authorization."

"Authorization?" Garrett growled, taking a step closer. "You need to understand something, Daveen. The stories you've heard about demons? They're all true. The High Cleric is the least of your worries right now. I'm not even going to bother threatening physical pain, or threatening your family. No..."

He bent down and clamped the man's trembling jaw with rigid fingers, forcing Daveen to meet his eyes.

"... If you don't give me what I want, Daveen, I'm just going to delve into your sad little mind and *make* you do it." He squeezed harder. "I will *break* you. Do you understand?"

Daveen's attempts at a nod were so shaky Garrett thought for a second the man might be seizing. But he was almost to the tipping point. Garrett could feel it just as surely as he could feel the invisible pressure of the High Cleric's hand tightening around his still-active collar.

This was it. Alpha's Chosen or not, lies and half-truths aside, Garrett had crossed a line in coming here. He knew that now just as clearly as he'd known deep down what he was going to find the moment he'd stepped off that lift. He'd known all along, he realized, somewhere down in the sickened feeling he got every time he thought of Kovaks or Raish, or questioned why things were unfolding the way they were. Because he'd been right.

Something was wrong. And he needed to get the scud out of here.

Deactivate the collars.

Get Alexia.

Run.

That was all that was left for it. And his only answer to Step One was right here, shuddering in his hands.

He tightened his hold on the man he'd known as Watchtower. "So what are you going to do for me, Daveen?"

For a second, the tech-head's only reply was to shake uncontrollably. Then he opened his trembling lips and managed a few words. "There.... There might be a way..."

Garrett loosened his grip a little, just enough to demonstrate that cooperation would be rewarded. "Might?"

"I don't know. Maybe. There's... There's a feature. A loophole, maybe. Please... Please..."

Garrett studied the tech-head's face, looking for any sign of deceit, then finally released the man's jaw and allowed the man to slump back into a miserable pile, all too aware of how dead he was going to be if this didn't work.

"Start talking, Daveen."

2 6

YOU FIRST

"Did you confuse softsteel for caffa this morning?" One's harsh tone cut through the growing din at the head of the Great Hall, cranking up the burners on Garrett's already troubled thoughts and directing his attention over to where she'd just emerged—ostensibly from the High Cleric's quarters beyond the wall of the first plateau step.

"That might explain a few things," Garrett admitted, doing his best to push aside his immediate panic at seeing her and focus on the here and now.

She didn't know where he'd been that afternoon—what he'd learned about the "freedom" he'd been granted. Or maybe she did. Either way, his only play here was to do his part and standby while Haldin Raish met his public end.

Of course, he already *had* done his part, as far as he knew.

Drawn by that thought, his gaze tracked in the direction of the second plateau above, where he'd just delivered Raish to the archaic gallows and to the Tower's rotund simpleton of a hangman. After everything else that'd happened in the past few hours, he was still more than a little uneasy that the High Cleric had sent him—and not One, or anyone else—to collect Raish when the time had come.

It should have been comforting—proof that the High Cleric had no reason to suspect Garrett's disloyalty and treachery in paying a visit to Watchtower. Instead, Garrett could only worry that His Holiness *did* know and had in fact been watching Garrett from afar all along, waiting for his wayward Seeker to try something stupid.

Stop it.

He'd delivered Raish. He'd done his job. There was no reason for anyone to think otherwise.

So then why did he feel like he was going to be sick?

And why was One still watching him like a hungry hawk?

"Can I help you with something?" he asked, crossing his arms and reaching for his most salty smirk.

"Where the scud have you been?" she asked, apparently too irritated to bother with their usual sadistic foreplay.

"I got sidetracked trying to make sure Raish was actually secure. Not really any standard procedure for holding a demon captive. Not that anyone else around here seemed too worried about that. You all know something I don't?"

He doubted that turning the suspicion back on One would distract her from his scuddy excuse for his absence that afternoon—especially if she'd been in contact with the High Cleric and learned that he'd in fact disappeared from Raish's holding cell shortly after His Holiness and his alarmingly powerful telepathic companion had arrived. But it sure sounded a lot better than a more honest, *Oh, just plotting to shirk our lying master's chains and get the scud out of here before he can kill us all, you miserable psychopath.*

Whether or not One bought his act, he couldn't have said. She just glared at him a few seconds longer, then gestured for him to follow her across the front of the Great Hall. She turned, not waiting to see if he would, and set off along the wall of the first plateau step.

"His Holiness wishes for us to remain ready below his dais should Carlisle and the rest of his cohort attempt to interrupt the ceremony," One said without looking when Garrett caught up to her near the main entrance to the High Cleric's quarters.

Before Garrett could ask how likely they thought that possibility was, he realized he already knew the answer. They'd all talked about it during their meeting last night, after all. Carlisle and Raish had showed no lack of demonic audacity up till now, and there was no reason to think they'd start here. That was why the High Cleric had decided this would be the perfect time to reveal the existence of the enhanced. Part grand unveiling. Part insurance policy.

It all added up with such neat, tidy certainty that Garrett almost missed the telltale smudges of the dissonance at the edges of the memories.

Had those been tampered with as well, then?

He shot a sideways glance at One and wondered, not for the first time, whether he shouldn't come clean about what he'd learned that afternoon, or at least try to figure out if she was in the same boat he was. Was it so crazy to think that maybe she too was acting on blind faith, falsely believing that her freedom had already been granted by her beloved High Cleric? Maybe her memories had been tampered with last night as well. Maybe behind those cold eyes of hers, she was just as rattled as he was about what was happening here.

Maybe, he thought, as they passed the huge stone disc of the main entrance to the High Cleric's quarters and headed for the much smaller door beyond. Maybe.

But none of that changed the fact that breathing even a single word of his concerns to One could quite possibly mean death if he was wrong. It was inconceivably reckless. An unnecessary wrinkle in an already shoddy plan. Just plain stupid, really.

Which, for some reason, was all to say that it only seemed to make that much more sense when Garrett found his feet drawing to a halt, and his mouth moving to action of its own accord.

"One."

She paused, hand halfway to the discreet access panel beside the equally discreet side door, not looking at him.

Behind them, he was dimly aware of the thickening background roar of the growing crowd of spectators. He could simply let the moment pass, the desperate voice of reason pointed out. He didn't have to say anything more—would be an idiot to do so. And yet he couldn't seem to stop himself.

"Why don't I remember?"

He could have played it more cautiously—asked what she'd thought about last night's talks, or something equally non-specific. But if he was going to throw out a lifeline, he might as well mean it.

For a long moment, One didn't move, her icy blue eyes staring blankly through the wall, calculating. In that moment, Garrett was sure he'd signed his own death warrant. He waited, morbidly captivated by the spiraling host of the ways she might end it. With a quick draw shot or a cry to assembled Sanctum Guard. With a telepathic warning to the High Cleric, or a call to the enhanced soldiers within His Holiness' quarters.

Perhaps with her bare, frosty hands.

But when she finally stirred and glanced his way, there was something else in her eyes—something so faint that, at first, he wasn't sure it was really there at all. But the gaze lingered a moment too long, and there it was, unmistakable even beneath the years of layered ice. Something soft. Something he'd never seen in her before.

Something like caring.

It was such an unexpected look from One that, for a few seconds, Garrett forgot to breathe—forgot even to be afraid of the cold-blooded reptile in front of him. Because, in that moment, frozen and cocooned together in the growing din of the crowd, she almost looked human.

Then the moment passed, and the frosty gleam returned to her eyes. She palmed the access panel without a word. The door that had been laid to so unobtrusively blend in with the dark stone of the Great Hall's first plateau step slid aside, and she stepped through, leaving Garrett alone with hollow certainty that she knew exactly what he was talking about— and that he'd better not ask her again.

Garrett stared at the open door, wondering what her reaction had meant and, more importantly, what came next.

A fireteam of Onyx Guard, perhaps?

Alpha only knew. But the crowd was thickening throughout the Great Hall behind him, and every second of hesitation only made his case look that much worse. So Garrett took a steadying breath and followed One into the High Cleric's quarters, defenses held loosely at the ready, just in case of prompt gunfire or telepathic attack.

What he found, instead, was the High Cleric's entire entrance hall packed to the spacious brim with dark-clad troops standing in formation at eerily inanimate attention.

Enhanced. And so many of them. Far more than he'd expected. At least a hundred. Probably more.

"I... didn't realize there were this many already," Garrett said quietly, stepping over to where One was checking her palmlight inside.

"I wonder why," she said, looking up to glare daggers at him. "I really should kick your ass for leaving me to deal with these things on my own today, you know?"

Garrett said nothing, scanning the crowd of silent guardians. He knew how sharp their ears were. There was no way they'd missed One's comment. But if the enhanced objected on any level to being referred to as *things*, they gave no such outward indication. They only stood there, paying no mind to the acolytes, clerics, and Sanctum Guard shuffling to and fro throughout the cavernous quarters, tending to last minute details and preparing for the ceremony.

Above, Raish would be tied up and ready to hang by now.

After everything that'd happened—every hurt and headache the wild hound and his demon master Carlisle had laid on him—Garrett should've been relieved by the fact. Maybe that was actually why the High Cleric had chosen him to be the one to bring Raish to his final end. To remind Garrett who the true enemy was here. But escorting Raish up here...

There'd been a moment on the service lift. A moment when he'd thought Raish might show his true lunatic-terrorist colors and actually try to take down Garrett and two Sanctum Guard to escape, even with his wrists and ankles thoroughly shackled. But the kid hadn't fought. He'd shot Garrett one last look—one last silent, contemptuous look, begging the answer to how Garrett could possibly degrade himself to being a part of any of this—and then he'd marched himself out of that lift car, refusing to let his escorts prod him on toward what was coming.

Watching the kid shuffling along, chains rattling, bare feet padding across the dark stone floor, lingering on the myriad squares of sunlight from the duraglass ceiling like he was trying to bottle up the memory of that warmth, and of all the warm things he was about to leave behind...

Demon or not, the sight had tugged at something in Garrett's calloused heart. He'd actually felt for the kid. Or maybe it had really been Andre Kovaks he'd been feeling for. Or even himself. Scud if he could tell anymore. But damned if Raish hadn't picked himself up a little straighter when he'd shuffled into the Great Hall, casting aside any traces of fear, and shedding the would-be pity of anyone watching.

Whatever else he might be, the kid was a fighter. Not that it would save him now. No more than thinking about Raish right now was going to save Garrett. What he needed to do was pull his head out of his ass and—

"Come, my children," came the High Cleric's voice in his mind, so sudden and unexpected that Garrett jerked in surprise. *"I would have you by my side."*

A glance at One confirmed that she'd heard as well. And that she hadn't missed his reaction, either.

She held him on the end of a suspicious scowl, thoroughly scouring his very spirit for some sign of treachery, before finally tilting her head toward the rear of the High Cleric's quarters, where Garrett surmised the lift to His Holiness' private dais must lie, though he'd never seen the thing himself.

He should be thanking the High Cleric's timing, he supposed as he fell in step beside One, fingering the square drop case in his jacket pocket and thinking about the tiny vial contained within. If he was actually going to go through with this insane plan of his, after all, his best shot was probably to do it before His Holiness ascended to the fourth plateau dais above to address the Great Hall. Because after that... well, Garrett didn't know what then.

Perhaps Carlisle would descend for his protege with the horde they'd so mysteriously conjured for the assault on Sanctuary last night. Or perhaps Raish would be hanged without a hitch, and the High Cleric would be liberated to turn his skeptical attention upon the question of where exactly his not-so-loyal Seeker had wandered off to that afternoon. When it came down to it, there was really no limit to the number of ways this whole thing could fly off the rails at any moment. All Garrett really knew for sure was that the sooner he could get what he needed, the better.

Assuming his good friend Watchtower hadn't been spouting him complete bullscud all afternoon.

I'm not talking about his signature, for the love of Alpha, Daveen's words rolled through his head. *I'm talking biometrics. Fingerprints. Blood scans. The triggers use both.*

"And if I brought you both?" Garrett had asked, much to Daveen's wide-eyed, pale-as-the-moon horror, and a long, sputtering string of *hows* and *whys*.

Garrett, for his part, might have insinuated—or, rather, promised—that he would personally burn the White Tower to the ground and drag the High Cleric there over the ashes if that's what it took, and that Daveen had no unholy idea what Garrett was prepared to do to free his people.

He still wasn't really sure why he'd said the last part, or how much of any of it he'd truly meant. But that was hardly important at the moment. What mattered right now was whether or not the spiel had been sufficient to ensure Daveen would hold to his word and keep his cowardly mouth shut until Garrett brought him the goods, so to speak.

"Two."

Garrett froze at the sound of One's voice, cursing himself for having slipped so carelessly back into his own head even as he marched straight toward what was almost certainly the most dangerous appointment he'd ever willingly walked into. He looked over at his severe companion and was surprised to see that a shade of that odd humanity had crept back into her eyes.

"Things will be different after today," she said. "Just remember that."

The way she said it, he couldn't quite tell whether it was meant to be a threat or a plea. Maybe a little of both. Either way, it sounded like a warning. A warning to keep his head down and not rock the ship, no matter what happened. Whether she knew something beyond that or simply shared his own sinking feeling about this ceremony, he wasn't sure. She didn't stick around for questions.

They passed the last ranks of the waiting, rock-steady enhanced soldiers and left the High Cleric's entrance hall through the doorway beneath the enormous darkwood Alpha sigil on the rear wall. Half a dozen Onyx Guard lined the hallway beyond, the weight of their faceless black stares following Garrett down the path even though he swore none of them so much as turned their heads. But none of them made any move to stop him, either. That was all that mattered.

The muted sound of an argumentative voice drew his attention ahead, to the open doorway at the end of the hall where they were headed. A quick sweep with his senses confirmed the High Cleric was there, as was the frightening astral-body presence of his new gray-haired companion. But they weren't the ones arguing.

There was a third mind there, non-telepathic. A cleric, Garrett saw, as they reached the doorway and got a look at the spacious room beyond. And not just any cleric. It was Cleric Faden, the wide, balding man who'd taken up the mantle of head handler in the White Tower after Verner's not-so-mysterious disappearance. And he didn't look happy.

"Alpha forgive me for speaking this way to His Holiness," the cleric was saying, "but I simply do not see how those... those *things* can possibly have any—"

"I understand your concerns, Cleric Faden," the High Cleric cut in, turning from the ornate table of refreshments on the side of the room with a sparkling crystalline glass of water. "I do. And you can rest assured you are not the only one. But you know as well as I that it is not put to any of us to question His will."

Faden's reddening puffed cheeks made it clear what he thought about that excuse.

The handler had drifted into obscurity in Garrett's world shortly after his ascension, as the High Cleric had systematically loosened the handlers' holds on those few Seekers he'd entrusted with his newfound revelation in Alpha's Chosen. It had been seasons now since Garrett had last spoken with Cleric Faden. Having thought himself a free man, he'd nearly forgotten about the handler all together. Irrelevant or not, though, Faden clearly hadn't forgotten his duty. Lucky for him, he hadn't forgotten his place, either.

"Very well, your Holiness," he said with a stiff bow. "I understand. Blessings be with you for the ceremony."

With that, Faden turned to leave peacefully, only to draw up short when his eyes landed on Garrett and One.

It was the last misstep he ever made.

For a second, the cleric considered his two Seekers, his features flickering from surprise to disgust to suspicion. Then his face went oddly blank, and he teetered in place like he'd fallen asleep standing up. Garrett was only just beginning to register what was happening when Faden's head whipped around, wrenched by an unseen force, twisting until his neck broke with a deep, sickly crack.

Garrett could only stare as the handler collapsed to the dark stone floor, his head twisted around at an unnatural angle, his eyes lifeless.

Why?

He tore his eyes from Faden's body and took in One's look of surprise before forcing himself to look at the High Cleric. But His Holiness was only watching his silent gray-haired companion, pasty brow crinkled and one wispy eyebrow cocked. His silent companion didn't seem to notice.

He was too busy staring straight at Garrett. Scrutinizing him with those pale, deranged eyes like he'd just prodded an insect and was waiting to see what it might do in response.

A test. Was this some kind of test?

The sick bastard had just killed a man. Broken his neck with telekinesis for... for what?

"Don't," came One's tense voice in his mind. *"Whatever you're thinking, don't."*

Garrett froze, only then realizing that his hand was halfway to the holster beneath his jacket.

This was too much. Too much tension around every corner. Too much death waiting behind every look, behind every single twitch. Whatever was happening here, he no longer understood the rules of the game. He couldn't handle it anymore. The walls weren't just closing in. They'd crumbled completely, and it was everything Garrett could do not to draw his weapon and back out of the room shooting.

The reedy keening of the key pipes coming to life in the Great Hall above nearly sent him bolting. The sound took form, shifting into a ceremonial Sanctum tune. It was only then that Garrett noticed the artificial daylight dancing down from above had arrived at the telltale blood-orange hue.

Sunset had come.

And the High Cleric's gray-haired killer was still watching him, his demeanor as calm and patient as it was deadly.

The High Cleric glanced up at the lights himself, then set his water glass down and clasped his hands together like they'd all just finished a nice inspirational pep talk. "Very well, then. The time has come. We will discuss this later."

Discuss it later?

How could he say such a thing? How could he look so mind-groppingly casual as Cleric Faden's body lay cooling on the stone floor, his cold-blooded murderer standing there without so much as a single excuse or a remorseful look?

Garrett had no love for Faden, or for any handler. But as he watched the High Cleric stroll onto the great Alpha sigil on the circular platform at the center of the room, he realized that maybe he'd actually *meant* every grandiose word he'd said to Daveen, even if he hadn't known it at the time.

"For now," the High Cleric continued, stepping onto the platform ahead and looking up from his palmlight to focus on Garrett and One. "You two will wait here, prepared to join me above should anything happen during the ceremony. Understood?"

"Of course, your Holiness," One said immediately, head bowed deferentially.

In some dull corner of his mind, Garrett registered that he should also say something, but he couldn't seem to find the words through the shock. Shock not just at the violent surprises of the past minutes, but also at the High Cleric's impending departure, and the sudden and dreadful realization that he'd failed to do the one thing he had to do.

A drop of blood. One drop.

"Understood," Garrett agreed, nearly choking for the dryness in his mouth.

No time now. No way to reach the cleric before he ascended.

He'd failed.

"Splendid," the High Cleric said, his mouth curling in a bright smile, like he could taste the victory. With a flick of his fingers, the platform began to rise, taking him up to his holy dais at the head of the Great Hall, leaving Garrett alone with One and the nameless gray-haired killer. Alone with his failure.

"Alpha be with us all," the High Cleric called down.

And then he was gone.

27

UNVEILED

"Seeker."

Garrett fought back the biological urge to freeze at the single word—and at the voice that sent uneasy chills through every cringe-worthy part of his insides—and instead forced himself to finish slipping the imprinted film back into the open drop case in his palm. His fingers shook badly enough that he nearly dropped the film and the case alike, but somehow, he managed.

That done, he one-handedly closed the small case, slid it up his jacket sleeve, and turned to face the High Cleric's gray-haired killer, holding the half-full water glass in his other hand like a shield against any and all suspicion.

He knew. The creepy bastard knew.

"I was thirsty," Garrett said anyway, fighting to keep his voice level, and hoping his hands weren't shaking badly enough to be noticed. "You going to snap my neck for that?"

The nameless telepath only stared back for several long seconds. Too many seconds. The lifeless body of Cleric Faden lying undisturbed on the stone between them, lost to the murderer's emotionless gaze.

He definitely knew.

Garrett resisted the impulse to squirm, sure that the pale-eyed psychopath had already finished testing his admittedly guilty conscience and was now simply playing a sadistic game with him. Calmly and as casually as he could, Garrett took a sip of the water he had little interest in—although it wasn't unwelcome in his severely parched mouth.

The stare stretched on. Garrett stared back, saying nothing.

Then, without so much as a word or a nod, the gray-haired killer finally dropped Garrett's gaze and strode into the room, not backing down so much as disregarding Garrett completely, as if he'd simply passed from existence.

It was only then that Garrett noticed the six enhanced in tow behind the man.

When the creepy bastard had left without explanation, Garrett had jumped at the chance to lift the High Cleric's fingerprints from his discarded water glass, hiding his work from One with little more than his turned back, but not overly concerned about her, as rapt as she was with watching the High Cleric's speech above on her palmlight. The High Cleric's gray-haired attack dog, on the other hand...

He hadn't thought the man would be back so soon. And he definitely hadn't expected he'd bring company. But seeing as he seemed to be in the clear with his stolen fingerprints for now—and that asking questions of the man seemed about as intelligent as slapping an Onyx Guard—Garrett kept his mouth shut for the moment, and looked over to see what One thought of the development.

Not all that much, he gathered from her standard resting scowl. She was eyeing them both from where she stood on the returned circular lift platform, her cold eyes lingering on the enhanced for only a few seconds before she returned her attention to her palmlight, and the live WAN feed of the ceremony unfolding above.

Garrett let out a slow exhale and took another sip of water before setting the glass down and going to join her. Above, the High Cleric's well-amplified voice sounded to be well into one of his familiar sermons on the nature of demons, and the peril they posed Enochia when allowed to walk the planet unpunished, as Raish and his master had done. Familiar words, but delivered with the High Cleric's undeniable skill at finding new meaning in the old—and just as clearly delivered, Garrett thought, with the intent of steering the broader conversation toward the need for progress, once the deed was done today.

Progress like the enhanced, and maybe even like Alpha's Chosen.

Briefly, Garrett thought about opening his palmlight and quickly shooting off the message he'd drafted earlier for Alexia, doing his best to explain what was about to happen without actually making her complicit, should anything go wrong.

But no. Not yet.

There was still too much in flux. Too many unknowns. And not enough High Cleric blood tucked away up his sleeve. Without that, they were all just as trapped as they'd ever been, no matter what else happened here tonight. As tenuous as his position here felt, it was all he had.

So he stepped onto the central lift platform next to One, thinking innocent thoughts as he scooted in to watch the broadcast on her palmlight. Aside from a slight sideways frown, she didn't argue.

From the sound of it, the High Cleric was already drawing to the big moment. Faster than usual, Garrett thought. But then again, he had been a little distracted for the past few minutes. Maybe he'd missed more than he realized. Or maybe the High Cleric was just anxious to get the ceremony over with before Carlisle rode in on Alpha only knew what manner of demon's horde. Not that hurrying up the speech could change that.

If Carlisle was going to come, then he was going to come.

As promptly as Raish's execution had been scheduled, it wasn't like the time or location had been kept secret. The feed on One's palmlight was proof enough of that as it cut to a view of the reverent crowd—over a thousand loyal citizens of Divinity, all come to see Alpha's justice served. Or at least to see a man hanged. And the moment was approaching.

"Alpha grant you peace, Haldin Raish," called the High Cleric, his voice booming both from One's palmlight, and from the high ceiling above.

A rush of apprehensive nerves shot through Garrett—a sudden, ambiguous certainty that they weren't ready, that they'd overlooked something crucial. Probably just an aftershock of his failure to procure the blood sample he so desperately needed, he decided. But that didn't really explain why he found himself instinctively reaching out with his extended senses toward Raish, reaching through layers of stone and steel until he found the rickety grain of the old gallows wood, and traced it up, up, right to the shining floodlight of the kid's mind. And shining, it was.

Raish was in a blind panic. Garrett didn't have to delve into the kid's mind to tell that much.

It shouldn't have come as a surprise. He'd witnessed the dying revelations of more than enough apostates over the years, after all. But it did anyway. Maybe because he'd never seen a foe the likes of Raish or Carlisle brought to heel. Maybe because he'd sworn that the kid he'd watched marching across the Great Hall with his head held high never could have imploded like this. But in that moment, that was all Raish felt like.

A kid. Scared and alone, just like everyone else in the end.

Then the hangman threw the lever, and Garrett felt the platform floor drop out beneath Raish's feet, opening him to the lethal fall. Garrett felt a flicker of remorse and guilt. More than a flicker. Then his brain caught up, and he registered what his extended senses were telling him.

Raish hadn't fallen.

Garrett felt it in his senses just as surely as he saw it on One's palmlight display when he opened his eyes. The slippery little bastard had caught himself with telekinesis before he'd dropped more than a foot through the opening.

Suffice it to say, the loyal citizens of Divinity weren't prepared for that one.

Gasps and shouts erupted from One's palmlight feed. Someone screamed.

"Evacuate this hall, now!" Raish roared. "You're all in danger! Go! Run! Please!"

Understandably, he was met with little more than a thousand stares, each and every one of them equally dumbfounded by the teenage boy floating in midair before them, defying death, gravity, and pretty much every other given they'd assumed about their world.

"This is why we don't take prisoners," Garrett muttered, glancing down at the lift platform and wondering if this meant they'd be joining the High Cleric above after all. He tensed when he realized the gray-haired killer and his six enhanced had already joined them on the platform, moving so quietly Garrett hadn't even noticed. The gray-haired man was looking up with distant eyes, like he could see straight through the walls and ceiling, his palmlight unfurled and at the ready with the lift controls. Like he'd been fully expecting to go up all along. Like this was all part of the—

A shrill scream ripped through One's palmlight feed, markedly different than the first one had been. This one was stained with mortal terror, and it was followed by two more in rapid succession before One curled her fingers closed, killing the feed completely. She looked to the gray-haired man, who hadn't so much as twitched at the sounds.

Garrett looked between them with growing unease. "So are we going to do something about that?" he finally asked when neither of them spoke.

"Patience," the gray-haired man said in a flat tone, not bothering to look away from whatever the scud he was staring at.

But patience wasn't really an option. Even through the thick stone walls, it was impossible to mistake the growing roar of voices for anything but sheer, senseless terror.

They were under attack out there.

Carlisle.

Garrett woke his palmlight, thinking to glance at the WAN feed for some clue as to what they were dealing with, but One's hands closed around his wrist and fingers, curling his palmlight shut before he could.

"Protect the civilians!" the High Cleric's amplified voice boomed through the ceiling. "Seize Raish!"

"What the scud are we waiting for?!" Garrett growled, yanking his arm loose from One's grip.

She didn't try to stop him. The High Cleric's gray-haired killer finally turned to look at him, his expression betraying little but for maybe a hint of irritation.

Then a deep explosion rocked the Great Hall above, followed by another, and another.

"That," said the gray-haired psychopath. Then without another word of explanation or warning, he thumbed his palmlight and set them ascending toward whatever unholy scudstorm was unfolding out there.

THE FIRST THING GARRETT HEARD, when the intricate ceiling panels slid aside to permit their lift to the High Cleric's dais, was a blood hungry roar like nothing he'd ever heard before. It was taken up by another unnatural, beastly throat, and another. All to the stomach-clenching screams of the dying.

Garrett didn't have to wait until the lift brought them to the cusp of the Great Hall's fourth plateau step to know they were dying. There was no mistaking it. No un-hearing it. But even those horrific sounds didn't prepare him for the sight that greeted them when the lift finished its climb and delivered them just behind the High Cleric's dais.

It was a slaughter.

A bloody, unholy mess of a slaughter.

Legionnaires rappelled down from gaping holes in the great duraglass ceiling, firing on the crowd, dropping grenades and wild panic. The crowd below was a writhing stampede of screams and blood and frenzied wide eyes, pushing their way everywhere and nowhere at once, knocking their fellow servants of Alpha to the ground in their mad rush to escape the death raining from above.

Except it wasn't the legionnaires they were running from, Garrett realized. Or dying from. No. Those weren't lethal grenades they were throwing down, but thumpers. And the unruly mass of the crowd pressing *away* from the exit at the rear of the Great Hall, not towards it. Away from the exit, and away from the dark-clad *things* flooding into the Hall from the column-lined corridor beyond. As soon as Garrett spotted the things, there was no questioning it.

They were demons. Actual, honest-to-Alpha demons. Tearing into the crowd like wild animals, letting loose more of those horrific roars, faces disfigured and discolored sickly green, like some kind of reptilian half-breeds.

Just like... Just like...

A flash of crimson pain and an empty, burning pit at the core of his chest. He felt like he'd been punched in the diaphragm, though the sensation paled in comparison to the fiery rift at the center of his mind.

Just like those things from Raish's propaganda vid last night.

The one that had been all lies and mistruths?

Crimson pain and blurry edges.

Pitched screams and man-made thunder ripped him back to the sight of the civilian masses pressing themselves into the walls, with nowhere to run. The only exits were through the antechamber. Through the beasts. Legionnaires and Sanctum Guard alike swept into the fray, fighting to keep the beasts back from the unarmed citizens of Divinity. But it was hopeless. The beasts were too numerous, too wild.

And there, a hundred feet below, were Carlisle and Raish, staring up at the High Cleric and his gray-haired companion like this was all their fault—Raish's face twisted in a mask of cold fury, and Carlisle...

For the first time since he'd had the displeasure of meeting the demon, Garrett watched the unshakable Carlisle blanch at whatever he saw, his eyes locked on the High Cleric's companion with unmistakable recognition.

A pair of detonations snapped Garrett's attention forward to where the legionnaires had just blown a pair of openings on each side of the Great Hall, wide enough for their transports to scrape their tail ends in and start unloading more legionnaires. Where they'd come from or how they'd gotten here so quick, Garrett didn't know.

Below, Raish was pulling Carlisle away from the gallows, toward the main floor of the Great Hall, the Fields girl and the rest of their outlaw allies falling in with them, like they fully intended to skip their shot at the High Cleric and instead go down into the fray—to maim or protect, Garret couldn't have said. None of this made any sense. None of it.

But when one of the beasts leapt up and attacked one of the ceremony camera crew only to be violently hurled thirty feet into a stone wall by Raish's telekinesis, Garrett was afraid he had his answer.

"What the scud is going on, here?" he sent to One.

"I told you," came her telepathic reply. *"Things will be different after today."*

When he finally managed to pull his eyes away from the carnage below and look at her, her expression was grim, and maybe even a little horrified. But she didn't look nearly as shocked and confused as he felt.

Below, Raish and Carlisle were floating their little band of outlaw terrorists down to the main floor with telekinesis now. Down to the main floor, where those *outlaw terrorists* proceeded to wade straight into the thick of the fray, gunning down one feral beast after another, treading through piles of bodies and lakes of blood on dark stone to get to whatever civilians they could. To rescue them. To stop what was happening here. Which meant...

Garrett looked at the High Cleric and his gray-haired companion, both watching the slaughter below, both of them so calm, so detached. Inhumanly so. He pried his eyes from the pair and looked over his shoulder at the six enhanced lined up behind them, mind whirling, insides following.

It couldn't be. Couldn't.

He couldn't have possibly missed it. Not this. It was too big. Too mind-numbingly gropped to be real.

But then, as one, the six enhanced snapped to action and removed their helmets on some silent telepathic command, and Garrett had his answer, gaping in frozen horror at what lay underneath.

Their faces were a sickly, scale-flecked green, their eyes pale crimson, faces slightly elongated.

Just like the beasts below.

He felt sick. Couldn't look away.

All the lies, all the underhanded excuses, and somehow, he'd still never even began to imagine the darkness could run this deep, this spirit-crushingly black. He'd been too busy worrying about his own life. Too busy worrying that the High Cleric and his mysterious brethren might not intend to honor their promise of a new life for the Seekers once they had their new world.

Too busy to see that he'd been serving the demons all along.

Because that was the only explanation, wasn't it, when he cut away everything else and looked at what was happening here? That Raish and Carlisle, and even Andre Kovaks, had all been circling the truth with their madness. That the apostate terrorists had truly been trying to stop these things all along.

It was preposterous. Utterly unbelievable. Yet as Garrett turned back to face his masters, he couldn't deny it any longer.

It was all true. Or enough of it, anyway.

He didn't need to look any further than to the High Cleric, and the way the old man was watching him with a trace of that same bright grin he'd shown them before the ceremony. Grinning, here and now, even as his loyal flock was lost to the screaming slaughter below.

Garrett could've sworn he even saw the unholy bastard's eyes radiating with a faint crimson glow, but that was probably just his fracturing psyche adding its own colorful twist on the nightmare. Except...

Crimson pain. Blurry edges. Piercing bolts searing through his brain.

What in demons' depths had he done?

"Come, my children," said the *thing* masquerading as the High Cleric of Sanctum, turning back to the edge of its dais to survey the carnage below. "Come, and let us usher in our new era."

2 8

UNFORGIVABLE

I f ever there'd been a time Garrett was sure he needed to get the scud out of the White Tower and never look back, his descent down the plateau steps of the Great Hall was probably it. Given that he was stuck beside One, the gray-haired killer, and the *thing* that called itself the High Cleric for said descent, though, turning tail wasn't exactly an option. Short of that, he was half-convinced he might as well throw it all away, draw his weapon, and try his luck at ending the unholy trinity himself.

Whether it was some higher reason that stayed his hand, or just plain cowardice, he wasn't sure. But something told him the High Cleric or his gray-haired companion wouldn't be so easily ended as the simple pull of a trigger.

He needed a plan. And until he had it, it was all he could do to follow along, looking the part of the willing Seeker as best he could. He wasn't sure the High Cleric or his murderous friend bought it, but they were far more focused on the fighting below. If fighting was even the word for it.

Garrett had seen darkness in his life, had witnessed and even participated in some of the most overt acts of violence one human could enact on another. But he'd never seen anything like this. The ferocity of the enhanced. The thickening pools of blood congealing on the dark stone.

The sheer number of bodies strewn throughout the hall—hundreds dead in the first few minutes, civilians, legionnaires, and beasts alike.

It was staggering. So staggering that Garrett could hardly process any feeling at all aside from numb, deadened horror. That, and another bout of guilt and sickened disbelief as he watched the Fields girl save a young boy from one of the beasts with a quick spear thrust, while nearby, Carlisle and Raish tore through another trio of the creatures with daggers and a few slugs to pull a trembling huddle of four civilians to their feet.

They all fought on, escorting the survivors toward the evacuation lines that had formed at each side of the Great Hall—civilians waiting in rigid terror for the next returning transports to ferry them away even as they watched legionnaires and Sanctum Guard dying to protect them. Legionnaires and so-called terrorists, all fighting side-by-side to keep the ferocious beasts at bay while the High Cleric looked calmly on, like he was observing a grand play in his honor.

It made Garrett reconsider that simple pull of the trigger.

He didn't understand what was happening, or why. His mind was too clogged with scuddy half-plans and with the retracings of every insane accusation Andre Kovaks had made about dark forces—gropping alien beings, for the love of Alpha—invading the fabric of Enochia's infrastructure. Invading to the highest levels of world power, for reasons unknown.

Reasons like this? he wondered, eyes fixed on the back of the High Cleric's head, heart racing on pace with the cacophony of gunfire below. Trigger finger itching like never before.

His gun hand was already inching toward his jacket of its own volition when a low rumbling beneath his feet broke him free of the desperate spell. The grating sound of stone on stone. The High Cleric's main quarters entrance opening, Garrett realized—just before he also remembered the additional horde of beastly enhanced still lying in wait therein. And that wasn't all.

Hungry roars from the rear of the Great Hall announced the arrival of another horde of the beasts from the mag lifts in the entryway antechamber.

Demons to the wind, how many were there? And who was even controlling all of them?

"Go."

The flatness of the voice, and its proximity, startled Garrett, but he didn't jump. He was too overwhelmed to jump. He just turned to the gray-haired killer who'd spoken the word. The man was watching him like he expected Garrett to hop to and march into battle on that single command.

Beside Garret, One was eyeing him expectantly, looking ready to do just that. Ahead, the High Cleric remained at the lip of the first plateau step, apparently not intending to leave his perch and join them.

Garrett hesitated, distantly aware of the fresh wave of beasts surging forward to exit the High Cleric's quarters below. He didn't know what to do, who to help. He didn't even know if he had a side in this fight. All he knew was that someone needed to stop this madness, and that right now, he was the one who had a shot at the High Cleric.

And yet he hesitated. Because he wasn't sure, *couldn't* be sure. Because it was all too gropped to make any actual sense. Or because he was too afraid to see that it in fact did.

In that moment, he felt his mind flirting with the bright light of clarity. Then One shoved into him hard enough to point them both toward the stone staircase at the side of the first plateau, and Garrett relented, his moment past.

"Don't fight this," One sent. *"Just remember what I said. We help take down Raish and Carlisle, and we're set."*

Set? Set for what? For freedom, just like last time? For this new world of the High Cleric's, born in on a river of innocent blood?

Garrett said nothing. Just marched along beside One, acutely aware of the presence of the High Cleric's gray-haired killer ghosting along right behind them, ready to do Alpha knew what to Alpha knew who.

"Cut the chatter and stow the frillies, soldiers!" one of the legionnaires roared across the hall as his panicked line prepared to engage the new flood of beasts charging into the Great Hall from both directions. "We have civilians to protect here and exactly zero time for your sad bullscud. You *will* hold the line. Understood?"

The rallying cry of the legionnaires wrenched at his insides, demanding he do something, demanding he explain how he could stand by and simply watch while a pair of demons and a bunch of mindless grunts stepped up to do what was right.

Then the charging masses of enhanced beasts broke into the Great Hall from the columned corridor in the back, more streaming out from the High Cleric's quarters, and the fighting resumed in full. The Legion lines opened fire in deafening synchrony. The enhanced dropped in swaths, but the horde pressed on with unstoppable momentum. One fell, two more charged forward in its place.

Garrett stuck close to One, keeping his defenses raised against the inevitable stray fire as best he could, not bothering to afford the same protection to One or their gray-haired stalker. One hurried forward with purpose, seemingly unafraid of the thickening horde around them. And for good reason, apparently. The beasts avoided them with eerie precision, charging past on either side without so much as a sentient glance, like they were repelled from colliding with Garrett and the others by simple magnetism.

One pushed on through the sea of charging beasts, leading them straight for the place where Garrett could feel Raish and Carlisle holding the line, her presence swelling with a small ocean of channeled energy as she went, clearly preparing for something big.

And he couldn't let her, he realized.

It hit him like a softsteel cannon ball to the gut.

Years of hunting Carlisle. All the pain and humiliation he'd experienced at Raish's uncannily talented hands. All the righteous certainty that he and his fellow Seekers had been fighting the good fight for the safety of Enochia.

And now he couldn't let her stop these two demons. Because he'd been wrong about all of it.

But it was already happening.

Like an extension of One's will—or maybe the gray-haired killer's behind them—the sea of reptilian beasts parted before them in one smooth, synchronized move, leaving an open path straight toward Carlisle and Raish. An open path One wasted no time filling with a roaring column of fire.

Even from a distance, it was startlingly hot—a frightening reminder of just how strong One really was beneath that not-so-fluffy exterior. Raish, at least, look rattled as he raised his hands in defense. Carlisle, though, raised a hand and broke the column of fire on an invisible barrier without so much as a ripple in his calm composure.

Garrett shouldn't have been surprised, he supposed. It wasn't the first time he'd seen the man work a casual miracle. What he wasn't ready for, though, was how deftly the tricky bastard turned the attack aside, not just quelling the flames, but instead splashing thick waves of fire straight over the parted walls of beastly enhanced.

Maybe Garrett should've felt satisfied at the choir of inhuman screeches that filled the air. It was kind of what he'd wanted, wasn't it? But somehow, the visual reminder of the depths of Carlisle's power shook his resolve. Or maybe it was just the haze of greasy smoke, and a disturbing scent of burnt meat that filled the tense air in the resultant ceasefire.

Ahead, through the smoke of charred enhanced flesh, Carlisle lowered his hand. Around him, wide-eyed legionnaires broke into a round of victorious cheers. One started forward, apparently unperturbed, only to be promptly met with a lone gunshot from the red-headed legionnaire Garrett vaguely remembered from Raish's files as Johnathan Wingard.

One was ready for the shot. The slug snapped to a midair halt a foot from her chest, and she thrust her hands out in Wingard's direction, preparing to counter. Raish hit her with a telekinetic blast before she could, and then the scudstorm kicked right back into high gear real fast.

Gunfire erupted. Enhanced beasts roared. Garrett did his best to not die—a point which the legionnaires seemed rather insistent to fight him on.

Those soldiers who still had a line on them through the seething ocean of enhanced fired a heavy river of high-velocity softsteel at Garrett and One. Garrett focused on deflecting rather than catching the shots head-on, saving himself considerable energy, with the added benefit of "accidentally" taking down at least a few of the beastly enhanced around him with wild ricochets.

Before he could so much as think about next moves, the High Cleric's gray-haired killer sprang past them, bound straight for Carlisle with inhuman speed. Beside him, One took advantage of the momentary distraction to loosen her defenses and roast two legionnaires with a smaller lance of flames. Garrett only half-registered the barbaric abuse of power.

His focus was locked on the High Cleric's man as he tumbled into an impossibly fast tangle with Carlisle. But it wasn't the speed of their movements that stopped Garrett's breath. It was the man's—the *thing's*—eyes.

They burned like twin orbs of crimson demon fire.

Crimson... Crimson pai—

"Hey!"

One's voice snapped Garrett back to the scudstorm of battle, and to the sight of Raish charging toward them, the Fields girl by his side, and Wingard and Phineas Hammer at their flanks.

"I've got the girl," came One's voice in Garrett's mind.

He shot an incredulous glance over at his psychotic partner, who was licking her lips, fixated on Fields with disturbing intensity, a tiny flame flickering to life over her open palm.

How in the demons' depths had he ended up here? Garrett numbly wondered as his eyes flicked back to where Carlisle and the crimson-eyed monster were trading blows faster than he could follow. And what the scud were these things?

A peripheral warning of movement was all he had before he realized it was already too late. Raish was pitched back, ready to throw his dagger for the kill shot, and Garrett was completely frozen, reflexes failing him, too overloaded with the sheer shock of everything happening around him.

For a split second, he was sure that was it. The pathetic end to what turned out to have been a useless existence, built on more lies than he'd ever have a chance to comprehend.

Then a flicker of motion above caught Raish's attention, and he abandoned the throw, shoving Fields off her feet and diving the other direction himself—just before two figures smashed down side by side, shattering the dark stone where they'd vacated.

Garrett blinked, only growing more stupefied as he recognized the well-garbed backs of High General Kublich and the High Cleric himself. Phineas Hammer, on the other hand, didn't bat an eye. The burly outlaw cocked back and hit the High Cleric with a prosthetic-powered punch that easily could've killed a man. The High Cleric, though—the frail, old High Cleric—only stumbled backward with a deep growl, clutching at his jaw.

His eyes were filled with crimson fire.

Kublich lunged in to repay Phineas in kind. Wingard stepped forward and shot him in the head before he could. Twice.

Kublich didn't go down. But his eyes did go crimson.

What in the unholy scud *were* these things?

Before Garrett could wrap his head around any of it, Carlisle swept in and blasted Kublich off his feet with telekinesis, the High Cleric's red-eyed killer hot on his heels. Off to the left, One was already charging at the Fields girl, who was still pulling herself to her feet after nearly being flattened.

Garrett shook his head clear and started toward them, not sure what he was even planning to do, only that he had to do something to help. Instead, he nearly ran headlong into Raish before he'd taken more than a few steps.

"Wait!" he snapped, sliding to a halt, hands outstretched.

But Raish had already let his knife fly, launching it straight for Garrett's heart like a telekinetic mag bolt. Whether it was Garrett's single word or simply Raish's distraction over Fields, the blade wavered mid-flight, slowing just enough that Garrett managed to catch the weapon with his own telekinesis a foot short of his chest.

Raish snarled in frustration, eyes darting off to the left, where a flash of heat and light suggested One had taken her shot at Elise. Garrett was reaching out to tell the wild hound to stand down and let him help when he caught sight of the High Cleric's gray-haired, red-eyed killer rushing in to knock Raish's head off from behind.

There was no time to warn him, but Raish didn't need a warning.

Moving almost as deftly as his master, he ducked the blow he couldn't have seen coming, dodged the follow up, and drove a brutal straight kick into the monster's planted knee. The strike looked like it should've left the gray-haired man permanently and violently double-jointed at the knee, but the creature barely seemed to notice, and Raish didn't seem the least bit surprised about it. Instead, he lifted the gray-haired monster a few inches from the ground with telekinesis, furiously backpedaling to buy space.

Raish didn't make it far, though, before the gray-haired creature's crimson eyes flared brighter, and Raish slammed down to his knees, crushed under a violent wave of telekinetic force. He was pinned, Garrett realized with a ripple of surprise. Helplessly pinned as the gray-haired killer thudded back down to the bloody dark stone and stalked forward with finality, holding his prey firm in his snare.

And Garrett was just watching like a gaping child.

He looked down at the knife he didn't even remember having called to his hand. The same blade Raish had tried to drive through his heart. But that hardly mattered now. What mattered was that people were dying all around him—bloody, violent deaths at the hands of inhuman abominations. He didn't know why, or what for. All he knew was that Raish and his frighteningly powerful master were trying to put a stop to it. It was all Garrett needed to know.

All he needed to know to dart forward and jam his blade straight into the gray-haired killer's neck.

29

EQUIVALENT EXCHANGE

It was a stupid plan. Not even a *plan* at all, really. Especially not after he'd already seen one of the red-eyed monsters survive two gunshots directly to the head.

But none of that managed to fully process before Garrett leapt forward and jammed Raish's dagger into the side of the gray-haired killer's neck, straight for the cervical spinal cord. Only the blade didn't make it that far.

The knife jerked to a halt in his hand like it was a block of hardwood he'd stabbed, and not a living, breathing monster. Time seemed to slow as Garrett gaped at the spot where the blade had barely sunk a half-inch into the thing's flesh—no, it's *hide*, he realized as dark green streaks rippled out from the point of impact, like some kind of reactive armor. Then time sped back up, and the gray-haired killer turned, crimson eyes burning, and hit him with a backhand.

Outwardly, the motion looked so casual that Garrett almost thought it was a joke.

And that was just about the last coherent thought he had.

The impact of the blow was of a magnitude he'd never known existed —worse than being blasted out of a moving tram. More like being hit by one. A red-eyed, super-powered lackadaisical psychopath of a speeding tram.

That gray-haired bastard hit him so hard his mind just went blank, certain it was already dead. For a time, there was little to refute the idea—a whirling of sight and sound, none of it making any sense. The distant jostle of secondary impacts. Landing, maybe. That seemed right. That was what bodies tended to do after their owners died.

It all made sense, really, in the twilight of his dwindling consciousness.

Only some stubborn little tendril of him kept clinging there, aware that he wasn't quite dead yet. He couldn't have said how long he hung there in that gray space—only that it felt both like a brief instant and a small eternity before he noticed the first touches of pain creeping forward. Creeping forward like the soft kiss of a red hot wire brush raking across his flesh.

Definitely not dead. Which meant...

Sight and sound began to resolve into something half-sensical again. He saw that he'd flown at least a good twenty-five feet on the Backhand Express, and with that realization, the wire brush pain that had been lingering at the fringes gladly flooded forward to where he could properly appreciate it.

Something was broken. A lot of somethings.

But now wasn't the time to be lying around, he remembered, as his surroundings slowly began to take shape again. The sounds of fighting had stopped. How long had he been down?

Garrett tried to move, but his body wouldn't respond. Someone was shouting wild obscenities. Another voice cut over it, deeper and more guttural than any human voice he'd ever heard.

"Enough," it boomed. Not a human voice at all. "Lay down your weapons."

A scream ripped through the haze, punctuating the demand. Raish's scream, Garrett realized. He managed to turn his head far enough to see that one of the beasts had Raish by the throat, its clawed thumb buried into his back like a dagger. But not just any beast, he realized, taking in the insignia on the thing's dress tunic.

It was High General Kublich holding Raish, crimson eyes ablaze, gleaming fangs bared.

Elise Fields stood next to them, hands raised in surrender, face twisted with helpless rage. Ahead, the clatter of metal on stone drew Garrett's eyes to where Carlisle had just dropped his daggers and followed her example.

No.

Wingard stood beside Carlisle, warily facing the gray-haired killer and the High Cleric, but both of the red-eyed monsters were focused on Kublich and Raish, the former looking annoyed, and the latter victorious.

Because they'd won.

They had Raish in their claws—even had his mind on lockdown, Garrett realized, reaching out—and neither Carlisle nor the others were willing to ignore Kublich's threat and fight on. What few legionnaires remained watched from beside the ramp of the lone transport, guarding the last few boarding civilians with weapons at the ready, seeming to understand that they wouldn't be enough to help Raish and the others.

Whatever Raish's friends had come here to do—whatever had convinced these legionnaires to turn against their own High General— they'd all failed. Just like Garrett had failed. Because he wasn't getting out of here alive. Wasn't even sure he could stand. Certainly wasn't in any position to finish severing the High Cleric's control of the collar system.

What would these monsters do to the rest of his fellow Seekers when they were done here?

What would they do the rest of Enochia?

"Kill them all," growled the gray-haired killer, breaking the thick silence with a clear answer, and the unmistakable air of absolute authority.

Distantly, Garrett noted with a certain amount of bitter amusement that he'd been too far in the dark to even realize who was truly in charge of this demon brigade until that very moment. But it hardly mattered anymore.

They were all dead.

The Great Hall exploded into action, enhanced beasts snapping free from their creepy attention with hungry roars even as the remaining legionnaires opened fire. Kublich and the High Cleric sprang to obey their master's command, the High Cleric stepping up to remove Wingard's head as his master charged Carlisle.

Carlisle's hands shot out, ripping Kublich away from Raish with telekinesis even as he plowed the High Cleric clear from Wingard mid-strike, whirling all the while to meet their incoming master.

Not fast enough.

The gray-haired killer's clawed hand tore through Carlisle's abdomen with a sickening wet thunk. Carlisle jerked to a violent halt, mouth agape, eyes wide. Already dead, Garrett thought.

He turned, thinking to help Raish instead, or at least to capitalize on whatever rage-fueled scudstorm the kid was about to call down at the sight of his maimed mentor. But his body was broken. He wasn't going anywhere. And neither was Raish, he realized, seeing Kublich approaching the young apostate with halting steps, both of their faces oddly blank.

Because they were still fighting for mental control, he realized in a flash.

And just like that, he knew what he had to do.

Gathering his will, Garrett did his best to push aside the pain in his physical body, not bothering even to worry about keeping his own mental defenses tight. It wasn't like his broken body was worth a damn to anyone, anyway. But Raish could still fight, could still finish this.

So Garrett set everything else aside and threw his mind at Kublich's with everything he had. He tore at the monster from the outside, seeking the weak points, feeling for where Raish was trying to buck free, and helping to pry Kublich's grip loose as best he could.

But it wasn't enough.

Kublich was strong. Beyond strong.

"C'mon, kid!" he sent to Raish, struggling on. *"Fight the bastard!"*

He felt the flicker of Raish's surprised recognition through the maelstrom, then the kid redoubled his efforts, throwing himself at Kublich's restraints like a wild animal. Garrett applied his own leverage, working alongside Raish wherever he could, until the red-eyed monster had no choice but to give an inch to their combined minds. Then another. And another. Then Elise Fields crashed into Kublich with a hard kick to his scaly green head, and the High General's hold broke completely.

After that, Garrett almost felt bad for the High General.

Almost.

Enraged by the sucker kick, Kublich swung for the Fields girl and promptly found himself skewered on the combination of his own momentum and her well-planted spear. Finally free, Raish spun on the High General, a hoarse cry tearing from his throat, and proceeded to slam him bodily into the floor with telekinesis, hard enough to shatter stone. Then he lifted the general and slammed him down again. Again and again, screaming like a mad demon all the while, until the dark stone floor was utterly pulverized, and Raish had collapsed to his knees from the exhaustion.

Garrett was screaming too, he realized, telepathically spurring Raish on, adding what telekinetic aid he could to every brutal slam.

Kublich wasn't fighting back anymore. Fields was calling Raish's name, fear in her tone, trying to pull him away. But there was no stopping him. And somewhere between his tenuous link to Raish's mind and the cracking lines of whatever had been done to his own memories, Garrett understood why.

It had been Kublich, not Carlisle, who'd killed Raish's parents. Kublich who'd pushed Raish into all of this. Garrett couldn't quite recall how he knew it—only that he did. And that he was more than ready to help Raish exact his vengeance.

But then a strange energy surged through the Great Hall, and even Raish turned to investigate. It was unlike anything Garrett had ever felt, swirling through the enormous space in viscous waves, building and building, speeding up until the air was positively howling with it.

And at the eye of the bizarre storm sat Carlisle, decidedly not dead, head rocked back and a peaceful smile on his face, of all things. He held his gray-haired killer's face cupped in both hands like he was greeting a long-lost loved one, his fingertips radiant with a crackling violet light that was spreading across the his killer's face. Consuming it. The energy building all the while. Building like an awakening mountain glacier.

For a long moment, it was all Garrett could do to stare. He didn't understand what sorcery Carlisle was working—or even how the man was still alive. And neither, it seemed, did Carlisle's victim, who sat frozen in his glowing grip, eyes wide, crimson fire dimmed almost to nothing.

Raish was watching Carlisle, eyes brimming with tears as something passing between the two of them, Kublich all but forgotten. At least until the High General stirred from his pulverized crater and bellowed, "Kill the Shaper! Kill him now!"

As one, every remaining enhanced beast in the Great Hall turned from the legionnaires and charged for Carlisle. The thrumming power flared brighter through the air, pulsing from Carlisle like a giant bomb, preparing to explode.

The enhanced didn't stand a chance.

The eerie violet wind whipped harder. Garrett cringed at the flare of channeled power. And then Carlisle swatted over a dozen incoming beasts across the Great Hall like so many polymer dolls. Whatever was happening to him, the man didn't seem even remotely hard-pressed by the monumental exertion. Nor did he have trouble reeling Kublich into his fold at the same time, despite the fact that the High General was literally punching holes through the stone floor in search of a strong enough handhold to resist.

He didn't find one.

So maybe Alpha had been paying attention all along. That was the only explanation Garrett could lay on any of this, as he clenched his teeth and struggled to rise to his feet, only to find that his legs still wouldn't cooperate. It wasn't just the pain, either. That, he could handle—*did* handle, as he scrabbled around on the power of his arms. But his legs were too weak. Practically unresponsive.

Something was horribly wrong with him.

He looked over to where Fields was pulling Raish toward their friends, and toward the few surviving legionnaires who were waving furiously for them to get their asses over there and board the last transport before Carlisle's seemingly divine intervention puttered out. For a second, Garrett was gripped by the the overwhelming urge to call after them, to beg for them to come back and help him out of that nightmarish place.

But his job wasn't done yet.

Whatever the crazy bastard was doing, Garrett got the distinct impression that there was no longer any turning back for Carlisle. The man still had a fist-sized hole through his insides after all. No. Carlisle was already as good as dead. And clearly, he was intending to take every last one of these monsters with him. Garrett wasn't sure exactly how this would end. Only that before it did, he needed to get the High Cleric's blood in that drop case—if it was the last thing he did.

And lucky for him, he realized as he looked around, the treacherous old bastard was headed straight for him.

The High Cleric's crimson eyes burned bright as he skirted through the howling winds, keeping low like he was afraid he'd be spotted among the piles of the dead. One was with him, looking like she'd just been pulled from one of those piles herself, her face ghostly pale, and her right arm clutched close to her side, like she was trying to protect an injury.

There was no glib victory on the High Cleric's face anymore. He simply hurried to Garrett's side, bent down without a word, and hauled him from the ground with an ease that would've been out of place for even the strongest man in the prime of his years. The dilapidated old High Cleric didn't even loose a stray grunt as he slung Garrett over his silky white shoulder. Not that Garrett cared in that moment how inhumanly strong the creature was—or even about the pain that racked his body with every abrupt jostle.

All he cared about was the dark trickle he saw running from the side of the High Cleric's head as he was manhandled into position.

Blood?

He had no idea. It was darker than any he'd ever seen, and vaguely greenish in hue. For that matter, he wasn't even positive this red-eyed thing was really the High Cleric at all, and not just some demonic abomination who'd eaten the man and taken on his form.

He had no idea about any of it. But that rivulet of dark blood stuff was all he had. There was no backup plan. No hope of surviving long enough to find one.

So he dug into his pocket and retrieved the small drop case from his jacket, squeezing with white knuckles to offset the chances of dropping it on a sudden movement or a spike of pain. He worked the clasp open with shaking fingers, bouncing on the High Cleric's shoulder every step of the way. Moving with painstaking care not to lose the fingerprint film inside, he slid the slip of absorbent fabric free from the case.

Just one drop. And it was right there.

But then the energy in the room surged violently, and the resultant wind nearly ripped case and cloth alike from his hand. Garrett clutched tight, tensing as the High Cleric swayed and One staggered into them. But then both his abductors caught their balance and kept moving. Heading,

Garrett could feel now, for one of the breaches that'd been blown in the wall for the arriving Legion transports.

Trying to escape?

It didn't matter.

Pinching the cloth tightly between thumb and forefinger, Garrett reached up to where his right hip was riding against the High Cleric's head, and proceeded to swab every square inch he could reach, trying to mask the awkward attack as a weak, pawing struggle to escape.

The High Cleric didn't play games. Pin-pricks of fire erupted from Garrett's right leg—the High Cleric's claws, he registered, puncturing his thigh in warning to be still like a good abductee.

At least that confirmed his lower extremities were still perfectly capable of sensation, even if he couldn't seem to move them right now. But Garrett forgot all about the pain in his legs as soon as he got a look at the cloth in his fingers.

It was stained dark green.

That was it. Whether it would work or not, he couldn't begin to guess. But he'd done what he could. All that he could. He didn't struggle as the High Cleric carried him onward. Not as his thoughts turned to what lay in store for him should the High Cleric reach that breach and escape. Not even as another surge of energy spiked through the air, birthing a gust of wind that nearly slapped the High Cleric off his unholy feet.

He just tucked the precious contents back inside the drop case and gripped the thing like his life depended on it. Like Alexia's life depended on it. Because that was all he could hope for.

Or so he told himself until he heard the faint, tight tones of familiar voices on the howling wind nearby.

Unable to get a proper look past the High Cleric's torso, Garrett reached out with his extended senses instead, feeling his way toward his last miniscule shot of survival. And there, not so very far away...

"Raish."

Across the way, he felt the kid look around at his voice. He hesitated, not daring to hope, afraid to even ask. But demons to the wind with it.

"I was ready to die like a good boy," he sent. *"But I'd rather not stick with these crazy bastards, if you're feeling charitable."*

He felt Raish falter several yards short of the transport's waiting ramp, glancing uncertainly from Garrett's direction back to where his friends were already boarding. That hesitation was all the answer Garrett needed. He wasn't sure why he'd even bothered to ask.

Raish wasn't going to help him. He'd tried to kill the kid, for the love of Alpha. More than once. Had even mind-jacked his girlfriend to do the deed. There was no forgiving that.

Which was why Garrett was too shocked to even react when the inhumanly strong High Cleric suddenly buckled beneath him like Alpha himself had reached down and smote his unholy representative.

Garrett crashed down on top of a soft body. A dead body, he realized with a flash of nausea. He rolled off the bloody mess and hit the wet stone crawling, expecting the High Cleric's claws to close around his ankles any instant. Except the High Cleric was dealing with his own issues, Garrett saw. Sliding helplessly in, straight toward Carlisle, despite the fact that the man was already working to keep Kublich, the gray-haired killer, and a dozen enhanced all contained.

Garrett's eyes lingered on Carlisle, tunic billowing in gale force winds, tiny streaks of violet lightning arcing from his radiant form. He looked like something out of the old legends. Garrett wanted to thank the man, but it was all he could do to keep frantically crawling for Raish, chest burning with the effort, legs trailing limply behind. All he could do to take the gift he didn't deserve, and survive.

Then there was a surge of channeled energy behind him, and a string of sputtering pops and groans ahead announced the eminent death of that goal. Raish whirled at the sound of Fields' startled cry, just as the transport lurched clear drunkenly out of the breach on dying motors, pitching her and a wounded Phineas Hammer into open sky outside the White Tower.

Fields hit the side of the building and caught on, the transport plunging out of view behind her, trailing smoke. Phineas Hammer floated in midair above her, apparently caught by Raish's telekinesis. Garrett didn't have a chance to find out for sure.

Strong arms scooped him up before he could fight them. He caught a single glance of One standing with her good hand extended toward the wrecked transport, and then he was back over the High Cleric's shoulder, and they were moving.

"You don't belong with them," came One's voice in his mind, a moment before she slid into view, slung over the High Cleric's opposite shoulder with a grimly satisfied expression, like she wanted to be there.

Because she did, he realized. She'd fried the transport's motors to buy them a distraction. The High Cleric must've slipped Carlisle's control in the chaos. The specifics hardly mattered. Not as the High Cleric turned for the empty breach just ahead, and the dark night sky beyond.

Garrett thought about fighting, about telekinetically prying himself free. But the pressure of the High Cleric's grip told him that wouldn't end well for him. It was too late anyway. Too late to fight. Too late to even hope as Raish spun back from helping his friends, searching for Garrett.

"Nice try, kid," he sent.

Then the High Cleric sprang through the breach, and they were falling. Falling to their collective deaths, Garrett could only pray. But he knew better than that. He felt One casting her mind around the three of them in the dark rushing air. Even as injured and drained as she clearly was, she wasn't done yet.

Their wild fall began to slow. It was only a little at first, but then again, they'd also fallen from nearly two thousand feet above street level. Telekinetically lowering three people over that distance wasn't something you rushed into all at once. Not if you wanted to see to it everyone survived impact.

"Help your sister, child," came the High Cleric's voice, his iron grip tight as ever across Garrett's legs.

Garrett considered telling him to shove it, shortly followed by the equally tempting thought of deliberately disrupting One's telekinetic deceleration. Exhausted as she clearly was, he had little doubt she was capable of pulling this off solo if he didn't stop her. But no matter how insistently he told himself he was ready to die if it meant taking them with him, he couldn't bring himself to do it. Not yet.

Instead, he flicked open his palmlight and sent his waiting last words to Alexia with a few decisive jabs of his thumb. That done, he activated the drop case's nav beacon with another palmlight command and flicked the case into the open air, aiming as best he could for the lush gardens at the border of the pedestrian way below—so far below that he could barely make them out in the nighttime lights. He prayed to Alpha the case would survive the fall, like it had been designed to do.

In a perfect world, he would have waited until they were low enough to ensure a safe drop. But this wasn't that. Not a perfect world. Not even a half-decent one. Not as long as beasts like the one that called itself High Cleric could commit such atrocities and get away with it.

Garrett gathered what little strength he had left, dimly aware that One was asking him what the scud he'd just done, even as the High Cleric dug a warning claw into his leg, demanding that he obey and assist One's efforts. It didn't matter anymore. None of it mattered.

He'd done what he had to do.

So he focused his will one last time, and he threw his mind at One's, ready to take them all down like the falling mass of unholy, scudspouting evil they collectively were.

But the High Cleric was ready for him.

He'd barely kicked the surface of One's jagged mental fortress, accomplishing little more than to jerk their fall into a slow spin, when the High Cleric's presence swept in around him like a dark, angry river.

It was only then Garrett registered the High Cleric was behaving as if he wasn't capable of using his own abilities to catch their fall. Like One and Garrett were the only things that could keep him from plummeting to a squishy death. But that wouldn't matter either if Garrett didn't fight his way free of the bastard's mental chokehold. And fast.

He kept the pressure on, doing his best to kick One's focus loose without collapsing under the High Cleric's weight entirely. For several precious seconds, the three of them all struggled, locked together in the mental plane even as they all plunged for the hard street below.

Then the night sky came alive with a blinding flash of violet fury, and the air exploded with the most violent boom Garrett had ever heard. Carlisle, he dimly noted, as the first slap of the resultant shockwave hit, whipping at his clothes but doing little to pry him free from the High Cleric's hardsteel grip. Carlisle, finally losing his hold on whatever boundless power he'd tapped back in the Great Hall. The crazy bastard.

But even that no longer mattered. Not as the violent light receded, leaving a sickly greenish-yellow glow burned across Garrett's vision of the pale moonlight reflected from the White Tower. Not as the dark permacrete raced up to meet them—fast, but not fast enough. And not as Garrett tensed to redouble his mental assault on One, only to realize he'd already lost.

"Sleep, my child," the High Cleric cooed deep in his mind, pushing him down, down into the darkness. Smothering him with it. *"Sleep, you insolent little wretch."*

An edge of alarm kicked up from the blackened depths. Panicked voices shouting. Rushing lights, far away. A distant jolt, even farther, yet resonating down to the center of his being. A terrific jolt. The last jolt. Darkness closing in.

This was it, Garrett realized.

This was it.

30

LOW PLACES

Garrett snapped awake to the stink of mildew and dank, poorly ventilated permacrete. He blinked around at the dim gray walls. Cell walls. He was in a dimly lit cell, the hard cot buzzing faintly beneath him. Electronics, he realized. Large electronics, running somewhere nearby, their vibrations transduced through the floor and the cot, right into his buzzing skull.

Where the scud was he?

He'd dreamt of something... something terrible. Something horrific. Or had he? He couldn't remember. Felt like he'd been knocked unconscious, or like someone had taken his mind and—

It all came back in a sudden, vivid rush that left him gasping, clawing at the stiff cot in a frantic race to sit up. He pressed his back against the dank permacrete, only distantly noting the aching protests of his battered body.

Horrific didn't even begin to describe it.

The Great Hall. The people. Those *things*. Raish, and Carlisle, and—

The explosion!

He swung his legs off the cot to stand—not sure where he was going, only that he needed to move—then nearly pitched into a wild fall instead when his legs remained stubbornly strewn across the bare cot. He righted himself, staring at his still legs with deepening dread, panic building as he tried again and again to swing them over the edge of the cot.

They barely even twitched.

The icy fist tightened around his insides, panic fixing to overwhelm his senses. Paralyzed? He was... That couldn't be... Not like this. Not from a single backhand.

Had it been the fall, then? Had he succeeded in crashing One and that thing that called itself High Cleric down to the streets with him? He couldn't remember anything beyond that violet flash of light—the spillover of what had to have been Carlisle's final act.

Had he taken Kublich and the gray-haired killer with him? Alpha, Garrett hoped so.

Clearly, though, someone had survived to bring him here—wherever *here* was.

Before his racing mind could turn to wondering who, or why, or finish unpacking the thousands of questions for which he knew he had no answers, the rusted cell door gave a few rattles of outside activity, then swung inward with a mournful creak.

Garrett wasn't sure who or what he'd been expecting—sharp claws and demon fire eyes, he supposed. Whatever it was, he was surprised to see One standing in the open doorway, alone, and even more surprised to see the look on her face.

She looked like she hadn't a care in the world. Like she was simply coming to collect him for another day of putting in the work, in the name of Alpha. If anything, she actually looked happier. Like she *hadn't* just watched—and even helped—an army of reptilian monstrosities slaughter their way through hundreds of innocent civilians and legionnaires.

"What the scud's going on?"

Much as he loathed how damn vulnerable and clueless the words sounded leaving his mouth, Garrett couldn't help but start with the obvious question.

"Revolution," she said, as if it should've been obvious. Then, stepping into the cell, she added, "Everything we've dreamed about for the past two years. Our new world. Safety for Alpha's Chosen. It's all finally happening, Two."

"Safety..." he echoed, trying to process what she was saying, and the depths of the insanity therein. "All those people. Those—Those *things*. This isn't... I can't even move my Alpha-damned legs."

He wasn't sure why he added the last part. Given the magnitude of everything else that'd just happened, it sounded pretty damn self-centered. But it came out anyway, and if One thought it odd, she didn't say so.

"That too can be mended," was all she said, but he couldn't miss the suggestion in her tone. Like there wasn't anything under Alpha's sun and stars that *couldn't* be mended for their oh-so-noble cause—bloody public massacres included.

He looked at her more closely, gauging her frosty eyes for any hint of remorse or doubt.

There was none.

"I don't know what you signed up for," he said, drawing his mental defenses tighter, painfully aware of just how trapped he was anyway, with the state his legs were in. "But I'm not okay with any part of—"

"Oh, cut the bullscud," she snapped, her expression hardening. "You knew how much would have to change for people like us to exist outside of the shadows. You knew all along how violent the shock would have to be when the time came. Don't pretend like you didn't."

"Pretend? Pre—" Garrett shook his head, a fresh wave of nausea rolling through his gut at the bloody memories of the Great Hall. "They slaughtered those people, One. Slaughtered them. What the scud point did that serve?"

"An example needed to be made," she said, shrugging it off like it was an unfortunate but minor expense she was talking about. "A demonstration of our power. You know that. You can't lie to me about it, either. I've been inside your head, remember?"

He stared at her, scattered fragments of memories trying to piece their hazy way together.

"Oh, that's right," she said, grinning at the stupefied look that must've been resting across his face. "I guess you wouldn't remember, would you?"

Son of a...

So it *had* been her, then. Her who'd muddied the waters of what had happened the night they'd captured Raish. Her who'd planted Alpha knew what manner of delusions and outright lies there. But why? To keep him in line? Did she even know herself?

Did she know that the "harmless" collar at her throat was still primed to blow, and that her precious High Cleric was a lying piece of demon scud?

He didn't know. Couldn't know. Couldn't even trust anyone or anything to give him the truth of the matter. All he knew was that he could never be on board with any of this. And if she honestly thought that he could... that he could sit by and watch as those things ripped their way across Enochia...

"How can you stand for this?"

The words left his mouth before his better sense could stop them. Alpha, he sounded naive. But to his surprise, though, One's smug confidence actually faltered for a moment. It returned quickly enough, bolstered by an extra glint of fanatic energy in her eyes. But not so quickly as to hide the fact that she apparently had reservations of her own resting beneath that hard exterior.

"There's nowhere else *to* stand, Garrett," she hissed. "Don't you see that? Don't you see the gift that Alpha is offering us here?"

Obviously, it was her turn to take a sip at the naivety bowl. He wanted to smirk, but he was too busy stifling the flinch that ran down his spine at the sound of her lips uttering his real name.

So she *had* been in his head, then. But as for the rest of it...

He held her fanatic gaze, wondering whether it was truly him she was trying to convince of the rest of it, or herself. The maddened stare stretched too long. He dropped her eyes, wondering if he should ask. It was only then that he noticed her right hand. The one he could've sworn had been a bloody mess back in the Great Hall. It looked perfectly fine now, albeit a bit pink and raw. Like it had just finished healing.

How scudding long had he been unconscious?

She followed his gaze down to her hand then looked back to him with a smug grin. "Yet another gift," she said, brandishing her too-pink fingers in his face for emphasis. "Proof that the raknoth can create just as easily as they can destroy. It's why He sent them to us, Two. Why he sent them here, now, to the two of us. Imagine what we could accomplish now that..."

She kept talking, going on and on about the freedoms and power that would be afforded to them in this new world of theirs, and all the injustices for which they might, at long last, claim their rightful revenge. Garrett was only barely listening. His mind was still focused on that singular word—the one that sent dissonant vibrations rippling through his faulty memory.

Raknoth.

The *raknoth.*

Those scattered memory fragments swirled, hazy edges forming tenuous connections, resolving bit by bit until he was sitting right back in that skimmer, inbound for Sanctuary, Haldin Raish's voice speaking from his palmlight even as One's demands for him to silence the scudspouting racket grew increasingly more threatening.

They're called the raknoth, came Raish's voice from the palmlight, *and they already control half of the planet.*

Pieces began falling back in fits and rapid flashes, then, like the roaring flood of a unstoppered dam taking to the barren dirts. The enhanced beasts—hybrids, Raish had called them—engineered from unwilling captives via some manner of raknoth genetic infection. The dozens of Vantage employees who'd been imprisoned and held comatose, to be used as human blood bags to feed the growing hybrid army. Just like the raknoth were planning to eventually do to all of Enochia, starting with Vantage's shiny new "production" facility.

Alpha be sweet, could it all be true? Had he truly been patrolling the streets of Divinity alongside the victims of a gropping alien genetics experiment, using their uncanny senses to hunt the very two men who'd been trying to expose the creatures responsible.

It was impossible.

Almost as impossible as the idea that he could have forgotten all of this, even for a second. But it was all coming back now, whether he liked it or not.

"—to do is stop being such an Alpha-damned scudboots about all of this," One was saying back in the harsh reality of Garrett's damp cell, her arms aggressively crossed. "Try to keep things in perspective here, will you?"

Keep things... in *perspective?*

It was too much. So much so, in fact, that part of him—and not a small part—was just about ready to throw the curtain over his erratic memories and assume that there'd simply been some critical misunderstanding somewhere along the line. That was the only way any of this could possibly make sense.

But he knew what he'd seen in the Great Hall. And, whether it was worth a damn or not, his gut knew that Haldin had been speaking the truth in that vid—or as much of the truth as anyone knew, at least. Which all meant that what they had here was no mere fault in communication, or in Garrett's perspective. It was a fault in One's brain wiring.

A fault, he was starting to get the feeling, that might well be the death of him if he wasn't careful. But she was watching him like she wasn't going to take silence for an answer.

The words fell out of his mouth before he could think better of them.

"I always knew you were a psychopath..." He looked up at her cold eyes, half-expecting her to punch him, but she was only watching, waiting. Having already gone too far to quit, he shrugged and finished the thought. "I just somehow never figured you for steel-sipping insane. Not until now, I mean."

Her thin lips broke their icy standstill and curled into a dangerous smile. She took half a step forward, reaching to grab him by the front of the shirt, imminent violence clearly on her mind.

"You judge too quickly, child," called a voice from a ways down the dim corridor outside. A voice that chilled Garrett's insides.

The High Cleric.

One had frozen in place at the sound as well, though the look that came over her face was hardly one of horror. More like... reverence. Reverence for her honored master. It only deepened the sickened revulsion twisting in Garrett's gut.

"What one man calls insane," came the High Cleric's voice again, closer now, "might well be called visionary by another."

The unholy bastard appeared in the open doorway, and Garrett's newfound paralysis reached his lungs. Not because of the blood-stained tatters of the man's once pristine ceremonial robes. Not even at the shock of seeing the High Cleric *thing* standing there at all after their fall from the White Tower. No. What he was taken aback by was the fact that the High Cleric once again looked like the High Cleric. No green, scaly hide. No burning crimson glare. Just papery old skin and a pair of rheumy blue eyes staring right back at Garrett, a wispy, almost abashed smile pulling at the man's lips as he continued on.

"The truth of the matter is, itself, a question of perspective, my child. You see?" he added, waving a demonstrative hand in front of his plain human face.

Apparently, he hadn't missed Garrett's shock at his de-beastification.

Garrett probably shouldn't have been surprised by the shift. Clearly, the High Cleric was two-faced. It wasn't much of a stretch to imagine that status was more than figurative. He had watched the unholy bastard and his red-eyed friends shift from Enochia's finest into fiery-eyed monsters during the fighting in the Great Hall, after all.

But none of that made it any less disconcerting to see One turn and bow to what looked by all means to be the frail old High Cleric of the Sanctum, and not the monstrous, fanged raknoth *thing* Garrett knew was lurking just beneath that pale, wrinkly surface. Somehow, the deliberate appearance of frailty only made the raknoth feel that much more dangerous.

"Why do you not rejoice this day, child?" the High Cleric asked, stepping into the cell and paying little mind to the way One hurried to make room for him. "Have you not explained to him what tonight's unveiling meant for the future of Enochia?"

Tonight? So maybe he hadn't been out as long as he'd feared. That didn't explain One's miraculous recovery, but maybe he'd simply overestimated her injuries before.

"I have tried, Master," One was saying, her dark-haired head bowed apologetically. "He does not understand the necessity of tonight's unveiling."

"Ah." The High Cleric looked to Garrett with a mildly flummoxed expression, like he couldn't quite grasp why someone might make such a fuss over a little harmless slaughter. "Well, perhaps he will feel differently once the rest of your colleagues can be assembled here, and the work to remake Enochia can truly begin." A knowing smile curled his lips. "Perhaps once he has his precious Alexia here to motivate him."

At the sound of her name, and the look that crossed One's face when he said it, Garrett tensed, immediately ready to throw himself off that cot, worthless legs be damned, and strangle the life from both of them.

Alexia.

Had his message made it to her? Had Daveen come through? Had any of it worked?

Was Alexia safe?

"If either of you hurt her," Garrett growled, "I swear to Alpha, I'll—I'll..."

But he trailed off, impotent rage shriveling at the seemingly genuine surprise etched across the High Cleric's brow.

"*Hurt* her?" the cleric asked, his tone equally shocked to match his expression. "Merciful Alpha, why would I want to *hurt* her? The Seekers are the only thing of interest you humans have to offer. Why do you think I allowed *you* to live all this time?" He shot a meaningful look at One before turning back to Garrett to continue with a cold smile. "Certainly not because you are good company. No. A pain in this wrinkly old ass, that is all that you have been, my child. But even *you* have an unmistakable role to play in remaking Enochia."

For several seconds, Garrett could only stare. He didn't understand any of this. Was still trying to wrap his head around what was even happening outside of this dingy cell. But he was too stuck on those two little words to make it very far.

You humans, the High Cleric had just said.

Like he wasn't one of them.

Because he wasn't, was he? Of course he wasn't. It was beyond obvious, when Garrett actually stopped to think about it. Scud, Raish and Kovaks had been shouting it from the towers all along. But even after everything—even after witnessing the demon fire eyes, and the impossible physical strength and durability—Garrett's mind had somehow remained stubbornly obstinate to the fact that he was dealing with a creature that was simply not of this world. An alien. A demon. It hardly mattered. This thing wasn't supposed to exist. Not like this.

"So just to be clear," he said quietly, his voice cracking a little in his parched throat. "By 'remaking Enochia,' you *do* pretty much mean 'killing everyone and turning them into scaly mutant freaks,' right?"

The High Cleric only smiled. "You have always struggled to grasp any concept beyond the pull of a trigger or the warmth of forbidden flesh, haven't you, child? Even now, after everything you have born witness to, you still fail to see what is so blindingly obvious."

Garrett looked to One, not waiting to see if the cleric would bother pointing out that blindingly obvious bit of wisdom he'd apparently missed somewhere between his lessons on basic morality and abject gropping evil. He didn't even need to ask One how she could be a part of this. His expression must've said it all.

"Those people out there," One said, waving her too-pink fingers toward the world at large, "they're no less monsters than the enhanced you saw in the Great Hall. You know that. You've seen what they do to each other, what they'd do to us if they had the chance. At least this way, they'll be obedient monsters. Obedient monsters *we* control. Don't you see that we are the next reasonable step for this planet, Garrett? We are Alpha's Chosen. We can transcend our ancestors' wildest dreams, if only you'd stop clinging to your own chains."

The High Cleric was nodding along with a vaguely amused look, as if he were listening to a child recite their vows of loyalty to Alpha. "Yes..." he soothed. "Yes... And so you shall, my child. Just as soon as I take my next vessel."

Something about the look he gave Garrett while he said it sent a whole nest of cold dread worms slithering through his insides. His *vessel*? His *next* vessel. Implying that...

"Master?" One asked, finally tearing her fanatic gaze away from Garrett and turning to see what the High Cleric was talking about. Turning just in time for High Cleric to catch her by her pale, elegant throat.

The High Cleric broke her neck with all the gravity of a child idly snapping a twig.

It was done almost before it had begun. Garrett watched, mouth frozen in a silent scream. The cleric blew out a hefty sigh and tossed One's limp body aside as he turned for Garrett. He was still fixated on One.

She was dead before she hit the floor. And the High Cleric was on Garrett the moment after that.

Garrett raised his hands to defend himself, knowing as he did that it was pointless—that this monster, this *raknoth*, was infinitely stronger than he ever could be, even if he'd had time to gather his senses and use his abilities. But he didn't.

The High Cleric slammed him into the wall hard enough to knock everything but the barest strip of consciousness clear from his throbbing head. For the next few minutes—or maybe it was seconds, he couldn't have said—all Garrett really processed was that there was violent motion, and hard impacts, and pain. Plenty of pain. Too much.

When it had all stopped, some indeterminable time later, Garrett lay trembling on the damp permacrete floor, upper body curled into a tight ball beside One, his legs splayed out behind him, worse than useless. He wanted to fight back. More than anything, he needed to focus, to gather his will and telekinetically bury a hunk of permacrete through the bastard's brain. He needed to avenge One. No matter what she'd done.

But then the raknoth cuffed him again—a casual blow, like the light kiss of a falling pulse hammer—and his thoughts of retaliation exploded right alongside the iridescent stars spinning through his vision.

"Are you ready to accept Alpha's gift, child?" came the High Cleric's voice from somewhere above. "Or will you waste your friend's precious gift?"

At first, Garrett's brain was too rattled to understand what he meant. Then his vision resolved enough to see that the cleric was looking down at One's body.

"You have no idea how she fought to keep you safe in all of this," the cleric said. "How she begged us to give you but one more chance when Haldin Raish's propaganda proved too compelling for your... sensibilities. Then again when we arrived at this facility, mere hours after you had attempted to engineer our quite literal downfall. Even then, she swore she could convince you. That she could accomplish with words what she'd failed to accomplish in reconstructing your problematic memories."

The High Cleric pried his gaze away from One and frowned down at Garrett.

"Yes, her work is unraveling already. I can see it in your eyes." He shook his head. "It was pointless to let her try in the first place. I knew it all along. Pity, really. But then again, I suppose I might be owed a portion of the blame. I was the one who impregnated her with the underlying certainty that this was all going to somehow arrive at a desirable conclusion for the both of you."

The High Cleric looked back to One, his expression thoughtful, perversely calm. "Perhaps I've been infected with your maddening human propensity for blind, naive hope in the face of cold reason. Better, I think, that I'd simply killed you and allowed her to get over her pathetic little infatuation."

"So why am I still alive, then?" Garrett finally groaned, when it became clear the raknoth wasn't going to say anything more. He didn't really want to know the answer, but anything was better than simply laying there, not knowing which moment would be his last.

The High Cleric looked at Garrett like he'd nearly forgotten he was there. "Like I said, you and your kind are... interesting to us. Your gifts are unlike anything we've ever encountered before. Insolent and problematic as you may be, we still have much to learn from you. Perhaps, with the proper conditioning, you might even be forged into a useful servant, like your colleague here was, until circumstance forced my hand in the matter."

"She..." Garrett groaned, trying and failing to pull himself up against the side of his cot. The pain was breathtaking. He didn't want to know how many of his internal organs were currently bleeding.

He slouched back to the cold permacrete, unable to look away from One's vacant blue eyes. "She gave you everything you wanted."

He felt more than saw the High Cleric nod his agreement. "She did."

And you still killed her anyway.

Garrett didn't say the words. Wouldn't give the unholy bastard the satisfaction by playing into his theatrical game here. But the next words slid out anyway, propelled by the weight of their own gravity.

"You're a gropping monster."

The High Cleric tilted his head, conceding the point. "By your definition, I suppose I am. Contrary to what you so righteously believe, though, your friend here is, in a manner of speaking, getting exactly what she wanted. An eternal place in our new world. A chance to ascend." He smiled down at Garrett, his eyes coming alive with crimson fire. "A chance to truly become Alpha's Chosen."

Garrett stared at those fiery eyes, and the darkening green of the High

Cleric's skin, cold horror creeping through his insides as the creature began to change right before his eyes.

"What are you?"

The High Cleric bared a mouthful of elongating fangs in a demonic smile, crimson eyes pulsing brighter. When he spoke, his voice had dropped precipitously.

"I am your Alpha, my child."

And with that, he took Garrett's jaw in his hardsteel grip, slammed him to the cot, and pried his mouth open, leaning in until his face hung bare inches above Garrett's, a trail of unsightly green something dripping down from the corner of his thin, grinning lips.

"Now open up," he said, prying Garrett's mouth wider, more of the sickly ooze spilling down his chin, "and receive my blessing."

In the dim, dank cell that smelled of slow-rotting permacrete, trapped with the cooling corpse of One and the red-eyed thing that had once been the High Cleric of the Sanctum, Garrett gave in. He opened his mouth. And he screamed.

31

SIREN'S CALL

Alexia reached the shuddering peak of her climax just before the mark died.

It rolled through her body in shaking, overflowing waves of ecstasy, too strong to turn away from, washing away the labored burning of her hips and legs. Washing away the guilt. Washing away everything—right up until, riding out the last trembling waves, she breathed a ragged sigh of relief and sat back up. Back to the real world. Back to the mark who'd gone perfectly still beneath her.

Not dead yet, she noted by the weakening thuds of the man's heart, the muscles of her own hips and legs still burning pleasantly with the delicious intensity of those last few moments. He was only unconscious. Death would follow soon enough, drifting in on the insidious kiss of the poison the dumb bastard had so eagerly drank—no question, no second thought. Like he'd known what was coming, and had decided it was well worth it anyway.

And maybe it had been. There were far worse ways to go, she reminded herself. And it wasn't like the man had had any shot whatsoever at escaping death, anyway. Not after he'd decided to forfeit his life by breaking into the dark market field of telepathic blackmail with all the soft-footed subtlety of a battering ram.

It was no mystery where the man had derived inspiration for his bedroom technique.

But neither derisive mockery nor stale rationalizations could stay the coming darkness from her blackened spirit. She knew that well enough by now. So with one last sigh, she slid herself off of the mark's shriveling beardsplitter and stood, straightening her skirt and not bothering to fight the familiar heaviness that settled in on her heart.

There were no clothes to gather. She hadn't bothered taking any off. If her lust-crazed mark had had any complaints about her state of dress during, he hadn't managed to gasp them out between his wheezing breaths. She was half-surprised the man hadn't died of a heart attack the moment he'd entered her. It wouldn't have been the first time, after all. But things had all gone exactly as planned. Exactly as she preferred.

The rest of the cycle practically wrote itself.

After reaching out with her senses to confirm that the man's vital functions were in fact fading, she stepped back and waited for it to happen. She thought of Garrett in that moment, as she always did. Not in the fae-tale-princess-bullscud kind of way she'd done in the first year or so of the job. No. That hopeful longing that she'd see him again, that he'd come swooping in to sunder her collar and carry her away from this life... That had all died a long time ago. This thought was fleeting. Little more than a sad smile and a pang of longing for the too-brief kiss they'd shared, and the warmth of his hands on her. It was the last touch she could remember having derived any actual meaning from, outside of death, or fear, or mindless pleasure.

So she thought of Garrett, as she always did, until the mark's heart stopped beating. Then she gathered the requisite evidence and turned to leave, ready to report to Serenity and, finally, to take up her lash and complete the cycle with powerful sensations of a different flavor.

Maybe she'd even have time to squeeze in a nightcap afterward. The vid replays of Raish's execution would be flooding the reels by the time she returned. She might even catch a glimpse of Garrett somewhere in there, if she was lucky. Maybe.

Except before she could take three steps to the door of the mark's grimy hovel, her palmlight buzzed, breaking the cycle right in its well-lubricated tracks.

Alexia paused for several silent seconds before even looking at the device, acutely aware of the gut feeling that something was amiss. The handlers rarely bothered her in the field. No one did. She was remotely monitored, sure. All the Seekers were when they were in the field. It didn't matter that her methods were drastically more carnal—and, dare she say it, intimate—than most of her compatriots'. They all did their jobs. And as long as they did them well, they weren't bothered outside of routine debriefings upon return.

Oddly enough, if anyone had ever taken qualms with her bedding her marks—even on those occasions when it proved technically unnecessary, as it had tonight—they hadn't said anything about it.

They were too busy monitoring.

But now...

Slowly, she unfurled her fingers, waking her palmlight, all too aware of the familiar tingling sensation at her throat, right where the thin dark strip of her collar exerted its steady death hug. She looked at the display, expecting chastisement, or worse.

But it wasn't from Cleric Kellen, or Ardova, or anyone else at Serenity Tower.

It was from Garrett.

<<*Six,*

We have an important mark to discuss. One that might require both of us. Find me by the fire. If I'm unavailable, look to our old eye in the sky. Trust me. Be safe.

-Two>>

Alexia read and reread the message at least eight or nine times before she finally managed to start thinking on the contents therein. It was only then that she noticed she'd absentmindedly sank down onto the mark's dirty couch, shocked as she was to see the ID signature on the message. So much for completing the cycle.

Garrett.

She stared at their respective call signs, marveling at their proximity, right there in the same message.

Six. Two. After all this time... All the nights she'd spent lying awake, staring at his ID on her palmlight, longing to hear his voice, knowing that such careless weakness could well be the death of both of them...

All this time with nothing but the few infrequent, utterly impersonal messages in their first seasons apart. Those bland, faceless messages had been worse than dead silence. And yet she'd continued to play along, bitterly glad for any contact at all, until the handlers had come to her with one too many warnings, and even those emotionless snippets had died a quiet death.

And now this, after all this time, out of nowhere.

Why? What had changed?

She read the message again, turning over each and every word. It was unusual for Seekers—especially those at different posts—to contact one another about new assignments without first hearing of it from their respective handlers. Unusual, but not completely unheard of.

Asking for a meeting, though, and so cryptically at that... That wasn't going to fly with the handlers.

This wasn't simply about a mark. Couldn't be. No. He was trying to tell her something much more important than that. Several somethings, maybe. And he wanted to tell her in person, by the fire.

The fire...

The slums. That had to be it. The back alley, fire-lit gambling rings where she'd taken her first fallen mark—and where she'd so foolishly initiated the contact with Garrett that had gotten her transferred halfway across Enochia to keep them apart.

But why there? Why meet at all? He knew better than she did that doing so without approved handler permission would be suicide for both of them. Wouldn't it?

Almost certainly. But then what the scud was he expecting?

For a long few seconds, she was almost overwhelmed by the urge to just call him and ask what was going on. But that would be supremely stupid. Even more stupid than sending this message had been, if he'd had any choice in the matter. Which meant he probably hadn't. Unless he'd lost it.

We have an important mark to discuss. One that might require both of us.

Was she missing some hidden meaning in there beyond the obvious, *"We need to talk,"* or was that line solely intended for the peace of mind of whatever member of the handler team happened across this message and had to decide whether or not it was alarm-worthy?

She didn't know. But the last lines hardly inspired confidence.

If I'm unavailable, look to our old eye in the sky. Trust me. Be safe.

She was guessing that the "eye in the sky" he referred to was the omniscient presence of Watchtower—the man, or the team, or whatever, who ultimately had eyes and ears on every bit of data the Seekers and their handlers collected or produced. She hadn't heard so much as a peep from the mysterious Watchtower since her transfer, given that Serenity Tower had its own operator node that ran whatever occasional remote support was necessary on her assignments. But she knew Watchtower was still out there, living up to its name.

Scud, Watchtower was probably reading Garrett's message to her right now, and waiting to see what she'd do about it.

The thought sent tingles down her collared neck.

Had Garrett found Watchtower? Sweet Alpha, could they actually be working together?

She didn't know. All she knew was that it sounded like Garrett was in danger. And unless she'd completely misjudged the man who'd so captivated her that she'd spent two years dreaming for the impossible, the fact that he'd even tangentially involved her in this thing only doubly confirmed how important it must be.

"What are you up to?" she whispered under her breath at her palmlight.

Her heart leapt when the device buzzed in response, her imagination springing to life with fanciful snippets of Garrett on the other end, or of Watchtower himself, calling to tell her she was free, and happy trails. Then she saw the ID tag on the incoming call, and her heart fell back down into its rightful pit.

"Get back here immediately," came the firm tone of Cleric Ardova almost before the connection was even established. "There's been an attack."

Alexia stifled the would-be outpouring of pedestrian questions, and forced herself to act like the cold professional she was supposed to be. "Where?"

"The White Tower. Haldin Raish's execution ceremony. A rescue attempt was made."

"Carlisle?" she asked, pretty sure she already knew the answer, as well as the likely outcome.

Whatever darkness had touched fallen like herself and the mark she'd just finished snuffing out, it was undoubtedly nothing compared to the demonic powers wielded by Carlisle and his young apprentice. The events of the past cycles had made that clear enough. She still didn't understand why the High Cleric hadn't recalled more Seekers to Divinity to deal with the pair, other than that doing so would break the sacred Rule of Threes.

Somehow, the emergence of seemingly unstoppable demonic terrorists seemed to her like a fair reason to make an exception.

She blinked at her palmlight, realizing she hadn't registered Ardova's answer. In fact, she was pretty sure he hadn't answered at all. And given how much it *wasn't* like him to be distracted...

"Did they... succeed?" she asked, struggling to even suggest such a thing was possible, despite the sinking feeling in her gut that told her she already knew that answer as well.

There was an audible drawing of breath on the other end, like Ardova was bracing for something.

Something was seriously wrong.

"The High Cleric is missing," Ardova finally said. "Look, just... Cleric Donner has ordered that all active Seekers to return to their posts immediately. That's all you need to know right now. Do you understand?"

There was very little Alexia understood in that moment, save for the fact that this simply wasn't possible and that, seeing as it had apparently happened anyway, this had to be connected to Garrett's message, and why he'd sent it when he did.

But that wasn't what Ardova needed to hear. What the cleric needed to hear was that she would return to her post, immediately, and that she'd wait there like a good little girl until the handlers could get a handle on things. Or until they could officially decide they'd completely lost said handle and thumb the detonators on their dirty little Seeker core, just to be safe.

She needed to tell him anyway. Tell him that she understood. Tell him that she was on her way. Except her mind couldn't stop roaring with questions about how this had happened, and about how bad the damage was, and if Garrett had been there, and if he was okay, and if—

"Six."

Cleric Ardova's harsh tone snapped her back to her mark's dingy hovel, and to her waiting palmlight.

"When did this...?" She stared weakly. "How did...?"

So much for cold professionalism. She felt like she was going to be sick.

Ardova's huff of irritation declared she'd better get it together and do it on her own time. "Just get back here," he said. "Now. That's an order."

"Under—Understood, Holiness," she said, bowing her head reflexively, even though it was only an audio connection. "Might I just ask, though... Apologies, Cleric Ardova, but before I go... The Divinity Seekers. Has there been any word of—"

"We don't know," Ardova growled, an edge of mania slipping into his tone. "They're missing. Everyone is missing. Those cursed demons took the entire Great Hall with them, and just..." He paused to compose himself. "Just get back here. Right now."

"On my way, Holiness," she said, knowing all too well how unwise it would be to dismiss the bristling *or else* rearing up beneath Ardova's growing irritation.

As if to confirm the point, Cleric Ardova killed the connection without another word, leaving Alexia alone in the quiet hovel, sitting on the dirty couch of the man she'd just killed in service of the holy father who'd just gone missing.

What in demons' depths was going on out there?

And Garrett... Where was Garrett?

Those demons took the entire Great Hall with them, Ardova's voice echoed in her head. *Everyone is missing.*

Had he survived?

Merciful Alpha, had she lost him while she'd been too busy swiving a man to death, chasing a single moment of mindless pleasure?

No. She didn't know. Didn't even know for sure if he'd been there at all. And if he had...

She swiped out a quick message and sent it to Garrett before she could stop herself.

<<Please tell me you're still alive.>>

She stared at the words as they danced out onto the Lights, beyond her ability to retract. Probably, she could've been a bit more professional, a bit less worried-wannabe-girlfriend. The handlers might have something to say about the concerning sign of familiarity. But she didn't give a damn. The clerics had more than enough to worry about right now anyway.

So she waited, trying not to stare at the palmlight. Trying to tell herself that she was worrying pointlessly, that he must've survived. Of course he had. The damn message had said to meet him, hadn't it? That wasn't something you said when you were in mortal peril.

She checked her palmlight. Nothing.

That wasn't something you said while in mortal peril, whispered the cursed voice of logic in the back of her head, unless you'd written the message in advance, because you suspected an attack was coming, and expected the worst. Maybe Garrett had known. Maybe he'd sent that message in advance, or in his last moments, knowing that—

No.

She shook her head sharply, refusing to let the idea take root. Refusing even to check her palmlight for the message that obviously hadn't come. It didn't matter. He wasn't dead. He couldn't be. Because... Why?

Because she would've felt it happen, from a thousand miles away? That was fae-tale-princess bullscud, right there.

And yet she believed it, she realized. Had to believe it. Because otherwise...

No. *Otherwise* didn't bear thinking about. He was alive. And even if he wasn't...

No.

He *was* alive. And whatever else was happening out there, she was pretty sure he needed her to get her scud together and come find him. For *what*, she didn't know. Hadn't the faintest clue, really. But she knew that it was important. Maybe the most important thing there was. And she knew where to start.

"Hang on, Garrett," she whispered, standing from the dead man's couch and sparing the fallen one last look before turning her back on the silent room forever. She pried open the creaky door and left, bound for her skimmer, not even remotely sure how she was going to pull off what came next, and especially not without losing her head to an explosive misunderstanding.

But she knew where to start.

It was more than enough.

"Hang on, Garrett..." Alexia repeated under her breath, holding his image firmly in mind as she stepped out into the streets of Serenity, ready to turn every bit of fae-tale-princess-bullscud there was straight on its ignorant ass.

"I'm coming for you."

THE END

A LETTER FROM THE AUTHOR

"Well demons to the wind, that took a turn, didn't it?"

That, Dear Reader, is more or less what I was muttering to myself as I typed out the last chapter of this book. Which was kind of exciting at the time, seeing as I'd previously been *sure* I already knew how it was all going to end.

See, the thing about *Fallen*—the thing that was unique to this project—was that it was basically written before I even started trying to put it down on the page.

Allow me to explain.

If you're already a loyal reader of mine, you probably know that this book, Fallen, is a "side story," of sorts. *(You probably ALSO know that I love and cherish you and your book-loving soul. But that's neither here nor there...)*

If this book was only your first dip into the world of Enochia, however, well then boy, do I have some exciting news for you.

For one thing, Garrett's story was only the beginning...

If you enjoyed this book and want to know more about the raknoth and those dastardly demons, Haldin Raish and Carlisle—not to mention what lies in store next for Garrett and Alexia—well, there's already an entire (completed) trilogy waiting to tickle ALL of your adventurous fancies...

(Or, you know, most of them, at least. We're only just getting to know each other, after all. But I digress.)

Point is, if you're ready for more Enochian adventures, the Enochian War Trilogy is the place you want to go. And better yet, you can grab the first book free today!

Just go to *lukermitchell.com/fallen-signup* to join my mailing list and download your free welcome copy of *Shadows of Divinity* today! (Plus the exclusive Enochian short story, *Eye of the Storm.*)

In addition to these shiny new Enochian War stories, as a member of the list, you'll also get access to free books from all of my other fictional worlds—as well as discounts and short stories you won't find anywhere else, plus the occasional rant and/or behind-the-scenes shenanigans from yours truly.

(It's a pretty good time.)

If newsletters and email shenanigans aren't your bag, though, no worries. You can always visit *lukermitchell.com/books* to find the complete list of my published works—and to grab *Shadows of Divinity* (Book One of the Enochian War Trilogy) and "begin" the series today!

Lastly, whether you're set to move forward with the Enochian War trilogy or planning to simply ride off into the sunset like some kind of badass book-slinging cowboy, never to be seen again, I just want to take a moment to say thanks.

Thank you, Dear Reader, for taking the time to come on this adventure with me. I had a blast writing this book, and I hope you had every bit as much fun reading it!

I can't wait to share more stories with you.

Till then, though... happy reading!

Cheers,
Luke Mitchell

ABOUT THE AUTHOR

Not a llama. Mostly human.

Luke is a storyteller whose dreams include learning the ways of the Force, becoming a sentient robot, and maybe even one day growing up. Also, lots of zombies... Don't ask.

Oh, and that "growing up" bit? That was a lie.

After studying engineering science at Penn State and neuroengineering at Drexel, Luke finally decided to throw in the towel on building a working Iron Man suit and opted instead to simply make things up and write them down. Boy, is he having more fun now.

When he's not holed up in his writing cave trying to string words together, he can often be found powerlifting, video-gaming, reading, and/or drinking the darkest, most roasty beers he can get his mitts on. Sometimes all at once.

But you know what? That's enough about Luke. He's really not that interesting. Still, if you'd like to say hi to him for whatever reason, he'd probably be glad to hear from you!

Go to **lukermitchell.com/fallen-signup** to join the mailing list and grab your free copies of *Shadows of Divinity* and *Eye of the Storm*!

Additionally (as you wish)...

Follow me on BookBub for new release alerts
bookbub.com/authors/luke-r-mitchell

Browse the rest of my published titles
lukermitchell.com/books

Join the Patreon team for digital copies of ALL of my work (past, present, and future) — and much more!
patreon.com/lukermitchell

Thank you for reading!